BRIGHT SANDS, DARK SKIES

A ROMANTIC THRILLER

CHRISSY JOHNSON

BRIGHT SANDS MEDIA

Published by Bright Sands Media

ISBNs: 979-8-9941012-0-9 (trade paperback), 979-8-9941012-2-3 (hardback), 979-8-9941012-1-6 (ebook)

Printed in the United States of America

10 9 8 7 6 5 4 3 2 1

PROLOGUE

Edward.
This story starts with Edward—not the pale-faced teenage vampire, but a Marine... and, believe it or not, a billionaire.

CHAPTER 1

Poland - 2014

Gunfire cracked through the speakers.

The Ukrainian translator jolted beside me, knocking over a half-empty cup of coffee.

It splashed across his keyboard, but he barely noticed.

"The Russians are inside!" he yelled, voice shaking.

Then—more gunfire in sharp bursts. Shouting tangled in static.

A grenade went off, rattling the room.

"Four guards... uh, five guards down," he translated as fast as voices screamed. "They're already upstairs. Ten or more—they're everywhere. They don't know where they came from. They're trying to breach the safe room—"

The ops center exploded into motion.

I scrambled to make sense of the screens, pulse pounding.

I wasn't in Ukraine. But I felt like I'd been dropped into the firefight—

the worst-case scenario unfolding in real time.

One second, the safe house was secure.

The next, commotion.

Bodies on the ground.

Bright red painting the walls.

Then, another large blast—louder.

"They're in!" the translator exclaimed, hollow—like he was somehow to blame.

I scanned monitors as they flickered.

Confirmed. The safe room was compromised.

* * *

Three days ago, I'd been pulled from a field assignment in Ukraine without warning. Hurled into a seat in an ops center in Poland.

Told to follow orders—just sit tight. Watch the video feed.

It wasn't protocol or part of my job description.

When I asked why, my boss just shrugged.

"Not sure, Allie. Just do it."

So I did—monitoring a live feed inside a safe house, waiting for Mikhail Zlenko to make a nation-shattering announcement: conceding his "defeat" in May's snap presidential election.

The truth was, his opponent—Igor Ivanenko—hadn't won.

But the media—backed by the CIA and other Western powers—manufactured a different narrative.

Zlenko was a Ukrainian nationalist. Loyal to his people. Resistant to foreign interests.

That made him inconvenient. A problem for the West.

So under mounting pressure and ominous threats—and with his family held hostage—Zlenko caved. He would soon accept his rival's "victory" on national television.

The CIA had Ivanenko—their puppet—under lock and key at the safe house until then—ready to install him as Ukraine's new leader.

* * *

None of it made sense. *Until now.*

The room hummed, growing more chaotic by the minute.

Phones ringing. Voices barking orders.

Joe Turner, the agency's Kiev Station Chief, stormed in out of nowhere—eyes wild behind round glasses, already screaming:

"Somebody explain what the fuck is going on! Who are these guys and how the hell did they find him? Get the QRF team to respond! Now!"

"Team is en route, sir. Less than five minutes out," someone behind me said calmly.

Joe was slender with mousy brown hair and beady eyes—and a reputation as a prick.

I tried to avoid him whenever possible—but when the explosions started, he'd scurried in.

Why was he in Poland, too?

Whatever it was, it reeked.

I settled back into my seat, toggling between feeds—until several voices emerged.

Not Russian.

I shouted to a translator behind me. "Are you hearing any Russian right now? *Anything?*"

She shook her head.

Then, in a distinct Midwest accent:

"We've got less than five minutes, boys. In and out. No mistakes."

Shit. I threw up a hand. "Chief! These guys aren't Russian— they're American!"

Joe spun around, startled to see me.

"What are these imbeciles doing fucking around in my AO? Tell them to stand down!"

"I would, but—"

I scanned radio traffic and the locations of the agency's assets— nothing. *How was that possible?*

I could feel Joe's eyes burning into me as I muttered, "I have no idea who they are."

"Then get your head out of your ass and find out! Get EUCOM and JSOC on the line!"

"On it, sir," chirped a redheaded analyst behind me as I heard the tail end of radio chatter: "...stand down immediately. Deconfliction required. Await further orders."

Then more shouting, static, and confusion.

I flipped through audio and video feeds until I heard a new voice upstairs.

A faint southern drawl over background noise.

"Yo, Boss Man, think we got him! Sending biometrics. Standby."

Another voice cut in from a feed on the rooftop—quieter, no interference:

"Confirming. Got eyes on at least four Land Cruisers lining up at the intersection. Rockstar, Super Doom—recommend we get ready to *vámonos* in three minutes, tops."

"Where's the fucking QRF team?" Joe breathed, slow to track.

"At the intersection, like he said," a young analyst mumbled, then stopped. I lifted my eyes just in time to watch the color drain from his face.

"Pick up your shit and get the hell out!" Joe shrieked. "And tell these guys to stand down—I want their boss on the line. Now!"

Upstairs, one guy laughed—bigger, taller than the rest. "Damn! Where they at? Bros, Boss says we're on the agency's big screen. Everybody look sharp!"

"Hell yeah!" another replied from the hallway, flexing for the camera overhead while standing over a pile of zip-tied guards.

These guys weren't just American Special Forces. They were a show. And a storm.

"If these are the jackasses from Special Activities, I'm dropping a bomb on that fucking safe house," Joe sniveled, shaking as he fumbled with his glasses.

"Sir, all teams are accounted for. They're not ours," someone confirmed.

"Chief, no match on call signs."

Joe's face contorted. "Did you morons talk to the LNO at JSOC?"

"They're not JSOC. Already deconflicted, sir."

"Then run them through facial rec!"

We exchanged looks.

The team wore full black tactical gear—NVGs, face wraps—not a millimeter of skin exposed. Joe hadn't noticed.

Then, the guy with the southern drawl:

"Yo, Joe Turner! How's that young mistress you got in Mariupol? Heard you got a kid on the way."

The room whipped around.

Joe froze.

"Who are these guys?" his voice croaked. "Give me something!"

"Hah, looks like Joe's upset," the tallest guy said upstairs. Then: "Got it! Boss, last chance. We bringing Igor in or dropping him here?"

A pause.

"Affirm. Boss says drop him."

The tallest guy shoved Ivanenko to his knees. "Sorry, Igor. Boss has spoken. Word of wisdom for your next life—don't get mixed up with evil."

Three seconds later: a suppressed shot to the head then double tap to the chest.

The agency's puppet was dead.

Shock shot through my veins.

"Target neutralized," someone said upstairs amid pleading in Ukrainian.

Joe screamed, "Ah, fuck this! Get the White House on the line! Who the *fuck* do they think they are?"

"Sir," someone muttered, the live feed flickering on screen.

The tallest guy waved. "Joe, you didn't think we were just gonna let you get away with the Igor switcharoo, did ya?"

"Fuck you, motherfucker! Send in the QRF team! I don't care who they are."

The Midwest accent cut in: "Let's pack it up, boys. Rockstar, team's ready to roll... just waiting on you."

"Nice. On our way down. This Igor dude is super dead. Super Doom's just snapping a few pics in case they try a body double tomorrow."

Then Rockstar turned, staring straight into the camera.

His posture said everything.

"Hey, Joe—get ready. We're coming for you next."

The screen cut to black—audio and video gone in an instant.

When it rebooted, a single still image: Joe, kissing a visibly pregnant girl.

Whispers filled the room.

Joe kicked a chair on his way out, almost falling to his knees. Fury in his eyes.

I readjusted in my seat, pulse racing.

It wasn't the first time I'd watched a hit team take someone out—but this felt different.

This wasn't *just* a hit.

It was a message. A provocative middle finger to the agency—the establishment.

I'd always thought my job was about truth and doing the right thing.

About protecting national security.

But watching this?

For the first time, a poisoned whisper tainted my mind—

Was I on the right side?

It didn't feel like it. Not when the agency engaged in kidnapping. Lies. Overthrowing duly elected leaders.

Not when a rogue American hit team did what no one else dared.

I shivered as it hit me—this wasn't a coincidence.

Someone sent me to Warsaw. Someone *wanted* me to watch.

CHAPTER 2

Florida – January 2022

It wasn't much. Just a mimosa.

But for me, it was freedom—the kind I hadn't tasted in years.

I sat at a bar in Siesta Key—a tiny island off Sarasota—sipping in the sunlight on a beautiful Sunday afternoon.

It felt too warm for winter, but I didn't mind.

It was my first solo outing in ages—*unless grocery store runs counted*—and I was determined to enjoy it, one small moment at a time.

I'd become a homebody over the years—for good reason—and Blake didn't approve of me going out without his protection: his biceps, which he affectionately referred to as his *guns*, and the Glock 43X tucked in his waistband.

But we hadn't spoken since before Christmas.

If I called, I expected he'd give me the same stay-safe lecture I'd heard a thousand times—effective once, now suffocating.

Especially in Siesta Key.

I was bored. Lonely. And done asking permission.

I needed a reset—and a return to normalcy.

Today was that day.

* * *

That day may've never happened if it weren't for an older gentleman at the grocery store two days earlier. Classic red Marine Corps Vietnam Veteran hat.

After trailing me for several aisles, he boldly asserted:

"Miss, a girl like you shouldn't be grocery shopping on Friday night."

I couldn't argue. I should've been out at some restaurant downtown.

But I wasn't—because I was happily married.

Well... *mostly.*

At least *semi*-happily.

Regardless, going out sans my husband didn't feel right given my circumstances.

Back home, I whipped up a bowl of popcorn and opened a bottle of red wine.

By my second glass, an old itch drew me to my closet—fingers grazing silk. Cold satin. Sequins that once caught a congressman's cufflink.

A life I barely remembered.

Glamorous. Daring. *Invited.*

I paused on black lace, sighed, then quickly talked myself out of it.

* * *

On Saturday night, I drifted to my closet again. Assessing.

As a transplant from D.C., my wardrobe was a collection of designer staples in black and navy.

Business suits for Capitol Hill briefings. Gowns for military balls and fundraisers. Cocktail dresses for nights drinking with the rich and powerful.

But Sarasota wasn't D.C. Far from it.

I had plenty of dresses—but they were all too dark. Too formal for a routine Saturday.

I huffed. I had nothing to wear that wouldn't make me stand out—
and standing out wasn't what I needed. So I went to bed, resigned to
isolation.

* * *

I woke refreshed on Sunday and went about my routine:

A brisk 30-minute walk on a secluded stretch of beach.

Coffee on a point in my neighborhood overlooking the calm Gulf.

Then a long, relaxing shower.

Steam whirled around me as I dried off, the scent of a new plume-
ria shampoo vibrant and tropical—inspiring me to do something bold.

Brunch.

I quickly threw on a sundress, wedges, and a pair of glamorous
sunglasses—a splurge from the south of France—then drove to the Village before I had time to change my own mind.

There was nothing wrong with going to brunch alone.

Siesta Key was safe.

* * *

I parked just as the hostess was unlocking the doors—a swanky-
upscale bar and restaurant on Ocean Boulevard.

As people wandered in, the restaurant came to life.

The young, tattooed bartender gave me a once-over as I entered—
probably wondering if I was starved for company or just a little too
eager for alcohol. Maybe both.

I adjusted my sunglasses and smiled, trying to disguise the nervous
tremble in my cheeks.

I deserved this—didn't I?

Sunlight sparkled on the mirrored bar—and I forced myself to relax with a long exhale.

I chose a window seat at the far end, back to the wall, eyes on the
street.

One of my favorite spots—perfect for watching people without being seen.

* * *

I'd grown up watching people at the local park with my dad every Sunday morning as he skimmed the newspaper and drank coffee from a Thermos.

Even in the dead of winter, snow falling, we'd arrive early to claim his spot—a rickety wooden bench with direct line of sight to the entrance—then listen and observe.

Sometimes we'd be approached by gentlemen he knew, carrying on conversations in his native tongue. But often, we just watched.

People-watching became one of my best skills—honed over years surveilling targets.

Reading people—their voices, clothes, body language—brought me an unusual sense of joy, and I hadn't realized how much I missed it until I sat at the bar, taking it all in.

It felt good to be present. To watch people.

Something inside me reawakened.

* * *

"What can I get you?" the bartender snapped.

I met her eyes. "A mimosa, please."

I'd have preferred my usual—red wine, or even whiskey—but both seemed too heavy for brunch, and I didn't want the judgment.

I wasn't an alcoholic—*at least, that's what I kept telling myself.* Drinking was just my only way to escape.

Some days I wondered if I was drinking too much, but it numbed my pain and made the time pass faster—and Blake never seemed to notice—or care. Besides, he drank more than I did.

"That it?" she asked.

"I'd love to see a menu, if you have one."

I managed a polite smile as she rolled her eyes.

She slid the drink over seconds later, one brow arched.

I raised the flute triumphantly to my lips—the taste crisp and bright—a seemingly perfect choice for Florida and my new life.

I felt myself unwinding as I peered out at the cluttered sidewalk—sun shining on vacationers in flip flops and tank tops. Parents chasing kids. Chairs being dragged across a sandy street.

I caught a whiff of coconut—pulling me back to a trip to Hawaii.

The memory of freedom before surveillance and secrets, making my chest ache.

One small sip. One small step back into the light.

Chapter 3

The hum of music drifted in through speakers overhead, muffling the sound of clanking in the kitchen.

I lifted my mimosa for a second sip as my world stopped—and the most handsome man I'd ever seen casually strolled in.

Early forties. With a commanding presence that made people look twice.

The bar adjusted to him—chairs scooting in, conversations softening, eyes lifting.

From his designer suit to his vintage half-million-dollar watch practically begging to be seen, to his blinding monogrammed diamond cufflinks—he was dressed to be noticed.

Flashy didn't faze me—I'd spent a career around it—but this seemed over-the-top in laid-back Siesta Key.

He chatted briefly with the bartender before ordering a dirty vodka martini.

I smirked.

Interesting brunch choice—*but who was I to judge?*

He could've been a borderline alcoholic, too.

Moments later, he took a phone call. I caught snippets:

"Yeah, took care of it. It's done. I'm in the Village right now... that sounds fine... sure, bud, I'll hit you back."

Brief. Calm.

Thankfully not obnoxious.

The last thing I wanted was for my outing to be spoiled by children, drunks, or a rich jerk on his phone.

And he was undoubtedly rich.

People who weren't couldn't afford a security detail.

He was preceded into the bar by an attractive older gentleman in a suit—a silvery-gray high and tight—seated just beyond me.

A younger guy entered soon after him taking a seat by the door—trying—and failing—to blend in with a visible earpiece.

A blacked-out SUV idled out front with two bodies staged inside.

I'd seen wealthy types in Sarasota before—Bitcoin bros, trust fund kids.

But something about him didn't add up.

And that's exactly why I couldn't look away.

* * *

I flashed back to a hotel bar in Mexico City.

A rich Egyptian businessman cruised in, flanked by six guards with poorly concealed sidearms.

The place whirred in conversation and laughter—until a Mossad hit team arrived minutes later. A team with no regard for civilian casualties.

What were the odds I'd end up in the middle of another assassination attempt?

Incredibly low in Florida, I told myself.

Then again, my luck had been nothing short of cinematic—devastating, dark, and wildly unpredictable.

And of all days, I'd left home unarmed.

A terrible oversight.

* * *

I scanned the room again, my brain wired to observe—even when I didn't want to.

Evaluating exits. Assessing threats.

I stole another long glance at the handsome stranger.

Well over six feet. Dirty blond hair. Light green eyes. A jawline to die for.

With the ideal build—lean but strong.

Despite seeming familiar, I couldn't place him.

And I usually could—faces stuck with me, even those I'd only seen once—a talent that served me well in HUMINT.

Maybe I'd seen him on TV or in a magazine.

I offered a faint smile as he set his martini glass on the bar with a soft clink.

Before I knew it, he rose from his seat, moving toward me.

I told myself to keep cool, but it'd been a while since I sat at a bar.

Let alone talked to a man—*especially* one like him.

I was trained to blend in. To be invisible. But in that moment, all I felt was exposed.

He pulled out the chair beside me as our eyes met, heat immediately rising in my neck.

Then his cologne hit—a swirl of cedarwood and a note I couldn't name.

Sharp. Expensive.

"Mind if I join you?" he asked, smiling before slipping off his jacket to reveal a pristine white dress shirt clinging to dewy skin and a muscular chest.

A walking daydream.

I tried not to gawk.

"Unless you're a billionaire, this seat's taken," I said, swirling my mimosa with a smile.

Sometimes I amused myself. If I was going to cheat on my millionaire husband, it certainly wouldn't be with *another* millionaire. Same money, same problems.

He flagged the bartender for a second martini.

"What's your gut tell you?"

"About you being a billionaire?"

"Yeah."

I gave him a thoughtful once-over.

"Well, your detail tells me you're rich, but in Sarasota, rich is normal. And I haven't met many billionaires... but even if you're not, I'm guessing you're about to say you are. Am I right?"

"That's fair," he laughed. "You seem to know a little about details. Where's yours this morning?"

Smooth. "You flatter me, but I'm far too unimportant."

I sipped as he glanced me up and down, eyes lingering on my neck—a Cartier pendant—and wrist—a diamond Lady-Datejust—then the handbag sitting beside me—Chanel, vintage.

"That's not the vibe I'm getting. I mean—what's a woman like you doing brunching alone?"

It was a valid question.

One I didn't have a good answer for.

Our eyes met again—the moment unmistakably charged.

He studied me—not just with attraction, but real interest.

Something I hadn't experienced in... years.

It startled me.

"I'm married," I blurted—enthusiastically.

Far too enthusiastically.

"Yeah, I figured," he replied with a soft chuckle. "Hard not to notice the giant rock on your finger."

He tapped his own ring on the bar, catching my eye. A class ring.

"Harvard," he said, noticing.

I nodded—caught.

"You're younger than I expected."

"I wish! No... it just took me a long time to graduate. I'm a serial underachiever." He smiled—mischievous.

"So, where's the guy that bought you that thing?" he asked, gesturing to my engagement ring—a four-carat diamond, halo-set.

I twisted it, aware of its weight. It was a statement piece. Bold and impossible to miss.

Which was exactly the point.

Blake bought it to send a message:

She already has a rich husband. *Keep fucking moving.*

"He's out of town for business," I said, immediately regretting it.

Blake really was out of town. More accurately, he was out of the country—which one, I wasn't sure. Not because he couldn't tell me—but honestly, I hadn't cared enough to ask.

And his business? Well, that was sometimes classified.

Then he asked: "Saving the world one business trip at a time, eh?"

The way "saving the world" landed seemed too curious.

"I suppose you could say that."

I pivoted.

"I hate to be rude, but have we met before? You look remarkably familiar... although if you're a billionaire, maybe I know you from the news."

A sly smile. "Unlikely."

"So, what brings you to Siesta Key?" I asked. "You're clearly not from around here if you're sporting a Tom Ford suit."

"You know your designers," he teased.

I fluttered my ring. "Yeah, occupational hazard."

He grinned. "Well, I actually *do* live here. But I just got back from D.C. this morning—was catching up with a Marine buddy who works on the Hill."

I took a sip of my mimosa, trying to mask the smile forming on my lips.

Perfect.

A Marine.

Just what my life was missing.

"What's so funny?" he asked.

"Sorry, I shouldn't have laughed."

"Do you hate Marines?"

I debated telling him I was one, but often guys laughed when I told them—even some Marines.

I didn't fit the stereotype. I was in shape but not overly muscular, dressed fashionably, wore makeup, and enjoyed being feminine.

Anyway, it seemed easier to dodge the topic of myself entirely.

It also meant avoiding a long-winded exchange of units, ranks, and duty stations until eventually we'd find someone we knew in common. It was a small Marine Corps.

I replied. "More often than you know. My husband's a retired Marine."

"Oh, nice. A retarded Marine. Me, too—well, sort of. I was medically retired in '09."

"Was that before or after you made your billions?"

"Touché!" he laughed. "Would you believe me if I said *after*?"

I downed what was left in my champagne flute. "Depends how good your story is."

He signaled the bartender for another round.

CHAPTER 4

Edward

He wasn't born billionaire-rich, but his family didn't struggle. His ethnically Russian mother, Eva, was a few years shy of fifty, and his dad, Erik—a giant Norseman and first generation American—nearly fifty-five when they had him, by absolute miracle.

Growing up an only child in small-town Ohio, Edward had a hard time fitting in.

He was the consummate student with an IQ over 170—brilliant, reserved, and according to himself, *formidable*.

Relating to other kids didn't come naturally, so his parents encouraged sports. Given his height, volleyball seemed an obvious choice—and he was a quick star. At fourteen, his parents even uprooted their life and moved to Florida so he could play year-round.

Then tragedy struck. Shortly after his sixteenth birthday, they died in a plane crash.

Some accounts called it mysterious while others chalked it up to pilot error in stormy weather.

Either way, he was orphaned with no blood relatives and sent to live with his godfather—also named Edward, better known as Ed—his namesake—a friend of his father's from Harvard Law.

Ed was a serial bachelor from an extremely wealthy and well-established American family. He told me to think along the lines of the Carnegies and Vanderbilts.

When Ed was named as Edward's godfather, he was engaged—though that was short-lived. He never married, and for reasons Edward couldn't understand, his parents never designated anyone else his guardian.

So, at the impressionable age of sixteen, Edward was traveling the world, drinking martinis at dinner parties, and playing wingman to the straight but incredibly flamboyant Ed—a man he barely knew.

I laughed, thinking a playboy lifestyle couldn't possibly have been what Edward's parents had in mind for their son. But no one really expects to die in a plane crash. Especially a mysterious one.

The story was certainly intriguing—if any of it was true.

After recounting his childhood, Edward jumped ahead to 2004, "sparing" me details of his boarding school days in Switzerland, time at Harvard, and many escapades around the world. That's when his life took another turn.

While sitting beside Ed at breakfast in the Hamptons, he suffered a massive heart attack.

"One second, he was reaching for a biscuit, the next, he was just... dead," Edward said, flatly. Then, without missing a beat:

"So I enlisted."

"Why would you have done that instead of graduating from Harvard?"

He shrugged. "I thought it would be fun?"

He recounted a conversation he'd had with Ed months earlier—about being so handsome, cunning, and charismatic that one day he'd be expected to run for office—which would be easier if he'd served.

I shook my head in authentic hilarity.

"How am I not surprised by that answer?"

"I didn't make that up! Honest to God!"

"*Mm-hmm.*"

Edward shipped to boot camp in early 2005, and by year's end, PFC Anderson—he said, referring to himself in third person—was in Iraq for his first combat deployment.

As I sipped my third mimosa, I couldn't help but envision him as the most attractive PFC the Marine Corps had ever seen. And possibly the most commanding. Presidential-level was no exaggeration.

While deployed, Ed's estate settled, and Edward was shocked to discover he'd been left a fortune—a little over three-billion-dollars.

Overnight, he had what he described as "fuck you" money.

He inherited Ed's mansion, a villa on the Amalfi coast, a château in France, and a dozen other properties around the world—some in places he'd never even heard of. Plus, a yacht, helicopter, and private jets to get him from mansion to villa to château.

The kind of money that allowed him to do almost anything he wanted.

He laughed, recalling how Ed's lawyers counseled him to report his new wealth, knowing it would swiftly get him separated from the Marine Corps. But he didn't. Instead, he concealed it, paying a team of professionals to manage Ed's businesses and foundations while he continued to serve.

He said he was young, stubborn, and lived with an air of invincibility.

I suspected Edward hadn't changed much.

In mid-2007, he deployed to Iraq a second time. Then, three months into his seven-month deployment, tragedy struck again. His convoy hit an IED.

He lost most of his squad. Luckily, everyone in his vehicle survived—but not without serious injury.

One buddy lost a leg. Another an eye and a leg. All suffered traumatic brain injury. Edward sustained a testicular injury and third-degree burns to the fronts and backs of his legs.

I fumbled my flute—glass clinking loudly against the bar.

"Where was I?" Edward asked with a grin. "The doctors almost took my legs. I was lucky—well, aside from the loss of mobility and years of rehab."

I tried not to smile but couldn't help it.

He was charming. His tale, gripping.

Maybe he wasn't so full of shit, after all.

Behind us, a server dropped a plate.

It shattered on the floor as the room lulled.

"I'm sorry to hear that," I said quietly. "Losing a testicle must've been difficult."

He laughed boisterously, drawing attention our way.

"That whole story, and that's what you got out of it? That's kind of fucked up," he said before taking a sip from his martini. "Bad news is, I can't father children. But don't worry—everything works mostly as it should..."

His face morphed—suggestive. "Sometimes I just require a special touch."

I blushed as his gaze pierced through me.

"So—what's your story? You clearly ditched your detail. What do you do?" he asked.

I reassessed Edward for a beat. The question was almost too smooth.

I was once an Intel Officer in the Marine Corps. Then a CIA Targeting Officer before I was blackballed. Now? Nothing. And that was exactly the vague answer I was going to give him.

"Me? I'm boring. I bounced around a lot. I only moved to Siesta Key recently... I suppose now I'm just a housewife."

He smirked. "Well, it seems to agree with you."

Then:

"Tell me—how do you like Siesta Key, Allie?"

I started to respond. "It's really lov—"

Wait—

I froze.

The room blurred, noises suddenly distant and muted as I replayed our interaction—every word we'd exchanged.

My tradecraft kicked in—late. *Embarrassingly* late.

This wasn't brunch. It was a setup.

Edward dropped my name casually, like it wasn't the first time we'd met. Like he already knew me. But I hadn't introduced myself by name.

Even if I had, I wouldn't have used my real name—I didn't do that with strangers.

Ever.

"I'm sorry, did you just say, 'Allie'?"

He appeared startled.

"No... I don't believe so."

I scanned the restaurant and abruptly rose from my chair, the noise causing his security to alert.

My defenses surged as reality snapped into place—someone sent him.

Someone who knew exactly how to get me to lower my guard.

A charming and patriotic man. A Marine.

It was textbook. And I fell for it.

I clenched my jaw so he wouldn't see my panic, then fumbled for my wallet—stopped, and let out a tight laugh.

"Oh wait, I forgot you're a billionaire. You've got this covered, right?" I scoffed, savoring the idea of the agency footing the bill.

Losers.

As I hurried to leave, I caught Edward's expression—his brow furrowed in regret.

He'd screwed up.

"Are you sure you have to go?" he asked, voice low.

Seriously? He was working me. And he wanted me to stay to chit-chat?

I assessed the body language of the kid by the door—unseasoned—the weakest link. He fidgeted with his earpiece, eyes focused on the SUV outside.

I looked around for makeshift weapons. A heavy salt shaker. A fork. A bottle of vodka. None gave me decent odds against armed men.

I felt my lungs tighten, ready to scream. To make a scene.

"Why—if I try to leave—are you going to shove me into the SUV parked out front?"

"God, no!" Edward replied, looking genuinely disturbed.

"Well, that's a relief, because I was hoping to avoid getting kidnapped today," I sneered.

"Allie, could you please give me a second to explain?" he pleaded, sliding me a business card. In my haste, I didn't grab it.

Edward pushed his chair back—loud, sudden—so I improvised, fumbling in my purse like I was reaching for a gun.

A gun I'd stupidly forgotten.

He put his hands up in surrender and signaled his guys to keep cool.

I watched the young one send a text on his phone as I stumbled outside—the day gorgeous—sunlight blinding, air perfectly warm.

So much for a pleasant brunch outing, I thought, my heart racing with fear I hadn't felt in years.

I took stock of my surroundings.

A work van—no windows. People loitering in the parking lot. A man with mirrored aviators sitting in the ice cream shop across the street.

I memorized the plates of the SUV, then made purposeful eye contact with the driver—a smaller guy with a scraggly beard. Ex-military. He kept his hand on the wheel and gave me a wave.

A guy in a black polo rolled down the back window with, "What's up?" and a head nod. Almost disarming, but I knew better.

I glared as I got in my car and sped away, hitting the main street.

Then panic.

For the first time in decades, I had no escape plan.

Frustrated, I slammed the steering wheel.

What was my move?

I was trained in countersurveillance and evasion.

I should've turned off my phone and gone dark. Disappeared.

Instead, I looped the Village three times—clearing my mind, watching for tails.

I didn't see any... so I thought I'd lost them—

Until the same SUV glided around the corner behind me.

My efforts were useless. There was no ditching them.

They knew who I was. And where I lived.

I'd been targeted—probably long before brunch.

I was tired. Unarmed.

So I did the worst thing I could've done: I drove straight home.

CHAPTER 5

Heat rose from the asphalt as I approached my gated neighborhood—warping the SUV behind me like a hallucination—a projection of fear, closing in.

A lone figure leaned out of the guard shack—a veteran in his early seventies.

"Hey, Jeremy. See the black SUV behind me? Followed me home from brunch. Don't let him in, okay?"

"Not a chance! Want me to call the Sheriff?" he asked eagerly.

"No, I think the guy's just drunk."

I eased forward and watched as Jeremy stepped out of the shack, hand on his holster.

Once the gate closed behind me, I exhaled—what felt like my first breath since leaving the bar. No more tail.

The tightness in my chest loosened, and I let out a laugh—until it caught in my throat.

How could I have been so naive, so mesmerized, that I hadn't even realized I was the mark?

I pulled into my garage moments later, killing the engine. Listening.

Past the gate, everything looked normal—no suspicious cars, no unfamiliar faces. But then again, I hadn't been paying that close of attention. Not anymore. Not in Florida.

Escaping the constant paranoia of the D.C. beltway was the reason I'd moved.

* * *

The neighborhood was beautiful, but otherwise unremarkable—a mix of retirees and wealthy young families living uneventful lives, as far as I could tell.

The house had been offered to me by my closest Marine friend, Mike—a retired O-6.

It felt more like home than anything I'd known after years of bouncing between assignments. A flurry of hotels and apartments—each one only temporary. Unpacking for a few months just to repack and start the whole cycle over. Sometimes with nothing more than a suitcase.

I'd hoped to finally settle down and buy a place of our own, but Blake was set on moving back to a family estate in Texas in another year, and after one too many arguments, I let it go.

Renting it was.

One of Mike's friends owned the house and claimed he needed a reliable tenant to keep it from sitting vacant. Mike offered me a generous deal—handshake only, no lease—and I wasn't about to question it.

He'd always looked out for me—even when I insisted I didn't need it. This house was just another way for him to keep me on his radar. He knew I wasn't okay—but he claimed the Florida sun would melt all my worries away.

If only it were that simple.

Mike had been my only real family for years. He'd taken me under his wing on my first deployment—like an older brother. Watched out for me.

When I first started seeing Blake, he warned me not to get involved—for the sake of both our careers. It was sound advice, but I failed to take it.

Later, when Mike and his secretive silent partner started his company—Dark Skies—he crashed at our condo in D.C. That's when he came around to Blake, a man he originally hadn't cared for.

Or at least, he pretended to—playing along for my benefit.

On paper, they were cut from the same cloth—southern boys, same uniform, same loyalty to the Corps.

But they couldn't have been more different.

* * *

As the door swung open, I listened. The house was still except for the faint hum of the refrigerator. No movement or shadows.

Everything seemed in place.

I double-checked the alarm system, eyes scanning nervously—mortified I hadn't enacted tradecraft in over two months.

But why?

Because part of me had given up.

It was exhausting, constantly looking over my shoulder for threats that might not be there. But I couldn't tell anyone that.

The truth was—my life wasn't good. Far from it.

I was depressed.

My marriage was crumbling.

I didn't have any friends besides Mike thirty minutes away, and Liv—a housewife with four children under the age of ten.

I'd been forced from my career—one of the few things that motivated and inspired me—and lost my sense of self.

Maybe that's why I'd gone to brunch alone in the first place.

I wasn't trying to meet someone. I just wanted to feel again.

And Edward made me *feel*.

First intrigue.

Then terror.

I passed the hallway mirror and stopped cold.

The woman staring back was nothing but a shell of the woman I once was.

Now fragile. Frail. Unnerved.

God. Was this who I'd become?

* * *

Before bed, after sitting for hours on the couch half-comatose, I considered doing nothing—leaving the front door unlocked, disarming the alarm.

Let them take me. Put me out of my misery.

Then I pictured Blake.

That look that said, "Darlin', really?"

I owed him more than that.

So I secured the house. Slid a gun under my pillow. Tipped a chair against the locked bedroom door.

Put surrender off another day.

* * *

I tossed and turned in bed, replaying every word and detail.

Edward's security. His clothes. What he drank. The way he spoke with the bartender.

He couldn't have been agency. If he were, I would've heard about him. *That,* I was certain.

If not agency... then *what?*

A contractor, maybe? But no contractor I'd ever known wore a ten-thousand-dollar suit and vintage collector watch.

He claimed to have gone to Harvard—so maybe he was already wealthy?

Then it hit me.

I let out a shrill laugh—the kind that flirts with insanity.

His whole story—Harvard, being a billionaire, Siesta Key—was bullshit. A cover.

Then a darker thought crept in—

What if Edward wasn't a man at all, but a test? A red cell?

No... Mike trusted me. He wouldn't pull something like that.

I debated calling him, but what would I even say?

That I went to a bar alone and let a man flirt with me?

That the man knew my name?

That maybe Florida wasn't as safe as he'd promised?

Still... something about Edward felt real.

The way his voice broke when he talked about his friends.

The way he said *we*.

He was a patriotic American. I believed he was a Marine.

But professional hitmen didn't make mistakes.

Edward had—my name.

What was his angle?

I wished I'd taken his business card.

* * *

A car made an unexpected U-turn in my driveway, its headlights sweeping across my bedroom like a searchlight.

As it drove away, I sighed with relief and refocused, my mind cycling through our interaction again.

This time, something clicked.

Edward had referred to himself in third person—PFC *something...* starting with an A.

But what was it?

It sat on the tip of my tongue—jeering.

I pulled out my phone and searched for last names starting with an A, and there it was—Anderson.

Edward Anderson.

I searched him, my eyes glued to the screen as I scrolled. Stunned.

Edward Anderson had, in fact, attended Harvard.

He was a combat-disabled Marine. A Silver Star recipient.

A billionaire. A philanthropist.

Once named Florida's Most Eligible Bachelor... I nearly choked. *Of course he was.*

Then it got worse.

My skin crawled.

Edward had once been named a *Future Leader of the World* by a panel of global elites—the kind of title people traded their soul for.

The military record. The Harvard diploma. The smoldering backstory.

An entire persona carefully crafted. Weaponized. Groomed for power.

Suddenly, Edward read like a threat assessment—every detail a giant red flag.

Brunch wasn't a coincidence.

It was a meeting—staged and deliberate.

I felt myself falling into a part of my life I thought I'd left behind.

* * *

After staring at pictures of Edward online for hours, I couldn't shake the overwhelming sense that I'd met him before—his eyes so familiar.

Then I stumbled across a picture of him as a younger, slightly thinner Corporal Edward Erik Anderson being awarded the Silver Star at the Pentagon.

He looked almost exactly the same.

I couldn't have met him.

I would've remembered meeting the most handsome man in the world.

* * *

I woke Monday morning and made myself a promise:

No more living in fear.

Whatever was meant to happen would—but I'd put up a fight.

I channeled the woman I once was then slid a gun into my waistband, threw on a light sweatshirt to conceal it, and headed out for my usual morning walk—reminding myself, step by step, not to let them steal my confidence.

As I returned, a dark SUV caught my attention, turning on the street before mine, so I detoured for a better look.

Everything appeared normal on my street.

I exhaled—pushing the paranoia aside.

I was good. Steady.

Until I reached my front door.

There it was—that spiny sense. The instinct that something was wrong.

Over the years, I'd learned to lean into it.

I trusted it to keep me safe.

And it wasn't just nagging.

It was screaming.

As I turned the key, I caught a hint of cologne.

Earthy and warm with a faint smokiness.

I shivered before hastily drafting a text:

Hope you're enjoying your trip. Nice day here, but I'm feeling sick. Think I'll watch our favorite movie and rest. Call when you can. XO

After years of cryptic texts and secret codes, Blake would know what it meant. My finger hovered over send as a wave of panic sent goosebumps up my arms. *What if Blake sent someone to check on me—and everything was fine?* I'd seem crazy. Irrational.

Exactly how he liked to paint me.

He'd hinted before that I needed help.

The last thing I wanted was to prove him right.

So instead of trusting my instincts—and my training—I deleted the text, slipped the phone in my pocket, and let doubt win.

I didn't bother to clear the house—I just walked in, swiped a bottle from the bar, and collapsed into the couch.

There, I stared blankly at the wall—caught between laughing and crying.

Until I caught it again. The same scent of cologne.

Warm. Smoky. Undeniable. *Recent.*

My stomach turned.

Someone had been *inside* my house.

CHAPTER 6

The family room was dim except for the flicker of the muted television in front of me. Subtitles were on, but I focused only on the whiskey in my hand—petrified my house was bugged.

I considered putting on a show—waving my gun, spiraling on cue—just to prove they'd finally broken me.

Maybe then they'd leave me alone. Let me go about my new life in peace.

But would they *really?* It was unlikely.

I took another slow sip, the burn in my throat a welcome distraction from the thoughts looping in my head.

How had I become such a paranoid person?

I was accomplished. Poised. A perfectionist who'd built her life on rules, loyalty, and hard work. An athlete. A patriot. An expert in my field. At one point, a rising star within the agency.

I could walk into a room full of men—high-level government officials, generals, politicians, donors—and own it. Confident. Unapologetic.

I was accustomed to danger. For years, I'd volunteered for assignments that put my life at risk for a cause greater than myself—my country.

I'd testified in classified hearings before Congress, answering tough questions honestly but diplomatically, because that's what D.C. required.

I was known and trusted in D.C.'s social and political circles.

My nights and weekends were crammed with cocktail parties and charity galas.

I thrived.

The heels, the gowns, the champagne.

I used to be someone.

I shuddered as I caught a glimpse of my former life, and for a moment, my mind latched onto Blake.

Back then, his presence was addicting—the weight of his name, the way he carried himself, the doors he opened. He gripped my mind and body like a drug I couldn't quit.

His power and influence helped mold me into that woman.

The one who got the best assignments.

The one people had on speed dial—the call they made when stakes were high and results mattered.

Together, we looked like a coveted power couple, and he let D.C. believe it.

But the truth was, I was there to polish his image, never to outshine him.

Would I ever have amounted to anything on my own without his wealth and pedigree?

Worse, was that strong, confident version of myself even real—or just a woman propped up, playing pretend?

My eyes welled as old memories twisted to doubt—

And a nostalgic ache for a life I'd never get back.

A life I wasn't sure ever existed.

* * *

I slumped into the couch, letting it swallow me as I sipped and spiraled.

My past hit in stinging blows—sharp and unforgiving.

Ever since I'd been suspected of leaking classified intel on dark web forums, alongside a handful of others I'd worked with, my perfect life had shattered.

I was the target of non-stop intimidation and harassment—and something more.

Psychological warfare. What the agency did best.

Surveillance teams idled outside my house. Engines humming at 3 a.m. Dark figures behind tinted glass. Always watching.

Then came the calls. The texts. The threats.

It all chipped away at me until I barely recognized myself.

I should've sought help—but it was never really an option.

I was part of a generation that compartmentalized trauma.

It was expected, and therapy was a liability for my clearance and career.

So I sucked it up and stayed silent.

But the sickest part?

The agency trying to break me was the same agency that would've punished me for it.

I found other ways to cope.

Late night wine turned whiskey.

Security cameras.

Weapons staged strategically throughout the house.

I told myself I was just being smart. *Prepared.*

But deep down, I knew what it was—fear—and the only sense of control I had left.

And Blake?

He said all the right things, but he never really listened or helped.

He seemed to enjoy pointing out how fragile I'd become.

So I retreated into my shell, no longer an extroverted introvert—just an introvert.

And the alienation wasn't just painful.

It changed me.

* * *

The thing was, while the agency assembled its shortlist of suspects with access to the classified files, I was quietly building a whistleblower complaint of my own.

Anonymous.

The goal?

To expose wrongdoing inside the U.S. government and intelligence community—threats to national security too big to ignore.

I wanted full-scale investigations.

Real accountability.

Heads to roll.

The problem?

My complaint mirrored intel being leaked online.

Some of it even matched testimony I'd given to Congress. Not by choice—but because I was compelled. Under oath. My every word on the record.

It made me a prime suspect.

And just like that, I could feel the darkness closing in.

* * *

I raised the whiskey to my lips, weighing my decision before taking another long sip.

It did little to dull the pain or paranoia.

I glanced around, the light from the TV casting eerie shadows that danced on the walls.

I knew I needed to stop drinking before my mind wandered to memories I couldn't escape.

The TV went dark for a split second. I jolted, fearing someone had cut power to the house.

And for a moment, I wasn't in Florida.

I was back in Iraq.

Alone in darkness.

Standing helplessly a hundred yards from a burned-out building along the Euphrates.

The screaming and horror.

Listening to my team get killed.

No backup within range.

Sixty seconds. Five lives.

All because one guy wanted to impress a female Black Hawk pilot.

The TV flickered back to life in front of me as I caught my breath and pulled myself out of the nightmare.

* * *

I thought I'd seen and heard it all after ten years at the agency. Scandal. Fraud, waste, and abuse. Cronyism. Government overreach. Money laundering. Drug trafficking. Even human trafficking.

My former boss used to say: "If you know, you know—and nothing can be unseen."

It sounded melodramatic.

But he was right—some truths ruin you.

I often wished I hadn't solved certain mysteries that had been nagging at me—unfortunate puzzle pieces that led to the first draft of my complaint.

Like Pandora's box—once opened, there was no closing it.

But for reasons I still couldn't fully understand, the complaint never saw the light of day.

At least, not through me.

I closed my eyes, the light of TV flashing behind my eyelids.

If this wasn't rock bottom... I might not survive it.

CHAPTER 7

I didn't know how long my eyes had been closed, heavy from whiskey—bottle still in my hand.

Minutes? Hours? The blur of too much drinking. Too much thinking.

On the TV: a documentary on Afghanistan.

Another place I wished I could forget.

Still, the memories came flooding back.

I was shaped by September 11, 2001. My whole generation was.

That day pushed me straight into the Marine Corps after college—and every part of my life since had been shaped by the War on Terror.

Serving gave me pride. Determination.

A love of freedom—and a need to do the right thing.

When the agency recruited me, I jumped at the opportunity.

I woke every morning with purpose, energized by the mission. Work didn't feel like work, even during hundred-hour weeks. My job was my identity—and I was fine with that.

Working there had been more fulfilling than I ever imagined—

Until the terrifying day it wasn't.

The day I realized I wasn't serving freedom anymore—but feeding something darker.

Warsaw, Poland—June 6, 2014.

* * *

Years into my work, I received an assignment to Eastern Europe—one that made me intimately familiar with the term *color revolution.*

Color revolutions were essentially sophisticated mind games: information warfare, psychological operations—designed to obfuscate the truth and bend perception as entire nations unraveled.

They targeted governments resistant to Western influence because they were cheaper and cleaner than direct military action.

No footprint. No attribution. But no less effective.

First, they'd contest electoral legitimacy.

Then came organized protests and mass civil disobedience—driven by media pawns ensuring favorable coverage in the Western press.

Then forced regime change—without a single bomb dropped.

Americans were conditioned to believe such things weren't real.

But within the right circles of the U.S. government, they were an open secret—quietly deployed around the world.

And I unintentionally became a leading expert in them.

Even as the U.S. government publicly dismissed them as conspiracy.

That was the strategy. Deny reality. Discredit anyone who claimed otherwise.

It wasn't just foreign adversaries they targeted—it was their own people.

Their own employees.

They weaponized doubt and drummed up confusion.

And if someone tried to blow the whistle on the truth?

They made them look crazy. Paranoid. Unstable.

I knew their playbook all too well.

I'd lived it.

* * *

I wasn't in Cairo or Tunis during Arab Spring.

I was stuck at a forward operating base in Afghanistan—catching bits and pieces of the news through choppy satellite feeds and misleading headlines, surrounded by concrete T-walls.

In 2011, it was just a story from another godforsaken place where time moved slow.

It wasn't until years later that I realized what happened in Syria was nothing short of an attempted color revolution by the West—stalled only by Russian support to the Syrian president. From there, it devolved into civil war.

Arab Spring didn't combust spontaneously. It was sparked, stoked, and fraudulently sold to the public—toppling governments through 'organic' uprisings that weren't organic at all.

At first, I assumed these operations—while morally questionable—were about geopolitics. Part of the chessboard controlled by the great power players.

If so, I could've looked away.

There was barely a foreign election the agency hadn't touched, going back decades. That wasn't news.

But color revolutions were far more devastating—more sinister.

They weren't just being used to feed the military industrial complex.

Or to enable money laundering at a colossal scale.

They were being deployed to fuel global human trafficking—

Including child sex trafficking—

Through unfettered, massive influxes of people across borders.

Without realizing it, the world witnessed this with their own eyes as the media swamped them with repeated imagery of thousands upon thousands of fleeing Syrians making their way to Europe.

But who were they? Mostly military-aged men. *And unaccompanied children.*

The Syrian humanitarian crisis opened the floodgates.

A dream scenario for human traffickers.

* * *

I had the data, sources, and expertise—ready to expose the whole ruse.

And then—the plot twist I didn't see coming:

A signal from someone staring into the same darkness.

CHAPTER 8

An envelope sat on the doorstep at 4 a.m. as I was stepping out for a run.

Heavy. Thick. Unmarked. My name scrawled in large blue caps across the front:

ALLIE BAILEY

Taunting me.

I brought it inside with gloved hands, praying it wasn't laced with anthrax.

It was something worse.

My blood ran cold.

The first page:

HE KNOWS

My heart rate skyrocketed.

One man came to mind: Joe Turner.

But what did he know?

I flinched.

More importantly, who was warning me that he knew? And why?

I set my alarm, closed the curtains, and rushed to the safety of my basement office.

It didn't take long for me to realize that the papers echoed my fears—louder, smarter, and more damning.

Classified operations. Transcripts. Affidavits. Financial records. Timelines. Photos.

Most chilling—a single verbatim line from my draft complaint.

I suspected it was written by a high-ranking official, a hacker, or a reformed member of the deep state.

Possibly all three.

I had a tough decision to make.

I called out of work, then went to urgent care for a strep test—just in case someone at the agency checked on my absence later.

I needed an alibi that was boring and believable.

When I got home, I whipped out a whiteboard and dumped a basket of burners onto the cold concrete floor—settled in, strategizing—like a woman preparing for war.

* * *

I needed a lawyer willing to take on the DoD and intelligence community—someone ambitious. Fearless. Unshakable.

Blake was deployed, so I called Mike.

I tried describing my situation without divulging too much, and we talked in circles for an hour, leaving us both frustrated.

But Mike came through.

"You're sure he's good?" I asked.

"He's a real shark," Mike said. "Doesn't scare easy."

So, I took a leap of faith—placing full trust in a man I'd never met—a man who could run into a firefight with nothing but a legal pad and somehow walk out unscathed.

At least, that's how Mike described him.

He set up a secret meeting for us in Savannah, Georgia, two weeks later.

The lawyer?

Spencer Goldman.

* * *

Six days later, another leak of classified information triggered a criminal investigation with talks of espionage charges. Capital punishment.

I no longer needed legal advice on a whistleblower paper—

I needed a lawyer to defend my name.

And maybe my life.

Because if *he* really knew everything—

I wasn't just a suspect.

I was a target.

CHAPTER 9

Historic Savannah was exactly as charming as I'd imagined.

Spanish moss dripped from the magnolia trees as I turned down a quiet cobblestone street with six or seven homes, all shrouded in a low fog.

I parked where Spencer told me: beside a carriage house with peeling paint and sagging shutters, then let myself in without knocking, per instructions.

Inside, the air was dusty and damp. Heavy. Almost stifling.

It looked like a time capsule—nothing updated since the '70s.

A yellowed corduroy couch. Green shag carpet. Faded wallpaper.

A creak sounded above me.

I looked up the staircase as a face appeared.

"Welcome, Allie."

Dressed in khakis, a pink polo, and a bright argyle sweater, Spencer was different than I imagined. Younger. More laid-back. Cheerful—but no less cunning.

We sat at a table in the dim kitchen and got to business.

No drinks or chit chat. Just a heaping pile of documents.

He spoke with laser focus and the learned cockiness of a Harvard Law grad—tracking my every word. Unafraid.

Just hours before our meeting, there had been another leak—fresh intel hitting the twenty-four-hour news cycle.

And it didn't seem like coincidence. It felt personal—like I was being framed.

I had a prime suspect in mind: Joe Turner—former Kiev Station Chief clawing his way toward Director.

He'd coached me to lie under oath. I hadn't—making me a liability with a dangerous voice.

Joe was morally bankrupt, and taking a life meant nothing to him.

He'd knowingly unleashed suffering on entire populations, deploying color revolutions like chemical weapons—brutal and without remorse.

And he'd killed before.

A young Ukrainian mistress and her child—*his* child.

Disappeared without a trace.

Framing me wouldn't be difficult.

Spencer agreed.

After redlining several sections of a document, he looked up.

"We'll need to get you into hiding if you submit this."

I blinked as a chill crawled up my spine. "But I didn't write it."

"You mentioned you know certain parts to be true, though. Correct?"

"Yeah... but these details are way above my pay grade." I pointed to the excerpt laying in front of us.

"They'll still think you wrote it."

"They *who*?" I asked.

"Take your pick." He shook his head. "It doesn't matter—you'll be the face of it."

"But..."

Spencer leaned in slightly.

"Mrs. Bailey, these situations ruin lives. Submitting supporting information that's already leaked will end your career—anonymous or not."

He paused, vibe ominous.

"Are you sure you want to do that?"

I shrugged. "I don't see a way around it. If not me, then who?"

Spencer reeled.

"I'd advise you not to make any hasty decisions. Sit on it."

He tapped a folder in front of him. "I'll lock this down. But you need to destroy everything... even your own draft."

Then his voice dropped.

"Because if they find *anything* in your possession—"

He hesitated.

"They'll bury you."

I sat back, weighing my options. The timing couldn't have been worse.

"Okay," I said carefully. "Can you think of any other reason someone would leave this on my doorstep?"

The question had been gnawing at me—that maybe I was being recruited into something bigger. A conspiracy against the U.S. government. I'd received a series of strange letters—nothing more than one or two lines—all addressed the same: **ALLIE BAILEY**

Spencer took a breath. "They wanted to stop you from filing your own complaint? Or frame you? Could be they wanted to blur the trail—make it impossible to ID the true source of the leak."

He folded his hands, assessing.

"I don't know. But as your lawyer, I'm advising you to stay alert. Burn the copies you have and watch your back. Trust no one."

Then a long pause.

"Taking off my lawyer hat—don't make this your fight. I respect your conviction, but... this could get you suicided. Do you understand?"

I nodded, his words haunting me for weeks.

There was more at stake than just my life.

* * *

When Blake returned home weeks later, I wasn't sure how to best deliver the news.

We sat across from each other at the kitchen table, storm clouds rolling in, breakfast going cold.

I explained what he'd missed, what it meant—and what I felt I had to do.

He just sat there, face taut, until eventually:

"Not your fight, darlin'. Time to focus your energy on more important things."

He smiled softly, but despite the rare moment of tenderness—
Walking away didn't feel right.

I wanted my husband to pick up a sword and fight beside me.

Instead, he shut me down—told me to stay quiet.

End of discussion.

But I didn't *want* to stay silent. I wanted to do the right thing.

To expose the perpetrators of color revolutions. Hold them to account for their crimes against humanity.

It sounded utopian.

It probably was.

But I believed it.

Blake didn't.

He was worried about my safety. *Our* safety.

So, I shut up. Burned the copies. Destroyed all traces of my complaint.

But in the months that followed, something between us started to unravel—slow and painful.

Blake thought my silence would keep us safe—but he was wrong.

* * *

We made a pact to stick it out—to weather the storm together.

But we were under constant attack and scrutiny. All for leaks I wasn't responsible for.

If the *ad hominem* smears and dead rats weren't enough, the agency's ideologue lawyers took it a step further with trumped-up charges and manufactured lies.

All at the direction of officials like slimy Joe Turner—if not Joe himself.

And it worked.

Couple by couple, our friends vanished.

I told myself good riddance—who needs friends without a moral compass, anyway?

But the truth hurt.

Our friends weren't cowards—they just couldn't afford to be associated with me. Not if they wanted to keep their own livelihoods. Their positions of power. Their platforms to do good.

It was a shame.

But it was how the agency worked.

How the Pentagon worked.

How the Hill worked.

And Blake wasn't immune to the witch-hunt.

* * *

I stood tall at Langley for months, confronting the rumors head-on.

I was reassigned to a menial desk job, but I kept showing up. Kept performing.

Until one day—I just broke.

I couldn't keep up the tough facade anymore.

Not when I was being followed.

Not when hang-up calls taunted me at all hours, forcing me to rely solely on burners.

Not when whispers chased me through every hallway.

Not with Blake's constant warnings.

Not with that inescapable sense that someone was always watching—one step behind.

It became too much.

I prayed it would stop if I walked away—so I did something I never had before—I stopped fighting and resigned.

I told myself I'd try to live what was left of my life to the fullest. To recalibrate what was important. Reconnect with Blake. Give myself a chance to finally breathe.

To be free.

But the result wasn't freedom. The threats kept coming. The harassment didn't stop.

My name was still blacklisted. My phone still tapped. My movements still tracked.

So, my goal changed.

I'd live my life to the fullest until I was imprisoned or killed—whichever came first.

Because it became clear:

I was a loose end.

Resigning wasn't an escape. It was merely an attempt at survival.

And I just barely made it out alive.

* * *

Blake was still at Ground Branch when I left the agency.

Part of me thought I was doing him a favor—I assumed if I quit, they'd leave us both alone.

I was only half-right.

The investigations into him vanished overnight—everything from embezzlement to trafficking weapons and drugs.

Poof. Gone.

But not for me.

I kept wondering—*why did he get to walk away clean?*

I tried to convince myself it made sense.

But it didn't sit right.

Still, controversy clung to Blake, and he was forced out under a cloud of scandal.

From there, he landed a contract with Dark Skies—a company focused solely on dismantling human trafficking rings.

The job was a lifeline—except Mike exclusively hired single operators. He only brought Blake on because he and I were family. The team didn't even know I existed.

Mike sought guys that were beat down and broken. Dealing with PTSD, addiction, burnout, anger management. His mission wasn't just operations—it was rehab, and Blake fit right in.

Dark Skies took everyone that could fill a billet: AFSOC PJs, Delta Force, aviators, Army doctors, Navy Corpsmen. But predominantly, Marines: Recon, Infantry, and MARSOC.

Mike's only hiring rules:

1.   Must be a loyal, like-minded patriot
2.   Must be single
3.   No Navy SEALs

Mike genuinely hated SEALs—and his reasons seemed mostly valid. Too much glory. Too many egos.

Dark Skies did everything the special operations community did but without the red tape and bureaucracy. They operated faster, safer, and they were paid fair wages for the danger they faced.

But the op tempo was brutal, and Blake was consistently gone eight months a year.

The isolation was tough, and the distance strained our marriage.

Though separation gave us less time to fight.

And fewer reminders of how broken we'd become.

Eventually I stopped pretending my life—*our life*—could go back to how it was.

I grew used to being alone—if not for the SUVs still parked outside—but even they seemed to tire of me after a while.

I stopped going out. Stopped socializing. Stopped acting like a threat.

I started fading away—and I didn't have the emotional energy to care.

* * *

Three years after the first leak, an anonymous source claimed credit—posthumously, through a Senator.

No evidence or interviews—just a statement, read live on the evening news as I was sitting in my kitchen, eating cold pizza. Blake deployed. Again.

Soon I was sobbing—ugly, broken sobs I didn't recognize as my own.

That night, I sat trembling at the table long after the news ended—staring into the abyss that had become my life.

I hoped my plight was over. That the record would be set straight and I'd be vindicated.

But no one came knocking. No one called with an apology.

All I got was more of the same threatening silence—

The same black SUV parked down the street, lights out.

Because truth *didn't* matter.

It never did.

CHAPTER 10

It had been several days since my startling brunch encounter, and my panic and paranoia started to fade.

But that didn't mean I wasn't still on high alert...

Waiting for a knock on the door. A call with no caller ID.

My instincts told me I was being monitored, so I did a discreet sweep of my house for bugs using the tools I had. I came up short.

I considered calling in a favor—asking an old friend for a professional sweep—but decided against it.

So what if someone was watching me?

I wasn't planning any top secret missions.

* * *

One morning, I caught my reflection in the bedroom slider, causing me to pause.

I had the same tired eyes, but I seemed steadier. More composed. Capable.

Maybe it was an illusion, or maybe I'd caught myself from spiraling out of control.

I decided to reclaim my life and get out of my own head.

* * *

It was getting late. I'd spent the early afternoon immersed in a bottle of wine—or two—on a formal sofa in the living room, staring at a cabinet full of sparkling crystal—the light coming in from the front windows, hitting it just right.

A kaleidoscope of color.

Spectacular.

But it bummed me out.

Expensive wedding gifts, precious heirlooms belonging to Blake's snooty family—and a single vase of my own. Inherited from my great-grandma.

Trapped in a mood, I passed out cold—deep enough that I didn't hear the first knock.

The second jolted me upright.

Startled, I gazed at the clock, then lunged for a Glock hidden in a side table.

Within seconds, I was at my front door, gun in hand.

I heard another knock—louder.

Then—a key.

My spine stiffened. Blake didn't have a key—not yet.

What if it was Mike?

I stepped back, three paces. Heart pounding. Gun still raised.

As the door swung open, I pictured a masked hit team. Silencers. My blood splattered on the tile. Game over.

"Ahhh! What are you doing?! I called you a bunch of times!"

It was Liv— immaculately dressed, full make-up, hair blown out— her usual when leaving the house. Always polished, even with four kids.

She froze.

Her eyes bulged, locked on the gun in my hand.

"Allie!" she screamed.

I lowered it instantly, switching on a light by the entryway.

"Shit. Sorry—I—"

"Ahhh, you're scaring me!" she exclaimed, catching her breath. Her entire body trembled. "I was on Siesta visiting my mom and thought I'd drop by. I would've stopped earlier, but there was someone parked out front... did you have a visitor?"

"*Was it a black SUV?*" I asked, panic knotting in my chest.

I knew it.

Liv shook her head.

"No, a lifted truck with Alabama plates. It looked a little like Blake's," she said in her typically cheerful tone—then paused, eyes wide. Face tight.

"Oh no. Please don't tell me you're being followed again."

I forced a casual shrug.

"No—it was probably one of my neighbor's kids visiting."

"You okay?" she asked, glancing around, like she expected someone might leap out of the pantry.

I needed an excuse—something believable.

I smiled. "Yeah, it's just Blake's owed me a call for a week, and I think something might be wrong."

"I'm sure he's fine. If anything happened, Mike would tell you."

"You're right... what am I saying? I guess I've had too much wine."

Liv eyed the open bottle and two empties on the counter.

"Looks like it. Maybe include me next time you go on a bender?"

I gave a sheepish smile.

The last thing she needed was more reasons to worry about me.

"This isn't just about Blake, is it?" she asked, quieter.

I didn't reply. I knew I couldn't tell her the truth.

She paused, nodding, then asked, "Want to join us for homemade lasagna tonight?"

I shook my head, sadly predictable. "Rain check?"

She gave me a pity hug—gentle with a pat on the back—like *Aw, Allie. You poor thing.*

"Then I'll bring pizza tomorrow. Six p.m.," she called, already halfway down the hall.

I leaned against the wall, watching her disappear out the door.

She was all light and brightness.

I loved her for it—but I was still trying to break free from the darkness.

I turned the deadbolt behind her then paused—spooked.

Feeling it again.

That sharp prickle up my spine—the instinct that something was wrong.

I slowly peeked through the curtains, scanning the street until I was satisfied the danger had passed.

No sign of the black truck.

For now.

I stepped back from the window and exhaled, pressing a hand to my chest. Trying to settle my inner voice.

And then—a thought of Edward slipped in—uninvited.

His voice. His stare.

I couldn't let him go.

* * *

At 3 a.m., I gave up on sleep.

I wandered into the kitchen barefoot, the floor cool beneath my feet, and started a fresh pot of coffee.

Then I dug through drawers for sticky notes, tape, markers—whatever I could find.

Ready to dissect the life of the mysterious Edward Anderson.

It was one of the things I did best.

Dissecting people.

Now it was his turn.

On a whiteboard, I taped an obnoxiously handsome photo I'd printed from the internet—

Florida's Most Eligible Bachelor.

I cleared space on my kitchen island and started pulling pieces of the puzzle together.

Public appearances. News articles. Timelines. His Silver Star citation.

Every tidbit he'd disclosed at brunch—all informing the larger picture.

Around his photo, I started filling in what I knew:

- Lives in Siesta Key
- Armed security
- Marine, 2005-2009
- 2x deployments to Iraq
- Silver Star
- Harvard
- Wealthy—inherited or fabricated?
- Future Leader of the World—2010

And then the more subtle things:

- Said my name before I told him
- Meeting controlled—possibly orchestrated?

I stared at his photo, adding another sticky.

Who's bankrolling you?

I stood back and let the question hang.

A word caught in my mind as my stomach clenched.

Bankrolling.

Wait—

I closed my eyes in concentration.

Could Edward be Mike's mysterious partner?

The one who bankrolled Dark Skies with millions in untraceable cash?

Ungodly wealthy.

A Marine.

Is that why I recognized Edward? It had to be. *Right?*

* * *

I impulsively cold-called Mike.

"Hey Mike, have a quick sec to chat?"

Groggy, he answered, "Uh, yeah, hey kid. Everything okay?"

"Oh..." I checked the clock. It was only 5 a.m. "Sorry for waking you. I didn't realize it was so early."

"It's okay. What's going on?"

I paused—my heart beating too fast.

"Umm, sorry this is out of the blue but do you know a guy named Edward? Last name starting with an A."

Mike cut in, voice tense. "Allie, who's asking?"

"Me. I had a guy hit on me at a bar the other day in Siesta Key. It's not what you're thinking—it was brunch. But is the Edward you know over six feet, green eyes, ridiculously charming? Possibly wearing a *very* expensive watch?"

"Depends who he's trying to impress."

"And does he usually have a detail?"

"Uhhh, kiddo... this is probably a conversation we should be having in person."

"Sure. When will you be back?"

"Might be a few weeks."

That wasn't going to cut it.

I video-called. I couldn't wait weeks.

I needed to know.

I figured Mike didn't want to risk a phone call—too easy for the NSA to intercept. They'd have to work harder for video. Not impossible. Just harder.

"This him?" I asked as I flashed Mike a picture of the Edward I'd met.

"Yeah, that's him."

"And you trust this guy?"

"With my life. And yours."

Mike paused, then, "He's a trusted agent, Allie. *Family.*"

"And you know about his... connections? Right?"

"He's not who you think. He's—"

"Say no more. That's all I needed. Give me a call next time you're in town, okay?"

"Yeah, kid, you got it," he said—wearing a puzzled expression as I hung up.

The memory raced in my mind—Edward relaxed at the bar, an amused glint in his eye like he knew what I'd say before I even said it.

The moment suddenly felt different. *Reclassified.*

I set my phone down with a tinge of relief.

Edward was Mike's secretive partner—the one I'd only ever heard about in whispers.

A figure with no name or photo—just a call sign: *The Punisher.*

Still, Mike's expression lingered in my mind—calm yet cautious. Cryptic.

His statement: "*With my life. And yours. He's trusted.*"

That meant... Edward had to be one of the good guys.

But, then why had he tried to manipulate me?

I stood in the kitchen, fingertips anxiously tapping the counter.

The air felt heavy. My instincts louder than ever.

It wasn't just his security. Or his expensive watch.

It was the way Edward interacted with me like he already knew me. Like he'd seen me before. Met me before.

Maybe he had.

Maybe I'd just been too tired or sad to notice.

I closed my eyes and exhaled.

This wasn't the time to spiral. I needed to focus.

I turned back to the whiteboard, eyes locking on his photo:

Underneath it, I scrawled a single line:

How long have you been watching me?

* * *

Liv texted from the road:

OMW! Yay!!

I'd cleaned earlier in the day—disposed of empty bottles, folded laundry, fluffed the couch so it didn't look like I'd been living and drinking on it for days.

Then I tucked the whiteboard out of sight.

For the first time in a long time, the house was presentable.

I glanced around, taking in the light, the furniture, the turquoise shimmer of the pool beyond the sliders.

It was beautiful. Luxurious. Serene.

Things I hadn't noticed while drowning in wine, whiskey, and paranoia.

Now I did.

In that moment, I felt better.

Mapping out Edward's life in a web of color-coded sticky notes—hazy picture or not—had given me back some semblance of control.

Proof I could still think.

Still be me.

I'd wasted enough time surviving.

CHAPTER 11

When Liv knocked on my door, I ran to answer it gleefully. Hair down, bare feet. Ready for a much-needed girls' night.

She was surprisingly fun—normal.

We had next to nothing in common, but that was part of her appeal.

She'd never worked in my world. Never been trained to see threats in every stranger or a lie behind every smile. Which meant some things were hard to explain.

But she never asked for explanations I couldn't give.

She showed up for me anyway—even when I was at my worst. When I was hellbent on charting the storm alone.

With brightness and cheer and stubborn loyalty. A shoulder to cry on.

It was the kind of friendship I wasn't used to.

And one I wasn't sure I deserved.

But that was Liv.

"Hey, girlfriend!" she exclaimed while bouncing in balancing pizza, voice full of sunshine. "I thought about using my key again but didn't want a repeat of the last time."

She held up her hand like a gun, laughing skittishly.

"Why didn't you tell me about your friend? He's so wow!" she gushed.

"What friend?"

"Your friend visiting his dad! *Edward.*"

My heart rate spiked. I yanked her inside and shut the door.

"Sorry, Liv, when did you meet Edward?" I asked, trying my best to sound casual.

"Just now! Duh!"

"Wait—he was outside?"

"Yeah! About to knock when I pulled in. I think he chickened out. Oh my God, he's so cute!" She beamed. "I don't know... maybe since Blake's out of town, it might be fun to have him join us for pizza night? What do you think?"

I pointed to the cabinets to distract her.

"Umm, yeah, sure, let me ask him. Why don't you get us set up in here? I'll be back in a minute."

My gun was in my hand before I could think, my body on autopilot.

I nearly ran through the door—weapon drawn, chest tight. Barely breathing.

Edward stood in the driveway.

I quickly scanned the street for threats.

The black truck—presumably his—sat parked two houses down, Alabama plates barely visible.

I evaluated his posture: relaxed. No bulge at the waist. No apparent ankle holster. His arms hung loose at his sides. Still, my instincts blared.

"What the fuck are you doing here?" I snapped.

I hadn't sworn like that in years—but I was in fight mode. Projecting power from my former life.

"Hi... uh, nice to see you, too... not the reception I was expecting."

He glanced at my Glock, his voice calm—entertained, even. Like I wasn't standing there with a loaded gun.

"Wow. Okay. Allie, I'm going to lift my shirt and show you I'm unarmed."

He raised his shirt and carefully turned in a full circle. No weapon.

Fine. He wasn't armed. That didn't explain why the hell he was at my house.

I didn't budge.

"How about this? I'll take a few steps back so you can lower your gun. Then I'll explain."

He eased back, slow and measured, hands up. Then—God help me—he smiled.

It was entirely disarming.

And worse, I smiled back.

My grip loosened as I half-lowered my gun—my body relaxing by reflex.

With nothing more than a smile, he'd gained control of the situation, rattling me.

"Why are you at my house?" I asked.

He didn't waver. Just said smooth, nonchalant: "I'm Edward Anderson."

Like he'd talked to Mike and already knew his name meant something to me.

"Yeah, got it. What are you doing here?"

"I work with Mike. Actually..."

He shifted his weight carefully.

"Mike works for me. So does Blake."

I was aware. But something about hearing it from *him* still made me flinch.

"Uh... yeah, I'm already tracking all that, but why are you following me? Was this Blake's idea?"

"No. This has nothing to do with him."

He hesitated with a slight shrug—casual, unfazed—then added:

"Also... this house? It's mine."

He gestured around, oblivious to the situation.

"Technically. One of mine. I was hoping to say hi and clear the air."

Was he a moron?

He should've known showing up unannounced was a recipe for disaster.

Surprising people like me wasn't a good idea. *Especially not the emotionally unhinged version.*

I studied him like he had three eyes.

"Well, like I said, it's *my* house. I stopped by yesterday... anyway, I wanted to talk to you about Dark Skies."

"What about it?"

"Allie, do you suppose we could go inside before we get into that?"

He gestured to the door.

"I'll be whoever you need me to be in front of your friend. I heard I'm visiting my sick dad across the street."

He chuckled.

"One more thing," he added as he held out his hand. "This is for you."

I peered suspiciously before realizing it was a business card—the same card he'd tried extending me at brunch. I approached cautiously and snatched it.

"Turn it over, please," he muttered.

On the back: **MAGICAL STARLIGHT**. An authentication phrase from Dark Skies.

Of course it was.

Because nothing screamed *trustworthy* like a handsome stranger showing up uninvited with an access phrase—for pizza night.

I rolled my eyes, nodded, and led him inside—my tradecraft clearly still on sabbatical.

It was a lot of trust to put in a stranger—but that was the thing: Edward wasn't a stranger anymore.

He was in Mike's trust circle. Part of Mike's family.

Which made him mine, whether I liked it or not.

* * *

The door clicked shut behind us with a thud that made my skin prickle.

His footsteps were soft on the tile, but his presence was impossible to ignore—unnervingly at home.

Fitting, I supposed, since he owned the place. And, apparently, the moment.

His cologne swirled in the air, already imprinting on my space.

I stayed a step behind, arms loosely crossed, gun in my waistband, trying to appear composed.

I didn't want to seem rattled or rude.

I needed to play nice—for Mike's sake.

And still—every instinct in my body screamed that something was off.

His charm, the timing—all calculated.

My gut didn't trust the truth.

Unfortunately, it was too late.

Edward was inside.

* * *

Three glasses of wine in, and Edward was positively wooing Liv.

He was sociable. Engaging. Mysterious. A billionaire.

Somehow that made him exponentially more fascinating than our own husbands with similar war stories.

He'd breached the perimeter and was compromising the targets. *10/10 tradecraft, Allie. God, I needed supervision…*

I lingered in the kitchen, pretending to rinse a dish. In reality, I was studying him. His cadence. His posture. His expressions.

It was like watching an interrogation play out in reverse—he wasn't extracting secrets. He was giving them away just enough to build trust.

"Wait—you spent a year in Africa doing humanitarian work?" Liv gasped, lighting up. "That's so amazing. Good for you!"

She didn't seem to track—Edward's "humanitarian work" was killing drug lords, but he didn't correct her.

Instead, he shrugged modestly. "I dabble. But now I mostly fund the people who do the dirty work."

"Wow." She was spellbound, hanging on his every word as she clutched the wine glass to her heart. "So how long have you and Allie been friends?"

She winked at me as I assumed a position on the couch across from her, topping off my glass.

Great. Just what the situation needed—Liv matchmaking.

Edward smirked. "I've known her a while. She's incredible, isn't she?"

"She is! You two'd make such beautiful babies," she giggled.

"My God! Liv!" I glared, nearly throwing a pillow at her.

"What?" she giggled again, cheeks flushed with wine.

I stared wide-eyed. "I'm married."

"Oh, oops. Sometimes I forget about him," she shrugged, tipsy.

"I'm calling you a taxi."

"Ugh. You're no fun!"

"I'll have my driver take you home," Edward said with a grin before quickly sending a text. "He'll be here in 10 minutes."

Liv swooned, leaning forward. "You have a driver?"

His eyes sparkled. "And a chef."

"Oh, wow... Allie, I think he's a keeper."

Edward smirked. I shook my head, then rose from the couch—clearing a wine bottle from the coffee table.

When Liv left minutes later, she didn't ask why Edward was staying.

She just leaned in—wine-drunk and glowing—and whispered, "Have fun..."

* * *

An uncomfortable silence fell as I wandered back to the kitchen, refilling my glass.

Being alone with Edward felt scandalous.

Not just because I was married—but because I didn't know what game he was playing.

"So, what was brunch all about?" I asked—short. To the point.

He smiled like I was joking.

"Other than the martinis and eggs Benedict?"

I shot him a look.

"Cut the crap. You know what I mean. Why the show?"

He exhaled through his nose.

"I wanted to meet you. Organically. Without the noise or expectation."

Without the noise or expectation? Yeah, right...

"And?" I folded my arms.

"I tried. For weeks. But you weren't leaving the house much, and my timing was always off."

"So, how'd you know I'd be at brunch?"

Wait—

"And how'd you know I hadn't been leaving the house?"

He shrugged. "Well, I was on my way over to say hi, and you were on your way out."

I stared.

"So... we followed you," he added. No shame. No fidgeting.

"Then why didn't you introduce yourself?"

He leaned in slightly as I stepped back.

"I wanted to see how we got off as strangers."

"So you were watching me? Testing me?" My eyes narrowed.

His smile came slowly. "No... just hoping to connect."

"Bullshit! You wanted to see if you could take me home."

Edward didn't flinch. He just muttered:

"Possibly."

Then he stood there, letting the weight of what he'd said hang between us.

Uncomfortable. Charged.

The worst part?

If I'd had more to drink—and if he hadn't slipped my name—he may have succeeded.

* * *

My instincts were screaming: Don't trust him!

I ignored them because there was an ease between us.

Because *he already knew me.*

Because he'd allegedly been on the periphery of my life through Mike for years—something I found bizarrely comforting.

Blake and I had less than ten people in our inner trust circle since I'd quit the agency—not even our families. So, if Mike trusted Edward enough to share details about me, that meant something.

At least, that's what he claimed. It was also past midnight and I was alone with him on my couch—so it's what I wanted to believe.

He swirled his wine as I studied him in the low light—half-drunk, half-hypnotized.

While his intentions were murky, I wasn't concerned he'd murder me in my living room.

Edward was who he said he was—*or close enough.*

So, I pushed my reservations aside and continued drinking—to calm my inner voice and keep my skepticism at bay.

But what I couldn't fathom was how a guy like Edward landed in Mike's trust circle.

I worried he'd slipped in through a cycle of introductions.

I'd seen it before.

One friend would vouch for someone new, and suddenly that person was in the trust circle—inside the wire. Unvetted. Above scrutiny. Trust-by-proxy.

He hadn't served with Mike—but business made them fast friends.

Common values, shared enemies—according to Edward.

That didn't mean Edward was clean. Not with his connections.

Not with the *Future Leader of the World* label clinging to him like a bad cologne.

Was it possible Mike fell for Edward's money—a means to an end for the mission?

I knew Mike. He had a soft spot for Marines. And he liked a good story rooted in patriotism and honor. Maybe that's all it took for Edward to creep past his defenses.

* * *

I must've been in a trance because it was almost 1 a.m. when he rose to leave.

I was twirling my hair—drawn to him like a moth to a flame.

I should've known better. But I was doing it anyway.

"Thank you for your hospitality."

He smirked as I followed him to the door.

"And thank you for not shooting me earlier," he added, flirtatious. "It would've ruined this lovely evening."

One foot over the threshold, he lingered—then turned back.

Our eyes locked.

I barely had time to react before he leaned in for a kiss—one meant for my lips.

In a panic, I turned my head. His mouth grazed my cheek instead.

I froze, voice wavering, "You know I'm married."

"I do," he said, flashing a mischievous grin.

"You should probably go…"

"Yeah."

Still, he stood there. Didn't move. Didn't speak.

I worried my delivery hadn't been forceful enough.

Then: "Allie, I have to admit—I came over tonight because I'd like to hire you."

I blinked. Hard.

"Mike says you're the real deal when it comes to mapping threat networks," he continued. "Your experience would lend itself to the important work I'm doing. I'd like you to start Monday."

"What?" I let out a single, stunned laugh.

He had *to be kidding.*

"I could really use you."

I scrambled for words... any intelligible thought.

That was his angle? Recruitment? It felt more like seduction.

"Uh... oh, I don't know. I haven't worked in a while. My skills have atrophied."

I'd been out of the field for years and was soberingly aware I'd suffered a lapse in tradecraft. And judgment.

Was I ready to jump back in? I didn't feel it.

"Nah, you'll do great. I'm picking you up at 8 a.m. Monday."

He stepped closer, hand grazing the small of my back. I didn't move.

Then another hug. And kiss on my cheek. Possessive.

He didn't wait for a response. Just winked and walked out into the night, calling back:

"Be ready to run! You'll need to keep up with the guys."

I stood rooted in the hallway—cheeks tingling—cold fingertips pressed to the spot he kissed me, as the rumble of his truck faded into the distance.

The silence that followed should've given way to calm.

Instead, every warning light in my mind flashed red.

Between replaying his words—and recalling the gentle touch of his lips—I barely slept.

My body buzzed like I was still in danger.

It's possible I was.

Chapter 12

Monday morning, regret was already running laps in my brain. I considered canceling before realizing: I had no way to contact Edward.

Besides, I'd made worse decisions—with far less attractive men.

At 7:45, I peeked through the window: Edward sat in his truck, still as a statue.

Stoic. Intense. *The Punisher* seemed to suit him.

At 7:55, he knocked.

I opened the door—his face lighting up gorgeously, a confident twinkle in his eyes.

He pulled me into a long, firm hug—his body pressing against mine in places it shouldn't. Just shy of inappropriate.

I should've pulled away.

Instead, I stupidly leaned in—pinned by his charm and a sudden loss of control I couldn't explain.

"You ready?" he asked.

"Yeah... ready as I'll ever be," I muttered, grabbing my phone and wallet.

I stepped outside in two sports bras, a tank, wicking socks, and running shorts that suddenly felt way too short.

No idea why I was running—or what exactly I'd signed up for.

But judging by the once-over Edward gave me, I was grossly un-derprepared.

He didn't comment. Just started the truck with a smile.

* * *

Edward made small talk as he drove—nothing I could retain.

My brain was too busy toggling between exit strategies and fanta-sies—and scrambling for a plan to shut him down before the situation turned into a mistake I couldn't take back.

I'd assumed we were headed out to Dark Skies.

But after five minutes, he pulled up to a gated compound on Si-esta Key, arm flexed casually on the door.

A kid in contractor attire stood at the gate. "Sup, Boss?"

With his meticulously styled strawberry-blond hair, tan skin, and muscular build, he reminded me of a Ken doll. I recognized him from brunch.

"She finally said, 'Yeah,' huh?" he laughed, flashing a smug grin before glancing at me. "Welcome, ma'am."

I rolled my eyes as he waved us through, looking to Edward.

"Really, ma'am?"

Edward just shrugged—unapologetic.

I tried to shut the skeptic in me off—but the thought lingered:

How long had I been watched—my movements tracked—before I said yes?

It was unsettling... but also... strangely flattering.

As we rounded the corner, my eyes popped. "This is paradise," I murmured.

A grand fountain sparkled at the center of a coral stone driveway.

Towering palms, bougainvillea, limestone columns.

Everything was spectacular, manicured, and opulent.

Edward pointed casually to a '60s-era beach bungalow tucked un-der several trees.

"That was my parents' vacation home. It's now our ops center so we don't draw too much attention."

"Too many operators hanging around don't raise eyebrows?" I teased. Just enough to test him.

"Not when you're a billionaire, love."

Love?

I resisted the urge to correct him—barely. I was used to pet names, but something about the way he said *love* made me want to shut him down.

"And what makes you think they're operators?" he added, grin sharpening.

I laughed.

Directly ahead, another stereotypical operator: 5'10", mid-to-late forties, closely trimmed reddish-brown beard, full sleeves, black camo PT gear. And a Marine Raider hat.

"Gee, not sure," I deadpanned, tone light.

I'd spent years out of rhythm—now I was starting to remember how the game worked.

The guy waved over excitedly like we were old friends.

"Hey, doll! I'm Cody—call sign Con Man. Welcome to Bright Sands."

Bright Sands... I guessed that's what they called the compound... or the team. Or both?

"Heard you're the agency chick joining us. I've gotta lot of friends over there."

"Oh, awesome. Thanks."

Edward shooed Cody off, but not before he gave me a booming *Oorah.* He knew I was a Marine.

"*Am* I joining?" I asked.

Edward glanced over. "Only if you want to."

He dropped the line like a challenge—casual on the surface, but loaded underneath.

Then, quieter, taunting:

"But I already think you do."

My eyes met his as he grinned.

"You didn't come out just for a run... but this isn't Dark Skies. We're higher risk, higher reward here."

"So Bright Sands?"

He nodded. "*My* team. Or private security, depending on who you're talking to. Ten guys—the best out there."

He stopped abruptly. "Well... we *had* ten. We're a man down since losing Rob last fall."

Then:

"We run the ops Mike would never sign off on. What we do is entirely unsanctioned. We're the ones carrying out extrajudicial punishment against human traffickers and pedophiles. Eliminating evil. Exposing corruption. And other shit I probably shouldn't tell you until you sign an NDA."

He laughed lightly.

For years, rumors circulated about a wealthy American that sponsored teams to take out pedophiles and cells responsible for killing servicemembers in Iraq and Afghanistan.

I suspected that American was *Edward.*

"The difference between Dark Skies and Bright Sands is simple," he continued. "Dark Skies skirts the rules. We write our own."

He leaned closer. "And I only play to win."

His gaze locked on mine—with a double meaning I felt everywhere.

I shivered.

Then lighter: "Mike's the guy you'd call if Blake went missing in Afghanistan. He'd work things out diplomatically using official channels... not me. I'm who you'd call if Blake got rolled up and was rotting in a Mexican prison. I'd bring in a team and break him out. *By whatever means necessary.*"

"That's why we had to separate operations. Mike thought I was too brash... maybe he's right. Anyway, this is the main house."

"It's beautiful. But I'd hardly call it a house." *It was enormous.*

"Wait—I *did* tell you I was a billionaire, didn't I?" Edward smirked, and to my shock, boldly pinched my knee—his fingers purposefully lingering.

I should've swatted his hand away—but I didn't.

Damn it.

Luckily, the moment was interrupted by an operator in his fifties jogging up to greet us.

As we hopped out of the truck, Edward received a, "Morning, Boss!"

"Hey, Zack. You remember Allie, don't you?"

I recognized him, too. Zack was the older gentleman from brunch.

"Sure do. How you doing, Allie? Sorry for the scare."

He extended his hand for a handshake. "Can't say the boys were disappointed to hear we were adding a young lady to the team— though they've been told you're strictly off-limits."

I laughed nervously, wondering if I was 'off-limits' because I was married... or because Edward called dibs.

Before Zack could say anything else, Edward interjected, "We're headed to the beach for a run," placing his hand on my lower back and ushering me away.

"Roger. I'll be in the ops center. Boys start shooting in about five hours."

Edward nodded.

After a few steps, I asked, "Edward, are you hazing me?"

He chuckled. "Maybe? Look, the guys know I need you for a few things—but they'll mutiny if you can't keep up. Think you can run five miles in forty minutes?"

"I thought you knew everything about me. Did Mike not mention I was a D1 runner?"

Edward appeared guilty. "He did... but when was the last time you ran?"

Oof. He had me there. I used to run thirty miles a week like it was nothing. That version of me felt distant now. My bleak smile must've given me away.

"Hey, not a big deal. You worry about running. I'll take care of the rest, because I'm the boss."

"Okay, *Boss*," I quipped, waiting for his response.

He shook his head, a darling grin.

* * *

"So, what's Mike said about me?" Edward asked.

"Let's see... I've heard you're a playboy benefactor. A major pain in the ass but generally decent. Mike only ever called you 'The Punisher.'"

Edward grinned. "That's not *that* bad. Benefactor is accurate. Playboy is questionable. But people often like to *incorrectly* conflate that with billionaire." He chuckled to himself. "Pain in Mike's ass? Sure. Punisher? Absolutely."

"So spot on?"

We exchanged smiles.

"Almost to the beach," Edward said as we approached a boulder in our path. "We keep this here to discourage trespassers," he added, lunging on top. "Put your foot there. And give me your hand."

He hauled me up with ease—like I weighed nothing.

I stumbled slightly, and he caught me—one hand on my waist, the other bracing my arm—pulling me flush against him.

I froze.

Not from the fall.

From the jolt that ran through me.

I hadn't felt that kind of charge in years...

I could feel the warmth of his skin through the fabric of my tank. The steady press of his body.

Edward held me there. Watching me. Reading me.

Then, softly, he asked, "Allie, when are you planning to leave Blake?"

I felt like I'd had the wind smacked out of me.

Hot indignation rose in my throat.

"Are you serious?" I squealed, shoving him away.

Without thinking, I scrambled to climb the boulder alone—desperate to put space between us.

"Allie, hold on. Where are you going?" He caught my hand mid-struggle, stopping me. "I heard it from Mike."

I jerked free.

"Is that what this is about—me leaving Blake?"

The picture suddenly came into focus. Edward didn't need me—he *wanted* me.

Guilt and anger surged.

"Have you been stalking me?" I challenged, a quiver in my voice.

"No—I've been *vetting* you."

"You know, vetting and stalking aren't that different where I come from," I managed, keeping my voice controlled, but all I wanted was to scream.

Edward intuitively relaxed his tone.

"I wanted to make sure you were as good as Mike said. Ready to work again. Do you not want to?"

Was he trying to rattle me? Or gauge my weakness?

"Then why the hell would you ask why I haven't left Blake? That's personal!"

"I didn't ask *why*. I asked *when*."

I grumbled. "You're unbelievable. What do you know about my marriage anyway?"

"Mike said bringing you on would end it. I know you haven't lived together in months..."

A lump formed in my throat. His words too intimate—too knowing.

"You seem upset," he stated thoughtfully.

I was livid.

"Of course I'm upset!" I shouted. "I'm trying to figure out if you're legitimately trying to hire me or if this is about sleeping with me to piss off my husband!"

Edward smiled faintly.

Blake didn't like Mike's partner. I recalled him once mentioning he was a 'rich boy who thought he could do whatever he wanted.'

Accurate. Edward's personality clearly made him someone people either loved or loved to hate.

He tried to calm me.

"Maybe I was too direct. Look, if you want to salvage your marriage, working at Bright Sands won't be easy. I'm being honest. I already talked to Mike, and if you agree, let's have a sit down—the four of us."

What he said sent a chill through my body.

Conversations. Schemes. Plans I was never part of.

About my life—made without my knowledge.

Or my consent.

I felt rage, betrayal, and...

"Are you always like this?"

Edward's forwardness was appalling. Off-putting.

"Yes, why?"

"This is absurd! First, you tried to pick me up, then you tried to kiss me. What are you trying to do—destroy my marriage?"

"Guilty as charged."

He playfully kicked sand as I groused.

"Allie, relax. I'm kidding," he grinned—like it was nothing more than a game. "I want you on my team. But when you *do* leave Blake, I won't have to manage his expectations—or his tantrums."

I should've walked away, but for some reason I couldn't pinpoint, I stayed.

I exhaled sharply. "Not that it's any of your business, but I'm still married to Blake because he stood by me through some rough times when I needed him."

When I said rough, I meant it. Blake was by my side when I was barely myself, even when it would've been easier for him to leave. I loved him because, by all reasonable standards, he *should* have left.

But that didn't mean I hadn't considered leaving him.

Many times.

Like the time he took a contract I begged him to turn down. Or the night I packed my car, ready to leave, only for him to come home with diamond earrings and apologies...

"That's valid. I respect that," Edward responded, turning back toward the beach.

I didn't move. Anger rippled through me as I watched his back.

"That's it?" I called after him, sharper this time. "That's all you wanted?"

He raised his shoulders. "That's it. If you're not leaving him, I'll need his buy-in. And that's going to be a challenge. He wants to keep you isolated, Allie."

Isolated struck an uncomfortable chord. My mouth tensed in a scowl. In a single statement, Edward had somehow flipped the script.

"He thinks he's protecting me," I added, trying to justify Blake's actions.

I wasn't sure I could.

Yes, my emotional state had been a roller coaster as I struggled with depression and anxiety—but Blake didn't have faith in my ability to return to work—ever.

He rubbed his eyes. "Well, now that you're all riled up, let's see what you can do."

"You are *seriously* ridiculous," I muttered, exasperated.

But another feeling stirred beneath the surface—

A sense I was done living in a bubble. The bubble Blake had resigned me to.

My focus snapped into place.

It scared me how quickly I felt like my old self again—how one infuriatingly handsome man and the thrill of a challenge could bring out the woman I thought I'd long buried.

"Alright, let's go..." I said, forcing my legs to move.

"Oh no, I don't run anymore," he responded, lifting his shirt to reveal red scarring on remarkable washboard abs...

Oh, for God's sake. I rolled my eyes.

He smirked. "Well, if *this* impresses you, just wait until you see the rest of me..."

I mumbled as I shook my head and took off down the beach, pulse already racing.

* * *

I pushed hard for five miles—barely squeaking in under forty minutes. Exhausted.

"Nice job!" Edward exclaimed from the water—his beautifully sculpted body strategically exposed—shirtless and sun-kissed—scars and burns peeking from above and below his shorts as he waved me in.

Sensing my hesitation, he followed up with, "It'll feel good on your body. You'll be sore tomorrow."

I peeled off my shoes and socks slowly, then stepped into the cool water.

He smiled, watching me with maddening confidence.

That same quiet intensity—like I was a compromised target walking straight into his trap.

I waded toward him. Irritated. Helpless.

* * *

Out of nowhere I heard a whistle, then, "Hey, Boss!"

I turned to see Zack barreling toward us in a golf cart, shouting, "We've got a situation up here!"

His words hit like a lifeline, relieving the tension. Edward and I were dangerously close in the water—my body inching toward his, yielding to a magnetism I'd tried to resist.

He was undeterred. But I took a step back—ashamed.

Caught in a moment I shouldn't have been—again.

I blamed the heat. The adrenaline. The way he looked at me—a terrifying trouble that made me tingle.

I knew better. This was how bad things started...

"What's going on?" Edward yelled as we scrambled out of the water.

"Shit went sideways down in El Salvador."

Edward shook his head in controlled panic before punching the air. "Fuck... how bad?"

"José was just detained at a checkpoint."

"Why the *fuck* did he go through a checkpoint?"

I picked up my shoes and we jogged up the beach toward the cart—sand soft and warm beneath my feet, breeze biting my wet skin.

Edward reeled, picking up his pace. "Where are Greg and Derrick?"

"Still in a firefight at the compound. They snuck José out with the kids. Guards are dead but local police are swarming."

"Fuck me," Edward murmured as he motioned to me. "I need to go, but could use your help if you want to get your hands dirty."

My heart was racing—this time for a very different reason. I wasn't sure if I was ready to be swept into their world, but it was too late to take a step back now.

A strange mix of dread and excitement pooled in my stomach.

"Sure, whatever you need, Boss."

Boss?! I cringed.

Had I really called him that? I prayed he hadn't heard.

When we reached the cart, Edward nudged me into the front seat with a crooked grin.

"So, I'm going to be your boss, huh?" he teased, eyes gleaming.

One minute I was trying to convince myself to walk away.

The next, I was leaning in—chasing chaos.

What the *hell* was I doing?

Chapter 13

Zack held the ops center door open, face neutral.

I caught his eye as I stepped past—a blast of cold air smacking me back to reality.

"Thanks," I said, voice steady.

Like I hadn't just been caught gravitating toward Edward in the surf.

"Anytime, ma'am. Secret's safe."

His smirk said it all.

It was a secret because it wasn't innocent. I'd crossed a line.

I sighed before he added, "Hope you're ready for baptism by fire."

* * *

The ops center buzzed—the hum of servers, rapid keystrokes, voices shouting over radio static. In the air, the smell of coffee mixed with men's cologne.

Screens lined the walls—satellite feeds, flickering drone footage, map overlays, dossiers. Even a live translation over audio.

The situation sounded bad. Detentions. A firefight. Kids stuck in the middle.

James stood at the center barking orders—confident, clear, and perfectly measured.

A charismatic leader, though it was obvious Edward was in charge. He scanned the screens like a hawk, then—his voice slicing through the noise:

"I don't care what it takes. Get them home."

James nodded.

Striking—mid-forties, midnight black hair parted with military precision, steel blue eyes.

Unlike the others, he was clean-shaven and meticulously over-dressed—slacks and a crisp Aloha shirt, unbuttoned a shade too far, revealing chest hair and bronzed skin.

The effect? Pure Tom Selleck in his *Magnum, P.I.* era. All he needed was the mustache.

After a quick intro, James sized me up, then said dryly, "Probably not the best time to plug in a newbie."

I straightened. "Try me."

"Careful. She's sharper than she looks," Edward added.

James shrugged. "Yeah, I'm starting to see that."

Edward's tone turned lower—firmer. "Bud, she's not here to watch. Just give her some screen space."

James gestured to an empty workstation. "Alright. Let's see what you've got."

I slid into the chair, fingers hovering steadily over the keyboard. "I'm not here to slow you down. Just tell me what you need."

James paused, studying me—calculating—like he was searching for the safest task he could hand off. One with margin for error.

Finally: "Let's get you on the phone. See if you can find someone to get José through a checkpoint near Ciudad Hidalgo—right at the El Salvador–Guatemala border."

I jotted notes as he spoke. James glanced at my notepad, then cracked a smile.

"You even spelled everything right."

That earned me a wink—and possibly a sliver of respect.

He called out, "Sammy, print me another list."

Out of the corner of my eye, I caught him watching me again—this time with something different behind his sharp stare.

Curiosity.

Edward's statement echoed in my mind—*"She's not here to watch"*—as the team's radio traffic crackled in the background.

* * *

Two Bright Sands operators were mid-firefight.

On one screen, a shaky drone feed showed them pinned down—fighting off dozens as gunfire flashed all around.

The compound belonged to Rich Vega—a well-known and powerful drug lord that controlled large swatches of territory within El Salvador.

I didn't know the team, but the sight was enough to cause a knot in my stomach.

A plane waited on the tarmac at a private airstrip in Guatemala for the team—José, Derrick, and Greg—in anticipation of them extracting two recovered American children—part of a child recovery operation thirty kilometers from the border.

But the pilot didn't want to be idle long and was getting antsy.

James circled a section in Sharpie then handed me a list with steady hands, gaze direct.

"These are all rich American expats or ex-agency folks with strings to pull. If you recognize any names, call them first. Say you're Amanda with the Discovery Program."

I nodded. "On it."

It'd been years since I'd worked in an ops center.

I'd almost forgotten how exhilarating—and nerve-wracking—they could be.

I took a deep breath and dialed, tuning out the noise around me.

My first call was Dr. Ricardo Sanchez. His secretary answered. The doctor was on a trip to Benin performing surgery—unavailable.

Up next, a rich businessman with no local contacts. Then a woman that yelled at me in Spanish and several voicemails.

Seven calls in, I spoke with a gentleman who claimed he could help.

I raised my hand to flag James as I put the man on speakerphone.

"Sure, sure. Yes, three Americans. What does he need to get them across the border?" I asked.

"Give me a second," I heard before the line went silent.

I muted and turned to James. "Am I negotiating with this guy? Who is he?" I asked, pointing to his name on my list.

James shouted to the room, "Ryder, run up Javier R. Gomez."

Seconds later, the man's bio was on screen. We quickly scanned it.

He was a wealthy American with a brother-in-law overseeing the private border guard at a handful of northern crossings.

"He's former agency. Corrupt as hell, but give him what he needs. Tell him we're on a tight timeline."

"Roger."

After a minute, I heard the man say, "Amanda, are you still there?"

"Yes, sir."

Edward approached to listen in.

"My contact's on the ground. They'll release them for 150,000 US dollars each."

My gut clenched. I hit mute.

That was a huge number—especially for a random border checkpoint.

I glanced at James. "Could it be Vega's guys?"

"Don't think so," he said. "They'd have shot José already...but let's get him through before they catch wind."

True. José was still breathing—as far as we knew. If it were Vega, it would be a recovery, not a negotiation.

"Who the fuck does this guy think he is?" Edward scoffed.

"He's some flavor of agency. Let it go. It's only money," James replied before his face morphed into a smirk. "Any means necessary... that's the motto, right?"

James tapped my desk. "Allie, just get the wiring instructions. We'll take care of the rest."

"You got it." I unmuted. "Thank you, Mr. Gomez. I'm standing by for wiring instructions."

As Javier provided them, Edward walked off to take a phone call, jaw tight, and I wondered who was on the other end—someone important, undoubtedly.

James hovered as the wire went out.

He gave me a thumbs up, and we waited, listening anxiously to local radio chatter.

Minutes passed.

James kept shooting glances at Ryder—a young, pale-skinned Marine in a USMC tee, buzzed head, hazel eyes behind wire-frame glasses. His right-hand man. Synced to James's thoughts and cues—verbal and nonverbal—like a carefully choreographed dance.

Ryder shook his head. "Still nothing."

* * *

Ten minutes after sending the wire, James piped up. "Allie, let's get Javier back on the line."

I redialed and gave James a nod when I had him.

He swiftly took the phone from my hand.

"Hey, man. It's Jimmy over here at Discovery Program. What's the status on the Americans?"

I couldn't hear Javier's response, but James followed up seconds later with, "Listen up, dipshit. If you don't get this sorted out in the next five minutes, extortion charges will be the least of your fucking worries. We clear?"

A digital clock flashed on the main screen—5:00.00—the numbers glowing like a caution light.

Ryder sat stiffly, eyes flicking between the screen and his workstation.

Each second thickened the tension in the air.

When the clock hit thirty seconds, I knew something was wrong.

I approached James cautiously.

"I know you have a better sense of what's going on than I do, and I'm not trying to step on any toes... but I do know the RSO in El Salvador if you want me to work diplomatic channels."

"No shit. You trust him?"

"Well, he's a Marine. And a friend."

"Right on. Hit him up, will you? Feel free to throw in that our operator's a Marine, and the kids are grandkids of an active-duty Marine that wears stars, if it helps."

As the words left his mouth, my breath hitched.

A Marine General?

This wasn't just bad—it was a disaster.

Mission failure could spiral straight to D.C. and set off an international shitstorm.

"Roger that."

I appreciated the vote of confidence. And the chance to do something useful, but the stakes had been raised. This was no longer a simple extraction.

Years prior, I'd become close friends with a hotshot Assistant RSO in Mexico City. We'd never crossed the line into romance, though he certainly tried, but a shared brush with death—a harrowing Mossad assassination attempt—bonded us for life.

I hadn't spoken to him in ages, but I was sure he'd answer my call—as long as he wasn't stuck in a SCIF.

James was standing in the back of the room talking to Edward and Zack. They appeared troubled as they monitored the situation. The incident would indisputably garner attention—none of it good.

I dialed.

Justin answered on the fourth ring. "God, Allie, *pleaseeeee* tell me you're not involved in this cluster. My ambassador's losing his shit... and our station chief's about to murder someone."

I promptly waved James over.

If Justin had caught wind, the media wasn't far behind.

"I'm surprised you answered," I said as James assumed a position beside me.

"It's been a minute. Pretty sure you ghosted me the last time I was in town, remember?"

Justin smiled through the line—and he wasn't wrong. He'd tried to take me out for drinks, but I never responded because I'd been in a terrible rut. I wasn't sure how to explain it to him then—or even now.

"What are the chances you'd be calling when shit like this was going down? No such thing as a coincidence, right? I believe you taught me that."

"So, what are you hearing?" I asked.

James muttered under his breath, just loud enough: "Glad we could reconnect."

I shot him a look, mouthing, *My guy. My way.*

"Please proceed," he said, brow lifted—amused—gesturing to the phone.

I caught the tail end of Justin's sentence: "...Americans fire-bombed Rich Vega's compound and they're having it out with his guards."

Justin paused, hesitant to ask what he already knew. "You working with these guys, Allie?"

I winced. A straight answer wasn't going to reassure him.

Technically, I wasn't sure what I was doing—but I was doing it.

"Umm... yeah. Do you have anyone that could lend some support? They were doing an extract of some American children. Grandchildren of an active-duty Marine General."

"Yeah, I figured this was tied to General Smith. We've been tracking that. Kids make it out?"

"Out of the compound, yes—but they've been detained at a check-point. I was hoping you could work your contacts to get them through."

Justin let out a long groan. "Uhhh, depends."

"I know it goes without saying, but we'd like to do this quietly."

He half-laughed. "Yeah, you and everyone else! Look, I'll do what I can." A pause. "What's the compound situation? Hearing it's dicey."

Zack shouted across the room, "Ask him if he's got any helicopter pilots! Otherwise, I'm sending a Dragonfly for close air support."

Naturally.

And judging by Zack's tone, *sending* probably meant *commandeering.*

By any means necessary.

The words sparked like a match in my brain—Edward's voice, smooth and unbothered, as if the team stealing a jet in a foreign country was just another Monday.

"Well, it's not good. Any chance you have a helicopter pilot on standby?"

Justin didn't skip a beat. "Yeah, sure thing. I'll send you info for a former Black Hawk pilot. Real salt dog. He's already fueled up and ready to go. One of those days."

"And the kids?" I asked.

"Send me their coordinates and I'll get it sorted out. Our QRF teams are chomping at the bit," he laughed.

If the agency's QRF teams were spun up, it was more than a bad day...

"Thanks. I owe you!"

"Yeah, I'd say!" he chuckled as I saw a text come through from an unknown number, presumably one of Justin's burners. "Here's hoping this won't get me hauled in front of Congress. Give me a few."

I hung up and stared at the screen.

A moment later, James tapped me on the shoulder. "Don't worry. Nobody's testifying. Ed will make sure of it."

I half-smiled.

Was that a threat? Or just privilege?

Either way, it was too late for me to wimp out now.

Not mid-op. Not after implicating Justin.

CHAPTER 14

Thirty minutes after sending José's coordinates, we were all still staring at screens.

Still no movement.

Still no answers.

Just more radio static and a sense of rising dread.

James and Zack maintained comms with Greg and Derrick, who were holed up in an upper bedroom of the compound, taking sustained fire.

They'd killed Vega's guards, but cars full of armed thugs and police on Vega's payroll kept coming.

"Rockstar, this is Innovator. What's the current situation?" I heard James ask.

"Bro—this is a shit sandwich! We're fresh outta grenades, 'bout to be outta ammo. Super Doom's guys are posted across the street—we told 'em to hold fire. No point in burning their location with all these fucking jalopies rolling in."

"What about the tunnel?" James asked.

"Negative. Bad intel. Sealed shut, so we're stuck in this tower on the far northeast side of the compound. Probably gonna be taking RPG fire soon. Shit's *not* lookin' good."

Ryder nudged my shoulder. "Rockstar's Greg."

"And Vega?" James asked.

"No leverage. Dude's super dead."

The phrase hit like a round to the chest. *Super dead.*

My breath caught. That cocky voice. I knew it.

The ops center slipped away for a beat—replaced by a grainy video feed I hadn't thought about in years.

June 6, 2014.

The day I watched a rogue hit team take out the agency's Ukrainian puppet president before he could be installed.

This was the operator.

Rockstar.

The balls. The bravado. The fucking chaos.

Bright Sands wasn't just a nickname.

They were *that* team.

I shifted in my seat, pulse climbing. Processing.

Ryder tapped me again—pulling me back to the room.

"Boys, this is Silver Fox. Chopper inbound. ETA fifteen. Hope you ropers brought your rope and carabiners—you're gonna need a hasty repel seat."

"Fuck, thanks, yo. But it better be rigged for SPIE cuz there's no fucking way a chopper's landin' anywhere near this compound," another voice cut in—Derrick, I assumed.

"Super Doom," Ryder clarified.

"Yeah, we're tracking," James replied, giving Zack a thumbs up.

Zack was speaking on another line across the room—presumably with the pilot.

"Bro, did Coyote make it to the plane with the kids?" Greg asked.

"Yep, they're clear," James responded—zero hesitation.

He glanced at Edward, who gave a nod of approval.

"Damn, well at least we'll die for something good, bro."

God.

I knew why James did it. I just hated it.

But sometimes the only thing holding a mission together was hope. *Even if it was false.*

I checked my phone. Nothing from Justin yet.

When there was a lull, I turned to James. "Is there a reason the guys across the street aren't reacting?"

"Greg made a call."

"But what if—" I stuttered, scared to ask what I was thinking— *What if they died?*

"Too much exposure," he answered.

I grimaced before James added, "I see you don't like that answer."

"No, but—"

"I'm gonna try to find some ammo or RPGs," Greg said on an open line. "Radio your guys and tell 'em to lay low, no matter what!"

Then: "Make sure the pilot knows it's gonna be a *super* hot extract. We'll run out on the balcony when we hear him."

"Roger. Hey, Godspeed," Zack replied.

"Fingers crossed. Love you guys."

Edward and James shared a thought as their eyes met.

Both nodded in an unspoken exchange before Edward ducked into his office.

We all continued staring at the clock in silence.

And I kept glancing at my phone every ten seconds. Still nothing...

Ten minutes passed. Then—

A single text: 👍

I flashed it to Ryder and James.

Ryder shifted in his seat. "I'm still not seeing anything. You?"

James shook his head. "Nope. Al, want to follow up to confirm?"

"Sure."

I texted Justin: 👍 *?*

Seconds later, he replied: 👍 *x !!!*

"Yeah, I'm pretty sure," I said, holding it up.

James studied a monitor then pivoted to Ryder. "Make sure that plane's ready for takeoff. If they're clear of the checkpoint, they should be about twenty minutes out. And make damn sure the pilot doesn't leave without them."

Ryder nodded before James added, "Listen. Tell him I'll personally pay to have him killed if he leaves. If that's not incentive enough, we'll snatch up his wife and kids in Seattle and hold them hostage until everyone's back safe."

Ryder hesitated. "Yeah, okay."

James snorted. "Man, I'm kidding. I'm not kidnapping anybody."

I wasn't so sure.

And judging by his face, neither was Ryder.

With no change in expression, he again replied, "Yeah, okay..." then got on the phone.

I stood beside James. "What can I do?"

He appeared pensive. "Do you pray?"

"Not really."

"Well, let's sit back and hope this 'shit sandwich' doesn't turn into an international incident. My guess is Ed's on the phone with the President trying to smooth things over with Bitcoin in exchange for grace and a media blackout."

I nodded—half-in awe, half-in disbelief—eyes still on the clock.

* * *

Zack had Greg on an open line as he ran interference with the helicopter pilot.

Then—

Muffled yelling. Flashbangs. A flurry of gunfire.

In the commotion, Zack lost contact.

With the pilot.

And with the team.

It sounded catastrophic.

My stomach flipped, already filling in the worst-case scenario—a failed mission, men down.

Edward tapped on the glass and gave Zack a thumbs up.

Zack's head shake said it all.

The ops center went still. Movement suspended mid-motion.

Across the room, I saw it hit Edward—shoulders stiffening, jaw setting like stone.

His face changed—focused, gutted—as he mouthed *fuck me*, then slammed down the phone.

"What happened?"

"Don't know, Boss," Zack replied, eyes wide in disbelief. "God damn it! Not my boys."

He looked around in a state of despair before kicking his chair, sending it tumbling, then: "Fuck!"

"Alright," James said—steady. "Let's not jump to conclusions. We may have just lost comms."

He took to his computer, typing furiously. "Give me a minute. Ryder, check the satellites."

Ryder froze, turning ghost white—*literally*—only a shade lighter than his already porcelain skin.

Eyes wide, mouth agape. He didn't say a word.

Twenty seconds passed.

Edward and James didn't notice—they were glued to the screen.

I held my breath.

"What's up, Ryder? Give me something!"

Ryder's silence was haunting.

Zack bust out of the ops center, the door sounding off like a gunshot behind him, causing Edward and James to finally look up.

Eyes locked on Ryder.

Ryder gulped—then slowly turned one of his monitors.

On it—

a satellite image of a fireball.

All air was sucked from the room.

But Edward didn't flinch. "What about Coyote?" he asked.

Not a hint of emotion.

Unsettling.

Stone-fucking-cold.

I shivered.

He glanced at me, then softened his stance—like he'd read my mind—placing a hand supportively on Ryder's shoulder.

Part of me envied it.

The stillness. The control. The absence of panic.

Edward made it look like strength—

Like a high-functioning sociopath.

"Ryder, stay with me," James added gently. "Breathe, okay? We still need to get Coyote and the kids home."

Ryder nodded, but he was trembling—doing all he could to keep himself together.

I felt for him.

I'd been there.

When a mission had gone so wrong, I couldn't even wrap my mind around it. Where all I wanted to do was quit—curl into a ball and cry—but it was still mid-op and people's lives depended on me staying composed under pressure.

He scanned the screen. "He's... he's, uhhh, ughhh..."

After thirty agonizing seconds, with a ragged breath Ryder managed, "Uh, he's clear! Five minutes from the airstrip."

"Fuck. Thank God!" Edward muttered as Cody and Ken ran into the ops center.

"Yipeeeeeeee!" Cody yelled, jumping up and down—amped like he'd just won a national title. "Ho-ly shittt! What *was* thaaaaaattt, bros!?"

My God. Really?

Edward frowned. "Bud, why don't you and Tanner step into my office?"

Cody didn't clock the mood.

"No wayyyy! We needa be celebrating! We got stuck on the phone with Super Doom's guys when shit went down—but damn, that was hard core!"

Edward placed a hand on Cody's shoulder.

He instantly simmered down, asking, "What? Were you bozos not watching?"

"Watching *what*?"

Cody shrugged Edward's hand away before boisterously shouting again, "One of the sexiest extracts of all time! In the dopest move in history, Rockstar RPG'd Vega's bedroom—strung up under the chopper. One shot. Upside down. Then flew away like a fucking badass. Call of Duty worthy, bro!"

James perked up. "Slow down. They cleared the compound?"

"Fuck yeah, they did!"

Cody paused—finally registering the energy in the room.

"Oh fuck... bro... did José and the kids not make it?" He clutched his gut like he might hurl.

"They're across the border," James said evenly. "But you're *positive* Greg and Derrick are clear?" His demeanor lightened ever so slightly.

"Yeah. Why?"

Cody and Tanner shared a look, eyes wide. Realization creeping in.

The silence wasn't for the kids. It was for Greg and Derrick.

"Bro, don't play with me like that—"

"We fucking watched 'em fly off," Tanner added. "They're good. Right?"

Cody pivoted to punch James in the shoulder. "Yeah, they're good. You'll see."

Then we waited. Again. Each second dragging like an hour.

We'd gotten Coyote out. But Greg and Derrick?

No one wanted to say it, but the longer the silence stretched, the worse it looked.

CHAPTER 15

In the ops center, phones rang. People exhaled.
The mood cracked—just enough—for cautious optimism to slip in.
Nervous jokes. Shaky laughter.

And a question burned in my mind.

I leaned forward, tapping Cody on the shoulder. "So why did Vega kidnap the General's grandkids?"

"He didn't," Cody replied, brow raised like I'd missed something obvious.

"But—?"

Cody kicked Edward's chair, causing him to look up from his phone.

"Bud, she's not read in yet. She started today."

"I'll tell her—but only if she made the run," Cody replied playfully.

"She did."

"No shit—really?"

"What's that supposed to mean?" I scoffed.

Tanner and Cody shared a skeptical smirk.

Edward's gaze cut sharp as Cody adjusted in his seat. "Fine, I'll tell her."

He perked up. "Uh, well, their dumbass mom's dating Vega. Took the kids down to El Salvador while their dad was deployed.

Vega didn't technically kidnap 'em—but he fucking held 'em hostage. Can you believe that shit?"

He laughed. "Greg did this as a personal favor. He owed Kurt. *Big time.*"

"Wait, are we talking about Major General *Kurt* Smith?"

"Yeah, you know him?"

"I do."

Kurt was a legend within the Recon and Raider communities. I'd socialized with him and his wife many times over the years. One of his younger brothers even owned a ranch in the same west Texas town as Blake's family—the two were chummy.

"These are *his* grandkids?"

"Yep," Cody nodded.

Wow. "Did he know you guys were conducting this op?"

"Well—" Cody started.

"He did *not*. But he and the rest of the world will when this hits the news," Edward interjected bleakly, glancing at his watch.

"Boss, I'm telling you... you shoulda sent me and my boy Tanner down there for recon! We woulda sorted out all that shit intel."

"Yes, I'm aware," Edward grumbled.

The room relapsed into tense silence.

Then Cody's phone dinged. He jumped to his feet.

"Hell, yeahhh! See, I fucking told you!"

He punched James in the chest, then fist bumped Tanner.

"They're all good! My boy just sent me a Snapchaaaaat!" Cody roared, turning up the volume on a video of an operator dangling from a helicopter, sticking out his tongue and flipping off the camera.

"Wooooohoooo, motherfuckers! Tell Boss Man he owes me another Rollie!"

I started smiling as the mood in the room transformed.

But Edward was aggravated. "You know how many times I've explicitly told him not to take his phone?"

"Chill out, bro! It's a burner!"

He rubbed his face. "Tell him to ditch the burner and wipe that account. Immediately."

Cody nodded—conceding—making it clear: Edward was boss first, friend second.

A minute later, José made contact.

He and the kids were airborne, en route to another airstrip just inside the southern Mexico border. From there, they'd take a chartered plane to a private airfield in Atlanta.

Instantly, everyone was high-fiving, fist bumping, and hugging.

"Nice work, gents!" Edward called out before locking eyes on me. "And lady."

Then with a smile, he added, "Welcome to Bright Sands, Allie."

And just like that, I knew—I wasn't just falling for Edward.

I was falling back into the world I belonged in—for better or worse.

A world I thought I'd permanently left behind.

God help me.

Cody leaned over, whispering, "You're gonna be pretty popular, doll," before taking a guzzle from a Marine Corps flask.

"Yeah, thanks..."

I used the celebration as my opportunity for escape—only to be caught by Zack, who was doing push-ups in the driveway, blowing off steam.

* * *

Zack was ruggedly attractive with grizzled stoicism and shiny gray hair—a true silver fox.

The guys called him "Team Dad" he explained—with only the slightest hint of irritation.

An OG Delta Force guy and Troop Sergeant Major, he'd connected with Edward as he was retiring—after nearly thirty years of service.

Edward had asked him to assemble the team at Bright Sands. He quickly brought in Super Doom and Rockstar—two high performers with zero fear.

When he talked about them, he got choked up—like a dad proud of his kids—and it took everything in me not to tear up, too.

Zack used a clicker in Edward's truck to get into my neighborhood, then drove in without direction. He knew the route. The house.

I gazed out the window.

How long had they been watching me?

Surveilling me?

I swallowed. "Thanks for the ride."

He gave me a nod, then replied, "Don't sweat it. We'll be seeing you," before pulling away.

A man of few words.

*　*　*

Alone, the adrenaline rush faded, but the day replayed in my mind.

Was I terrified, exhilarated, or... just crazy?

It was past 7 p.m. by the time I got into bed, exhausted and sore.

My phone beeped. A text:

This is Edward.

A moment later, it rang. I answered eagerly.

"Hey!"

"Hey, I just broke free," Edward started, and I could hear it—concern in his voice. "Would it be alright if I stopped by?"

I re-checked the time.

My nosy neighbors were likely to notice Edward's truck.

And given the way he'd looked at me, any socialization felt irresponsible.

"Umm... can we catch up tomorrow?"

"I'd like that. May I take you to breakfast?"

"Sure."

"Excellent. Then I was thinking we could head out to Dark Skies for some shooting—if you're up for it. The teams are overseas or off-site, so it's a good time to show you around. Discreetly."

"Sounds good. What time should I be ready?"

"How's 8 a.m.?"

"That works. See you then."

Edward paused then added, "Well done, today, Allie. Good night."

Chapter 16

I opened the door to Edward's knock. He stood with a coffee carrier in one hand, a bag of bagels in the other, smile radiant.

"Good morning, beautiful!"

He caught my raised brow and corrected. "Well, rather, good morning, *Allie*. I brought breakfast."

"Oh... okay," I replied, stepping aside to let him in.

He followed me to the kitchen, close—too close.

Like he had no concept of personal space.

The problem?

He did.

"So, what'd you think? Solid group, right?"

"Yeah, everyone seemed great."

I proceeded cautiously—flickers of memory coming back. The takedown of the would-be Ukrainian puppet president—an event that proved calamitous to the West's oil companies and the agency's hold on the region.

"Edward, I know your call signs. I was in Warsaw when the team took out Igor Ivanenko. I listened to your op in real time."

Edward leaned casually against the counter as though we were talking about the weather, not a covert kill—unaffected—then grinned.

"I know. I read your classified testimony."

"Why didn't you say?"

"You've heard about more of our ops than you realize..." He paused. "But we'll get into that."

Another beat.

"If it's any consolation, Joe Turner's still on the team's shit list."

I despised the man. "How do you know him?" I asked.

"I checked him out at a few D.C. functions." He shrugged. "He's an interesting cat."

"I hoped my testimony would bring him down."

"Unfortunately, it takes a lot to shelve guys like him."

I shivered.

"The upside is, his crimes are all on record. He's only alive because we want him that way—for now."

"*Oh...* who's *we?*"

"An assortment of good guys I know." He gave a slight tilt of his head. "Believe me, he didn't land himself a four-million-dollar mansion in Georgetown on a government salary. That was one hundred percent blackmail."

He smirked, suggesting his involvement.

"There are dozens of men and women like him. The team keeps tabs on all of them—which is slightly more satisfying than it sounds."

"So, what's the plan for me? Do you want me working in the ops center or—?"

"That'll be a large part of it." His tone sharpened, eager. "You can set your schedule with James."

"No travel?"

Edward appeared pensive. "Uh, well, I'd love to send you out on some lowkey ops with the team... but most of the work is too dangerous."

I recoiled, tearing off a piece of bagel, buying a moment to collect my thoughts.

I missed being in the field, but I'd seen too many smart women get hurt trying to prove they were as physically capable as their male counterparts.

Despite Hollywood portraying female CIA officers as invincible, I had no delusions about being an operator. I wouldn't last a minute in hand-to-hand with the men I targeted—nor most the guys on the team.

At 5'9" and 140 pounds, I could keep up at the range. But in a fist fight? Not a chance unless the guy was roughly my size or smaller.

"I understand."

"Are you accepting officially?" Edward asked, face lighting up with a boyish grin. "I'll send you for refresher training—whatever you want. Shooting, driving, language—anything. Just say the word."

God, I missed this. I needed this...

"Yes. Officially," I blurted.

A smile hit my face before the thought fully landed—I hadn't asked Blake.

I wanted to believe I was independent. That I didn't need permission. But this was a decision I shouldn't make alone. Not after everything...

Yet something in me bristled.

Why should I have to ask my husband for permission to work?

A man who hadn't bothered to call me in months?

"Well... *almost* officially," I backpedaled. "Sorry—I need to run it by Blake. Do you know when they're getting back?"

I sighed, knowing the conversation wouldn't go well.

"You can run it by him if you want..." Edward smirked, "but I think we both know who you're really answering to."

He leaned back, gaze sharpening. Piercing. Charged.

Why did he make me feel so powerless—like I was under some sort of spell?

Then he started in on small talk—casual, noncommittal. Nothing related to work.

I pushed back in my chair for distance—and suggested we head to Dark Skies.

He agreed, but his smirk stayed.

The maddening kind that knew exactly where the line was— and exactly how close we were to crossing it.

Chapter 17

I'd heard about the Dark Skies compound for years—whispers, rumors, bragging rights. But I'd never seen it.

The entrance was secluded and unassuming—with burned-out vehicles and piles of junk camouflaging the first stretch of driveway. If I hadn't known it was there, I would've driven straight past it on the way out to Myakka State Park.

At the exterior gate, about a mile down a dirt road, a young guard appeared.

Edward handed him two fake Florida drivers licenses to scan—*Edwin Smith* and *Allison Jones*.

The kid clearly had no idea who Edward was. And he seemed rattled by a female visitor—I was his first.

After a tense wait and a slow, methodical search, we were waved through.

I was unusually familiar with the process from years of getting "randomly" stopped by flirtatious base guards.

"I worried he might detain you," Edward said as we rounded the first bend.

"Yeah, I was a little worried about that, too. Good thing I know a guy."

We shared a look—and laughed.

"But why the fake IDs?" I asked.

"James wipes the data each time I visit, and I make sure I never see the same guard twice. It's just an extra layer of caution to avoid any unnecessary scrutiny."

I nodded. That was one way of doing business.

By the time buildings came into view, we'd gone through two more gates—both automated—passed a runway—capable of landing a C-130, per Edward—two helipads, a full-size hangar, several boat ramps, and a pool with a dive tank.

The dirt road curved again, canopied by thick oaks draped in vines and Spanish moss.

The main compound was neatly manicured and basic—like many of the nondescript offices I'd worked in.

But one detail gave me pause.

Mike's car was parked out front.

"You didn't tell me Mike would be here today."

"Oh, I doubt it—last I heard, he's stuck in D.C. He's rarely around."

"You two don't talk much?"

"In person. Or by carrier pigeon." Edward grinned. "But that's about it. He's busier than a one-legged man in an ass kicking contest."

"So, the Dark Skies guys don't know who you are?"

"Nope. Only Mike, my buddy Tank, and your husband—and they've all been sworn to secrecy under penalty of death."

His delivery was blasé.

"That's it?"

"Everyone else I've had to kill." Edward's smile faded as he watched my reaction, letting the weight of his statement breathe.

"Oh... *duly noted.*"

"Consider yourself sworn in." He paused. "You'll meet Tank today. We got blown up together in Iraq. He's planned some firearms drills for you in the shoot house."

"Nice!" I glanced around at a variety of other buildings within the inner perimeter. "What else do you have out here?"

"Brand-new surgical suites, our own ICU, old hunting cabins, four team houses..."

He pointed to a two-story Victorian building about a thousand yards off to the left.

"That's Mike's place."

It looked like a country bed and breakfast circa 1850. Not what I pictured for a man like Mike.

"And they just finished a resort-style pool and lazy river. It's basically a bachelor pad on steroids—except there are no girls allowed, despite a few well-planned breaches."

"Well, if there were women, it would explain why Blake never wants to come home."

God, why had I said that? I immediately regretted it.

"Sorry, I shouldn't have—" I muttered, looking at Edward—apologetic.

But he didn't flinch. He already knew.

His hand found mine on the center console, grip firm and warm. I fidgeted.

"Allie, you deserve joy. I don't—"

He stared at me for a second before he shook his head.

"Never mind, I'm not going to say it."

"Say what?"

"It's not important, but please, do what makes you happy. I hope working at Bright Sands will, but if it doesn't..."

My eyes welled almost instantly. *How did he understand me?*

He squeezed my hand again, then: "Anyway, we're here—and there's my bud, Tank."

He pointed to a stocky bearded operator, saving me from embarrassment.

"And yes, that's his real name. His dad was a Vietnam vet—a tanker. No joke! Phenomenal guy. Just don't let him get too handsy."

"Seriously?"

"No, I'm kidding... I'm the only handsy one here." He winked.

"Edward, you know I can't work for you if you think *this* is going to happen."

"Define *this*."

I exhaled, waving my hand like I could fan out the fire smoldering between us.

"*This*. Whatever *this* is."

"Ah," he said, gaze lingering far too long. "*That*."

"Please, you've got to be a gentleman. I can't—"

"I get it... you're not ready. I'll wait."

"That's not what I meant, and you know it."

He gave a half-smile. "Fine. Then I'll be the consummate gentleman... now go enjoy yourself."

* * *

Built like a tank, with a massive Marine Corps tattoo wrapped around his left bicep—an eagle, globe, and anchor, with several dates inked beneath for fallen friends—Tank was genuine, lovable, and nothing but respectful.

We were best friends within minutes.

Three hours flew by in the shoot house as we traded stories and ran drills. After that, we moved outside to the range, where he spotted me at 750 yards.

By the time Edward approached, we were laughing so hard we didn't even notice him.

When there was a lull, he yelled over, "You two interested in lunch?"

"Yeah, you buying?" Tank shouted back. "And how long you been watching us, creepster?"

"Long enough to see you two canoodling."

"Hah! We're not canoodling. I'm spotting."

"Yeah, whatever you say, bud."

* * *

Edward was grilling hot dogs when we joined him at Tank's team house.

There was an ease between them I envied. Unlike Edward's interactions with the guys at Bright Sands, Tank wasn't a subordinate—they were equals—and it was clear as they joked around.

But halfway through lunch, I noticed something was off when I caught Tank shifting in his seat, subtly rubbing his neck.

He continued moving carefully, wincing like he'd pulled a muscle.

Eventually, I noticed a small spot of blood on his collar.

"Tank, are you alright?" I asked.

He deflected before I pointed to the blood.

Edward chuckled. "See bud, you should've seen Dr. Gretchen. It's not too late. I have her on speed dial."

"Too late for what?" I asked.

"Don't be ridiculous. I don't need a plastic surgeon," Tank muttered before tugging his collar aside, baring a reddish-purple wound—*clearly field work*—stitches aligning haphazardly. "Took thirty-five stitches. *No bueno.*"

"Oh God. What happened?"

Edward cracked up, blurting, "He got stabbed by a twelve-year-old!" before Tank could answer.

Tank appeared embarrassed.

"Seriously?" I asked.

He let out a meek, "Yeahhh."

I examined the proximity of the wound to his artery. "They missed your jugular by less than an inch!"

Edward laughed even harder. "Yeah, well, *she* was only four feet tall. Hard to get up there."

He stabbed a finger at his own neck dramatically. "Little arms, low angle."

"You don't know that!" Tank shot back.

"Bud, that's what I heard... you saying Mike lied?"

Tank rolled his eyes before retelling the story about a child rescue nearly gone wrong, which resulted in us all roaring with laughter, so much that it caused my cheeks and abs to hurt.

It was the most joy I'd felt in a long time.

* * *

After a grand tour of the compound, I was tired—mind churning from the excitement of the day.

"Anything else you'd like to check out before we get back on the road... unless you'd like to stay for hog-hunting this evening?"

I paused, grasping for a diplomatic response.

Over the years, I'd been forced to hunt it all—pheasant, elk, fox. Even big game in Africa. Blake loved it. I hated it.

"No judgment, but I'm not really into hunting. Something about killing animals just doesn't do much for me."

"Me, neither. Seems we both prefer killing humans."

Edward gave a slow, diabolical grin as I stared in surprise.

It sounded perverse, but I supposed that *was* our business. I'd just never considered it in those terms.

I knew better than to flinch—*but I did.* Unintentionally.

"I haven't killed many people," I replied, quietly.

His smile faded slightly, and he tilted his head.

"I'll try to keep it that way. For what it's worth, I try to avoid killing anyone that doesn't truly deserve it."

He softened his expression.

"So, no to hog-hunting? You could stay in my secret room."

"*What?!*" I exclaimed.

He threw his hands up with a flirty smile. "Oh, no... not with me! I meant my old panic room. Extremely hush hush. I'd stay somewhere else... but I *love* that's where your mind went."

Oh, Edward...

I barely knew him, and yet I hung on his every word like a schoolgirl with a crush.

He made me feel giddy. Unsteady. Vulnerable.

Something I hadn't felt since before I was married.

I should've kept my distance—but I didn't want to.

His mystery. His edge. I wanted more of it.

More of *him.*

* * *

Edward occasionally glanced over on the drive back to Siesta Key.

He looked happy, and I felt it.

When we pulled into my driveway, he parked and came around to open my door.

"So round three tomorrow?" he asked, helping me out of his truck.

"Yes, please! I've missed this."

He paused, then: "Allie, Tank's looking into when Blake should be back. I'll keep you updated."

I nodded, already halfway to the door—hoping to avoid an uncomfortable hug.

He called out: "I've got a slew of calls in the morning, so James will pick you up. Same time."

My key turned in the lock, mind swimming.

I wasn't sure if I was walking into a job or a trap—

but part of me didn't care.

Not yet.

CHAPTER 18

I hadn't been home more than an hour.

I was reading on the couch when there was a knock at my door.

Cody and Tanner were on my doorstep, grinning like idiots, cases of beer in hand.

"Hey, doll!" Cody beamed. "We woulda texted but didn't have your number. You don't get seasick, do ya?"

"No... why?"

"Wanna do some offshore fishing with us? We're taking one of Ed's boats out. Gonna fish and drink and chill."

Exhaustion tugged at me, but I couldn't turn down the first real invite from the team.

"Ummm... sure. When are you leaving?"

"Like an hour?"

"Okay. Uh... I can be ready in about twenty. You guys want to come in?"

Cody smirked, lifting his twelve pack. "Was hoping you'd ask."

Then they strolled straight to my kitchen like they'd been there a dozen times.

As Cody brushed past, I caught it—earthy and warm, with a faint smokiness.

The exact scent that haunted my hallways.

Cody.

I stood, feet frozen to the ground, eyes locked, before I asked boldly, "So how many times have you been in my house?"

Tanner went rigid, beer bottle halfway to his lips, but Cody didn't miss a beat.

"Not sure what you mean. We're not stalkers."

Creepy answer.

"Well, you just walked in like you knew your way around."

He laughed lightly. "Oh, I mean—yeah. We've been here a lot."

Tanner shot him a look—clearly there was more to it.

"*Why?*"

Cody grinned. "You think we got your house bugged or something?"

I paused.

His answer was too specific. No one throws something like that out—unless it's true.

"Yeah," I said, louder than intended. "Actually, I do."

His smile didn't just falter—it disappeared.

"Whoa. You accusing me of breaking and entering?"

Cody nudged Tanner, who gave a nervous half-smile.

"Look, doll... if you're wondering why I know this place like the back of my hand—it's cuz my boy Rob used to live here."

Shit.

Rob.

The teammate who was killed.

"Sorry," I muttered, my chest heavy in guilt.

Still... it didn't explain the cologne.

It wasn't a real answer.

I let it go in the moment—out loud, at least.

"I'll go get dressed," I added, excusing myself before moseying down the hall, just out of view. Holding my breath. Listening.

Almost instantly they were whispering—urgent, hushed.

Voices wisping around the corner, too low to make out.

An unnerving chill crawled my spine.

My house was *bugged.* Monitored. Maybe from day one.

But I couldn't show fear or panic, so I got dressed and pulled myself together, smiled like nothing was wrong, and joined them for two rounds.

Business as usual.

* * *

I recognized the captain of the boat—Sammy, or *Mustang*—instantly.

Smaller. Disheveled brown beard.

The driver of the SUV at brunch.

I'd also seen him in the ops center, though we hadn't spoken.

He seemed friendly. Smart.

Next, Cody introduced me to José—call sign Coyote.

Average build, Hispanic. Salt and pepper freedom beard. Dark man bun.

And a bright smile.

The operator who'd just returned from the near-failed op in El Salvador.

He shook my hand, thanking me for the favor that got him and the kids home safe.

Pleasant. Personable.

* * *

As we made our way to the intercoastal, the guys passed around beers and turned up the music.

But by the time we hit the open ocean, I noticed something.

There weren't any fishing poles on deck.

My chest tightened.

What if this nighttime excursion was an initiation—*my* initiation?

I was immediately uneasy as I speculated what it would entail on a fishing boat headed miles out into the Gulf.

* * *

Sammy killed the engines eight miles offshore.

Surrounded by darkness and the sound of waves lapping the hull, we started floating.

None of the guys touched the fishing gear, though tackle boxes and live bait sat ready. *As decoys?*

They continued to tell stories and drink, occasionally checking our location and the time.

We were waiting.

But for what?

Suddenly, I panicked. I hadn't told anyone about my late-night fishing trip, and my phone would be of little help. Not this far out.

Cody eventually noticed me scanning the deck, drinking slowly.

"Look, doll, we're not gonna throw you overboard and make you fin back." He winked. "I see you're trying to figure out what's up, but we're the most solid group of guys you're ever gonna know. Promise. We're badass."

I fidgeted, trying to play it cool.

"I worked at the agency a long time... self-promotion isn't exactly reassuring."

They all laughed before Sammy cut in. "Just tell her what we're doing out here and stop being sketchy."

"It's supposed to be a surprise, Sammy!" Tanner retorted, annoyed, sounding like Napoleon Dynamite despite being an Irish kid from Brooklyn.

"But it's making her nervous. Just tell her."

Cody relented. "We're waiting on our boy Rockstar to parachute in."

He pointed vaguely to the sky and tapped his watch.

"In seven minutes, José's gonna send up a flare. Then we wait," he added, rubbing his hands together dramatically like a lunatic—the theatrics doing little to tamper my disquiet.

I assumed he was kidding and forced a feeble chuckle. "You're fucking with me."

They laughed in unison before Cody responded. "Nope, he was delinquent on his HALO jumps. Gotta keep up those skills."

"Yeah, I'm *sure.*"

Cody leaned in, voice soft. "I swear. That's what we're waiting on. You can relax."

He patted me on the back. "For real though, doll. We're just fucking around waiting for our boy. But you better not tell Ed we hijacked his boat, cuz he'll flip."

"Hey, he gave us strict orders to look out for you, and that's what we're gonna do. Okay? You good?" He extended his hand.

I hesitated, then took it.

Cody's handshake was kind. Convincing.

"Yeah... sorry. I haven't done this in a while."

"No big deal!"

I'd seen and heard them operate the day prior, and they seemed like a good group, so I took a deep breath and made a conscious effort to let my guard down.

Tanner handed me a cold beer with a knowing smile, grabbing the warm one I'd been nursing before tossing it.

Cody chuckled. "You know the reason God made beer, don't ya?"

I raised a brow.

"It's so we wouldn't be able to take over the world."

"*We* as in 'men' or 'idiots'?" I quipped.

He laughed, squeezing my shoulder. "Nah, doll, *Marines.* It's so Marines like *us* wouldn't take over the world."

I smiled. *They were my people.*

And just like that, my fear started to fade.

* * *

Five minutes after José sent up a flare, a sharp whistle cut the night air.

Tanner vectored the spotlight north, light skimming across the waves—then stopped.

And there he was.

Swimming hard through black water.

Smooth, powerful strokes.

A pale face under the beam.

Rockstar.

He *really* had parachuted in.

I watched as he hauled himself up the ladder then toweled off, water gleaming on his skin, muscles tight as he slipped into a dry tee and cracked a beer.

He and Tanner exchanged a few quiet words—and whatever Tanner said made him freeze for half a beat. A flash of surprise crossed his face before he molded it into a cocky grin and looked my way.

No question—they were talking about me.

But if he thought I'd shrink under the attention, he was wrong.

I raised my beer and smiled.

He gave me a nod, then walked over.

And something about Greg's face tickled my memory.

No. *Couldn't be...*

He punched Cody's shoulder. "Bro, you didn't tell me you were bringing a sweet vixen out tonight—I woulda dressed for the occasion."

With a twinkle in his eye, he offered his hand.

"I'm Greg Swaller."

I took it as recognition hit.

I *knew* Greg. Rockstar.

"Hi, Allie Bailey."

His grip was strong as he held my gaze. Unflinching.

Letting the moment linger longer than polite.

Heat lit up my neck.

It was the move of an alpha male.

A subtle challenge.

Focused. Intense. But laced with something darker—control.

And a tell—Greg was attracted to me.

I felt it. Instantly.

He was taller than the rest of the guys. Perfectly tanned skin. Sun-bleached hair. No beard—just a slight grizzle. Muscles everywhere.

A total hunk.

Years prior, I'd run into Greg at my apartment building in Virginia.

We'd talked, not once, but *twice*—the first time in my neighborhood. The second when he'd flagged me down on a run close to Fort Myer, giving me his number scribbled on a 3x5 card.

It wasn't a coincidence, but I wasn't sure if it was safe—or smart—to admit we'd met before. Not yet.

Not with eyes on us.

Not with all the other "coincidences" that didn't seem to be coincidence at all.

So, I kept quiet.

But after a round of shameless flirtation, Greg and I found ourselves alone.

Then: "Love the hair, babe. Super cute."

Great.

Another pet name. Love. Doll. Al.

Now *babe.*

"Thanks. I think it was darker when we met."

He smirked. "We've met? Nah, I'd remember someone like you."

Was he pretending? Or had I thought more of it than he had?

I paused, taking stock of the situation... no... I'd never been wrong about a face.

"We met at a coffee shop. You were detailed to a diplomat that lived in my building... in Arlington. You gave me your number."

"Did you call me?"

"No..." I blushed. "I didn't."

Greg immediately brightened, pinching my side.

"Must notta been me, then. No way you wouldn't call me, right?"

He winked before checking me out—again. Obvious. Slow. Dialing up the heat.

I redirected.

We talked about the Marine Corps, intel, people we knew—though I left out my ties to MARSOC... and Blake.

He was easy to talk to. Disarming.

A golden retriever in operator form.

But every now and then, something flickered beneath the grin—a shadow that didn't match the energy.

I struggled to reconcile it. How someone so deadly could be so goofy. Giggly. Sweet.

We'd be friends—but he'd be trouble.

The kind that slipped past your defenses when you weren't looking.

I was already keeping Edward at arm's length.

Now I'd have to keep an eye on Greg, too.

Two alpha operators, both used to getting what they wanted.

I wasn't about to let either of them break me—

not when I'd just started putting myself back together.

* * *

The guys drank and partied before meticulously prepping the boat for a speedy departure.

I didn't see any real danger of Edward finding out about our fishing trip, but much to their dread, James *and* Edward were standing on the dock when we cruised up.

Greg quickly ducked into hiding.

I watched nervously as Cody hopped off the boat to approach.

"What's going on, bud?" Edward asked, arms crossed.

"Nothin', Boss. Just fishin' and bullshittin'."

"Yeah, looks like it. Know where Greg's at?"

"Nope, haven't seen him. Shit, haven't even heard from him," Cody replied shrewdly. "You told him to ditch his phone. Remember?"

"Bud, I was born at night, but not last night. Why don't you go tell him I've got a quarter-million-dollar Rollie burning a hole in my pocket?"

Cody lit up, keen to deliver the news. "Badass! He's below deck! Wanna join?"

Edward smirked. "On *my* boat? Yeah... thanks for the invite."

Noticing me, he laughed.

"Already making you an accomplice to their crimes, I see."

I should've known.

I shrugged, letting out a conciliatory chuckle as Greg appeared.

Edward pulled him into a hug before:

"Bud, you had me fucking worried. What happened?"

"Calm down, bro! Nobody even got shot! We can't head back to Central America for a hot minute, but—"

"Yeah, thank God for Bitcoin. How's Derrick?" Edward asked.

"Super Doom is *super* jacked. His team's salty as fuck—but awesome. They'll be ready when we need 'em."

"Should I bring him home to reset?"

"Nah, wasn't his fault. We can debrief over a six pack tomorrow."

Edward nodded then reached into his front shirt pocket.

In it, a gold Rolex encrusted in diamonds and rubies.

"Okay, well here's that Rollie you requested."

Greg's eyes widened.

"*Buhhhh-ro,*" he muttered as he snatched the watch from Edward's hand. "Hot damnnn!"

"This the one you wanted?"

"Hell yeah," Greg grunted. "Where'd you find this rare beauty?"

"Flew her in from Japan this morning."

"Damn, I feel like this is too much."

"Want me to send her back?" Edward joked before Greg shook his head, putting it on without delay.

He flexed his bicep and turned his wrist, examining it before stating hysterically, "Makes me look operator as fuck!"

Edward nudged him toward Cody and the guys, who were visibly anxious to get a peek.

* * *

After filming an impromptu music video starring the "most badass watch ever," Greg and Cody joined the rest of us.

And Greg wasted no time asking me to dinner.

I choked in surprise before replying, "Sorry, I don't date guys I work with."

Greg grinned, stating flatly, "Boss, consider this my notice."

Everyone laughed—except one.

Edward.

Minutes later, Edward made a point of saying goodnight to me in front of Greg, touching my arm—hand lingering. Fire and unmistakable desire in his eyes.

It wasn't just a goodbye—it was a territorial display, and I, the new female, marched into a pride of lions.

Energy shifted—sharp and uncomfortable.

Greg clocked it. But not without a daring smirk and slow head nod, like *game on.*

Edward just shrugged. *Good luck.*

His position at the top of the hierarchy was clear—but not unchallenged.

The thing was, the pissing contest was entirely unnecessary.

I wasn't a prize to be won.

I was married. I'd made vows—even if I didn't always wear the ring.

And yet, I felt myself drifting toward something dangerous—

Men who might make me forget, if I wasn't careful.

* * *

As I lay in bed, eyes on the fan spinning circles overhead, trying—and failing—not to think of Edward, a chilling realization hit like an alarm bell:

Blake barely crossed my mind all night.

I knew better than to fantasize over Edward. I *felt* the danger.

A relationship—sexual or emotional—was out of the question.

Still, I craved the heat of his gaze.

The thrill of his touch.

Reckless.

Irresponsible.

Impossible.

So why couldn't I stop?

CHAPTER 19

By morning, the compound was an oven—sun blazing, heat bouncing off the pavers, trapped behind elegant fencing that looked more country club than covert op.

Inside the ops center, it was a different world—cold, dim, abuzz.

Edward hadn't exaggerated—the capabilities at Bright Sands didn't just rival the U.S. government. They crushed them.

James shrugged casually when I asked how that was possible, then deadpanned:

"The NSA stole all the patents I filed in high school. They were good, but they're still running beta. We're on version thirty."

A wronged tech prodigy. A fearless Marine billionaire. Going up against the most powerful system in the world?

It tracked.

James met Edward at Parris Island in 2005. After completing his enlistment, he moved home to Boston to attend MIT but dropped out.

Edward promptly hired him to design the ops center at Dark Skies and had him replicate it at Bright Sands months later—only much better.

"So, when did Bright Sands officially come about?" I asked.

"Officially? It doesn't exist."

"Then how do you get paid?"

"Duffel bags full of cash. Bitcoin. But, there's not much you'll need money for."

* * *

After a lengthy tour, James set me up with the accounts I'd need for research before we discussed my schedule.

He explained that nothing was set when it came to operations before adding:

"Sometimes I sit on this couch for weeks bored as hell writing code. Then sometimes I'm here for three months working eighteen-hour days, pulling shifts with Ryder. Other times, I'm traveling with the team. It all depends on what pops up. And there's *always* someone manning a desk if Edward's on the move."

"Always?"

"Always. That's me."

"Is Edward worried about getting kidnapped or something?" I asked.

"Not in Florida. But there's a short list of people who'd love to see him dead. I make it my job to know exactly what they're doing and who they're talking to."

He tapped a screen, pulling up a cascade of live video feeds.

"We scan everything on and off the island—every plate, face, and pattern. Same goes for anyone who passes our vehicles. We can't afford any surprises."

He glanced at me, tone even.

"Better hope we don't see you twice."

"Oh..." I nodded.

He continued, casually. "He's not expecting anyone to take a bullet for him. But with the kind of work we do, we stay packed and ready to go at a moment's notice."

"Makes sense."

Then he grinned. "He's the best boss. Even better friend." He nudged me with a smirk. "You'll love him."

His hint wasn't subtle.

And that was exactly what I was afraid of.

James leaned back, rattling off technical failsafes, but my focus had already started to drift—not from boredom, but information overload.

I jolted when an alarm blared overhead—**bonk, bonk, bonk**—and instinctively scanned for threats, heart thudding.

James just smiled. "Noon. Time to eat."

We stepped out to a wall of sunlight and followed a winding path toward the sound of country music and laughter. The transition from icy ops center to coastline was jarring—like stepping through a portal.

Down on the sand, Greg stood behind a hulking steel smoker, sweat slick on his arms as he flipped slabs of hog in board shorts and a tank that read: *Sun's out, Guns out.*

Of course it did.

Zack tossed me a beer and pointed to an empty chair.

I sank into it, taking in the ocean breeze, tinged with hickory smoke and pork fat, then smiled, looking around—guys drinking, joking, throwing a football.

It wasn't just a cookout.

It was a reset and a ritual.

And there I was—toes in the sand, drink in hand, sun on my face—

Laughing like I belonged.

For the first time in years, I felt it.

Not just peace.

Something dangerously close to happiness—

And not the fleeting kind.

The kind that settles in. Hits deep. Refreshes your soul.

* * *

Edward summoned me to the main house in the late afternoon.

I dusted sand off my legs and followed the path, dress hem brushing my ankles.

I wasn't sure what I expected—maybe more beach, maybe more beer—but when the door opened, Edward stood in a tailored suit.

Something in me stuttered.

"Ohhh..."

I glimpsed down at my floral dress and strappy wedges—my take on Florida business casual.

"I feel underdressed now."

"No, you look beautiful."

His fingers trailed across the small of my back as he hugged me.

I let out a half-laugh—nervous, unsure how to respond.

The words and intimate hug caught me off guard.

"I'm not usually in a suit, but I've been on a VTC for a non-profit for four hours. Incredibly stupid."

He grinned.

"Let me show you to the study, then I'll change into more appropriate attire."

Funny. Edward had summoned me—his suit was clearly a flex.

* * *

As he led me down one of the corridors, I tried to keep my expression neutral—no easy feat in a mansion that felt more like a museum.

Oil paintings. Antique weapons. Crystal chandeliers. Furniture worthy of Versailles.

The attention to detail was astounding—from the curtains to the crown molding to the way the wallpaper matched the upholstery.

Everything grandiose.

It wasn't just wealth. It was curated power.

Heirlooms from Edward's godfather, dating back centuries.

Surprisingly, Ed hadn't left anything to his blood relatives—not his sisters, not a single niece or nephew.

He left it all to Edward—his chosen heir.

Why? I wondered.

Because he trusted him? Loved him?

Or because he was grooming him—binding him to a legacy and a fortune he never asked for?

Maybe it was even darker.

My mind was swimming in theories by the time we reached the study—a stunning room with floor-to-ceiling windows framing the ocean.

But I barely registered any of it. Something else caught my attention first.

I dropped my bag, laughing—full body, can't-breathe, doubled-over laughing.

Hard.

"Oh my God, that's amazing!" I exclaimed, wiping my eyes, just to be sure I wasn't hallucinating.

Life-sized Edward stood over the fireplace—boyish, smug, impossibly extra.

Posed like a monarch in a black velvet dinner jacket, green tartan pants, and coordinating ascot. Gaudy gold jewelry. Velvet slippers.

One hand clutched a crystal rocks glass. The other, a pipe—with a wisp of smoke floating dramatically overhead.

The painting—and its thick gilded frame—were gorgeous.

Lavish. Absurd. Self-indulgent.

And yet... also perfect.

A glimpse of who Edward used to be...

Or maybe still was.

He raised a brow. "Be honest—do you love it, or is it totally ridiculous?"

For just a second, he looked uncertain—like part of him wondered if I'd laugh *too* hard. Like he genuinely cared what *I* thought.

"I love it. It's incredible." I tried to keep a straight face as he let out a relieved breath. "Where'd you get this magnificent piece of art?"

He grinned bashfully. "That's a good story, but let me change first."

As he disappeared, I relaxed into a crocodile wingback chair and let myself stare. Really stare. The portrait was... something.

Blake's family had money—old money—but even *they* weren't ostentatious enough to commission portraits of themselves posed like royalty.

They limited theirs to famous ancestors—long-dead Civil War heroes and politicians.

Yet there stood Edward, completely unbothered.

And I had to admit, it suited him.

* * *

I heard him before I saw him—the soft pad of loafers against stone.

I turned.

Linen pants. Patterned shirt.

Dapper, relaxed, and devastatingly handsome. His usual.

"I see you're still staring at me."

I giggled. "I'm sorry, I can't look away. You seem so real."

He beamed brightly as our eyes met.

"Okay, so long story short—my best friend Vlad from boarding school, son of a Russian oligarch—I'll tell you all about him sometime—well, he had it commissioned as a thank you for being a groomsman in his wedding. Mind you, he had one painted for each of us, so there were eight portraits in total."

"Oh, wow... that's—"

"An obnoxious waste of money?" Edward chuckled. "The best part was he did the unveiling while we were cruising the Adriatic for his bachelor party. I believe one may have even been drunkenly tossed off his dad's yacht..."

I laughed. "What a gift!"

"Yeah, I'm shocked you like it. Yours is the best reaction I've had."

"I guess I'm just easy to impress," I teased.

"I doubt that."

Edward gazed at me a second too long. Then he cleared his throat and focused hard on a notepad on his desk.

"Uh, one of my lawyers—Jake—is flying in to walk you through the contract and NDAs. Just don't throw me under the bus and mention you've already seen the ops center or been out to Dark Skies. He'll have a meltdown."

I held up crossed fingers. "You got it, Boss."

He laughed.

"Excellent. The second thing is—I'd like to leverage your expertise building dossiers and targeting packages for leaders of a child trafficking ring—the Black Roses. Have you heard of them?"

"Of course. Happy to help however I can."

The Black Roses were a familiar name—prolific in the world of organized crime with a foothold in Eastern Europe.

Drugs, small arms, ammunition, surface-to-air missiles, tanks, and allegedly even submarines.

Yet I'd repeatedly heard the media dismiss their ties to child trafficking.

Unfortunately, the two often overlapped—criminals were criminals, after all.

Edward could see my wheels turning.

"There's a lot more to them than meets the eye," he said, checking his watch.

"James is joining us in an hour. Until then, I'd like to talk you through the system we use to capture some of our trafficking leads."

* * *

"So, years ago, the government set up a tip line to report human trafficking. You've probably seen the number on posters in airports. Bus terminals. Right?"

I nodded.

"Well, it was designed to make the public feel like they were *doing* something. But... it was mostly used for evil. So, James worked with a close buddy at the NSA to clone the line. Now everything the government gets, we get, too... and we don't drop the ball."

"All tips are triaged by a three-man team in Colorado—real nerds—nerdier than Ryder, if you can believe it." Edward chuckled. "If a tip's validated, they turn it into an ironclad targeting package and route it to local law enforcement. Anonymously."

"Wow."

"But we like to take care of the most heinous offenders in-house. Usually a single bullet to the head. Just to make sure they don't slip through the cracks of justice."

Edward shrugged unapologetically, and I nodded—part admiration, part surprise.

"The problem is, there's so much secrecy and coordination among the rich that bringing down their networks is more difficult than you'd think. Not impossible. But when we take out a cell, another one pops up. It's like al-Qaeda."

He exhaled. "And... I can't tip my hand using anything I've been told or personally witnessed. We need to find it other ways. That's why I need you."

"I'm flattered—" I started, blushing as I realized what Edward had said.

He *needed* me.

Then his tone shifted—flirty to flat—as the door opened. Authoritative.

"Hey, bud. You're early."

James stood in the doorway with a projector, brow raised, unmistakable smirk.

"Uh, yeah. Sorry for the cockblock. Want me to come back?"

Smartass.

Edward looked slightly embarrassed.

"No, why don't you get set up? I'd like to grab some water before we get started."

* * *

In the study, a colossal web filled the wall. A constellation of names and faces, glowing red, yellow, and green—flicking like traffic lights.

I'd mapped terrorist networks before, but nothing came close to this.

"This is—wow..." I leaned forward on the couch, pulled in by the gravity of it all.

"It's pervasive," Edward said, positioning himself beside me. "I'll let James explain."

He glanced at James.

"Now or never, bud. Get us rolling."

James dove in, walking me through ten minutes of Bright Sands' intelligence collection capabilities before adding comically, "And if ever in doubt, I'll take a quick peek in JWICS."

He shrugged. "You'd be amazed what shows up if you know where to look."

From there, he moved into secret societies and fraternal organizations. He and Edward touched briefly on ancient bloodlines before pivoting.

Child trafficking. Pedophilia. And the media's role in burying credible reports—fed talking points by elites in Washington and Hollywood.

Their tone was clinical, not conspiratorial. The research, meticulous.

And it was horrifying.

Edward handled most of the commentary as James delivered stats like a machine.

Then Edward started to describe the "Apparatus"—a term I hadn't heard before.

We covered its "philanthropic" foundations, and darker practices—cannibalism, human sacrifice.

Things I'd never believed were real—until that moment.

According to Edward, the Apparatus didn't just operate like a global shadow-state.

It *was* the global shadow-state. The cabal I never knew the name for.

It single-handedly controlled most governments and intelligence agencies.

And much like the KGB or Gestapo, it had eyes and ears everywhere.

Yet it had no offices.

No org chart.

No centralized power structure.

It didn't leave fingerprints.

Its leaders weren't kings.

They were ghosts.

A terrorist organization by every definition of the term.

It levied destruction through false flag attacks and information operations.

It morphed and changed like a chameleon—using financial proxies and coercive manipulation to execute its agenda.

It was almost impossible to track.

And yet, Edward and James had a list.

Ten names.

Ten people they believed made up its nucleus.

Ten people whose fall could shatter the entire web.

Bright Sands' mission:

Destroy it.

"How do you know it even exists and isn't a myth?" I asked, a slight tremble in my voice.

Edward's eyes didn't flinch.

"Because I know a few people in it."

"*Oh,*" I murmured, startled—but not surprised.

Edward moved in elite circles. He knew the players behind the scenes.

He pointed to the screen. "This is our current kill list. My friend Vlad's guys help with blackmail, extortion, recovery—and executions." He nodded to James. "Bud, can you light up who we've eliminated?"

James hit a key, turning part of the network bright red.

"Oh my God," I whispered.

"It's not all good versus evil, Allie. We're not fighting the traditional bad guys."

He paused, thoughtfully.

"We're going after the bad guys no one talks about. The ones people are scared to touch. Talking about guys like this would shake humanity's reality to its core. Most people can't handle it. We've taken out about ten percent of the network."

I studied the screen, reeling from a sudden comprehension: what Bright Sands was doing wasn't just operational. It was geopolitical. Moral. World-altering.

Covert operations without the brakes. No bureaucratic oversight. No budget constraints. No hesitation. Just results.

And somehow, I had a password—and a role.

"Some of these people are famous. You really killed the French Defense Secretary?"

"I didn't kill him personally," Edward chuckled. "But our intel set it in motion. Coyote made it look like a murder by his lover."

For a split second, a flicker of unease cut through me—not at the targets, but at how easy it was to justify killing. On repeat.

I'd watched the team assassinate a would-be world leader without losing any sleep.

This felt bigger.

Not murky.

Not even gray.

Almost... godlike.

With monsters like this—pedophiles, human traffickers—it was open season.

And I had no reservations.

Some people just needed to be erased.

* * *

Over the course of the next two hours, I lost count of how many times I gasped—sometimes from horror, sometimes disbelief.

With each gasp, Edward would lean over, then squeeze my hand or softly touch my leg.

He whispered as James spoke, his breath intimate and warm on my neck—sending shivers down my spine.

It wasn't subtle or accidental.

He knew exactly what he was doing.

And worse—

I let him.

Chapter 20

"You look better than expected," Edward said, eyes sharp and assessing.

"Yeah... but I definitely need a drink... and I might not be able to eat for a few days."

James winced. "My fault. I should've pulled some of the more frightening images."

Edward added gently: "Allie, every kid you saw who wasn't dead—we saved."

"I'm sorry, that wasn't a criticism. All the images were... terrifying, but essential. Thank you for sharing."

The room fell quiet. The kind of silence that settles after truth lands heavy.

James gave a small, appreciative smile while Edward rose—his gaze already locked on mine, hand extended.

A gentlemanly gesture. Innocent on the surface.

But nothing with Edward ever was.

I should've known better than to accept.

I was a married woman.

I'd survived interrogation, betrayal, war zones—

But I couldn't seem to survive *this*.

His presence.

The quiet, calculated pull of his touch.

Like he *knew* I'd take his hand.

And I did...

The second our skin met, a jolt shot through me—hot, electric, divine—all in one devastating charge.

But it wasn't *just* desire.

It was guilt—coiled and searing—reminding me I shouldn't feel this. Not for him.

We stood, hand-in-hand.

A flicker of satisfaction in his eyes.

The air between us buzzing—

until James mercifully cut in.

"Everybody okay?"

Without breaking our stare, Edward replied, "Bud, why don't you go track down that bottle of Jameson?"

Then he leaned closer. "Did I already promise to be the perfect gentleman? I can't recall."

"I think you did," I said—too quickly. Too firmly. Forcing a breezy tone I didn't feel.

My cheeks betrayed me, warming anyway.

"Then we better go," he murmured. "After you, love."

That word again—*love.*

I rolled my eyes, half-laughing, then turned before he could see the effect he had.

* * *

The whiskey's warmth matched the flush of my cheeks—only magnified by my laughter.

James had been measured all night—observant, sarcastic, mostly listening.

Then he finally leaned forward, his Boston accent in full effect.

Edward perked up.

"Alright, so there I am, posted up at Al Asad," he said, hands gesturing like he was setting the stage. "It's 3 a.m. Quiet. Then all the sudden—this long-ass 'Meowwwww' comes over the radio."

I laughed at the delivery—his 'Meow' was crisp, practiced. *Ridiculous.*

"Everyone perks up. We're like—what the hell was that?"

He glanced around, drawing us in with theatrics.

Edward just shrugged at me. Amused.

James continued. "A minute later, another one. 'Meow.' Silence. Then: 'Meow Meow, you there?'"

"Next thing I know, the radio's a damn farm—'Moo,' 'Ribbit,' 'Woof,' 'Quack'—you name it. Every animal noise you can think of."

Empty shot glasses clinked across the counter, James animated, hands flying.

I shook my head, grinning.

"At one point, I could barely breathe or hear. I was crying too hard."

We all laughed.

"The Watch Commander starts losing it, screaming at the top of his lungs: 'Identify yourself, Marine!' Going on and on about everyone getting court martialed. But no one stops. It had us in stitches until sunrise."

James grinned, then: "Only years later do I find out who was involved. You'll never guess."

I looked to Edward. He shook his head.

"Nope. Sergeant Gregory Swaller. He was the 'Meow' that sparked the pandemonium."

I nearly spit out my beer. "What? No way!"

"Yep, he was banging my Lieutenant and needed her to create a distraction for his non-standard entry back on base."

"Seriously? Greg?!"

"It worked... but I don't think she appreciated her 'Meow' getting put on blast—if you know what I mean. Don't think he tried that again."

"Oh my God."

The story was hysterical.

And somehow so Greg.

And somewhere between stories and shots, laughter echoing, I realized I felt joyful. Just like I'd been with Edward and Tank.

Maybe I should've been taking mental notes—questioning everything, solving the mystery that was Edward—but I wasn't.

After his briefing, I trusted him. Against *all* logic, I trusted him.

He was on the right side.

Maybe not the winning side. But the right one.

* * *

After an hour, James excused himself to use the restroom.

Fifteen minutes later, he still hadn't returned.

"Should you go look for him?" I eventually asked, hoping he hadn't tipped over in a planter or fallen down a flight of stairs.

Edward chuckled. "He's fine. He executed a flawless Irish goodbye. You'll see him tomorrow."

"Oh." I glanced down at my watch.

I needed to go. It was late—and being alone with Edward wasn't smart.

"Thank you for tonight. I should probably—"

I was stopped mid-sentence.

Edward's hand found my waist, fingers warm through the thin fabric of my dress.

He pinned me—the cold edge of the marble hard against my back, his legs boxing me in.

"Edward—"

His lips were already at my neck, wet and insistent.

Oh my...

I pushed him back. Firm.

"Edward, we can't do this. Blake's due back soon."

He stared with a playful smile, one hand sliding softly down my arm, goosebumps racing along my skin. I was almost helpless to his touch.

"This has nothing to do with him. Allie, I can't get you out of my head."

The feeling was mutual...

Did I want Edward to stop? Absolutely not.

But I couldn't give in to temptation—not so easily.

"Let me remind you I'm married."

"Being married hasn't stopped—"

My body flinched. Edward wasn't wrong, but I didn't want to hear it—not from him.

I grumbled before he could finish.

"That's not fair. And, we've only known each other a few days. We're moving too fast."

Why had I said we're*? There was no* we.

That wasn't allowed. Or real.

"Allie, I've known you a long time."

"Ah, don't say that! It makes you sound like a psycho."

"I thought billionaires could pull off psycho, no?"

He winked.

I shook my head. "I really can't work here if things are going to be like this between us. You promised to be a gentleman."

I looked into his eyes—pleading. "Please don't take this from me. I'm so excited about working again."

Edward nodded silently before relenting.

"You're right. I'll exercise restraint."

He shifted on the stool.

"Will you promise? *Please.*"

"Yes." He put his hand to his mouth, biting his own knuckle before muttering quietly:

"But you need to leave, because it's taking every ounce of will-power I have not to lead you straight to my bedroom... and the things I want to do to you won't qualify as gentlemanly."

His words left me breathless, a tingling heat rising all over my body.

A sensation only magnified when I caught a glimpse of his lap.

Oh. My. God.

This wasn't just temptation. It was lust. Unapologetic. Unreasonable.

I fumbled clumsily for my bag—flustered, hands refusing to work, every nerve pulsing with my heartbeat.

"Okay, I'm going," I mumbled, finally finding words.

Several seconds later, I ran out the door nearly losing one of my wedges in the process.

"Thank you!" I yelled over my shoulder.

All I heard was a deflated: "Good night, Allie."

* * *

I laid awake for hours.

I couldn't stop thinking about Edward's lips on my neck—fantasizing about the ways the evening could've ended if I'd lost all self-control and let him have his way with me.

While I didn't want to admit it—I wanted him, too.

Desperately.

But I knew my lust for Edward was likely the sad byproduct of loneliness.

Blake had been gone a long time. And I *was* lonely.

If I hadn't been—I doubted I'd have been so vulnerable.

At least that's what I told myself.

* * *

Over the following week, I struggled to concentrate.

My mind often drifted to Edward.

I was confident James sensed my distraction based on his tactful comments and well-placed innuendos as he brought me up to speed on operations.

Like Edward, his personality and brilliance were endearing, and he was eager to teach me the ropes—allegedly so he could take a much-needed vacation.

I laughed, doubting he was short on vacations.

His desk was littered with dozens of photos of him at various land-marks around the world—Machu Picchu, the Colosseum, Burj Al Arab, the Great Wall, the Pyramids at Giza, Phang Nga Bay, the Kremlin, even Mt. Everest and Kilimanjaro.

And for days, Edward didn't make an appearance in the ops center.

It seemed obvious—he was avoiding me. I tried to convince myself I was thankful.

I wasn't.

* * *

Over the weekend, Edward sent a text:

Blake may have rotated into another thing. Might be a few weeks before he's back. -E

I exhaled, relaxing into an emotion I couldn't quite name—surprise, disappointment, or relief?

Having to talk to Blake about Bright Sands—and the state of our marriage—had been weighing heavy on me.

Maybe Florida was my chance for a clean break. I just wasn't sure if I had the courage to take it.

Soon I was doubting myself. My decisions. My thought process.

Was Blake really that bad?

Had I moved on too quickly?

I couldn't imagine us regaining what we'd once had.

But maybe we owed it to ourselves to try?

Another text dinged minutes later:

Want to head out to DS for 2 weeks of skills training?

Starts Monday.

My fingers hovered over the screen.

Sure. Sounds great.

Then:

Arrive at 0700. Tank will get you situated. I'll forward his #.

Have fun. -E

I stared at the screen, pulse quickening.

An invitation—and a test.

* * *

When Monday arrived, I made my way out to Dark Skies—joining a potential recruit and three operators recovering from injury.

Tank met me in the parking lot, sun blazing on the blacktop, wearing a gray polo and black 5.11s. His first words were, "You know nothing about Dark Skies. Bright Sands doesn't exist. And you've never met Blake. Got it?"

I nodded. "Affirm."

Then he pulled down his aviators with a smile. "Stand on your own quals. You got this, girl!"

He gave me a once-over—gray polo, black tactical pants, black boots—all brand new.

"You look... crisp."

I rolled my eyes. "Yeah, nothing screams 'newbie' like fresh gear, huh?"

Tank laughed.

"What happened to your old stuff?"

"I may've burned it all in a state of psychosis." I shrugged.

He just grinned.

"Well, you're gonna fit right in. Come on—I'll introduce you to the guys."

As we walked toward the team house, I straightened my shoulders and exhaled.

I took what he said to heart—

and channeled the woman I used to be.

The one who could walk into any room and own it.

A woman who knew how to wield a weapon, read the threat, and make split-second decisions—something my success and survival once depended on.

I wasn't doing this for Edward. Or Blake.

I was doing it to feel like myself again—a version of me buried, not gone.

Maybe I was still faking her. A little. But I could feel her rising.

And I needed her now—more than ever.

* * *

My adrenaline spiked seconds before the clock started.

Sean—a long-time Dark Skies guy—and I were tasked with a timed CQB drill in the six-room shoot house. And the last thing I wanted was to fold under pressure.

Seasoned operators critiqued us from above—skilled in clearing structures.

I was just doing my best to keep up.

Things were going well—Sean and I moved through the house with precision.

All our shots were clean, our communication textbook.

We were making great time—despite the blaring music overhead and distraction of flashbangs—firing on all cylinders until the last room where I fumbled a critical reload—a magazine somehow slipping through my gloved fingers.

It hit the floor. *Failure.*

"Ah, shit!" I yelled as the music cut and the lights came on.

I looked up. Tank shrugged before barking, "Reset. Again!"

I grumbled under my breath, teeth clenched in frustration. And embarrassment.

Rattled on our second run, I stupidly missed a hostile target—triggering a simulated kill.

"Damn it!" I muttered as I holstered my gun, grimacing at Sean. "Sorry."

He shook his head, handing me a water bottle.

The goal was to build muscle memory and make split-second decisions under high-stress. Right now, I was the weakest link.

I took a sip of water, the bottle trembling slightly in my hand. When I glanced up, Tank met my gaze and gave a single, sharp nod.

Sean adjusted his gear, readying for another run.

"Allie, you're thinking too hard. Trust your instincts."

I closed my eyes—visualizing the run, every move clear in my mind.

One more deep exhale, then go.

As we zipped around the corner, I hit a target clean as it popped up in front of us.

Then another.

And another.

We moved together perfectly through all six rooms—no errors.

Exhausted and dripping sweat, I braced myself against a wall as the lights flicked on overhead. The drill was complete. Flawless.

Sean cracked a smile before slapping me on the back. "Not bad for a girl."

Somehow, it was the emotional breakthrough I didn't know I needed.

* * *

On Wednesday, Jake texted me coordinates to a ranch outside Ocala, then:

No cell phones. Come alone. 9pm. Don't be late.

The road narrowed into a gravel track with a dead-end in a nondescript field, swallowed by darkness. My tires crunched loudly— breaking the silence.

This is how horror movies started, I thought as I took my foot off the gas, idling.

A lone black SUV sat under a twisted oak, headlights off before a single flash, signaling my approach.

I eased alongside.

Jake rolled down his window, then tapped the light in the cabin so I could see his face. He was no older than fifty with a toothy, trustworthy smile.

"Hey, Allie. Thanks for coming."

I expected the paperwork to be dense—and secretive—but Jake handed me a thin folder—in it, two pieces of paper for signature: an NDA and a one-page employment contract.

"This is it?" I asked, scanning the NDA. Standard.

"That's it. Edward likes to keep things neat. This isn't traditional employment. There aren't contract disputes."

He hesitated. "You either come to an agreement and walk away, or—"

His voice trailed in a pointed warning.

"Yeah, I get it."

"Any questions?"

I skimmed the employment contract—nearly choking.

A thousand dollars a day?

I tried to appear unfazed. Inside, I was practically levitating.

I scanned the numbers again. *Really?!*

It was an insane daily rate for a non-shooter—but it didn't stop me from accepting.

My signature slid across the page like a blood oath—easy, fast. No going back.

Jake smirked. "Like I said, Allie, not traditional employment." He closed the folder. "Edward knows your worth."

As I drove off, I smiled.

For the first time in years, I didn't feel like a liability anymore.

I felt like an asset.

CHAPTER 21

I was still waiting for someone to call me out—to tell me I didn't belong. But two weeks into training, I was somehow keeping up.

So, when Tank invited me to stay another, I didn't hesitate.

I said yes before my mind—or body—could protest.

Tank and I were fast friends, our interactions completely innocent. Platonic. Fun.

A stark contrast to Edward and the Bright Sands team.

No tension. Low pressure. Just focus.

And maybe because of that... I was thriving.

* * *

The salty air of Siesta Key hit me the second I opened my car door, the air balmy and breezy.

A welcome change from the swampy humidity of Dark Skies.

I had weekend plans with a few former agency friends renting a mansion nearby.

Although I'd never been one for girlfriends, I made an exception for Sandy and Celine.

They were low drama and loyal. Not petty. *Usually.*

Instead of tearing each other down, we'd found ways to help each other up—navigating the agency's bureaucratic mess together.

We hadn't talked much since I left, and honestly, I wouldn't have joined them at all if I weren't still riding the high from training. And Bright Sands.

One minute I was saying I'd swing by for a quick drink.

The next thing I knew, I was fully committed—squeezing into a tight dress and meeting them downtown—my first time dressing up in forever.

We barhopped before making our way to a hotel rooftop for live music and dancing—

and ran straight into trouble: Cody and Greg.

Sandy and Celine were instantly enamored, asking multiple times why I hadn't mentioned them.

My answer was simple—I hadn't known them well enough to ask if they wanted to party—turns out, they did.

We shut down the bars and had such a blast that Celine roped them into a pool party the next day.

* * *

As I rolled through the gate, it felt like a scene out of South Beach. The mansion was painted in electric magenta and metallic gold, with sweeping views of the ocean and pool, which was cluttered with iridescent unicorn floats.

Strobe lights pulsed in sync with the music, the entire backyard throbbing with house and tropical EDM—low, relentless, like a second heartbeat.

Celine and another agency acquaintance, Tara, were floating in the pool while Greg and Cody outrageously danced on the deck—drinking and, presumably, tripping out—as Sandy sunbathed on a lounger.

Cody wore a skin-tight crop top stretched over barbell nipple piercings, a provocative crochet G-string, reflective sunglasses, and a floppy hat—with a sucker in his mouth.

I blinked once. Twice. Then openly stared.

I ogled his two full-sleeves and well-defined abs—USMC tattooed across them in large block text.

He looked like an entertainer from a Vegas bachelorette party gone very, very wrong... or right.

Greg's outfit was equally deranged—tight-fitting American flag silkies revealing an *enormous* bulge—making me suspect his shorts were stuffed—a pair of aviators, and neon green sweatbands.

He was shirtless, showing off a thick gold chain and flashy cross with diamonds, his glistening chest and abs, and a handful of military tattoos.

The sight reminded me of a rave—or at least what I imagined one might be like.

Tara, Sandy, and Celine didn't partake in drugs due to random testing, but we were all accustomed to drinking heavily to keep up with our male counterparts.

Though I sometimes limited my hard alcohol intake in fear of becoming a true alcoholic—I made an exception for the day so I wouldn't be accused of being boring and dull.

And alcohol helped loosen me up.

Celine and Tara were head over heels for Cody and Greg, respectively, and the flirtation was thick as the four of them drank and floated—leaving me with Sandy.

Operators were Sandy's type—Greg particularly—but Tara, despite being married to a charismatic and attractive operator herself, called dibs on him.

After excusing myself to use the restroom, I stumbled into the kitchen—where Greg and Cody were lining up shots.

The tile floor was slick from wet feet. A haze of weed and sunscreen hung in the air.

I smiled and tried to slip past, but Greg stopped me with a grin.

"Hey," he said, waving the tequila bottle—eyeing me. "Wanna take some shots—and let me motorboat you?"

Tipsy, bold, and completely unfiltered.

He wasn't the first man to speak to me like that—but *still*. We barely knew each other.

"Greg, I hate to break it to you, but there's zero chance that's happening. Dream on."

I smirked then grabbed a beer off the counter. I could hold my own with these guys.

Couldn't I?

It had been a long time since I'd played this game—flirty, fast, biting without being bitter.

Back then, I was practiced. Smooth.

Now I wasn't sure if I was witty—or just winging it.

"What about me, doll?" Cody asked with a drunken grin.

"That's also a firm no, but thanks for the offer."

I rolled my eyes.

They were testing my limits... challenge accepted.

"Could be great for team building?" Cody muttered, shrugging casually.

"Oh yeah? Maybe I should blow you both instead?" I shot back, dry.

"Double barrel?" Cody grinned, hopeful. Then, with a laugh, "Hey, don't underestimate the power of team building."

Greg squeezed my shoulder. "I'd love you all over me, but I'm really more of a giver."

He stuck his tongue out and winked—obscene.

These two.

Really professional.

They'd clearly never taken a sexual harassment class... but then again, Bright Sands wasn't traditional employment.

While crude, I had thick skin—no stranger to the sexual advances of the men I worked with.

I'd learned to disarm it—lean in just enough to stay in control.

Thwart playfully.

Let them think I was unfazed, even while calculating every move.

My cheeks were warm, but I laughed anyway, shaking it off with a sigh.

"Oh, sorry, doll, we're just fucking with you. You're a good sport."

Greg burst into a grin. "It's gonna be awesome with you on the team. You're super fun!"

"I'm glad I amuse you."

Greg didn't laugh this time. Just looked at me—*really looked*—for a second too long. Maybe it was the tequila—but... at least I wasn't invisible.

Objectified, sure, but somehow that felt better than forgotten.

"Group hug?" Cody asked, extending his arms toward me.

The hug was happening whether I wanted it to or not.

"Yeah, just try not to touch me with that banana hammock," I replied as he purposefully swept it against my leg.

"Like that, huh?"

"Uh... well, it takes a secure man to pull off a see-through thong. Your confidence is admirable."

"Must be all that big dick energy," Cody stated with a cool wink.

I raised my brow. "Uh, yeah, if you say so."

"Burn, bro!" Greg snorted in laughter, then hugged me—with a quick pinch to my butt—murmuring, "Please have my babies."

"Greg—what did you just say?" I squealed, blinking hard.

"You heard me."

I gawked.

"So maybe?"

"You guys are insane," I replied, sliding my hands down my face.

What had I gotten myself into with this team? They were next level.

Cody intervened. "Doll, slap us if we get too lit and start acting like dicks."

"Oh yeah? You seem the type that might enjoy a good slap."

"Damn, from you... more than you know," Greg replied in a breathy growl as he directed me back toward the pool.

"Go on! You and Sandy are getting in. No more hiding this hot bod on the pool deck. Let's go get you *wet.*"

Oh. "I wasn't hiding. I was giving you space to make new friends."

"Uh-huh," Greg uttered before Cody added:

"Come on. Party time!"

It was so absurd, so chaotic. I wasn't sure if I wanted to roll my eyes or laugh.

It was different than the intensity with Edward. *Lighter.* Still no less inappropriate.

There was no doubt Greg and Cody were stereotypical alphas—bad boys with swagger and *extreme* confidence.

Yet at Bright Sands, they were devoted bravos driving Edward's mission to success.

The hierarchy fascinated me.

I found myself drawn to men like them. I *thrived* around them.

And after our kitchen encounter, they started treating me like part of the team. An insider.

* * *

The water shimmered with sunlight and spilled drinks. Laughter and music echoed off the pool deck, but beneath the surface, the undercurrent of shifting attention was palpable—Greg and Cody had their sights locked on Celine and Tara.

It was admittedly a relief to me, though it caused heartburn with Sandy.

She was pissed that Tara—a woman she believed was less attractive and far less intelligent—drew Greg and Cody's attention.

Still, we all enjoyed the beautiful day—drinks and sun, floating and singing, and abundant flirtation.

It was strange to feel so light after so many years of darkness.

But I embraced it—friends, fun, joy.

CHAPTER 22

Tara and Celine couldn't resist making plans with Greg and Cody later that evening, so Cody invited us to a place he and Greg often stayed, several miles south of Sarasota on Casey Key.

The mansion was owned by Greg's former CAG buddy, and they'd stay there when he was out of town—or at least, that's what Greg claimed.

Cody gave a grand tour, even allowing us a peek inside the walk-in safe—bigger than my first apartment.

Shelves stacked with rifle cases, surveillance gear, hard drives, radios, unmarked briefcases. Even grenades and what appeared to be an '80s era rocket launcher.

I was tempted to compare it to the bunker arsenal at Blake's family ranch but refrained—I'd let the guys think it was impressive.

Then we proceeded to party hard—taking shots and dancing. Even stripping.

Cody and Greg had already established themselves as characters in their own right.

But together?

Hysterical.

They'd first met at BRC in the late '90s, then split—Cody to 2nd Recon, Greg to 1st. They crossed paths again at MARSOC in 2006, before Greg moved on to more dangerous endeavors.

Bright Sands brought them full circle.

Now they were inseparable.

Around 8 p.m., Edward arrived with Tank—allegedly at Cody's insistence to even out the male to female ratio.

He wore a crisp linen shirt and boat shoes, hair windblown from the drive. Maddeningly perfect.

We teased and flirted, laughter dissolving lines that should've stayed drawn.

I told myself to stop. Part of me even *wanted* to stop.

But I couldn't.

Maybe I was in free fall, but I felt like I was finally living again. Free from anxiety and fear and self-doubt.

And maybe this life wasn't better than what I'd once had—but this one pulsed.

It was vibrant. Thrilling. Addicting.

I craved it more than I craved control.

* * *

I watched as Greg spun around a stripper pole mounted in the center of the living room—winking every time our eyes met—blowing kisses like dollar bills.

He certainly fit the operator mold—amusing and self-assured.

And yet he was gregarious. Giggly.

Two words I never imagined applying to a man who killed for a living.

But did that make him less masculine?

Oddly, not in the slightest.

His giggles seemed a glimpse into his soul.

In them, kindness. Joy.

Until he flipped a switch and the facade fell away.

I'd heard the stories about his brutality. His lethality.

He showed no mercy for pedophiles or human traffickers. *None.*

Maybe that's why he acted the way he did.

The drinking. The drugs. The sex. The outrageous humor.

On the surface, it looked like indulgence. Hedonism.

But it was survival.

Because how else do you walk out of *that* world—pedophilia, child sex trafficking—then throw on silkies and dance on a stripper pole—the life and light of the party?

This was Greg's version of coping. The team's version of coping.

I couldn't fault them. When you carry that ugliness—that darkness—you grasp for any light, any glimmer of joy you can.

* * *

Tank approached, voice low.

"Cody and Greg are *crazy* high right now. Sometimes you gotta put them in check. Greg's good when you tell him no, so don't be afraid. Cody's normally the one wrangling him, but he's high as a kite tonight, too."

"Thanks for the heads up, but I think I can handle them. They seem fun."

"Oh, they're fun, but sometimes their version of *fun* turns into *out of control* on a dime," Tank said with a hearty chuckle. "I've seen it."

"I can imagine you have. Honestly, it's just nice having friends again—you especially," I added, a fond smile.

Tank looked bashful. "Yeah, it's a good group. They'll look out for you when you're down range. Probably too close sometimes, but that's just cuz you're pretty."

I laughed. "Well, that's a compliment considering I'm forty."

"I never would've guessed."

"Tank, you're too kind."

He grinned. "Ed thinks you're pretty, too... but you didn't hear that from me."

"What do you think about that?"

"You and Ed? Or Ed thinking you're pretty?"

I smirked. "Me and him."

"No one's judging, if that's what you're worried about."

"Thanks," I said with a shy smile. "But don't you think it's strange? I'm still trying to figure out if he really wants me on the team or just wants to sleep with me."

"Why can't you do both?"

"Tank!" I slugged him lightly in the shoulder.

He shrugged sheepishly. "What?"

"I mean, I'm married, for starters."

But Tank had a point... if I wasn't...

"I don't think Ed cares you're married. None of the guys do." He paused. "Ah—sorry, that didn't come out right."

"Do you *know* my husband?"

"Yeah... been on some things with him over the years."

"Well, then you probably know he's going to flip about me working at Bright Sands. And..." I hesitated, voice lowering. "*Cheating.*"

Tank raised a brow. "Yeah. But here's how I see it—he's out operating and having a good time."

I gave a tight smile.

By *having a good time*, Tank meant sleeping around. It wasn't subtle.

My stomach twisted. So people *did* know.

He clocked the flicker of discomfort in my eyes and softened.

"I'm not saying two wrongs make a right. I'm just saying, why's he the only one who can operate and have fun?"

I didn't answer. Because I didn't know.

"Look... you can tell Ed to back off. He might still chase you, but that's when you come talk to your boy Tank, here. I'll put him in his place."

"Thanks, Tank." I smiled.

It was nice to know he had my back—no strings or judgment.

"You got it, girl! I'm a big teddy bear, but I got no problem whooping him. Wouldn't be the first time I whooped him or Cody or Greg."

He grinned wide.

"Greg tried to fight me outside a Marine Corps ball after getting wasted on Ed's detail. I had to knock him out and throw him in the bed of a buddy's truck to take a little nap. He's known for testing his limits." He made a silly face. "Well, Ed, too. But you already know that..."

"Oh, I do," I replied—just as Edward approached.

* * *

Around midnight, Cody and Celine excused themselves to bed, and Tank and Sandy wandered out to the beach to take a walk—leaving me, Edward, Greg, and Tara alone.

Tara made several rambunctious moves on Greg—in full view—making me cringe with secondhand embarrassment.

But Greg didn't flinch. If anything, he seemed into it.

He turned to me, nodding toward the bedroom. "Wanna join?"

My stomach lurched. I laughed—awkward, startled—eyes darting to Edward like a lifeline.

"Don't look at me," he said, hands up with a slight chuckle. "I'm not here to stop you."

I shook my head, declining Greg's offer. He was the epitome of a playboy.

And Tara? A magnet for drama.

We'd been friends on and off for years, but she enjoyed misbehaving.

I once heard she tried to seduce Blake—whether she was successful, I wasn't sure.

But we were never the same after that.

I guess I should've expected the night to end with her hooking up with *someone* in the house—and Greg seemed a fitting match for her wild energy.

Things got interesting not long after they disappeared into his bedroom.

I exchanged a look with Edward—equal parts horror and hilarity—but every crash and moan only sharpened the tension between us.

Eventually I grabbed my drink—desperate for air.

Edward followed, silent, as I made my way to the pool.

The night was balmy, the air thick with salt and humidity, and we ended up talking under a sky full of stars for hours—soft waves filling the space between our words.

* * *

After making our way inside—well past 2 a.m.—we stood in the living room, tipsy.

I busied myself rearranging pillows on the sofa while Edward watched.

Quiet. Calculated.

Like a lion—waiting for the right moment to pounce.

He hadn't touched me all night, but I'd felt the heat of his eyes.

Every glance, every movement, like he was holding something back.

Tracking me. *Stalking* me.

Careful not to startle his prey.

One touch, and I might forget everything—

Logic and the life I was pretending to protect.

Then he stepped closer, fingers grazing the inside of my arm—barely there—sending a shiver up my spine.

Patient. Precise. *Possessive.*

He was inches away, close enough to feel the heat of his body.

I stood—heart pounding—caught between instinct and desire.

My last breath before the ambush.

The chase. The take down.

And I wasn't sure if I wanted to run... or be caught.

CHAPTER 23

Edward held my gaze, my body trembling—his eyes telling me exactly what he wanted.

Me.

The moments leading up our first kiss stretched like the final breath before the kill—then he pounced, captured, and claimed.

His hands framed my face as he kissed me—mouth melting into mine—hungry, demanding—guiding me backward onto the couch, laying me out like I was his to devour.

Edward's kisses were all-consuming. Captivating.

I squirmed, breath catching as I felt him against me.

I moaned.

He paused—smirked—and pressed deliberately, reminding me who was in charge.

Then came his shirt—peeled off in one smooth motion.

His hand slid beneath my dress, fingers tracing me through lace as his mouth found the hollow of my neck.

Every move measured.

Like he had all the time in the world to tear me apart. To tease me. To take me...

"Oh God, you're so..." he murmured against my skin, his voice barely more than a breath.

I'd been fantasizing about this all night—*him*.

And he knew it.

But this wasn't fantasy anymore.

It was real.

And I was on the brink of crossing a very red line—one that was still intact, even if dangerously blurred.

Blake flashed in my mind like a warning flare.

I tried to focus—to remember the vows I'd made, the damage this would cause.

But desire had taken over.

I couldn't think.

I could just barely breathe—my lungs seized in the thrill—the weight of Edward's body, the heat of his breath, the way he moved against me with a slow, predatory hunger.

I whimpered, helpless, his lips finding my throat, then turned my face to create space—one last grasp at self-control.

He paused. Watching me. Reading me.

A slow inhale. His body still. Eyes ravenous.

But I didn't pull away.

I couldn't.

Not when his every kiss, every touch, lit a fire.

I knew what came next.

Then:

A scrape of ice—

shattering the moment.

* * *

We whipped our heads to see Greg's butt-naked body illuminated by the freezer's glow.

He waved in the dark as Edward hastily rolled off me and adjusted himself.

Like we'd been caught in the act.

"Uh, hey—needed some ice for temperature play. Didn't expect you to be out here fooling around," Greg explained casually.

I swallowed as Edward reached for the hem of my dress, gently tugging it down. Shielding me without a word.

Greg added, "Bro, pick a bedroom in this monstrosity and fuck like adults. Condoms are in the bathroom, top drawer."

He faltered, gathering his thoughts, then: "Uh, sorry... forgot you don't really need 'em cuz you're shootin' blanks."

Edward chuckled diffidently before Greg muttered, "Remember what we talked about. Her pleasure's the mission," and headed back to his bedroom.

When he was out of earshot, Edward grumbled, "Thanks, bud."

I laughed, but my nerves kicked in. I glanced at the hallway. Was Edward about to suggest we move to a bedroom?

Was I ready? Sixty seconds ago, I had been... but Greg's interruption felt like a sign—to stop.

Yes, my marriage was *probably* over—but I hadn't said it out loud. Not to Blake. Not to myself. And until I did, going further with Edward wasn't right. I knew it... but God, I wanted to.

Edward took a careful breath. "Allie... would you be interested in moving somewhere more private?"

I paused, pulse racing.

Was I really considering this?

I harnessed what was left of my willpower, finally managing a faint, "Not tonight." I gulped. "I haven't been with anyone else in a long time. And, this... matters to me. I want to be sure."

He exhaled, nodding. Almost relieved.

"Whatever pace you need," he said, voice low and calm.

He kissed me again—gentle, full of promise—and after a moment, asked softly, "Would you be okay with me sleeping next to you?"

"As in... snuggling?" I teased.

Edward gave a half-smile and a shrug. "Only if you're comfortable."

I settled in beside him and repositioned his arm across my stomach, scooting closer until our bodies fit together. Like puzzle pieces destined to find each other.

He adjusted behind me, his breath warm against my neck, body hard—before he started pressing, shifting, grinding.

After several moments, he muttered, "God, this feels amazing with you."

He rocked into me harder—his force setting my skin on fire.

One arm locked me tight against him as his other hand slid to my hip, grip growing stronger with each thrust.

I moved against him in a slow rhythm—tentative at first, then bolder—surrendering to his wants. His desires.

I bucked back, hungry for more.

His mouth found my ear, breath zinging my neck—sending goosebumps all over.

"Fuck..." he exhaled, barely audible.

His fingers wandered back to my panties, tracing slow circles over lace.

Then he teased them aside. I trembled to his touch—his fingers sweeping circles with soft, slippery precision.

"Oh wow..." I whimpered—pleasure building fast and hot.

His rocking grew rougher, moans louder... until my pleasure broke.

My body spasmed, breath ragged, pressing harder against him.

I moved his hand to my hip. He clawed into me, grinding until I heard a low, guttural moan—and felt a sudden rush of warmth.

He stilled, chest heaving, thirty seconds before he rasped:

"Fuck me... love, that was incredible."

I nodded breathlessly, his hands clutching me like I was already his.

He nuzzled into my hair, pressing kisses to the side of my neck, breath slowing until sleep took him.

I bit my lip. Wide awake, staring into the dark.

What had I just done?

* * *

When I woke, Edward was behind me—breath ghosting over my neck as his fingers gently tousled my hair.

"Good morning, love," he whispered, planting a kiss on the back of my head as his arm tightened around my waist.

I didn't roll over. I couldn't. I was surely disheveled with morning breath.

Then panic—everything rushed back.

The smell of him, the feel of him—still on me.

I didn't know if I wanted to relive it... or scrub it off.

Footsteps padded down the hall—Greg walking to the kitchen.

Thank God.

I mumbled about needing the bathroom and slipped away before he could follow.

The moment I closed the door, my back hit the wall. I gripped the edge of the sink, pulse thundering in my ears.

The night blurred through my mind in fragments—lips, hands, breath, heat.

His eyes watching me like prey.

But now, in the sobering light of morning, it all felt different. I saw it more clearly.

Edward hadn't just flirted—he'd *hunted.*

He studied my signals and waited until it was late.

When I was *weak...* desperate for comfort.

And I let him.

Worse—I wanted it. Craved it.

Him.

My boss.

I looked at myself in the mirror—puffy face, messy hair, smudged mascara.

I'd spent years keeping clean boundaries in high-pressure environments, around sexy men with similar moves.

But Edward tempted me in a different way.

He was brilliant. He treated me with an unexpected reverence.

He made me swoon.

And that scared the hell out of me.

Because last night wasn't just a moment.

It was the beginning of something I might not be able to stop.

But if Blake found out...

I rinsed my face, forcing myself to breathe.

By the time I emerged, I'd fixed my hair and washed the night away—but not the regret.

We lingered in awkward silence, the scent of coffee thick in the air.

I stood near the sink, avoiding Edward's eyes.

He stayed quiet.

Maybe he felt it, too—that we'd gone too far, too fast.

And neither of us knew what to do now.

* * *

"Not into girls, huh?" Greg called from across the kitchen island, breaking the silence while flipping pancakes with a grin.

"Uh... no," I managed. "Why?"

"You seemed super nervous last night."

I rolled my eyes. "It's not that I was nervous. It's that I wasn't interested."

"All good. I'm not gay either. But I'll be heteroflexible all night for the right woman."

"Yeah, I bet," I mumbled. "Do you shout, 'No homo,' before-hand?"

"Always. *Duh!*" Greg winked.

Edward added dryly:

"I don't seem to remember you shouting, 'No homo,' when Cody was doing lines of coke off your dick on the yacht in Ibiza..."

"Oh, so you and Cody are an item? That makes a *ton* of sense now!" I giggled.

"Hah!" Greg grinned. A twinkle in his eye. "Girls ate it up, babe. Awesome party trick. Story for another day."

"So why is it good to know that I'm not bi-sexual?" I asked—half-annoyed, half-curious.

Being a female Marine, I was used to being mistaken for a lesbian. But not usually by the guys I worked with—that was new.

"Now I know to keep things to you and *me* and—"

Greg's delivery was smooth.

My mouth gaped as Edward's jaw clenched in my periphery.

"Okay, bud," he interjected. "That's enough. Allie's part of the team."

Was Greg seriously alluding to me *sleeping with* him?

In what world?!

Greg chuckled and shrugged.

"Didn't seem to stop you, bro."

Tersely, Edward replied: "That's different."

"Oh yeah?" Greg challenged. "You hit a home run last night—or only get to third?"

Edward shook his head, glaring.

"Bud, out of respect for Allie, we're not going to talk about it."

"Yeah, okay, whatever you say, *Boss.*"

"You need to give it up."

"Yeah, yeah—I'll stop stating the obvious. Truth hurts, huh?"

"Fuck, Greg. Don't make me..." Edward growled, his voice tight with warning.

"Oh, *puh-lease.* You couldn't if you tried."

Greg winked at me and tossed his hands up, mocking Edward.

"I'll just tell you about *my* night, then. Your agency gal pal is super crazy—not unexpected. She begged me to face fuck her after I—"

"Again, bud. Can we *not* talk about it?"

Greg looked genuinely perplexed. "Yeah, okay. Whatevs."

I smiled uneasily, surprised by the topic.

He caught my reaction and muttered, "You're so damn cute," then grabbed a watermelon from the island, held it out, and pumped his crotch against it dramatically as the contents of his basketball shorts jumped.

I took a gulp of coffee, eyes wide. Impressed.

"The watermelon was her head." Another wink. "See? You coulda learned a lot."

I laughed, but my stomach twisted. It was all fun and games—until I remembered it wasn't.

Sensing my discomfort, Edward stepped in.

"Greg, I said *enough.*"

* * *

Cody and Celine emerged from an upstairs bedroom, smiling radiantly.

Tank and Sandy followed minutes later.

Sandy was adamant they hadn't slept together.

Tank's smirk suggested otherwise, so we exchanged knowing looks—and let it go.

Then around nine, Tara emerged from Greg's bedroom, acting dramatically like she couldn't walk.

She plopped next to me, gushing under her breath. "Holy fucking shit! The things he did—the positions—Jesus! Have you seen him? I used to think my husband was packing."

"Well, I hope you didn't tell him you *have* a husband," I replied softly, hoping to dodge further conversation.

"Fuck, no! They probably know each other from CAG back in the day," she said, taking a coffee from Edward, who smiled at me.

"Wait... did you two—?" she whispered.

"Oh no. I'm married, remember?"

As soon as I said it, I nearly cringed—the hypocrisy landing heavy.

I hadn't exactly acted married last night.

Sharp guilt followed.

* * *

While I hadn't heard a peep from Edward during my first few weeks of training—after our evening together, he was constant. Texting. Calling. Video chat.

He showered me with attention and affection—something Blake hadn't done in longer than I could remember.

At times, it felt overwhelming.

I hadn't experienced such raw excitement in years.

He was addicting. Talking to him energized me. It made me happy.

Yet I was gripped with guilt as our relationship drifted into inappropriate territory. It pressed harder with each call. Each text.

The problem? Happiness outweighed my guilt.

I knew the further I fell, the harder it would be to climb back out.

But part of me had lost all interest in climbing.

Chapter 24

The tiki bar was bustling on Friday evening—tourists and locals packed in to soak up their slice of paradise.

Weather perfect. Drinks cold. Vibe laid-back—Siesta Key-style.

Designer bags. Expensive watches. Trendy clothes.

Rich people playing casual like it was a sport.

Liv and I were sipping on Mai Tais in celebration of her birthday, listening to the cover band, when Edward showed up—after teasing our plans out of me.

A pair of shorts, Aloha shirt, and flip flops.

The most casual I'd *ever* seen him. Almost... stress-free.

Still, he managed to command the room.

And he wasn't alone.

With him were Greg and Tanner—who knew a thing or two about commanding a room themselves. Loud, confident, and clearly having a blast.

They were quick to introduce themselves as Edward's body-guards—part of his "billionaire babysitting duty"—sending Liv into a fit of laughter.

We all grabbed a table and swapped stories over multiple rounds, secrets spilling as freely as the rum.

Eventually, Edward excused himself to take a private call, and Greg and Tanner wandered off to the bar for another round.

The moment they left, Liv and I were approached by two yuppies outfitted in pastel polos and khaki pants. Out-of-towners.

"You and your girlfriend want to get out of here?" the bigger one asked.

"No, thanks. We're here with friends," I replied with a snicker, gesturing to the bar where Greg and Tanner were already watching. Assessing.

Greg gave a cool nod.

I'd only been part of the team a few weeks, but they'd slipped into protector mode fast—too fast, maybe.

"Those meatheads?" the guy mocked.

"You mean the gentlemen that could kick your ass with their hands tied?" I shot back.

"Yeah, right," the man's friend grunted.

"Whatever you say, tough guy."

"You good, babe? These jerkoffs bothering you?" Greg interjected, shoulder-checking his way between the two men.

One of the yuppies straightened, trying to puff himself up. "Jerkoff? I make more in six months than you've made in your life!"

Greg shook his head, amused. "Doubt it, bro. Keep moving."

The man ignored Greg and turned back to me as Tanner shifted next to him, placing a solid hand on the man's shoulder.

"You must notta heard him."

The man tried to shake Tanner off, then sniveled, "Get your fucking Neanderthal hands off me!"

Greg laughed. "Damn—bro's rich *and* funny!"

Tanner smirked. "Why don't you pull out your phone and show us all those commas?"

He and Greg fist bumped causing Liv to giggle as she slurped down her third Mai Tai.

"Look, why don't you just walk away? You don't stand a chance against these guys," I said, voice low.

Then came the word: "*Bitch.*"

A quiet mutter the man would regret.

I opened my mouth to say something, but Tanner was already moving.

In one swift motion, his knee drove into the man's leg before Greg snatched the back of his neck.

Greg's voice was steady. "Apologize to this woman, or I'm gonna take you *and* your bro outside and kick the shit outta you."

"My cousin's the Sheriff!" the man whined while his friend slowly backed away.

"They're not worth it, Greg. Seriously—"

He just winked. "Babe, I got this."

Behind us, Liv cackled, slurring, "Yeah, kick his ass, Greg!"

The situation was spiraling—comically.

Edward appeared beside us, out of nowhere, calm as ever—adjusting his collar like he'd just stepped out of a meeting.

"What'd I miss?" he asked.

Greg grinned. "This loser called Allie a 'bitch'... claims his cousin's Sheriff Thomas, so I'm debating if I should kick his ass."

He shrugged as Tanner held onto Liv, who was wobbling on her barstool—drunk and having the time of her life.

Edward's expression hardened. "I don't give a fuck. Did he apologize?"

"Negative. Doubled down."

Edward leaned in low. "Then this is well-deserved. You're lucky— I'd have killed you and dropped your body at sea."

Without hesitation, he slugged the man in the stomach with a sharp undercut.

The man keeled over, gasping. "I'm calling the Sheriff!"

"Yeah, go ahead. Tell him his biggest donor just punched you for disrespecting a woman. Name's Edward Anderson. A-n-d-e-r-s-o-n."

He gave the man a condescending nod as a crowd looked on.

Edward laughed slyly, swiping his hair back—no embarrassment, no remorse. He set three crisp hundreds on the bar, nodded to the bartender, and turned to leave—then caught my eye, giving me a slow wink.

* * *

On Monday, I returned to Dark Skies for a fourth week—at Tank's insistence.

Edward snuck out on Tuesday, violating his own rule about visiting the compound too often—just to bring me lunch.

He said he needed to discuss a work trip involving the Black Roses—a delicate job involving human cargo—but after a minute, we were lost in unrelated conversation—and flirtation.

Before he left, he pulled me into a hug—warm, lingering—then leaned down for more.

A kiss.

Soft. Confident. *Heavenly.*

"Allie, may I please take you to dinner on Friday night?"

I paused.

I should've said no—but I didn't.

I agreed.

* * *

As I lay in bed, Edward weighed heavy on my heart and mind.

I could quit Bright Sands to pursue a relationship with him, but the work gave me a sense of fulfillment—something my life had been missing.

And I didn't want to give it up just for Edward.

I mulled over my options.

Working at Bright Sands *and* having a relationship with Edward—as Tank once suggested—wasn't smart or professional, but I was willing to give it a try.

* * *

By Wednesday afternoon, Edward and I finalized our Friday plans.

I specifically asked for *normal,* knowing full well if I didn't, he'd orchestrate something extravagant—probably involving a yacht and fireworks.

He promised not to go overboard.

So instead... he rented out a friend's Italian restaurant—just for the two of us.

His version of normal was amusing.

Still, I kept toiling over how a relationship with Edward could possibly work when he was anything but.

* * *

On Thursday night, as I was readying my gear for my final training day at Dark Skies, a loud rap on the door startled me.

I glanced at my phone, smiling as I read a text from Edward:

Can't wait for our date tomorrow! I hope you'll let me kiss you!

It was 9:06 p.m.

I opened the door with a smile, expecting Tank.

Instead, my jaw dropped.

In an instant, everything changed.

CHAPTER 25

H ey, darlin'!"

"Uh... ummm, wow—I wasn't expecting you!" I said, pulse kicking.

I hadn't seen Blake in months. We hadn't spoken in just as long.

And no one had warned me he was coming home.

"Yeah, I wasn't expectin' to find you here, either. Didn't realize I needed to check with Mike to find my wife these days."

He gave me a quick hug and peck on the lips.

"Umm, yeah... I'm going to do a little bit of work. Start getting my feet wet again."

"Darlin', we talked about this. You don't need to work. I have money."

Blake had been trying to get me to quit my job and be a stay-at-home mom or housewife for more than a decade.

I was tempted to say, *"We've got enough money that you never have to work again, either,"* but played nice.

"I know I don't *have* to, but I want to," I replied, trying to avoid how the whole 'work' thing came about.

"We'll talk about this when we get home."

Peeved, I nodded. Blake's response was what I anticipated. He wouldn't shoot me down outright, but he'd do his best to discourage me until I changed my own mind.

He was a professional in mind games and manipulation—something I both admired and hated about him.

"Hey, want to grab a beer with me and some of the guys?"

"I'd love to, but I'm exhausted from shooting all day, and I need to be up early. Why don't you go unwind and we can catch up tomorrow?"

He promptly agreed—then the wheels in his brain started turning.

"Uh, *no*, I thought I'd stay with you."

"Oh."

Blake was home from deployment and wanted sex—that was the drill.

"Uh, how 'bout I give you a few minutes? I know you weren't expectin' me. I'm gonna go grab *a* beer," he specified, "but I'll be back in thirty."

I couldn't say no to his proposition, so I just replied, "Yeah, I'll be here."

My stomach twisted. Dread sat heavy in my chest.

I shut the door and grumbled *fuck* a dozen times—over and over—like a broken prayer.

Sex with Blake used to be easy—detached, practiced.

Something I could get through even when I felt nothing at all.

But now...

I ran through every possible excuse, but Blake and I had been married long enough—he'd see through them all.

And if I refused—something I couldn't remember doing unless I was physically ill—he'd jump to one of two conclusions.

I was cheating.

Or I was leaving.

Maybe both.

And he'd lose his *fucking* mind.

So, I took a shower and scrubbed my skin like it could wash away the dread of what was coming—

Sex. With Blake.

But it didn't help.

Because no amount of clean or calm could change the fact that all I could think about... was Edward.

The way I melted to his touch.

The way he made me feel alive.

I couldn't fake *that* with Blake.

But I was going to have to try.

* * *

When Blake returned, he was holding a bottle of wine and two glasses.

"I wasn't expectin' a rendezvous tonight, so this isn't very romantic, but it'll have to do, darlin'."

Typical Blake.

Sweet-talking Texas cowboy charm.

Never romantic.

We sat on the couch, sipping wine, and made small talk about his deployment—where he'd been and what he'd been doing.

I nodded at all the right moments, asked the right questions—like I cared. Like I was mentally there. But I was just barely paying attention, my mind focused on steering the conversation away from Dark Skies.

Hoping if I played it cool long enough, Blake would get tired and forget about sex altogether.

No such luck.

Halfway through his glass, he set it aside and moved toward me, kneeling at my chair, eyes hungry, mouth pressed to mine—hard and fast.

I barely responded.

His hands made their way to my blouse, tugging it open with impatient fingers.

Then his own shirt hit the floor.

Muscles taut—even in his mid-fifties.

All that testosterone... and whatever else he was taking.

He yanked me from the chair, dragging me to the bed.

I stumbled, caught myself on the mattress—then stilled.

Trying not to flinch.

Not to feel.

Seconds later, my shorts and panties were gone—peeled off like wrapping he didn't give a shit about.

I lay there naked.

Hoping foolishly for tenderness.

A kiss.

A whisper.

A smile.

Something.

Anything.

But nothing.

Blake went straight for the main course, dropping his pants and crawling on top of me—mechanical—like he was picking up where we left off months ago.

And I let it happen.

To keep Edward safe.

To buy myself time.

To make it through the night.

I shut my eyes as his body pinned me down.

And I disappeared the only way I knew how.

* * *

Blake and I'd met at a black-tie military social in D.C.

I was a Second Lieutenant in my dress blues.

He wore a tuxedo with mini-medals.

Because of the beard and his age, I assumed he was out.

So, I let him flirt. Buy me drinks. Spin me around the dance floor.

Even take me home.

We ended up having sex—the kind that made me hope it meant something. Just so it wouldn't feel like a mistake.

The next morning, as I got dressed for work, he asked if I could drop him at his hotel to grab his uniform.

"For what?" I asked, confused.

He responded smoothly, "Gotta go testify at some bullshit hearing at the Pentagon."

"In uniform?" I laughed in disbelief.

"Yeah. They just flew me back from the middle of fucking nowhere. What a cluster."

My stomach dropped. "Wait—are you still in?"

I prayed he wasn't about to confirm it.

He flashed a devilish grin. "Yeah, Major Bailey. Did I not mention that, darlin'?"

"Oh, I'm so fucked," I muttered.

Blake smirked. "Say the word, and I'll bend you over this couch and remind you just how fucked you really are."

He grabbed my hips and yanked me hard against him.

"Now... what time do you need to be at work, Lieutenant?"

Blake was supposed to head back to Asia the next day.

That's all we were supposed to be—a one night stand.

But the Marine Corps launched an investigation into his unit, leaving him stuck in D.C.

And one night turned into weeks.

Then it turned into something else entirely.

Our affair could've ended my career—and his—so we kept it quiet. Blake demanded it.

He was already under investigation. One more misstep and he was done—and he made sure I knew it'd be on me.

And just like that, I was the Lieutenant secretly screwing the Major under investigation.

Not talking. Not dating. Just screwing.

My compliance, justified by pleasure.

Years later, during one of our many rough patches, I found myself wondering:

Did I marry Blake... just because of the sex?

Not the romantic kind.

The kind that impairs your judgment. Holds you hostage.

Makes you think there's no one else in the world for you.

Then Edward happened.

And suddenly, I felt something I wasn't supposed to.

Feelings I hadn't let myself feel in years—maybe ever.

As I lay there, paralyzed by guilt and wanting, I wondered if I'd mistaken sex for affection. And love.

And built an entire life around the wrong thing.

* * *

My body moved, but my mind had been somewhere else.

I'd hoped to close my eyes and wake up to a new day—but he was still inside me, thrusting harder and harder until—

he gripped my body tight, letting out an animalistic groan.

Then he pulled out—quick. Careless. Unaware or uninterested in my pleasure.

I'd been used before.

But this time, I felt dirty.

As I started to get up, he glared at me.

"What's going on here, darlin'? You didn't do that thing with your ass and hips."

The words sliced straight through me.

"I'm... uh..."

"You gonna tell me what the fuck's up?"

I froze, my brain scrambling for an explanation.

"What do you mean?"

"Don't play dumb," he snapped. "You always do that. Tonight? Nothing."

I swallowed hard.

"Blake, I'm sorry. I'm just tired, and you surprised me. If I'd known you were coming home, I would've napped... had something to wear... been in a better headspace."

I forced a smile. "Can we please talk tomorrow?"

"Yeah. You're tired," he muttered, bitter. "Says the woman used to going seventy hours without sleep."

He flipped off the light.

And just like that, the conversation was over, but his anger lingered in the dark like smoke.

I lay still, heart thundering, waiting for him to fall asleep.

When he finally did, I snuck into the bathroom, phone in hand.

After splashing my face with water, I turned off all notifications and sent Edward a text:

BLAKE IS BACK!

Then, I defiantly changed my long-time password—in case he tried to snoop while I slept. He'd be suspicious—but at least he wouldn't see my texts with Edward and Tank.

That would send him into orbit.

I stared at my reflection—mascara streaked, eyes hollow—and my mind spun.

What would I say when we woke?

Should I come clean about Dark Skies and admit I'd been training for Bright Sands?

Should I say nothing and wait until we were home—a home he'd still never seen—to have a shouting match?

Or lie? Distort the truth? Say what he wanted to hear until I could figure out a real exit plan?

And what the hell was I going to do about Edward?

There was no good choice. Not one.

I looked at myself a moment longer, then killed the light and crept back to bed.

CHAPTER 26

I woke to Blake snoring beside me, his body strewn across the bed like he was staking a claim.

I turned on my phone.

A text from Edward waited:

I'm on my way out there. Call me.

My heart kicked.

I yanked on a T-shirt and khaki pants—hands shaking—then quietly brushed my teeth and snuck outside.

He answered on the first ring.

"Allie, I promise I didn't know."

His voice was low, tense. Not defensive—just regretful.

I swallowed my emotion. "What happened? How did you not know?"

"He caught a ride with one of the teams leaving Germany. I don't know *exactly* where he came from. That's on me—I should've caught it."

"Shit," I muttered. "I'm going to go home early... I'll let Tank know."

"Hold on, I'll be there soon. Can I meet you?"

"Okay, but—"

A call came through—it was Mike.

"Give me a minute... I'll call you back."

"Hey, Mike," I answered. My tone was clipped, exhausted.

"Hey, kid. Sorry for spilling the beans."

"You did."

"I'm walking over from my place now. Let's meet in my office."

Great. Why not loop someone else into my drama? Sounded smart.

"Sure. See you in a few."

I leaned against a palm, head spinning.

None of this was what I'd wanted.

But at least Mike was back. I might need him to break up the fight I knew was inevitable.

Blake could be violent—but he skirted the right side of evil by controlling it. Knowing when to unleash it. He claimed he only used it for good. And most of the time, I believed him.

But if he found out about Edward—

God help us all.

* * *

I helped myself into Mike's office, glancing around.

The air was stale and warm, like no one had entered in weeks.

Overhead, fluorescent lights buzzed to life.

Behind his desk: team photos, shadow boxes, a gold-cast M4.

I sank onto a dusty leather couch, hands clammy, gut queasy.

All I wanted to do was scream. Or cry. Or punch something.

My anxiety surged as I waited. And waited.

* * *

I knew Blake would be furious about Bright Sands—he didn't want me to work.

And he was always on edge after a deployment.

Dropping the news now may only make things worse, but was there an alternative?

Other than lying?

I replayed the night. The smell of sweat. His grip. My silence.

The shame.

The door creaked open—and Mike and Edward entered in sync.

Mike hugged me first. "Hey kid. Got a plan? How we telling him?"

"Not yet," I mumbled, eyes jumping to Edward—searching his face for backup.

He shook his head.

His eyes didn't quite meet mine.

But something flickered across his face.

A calculation.

Like he'd already made a call behind my back.

And I had a feeling I wasn't going to like it.

Mike clapped me gently on the arm. "I need to do my rounds. I'll keep an eye on him, but you better come up with something fast. Stay by your phones."

His tone was firmer—less paternal, more operational.

The shift wasn't lost on me.

He left without another word.

The door shut.

Silence thickened.

Edward stepped forward and wrapped me in a hug.

"I would have told you if I knew."

I nodded. I believed him—but that wasn't what wrecked me.

It wasn't Blake showing up.

It was what he'd taken.

What I'd let happen.

"Allie..." His voice softened. "Are you alright?"

I pulled back, barely able to look at him.

"No," I whispered.

I paused, swallowing a lump in my throat, hand over my mouth, fighting for control but bracing for the flood.

"Hey, what's wrong?" he asked, stroking my arm.

I flinched without meaning to.

I wasn't sure how to say it, but the words came out anyway.

"Edward... he stayed with me last night."

My voice cracked. Just the thought made my chest tighten.

I remembered the way I'd felt—suffocated. Trapped beneath Blake's weight.

I blinked, trying to force it away before Edward could see.

But he did.

He clenched his fists, then growled:

"Fuck me."

I recoiled.

An ironic choice of words...

His eyes turned moody like he might slam his fist through a wall—but instead, he reached for me again. Cautious. Tender.

And I let him hold me—his touch gentle despite the fury in his jaw.

No pressure. No insistence.

Just a steady, grounding presence.

It was enough.

As I waited for the next shoe to drop.

Chapter 27

Edward flicked his eyes toward the door as Mike pushed it open. I turned and stood instinctively, heart pounding with dread.

Blake stepped into view—aloof at first.

Then his face tightened. His eyes narrowed.

He snapped.

"Yeah, I fucking knew something was up!"

Perfect. Angry Blake was a recipe for disaster.

Mike raised a calming hand. "Brother, nothing's wrong. We're all here to talk and—"

Blake erupted.

"What the actual *fuck* is this? An intervention? You couldn't wait one more day?"

He jabbed a finger toward Edward. "And what the fuck is this dipshit doing here?"

Edward rose slowly—measured. "You've got the wrong idea, bud."

"I'm not your bud," Blake shot back, voice cold as ice.

I stepped forward, reaching for his arm, trying to ease him back.

He swatted me away.

"What is this?" he shouted, louder.

I channeled empathy, forcing a smile.

"Blake, it's *not* an intervention. I'm sorry—I should've known that's what you'd think."

Honestly, he may've preferred that to the truth.

I gave Mike a throat cutting motion. Abort.

Instead, he blurted, "Edward's bringing Allie on."

Wonderful.

Blake's jaw ticked in disbelief, then rage—as his eyes jumped from me to Mike to Edward.

Then he went still. Five seconds of silence before:

"Let me guess, he recruited you?"

I nodded slowly, knowing I'd walked straight into a trap. There was no right answer.

Blake's expression curdled into disgust.

But his voice cooled in unnerving control. "Darlin', could you give us boys a minute?"

A chill shot through me.

"Oh, please," Edward muttered under his breath.

I started to back away, obediently walking toward the door, eyes quickly scanning Blake's waistband—praying he wasn't armed.

Mike caught my hesitation and waved me off.

I held the door open a sliver, enough to see Blake pointing at Edward, his face twisted in pure contempt. Then he screamed loud enough to rattle the walls:

"You motherfucker! I told you—NO! She's not ready. Spend a few days with her before you pretend otherwise!"

My stomach dropped.

I told you no...

They'd had this conversation before. Without me.

No wonder Edward had recruited me while Blake was gone.

He didn't have Blake's blessing—and he knew it.

How deep did this go?

Mike stepped in, motioning for Blake to settle down.

I applauded the effort—silently.

The anger wasn't entirely Blake's fault.

He'd been blown up. He had PTSD.

Unfortunately, nothing but space ever worked to cool his hot temper.

I stood in the hallway, ear pressed to the door.

"Bud, I *have* spent a few days with her. Even some nights. She's ready. You just wouldn't know—you haven't been around. Where've you been? On some bullshit job in Africa or Asia or—?"

Edward's voice trailed.

The word *nights* detonated like a grenade.

I wasn't sure if it was careless—or calculated.

"Hey, Lance Corporal—why don't you stay in your own fucking lane and shut the fuck up?" Blake sneered, launching into a tirade.

Name calling. Character assassination.

"Oh, yeah? You want to go there?" Edward shot back.

Then his voice lowered, almost inaudible—like he knew I was listening.

"Allie's right outside. Let's bring her in here and clear the air. What do you say? I'm ready to put the past behind us. For good. You?"

More yelling. A lot more yelling.

Then Edward—sharp, seething: "Fucking dick."

Blake: "I'm going to fucking kill you!"

Mike burst out of the room, muttering, "Oh, brother."

I peeked in as the door closed.

Blake had Edward pinned against the wall by the throat.

He was in the black—eyes gone, rage in full control. I didn't dare move.

Within thirty seconds, the room swarmed—five, six team guys throwing wild punches. Furniture toppled, curses echoed. A blur of limbs and testosterone. Like a bar fight.

Then—Mike stormed in, baseball bat in hand.

He swung at the table. A loud crack.

Everyone froze.

My pulse pounded as the air in the room turned electric.

"Not today! One more swing and I'll break your fucking hand. Blake—that goes for you, too, brother."

I'd never heard Mike cuss.

He meant it—and everyone knew it.

In an instant, the fighting stopped.

One by one, the guys filed out.

Edward emerged, cool as ever, tugging his shirt into place.

He raked a hand through his hair like nothing happened, then stood several feet from the door—well out of Blake's reach.

Blake grinned wickedly as he exited, a swagger in his step like he'd won, before he grabbed my butt and said, "You were great last night, darlin'."

An obnoxious kissy face followed—not to me, but Edward.

I turned to stone—fear tightening my chest.

I knew Edward.

He wasn't one to back down.

Or let disrespect slide.

His gaze sliced like a blade, a guttural growl rising in his throat.

I saw him twitch—his best effort at restraint.

Then—too late.

He flew past, shoulder grazing mine.

His fist slammed straight into Blake's cheek with a sickening thud. Then another. And another.

Eight or nine sharp punches.

Fast. Brutal. Precise.

Like an MMA fighter.

Blake's face exploded. Blood everywhere.

Mike swung the bat again, hitting the wall. A muffled thump. "No more."

Edward stepped back, perfectly controlled. Nonchalant. Then smug: "All done."

Blake staggered, dragging his shirt across his face, blinking through the blood.

He let out a low snarl—like nothing I'd heard before. Anger boiling.

"Keep your hands off my wife or I'll fucking kill you. That's a promise. Not a threat."

He didn't say another word as he walked past—face plastered in disdain. Maybe even hate.

I stood still. Steady.

I'd spent years doubting myself. Wondering if I'd lost my edge.

But in that moment—surrounded by blood and violence—I didn't balk.

I felt the old part of me kick in.

Mike scratched his head, shooing the team guys off.

He stared at Edward for twenty seconds before asking, "What's going on with you?"

The realization dawned in real time. I saw his eyes widen. Then came the boom.

"Oh, no. No. No. No way... oh brother, this is... I will *not* be involved in this."

He threw his hands in the air. "All these years, I vouched for you. I trusted you with her."

Mike looked disappointed. And I felt ashamed.

He turned to me, shaken.

"Allie, I've known you a long time. This is—"

"Mike," I cut in, "it's not what you think."

He cocked his head. "Oh, yeah?"

I glanced at him, then Edward.

Shit! Why did I look at Edward?

I knew better.

I'd never had a problem skillfully lying to get what I wanted.

But this time, I faltered.

Had time and distance dulled my ability to lie without remorse? Or was it... growing up?

Maybe I should've been thankful.

I shrugged.

"Oh sheesh," Mike mumbled, hands on his head, mouth agape.

He had a zero-bullshit tolerance—and my face confirmed everything.

"I won't be part of this. I should've known. You let me down, brother!" he shouted—then hung his head, disappointed, and started down the hallway.

I caught a glimpse of Tank, head peeking out of his office. He mouthed *sorry* and ducked back inside. He wasn't getting involved.

* * *

I wanted to smooth things over with Mike, but I couldn't follow him.

What would I even say? That Edward and I weren't sleeping together... yet?

I doubted he'd believe me.

And I'd been with Blake long enough to know he was not in the right state of mind to talk.

He needed time to brood and party until he was mindlessly drunk at some strip club, bitching about my need to prove myself in work unfit for a woman.

I expected he'd eventually apologize.

At least he would've at one time.

But both of us had changed.

Our marriage felt less like a partnership—and more like a fragile ceasefire.

And for the first time, I didn't think I wanted him back.

That was the thought that haunted me.

It wasn't the outburst.

Or the fight.

Or even the damage to my reputation.

It was a reckoning of my loyalty.

A quiet understanding: I wasn't the same woman who'd waited faithfully through every deployment.

I was different.

Done.

CHAPTER 28

The wind whipped through the open windows of Edward's truck, but the silence between us thickened. I stared straight ahead, the road blurring with flashes of swampland.

It felt like a breakup.

And I wasn't ready for it—not after everything that had just happened.

"Edward, I don't think things are going to work out like you're hoping. I know we made plans tonight—against my better judgment—but we can't be involved."

"Nothing's changed between us. So what—Blake's pissed? We both knew he'd be."

I folded my arms, jaw tight, biting back the urge to shout. To thrash. To claw at something. To wake myself from the nightmare before it drove me mad.

"You implied we're sleeping together! What the hell was that about?"

"I'd love to throw Blake under the bus, but you'll have to ask him."

"Well, you clearly have history," I muttered. "What's up with you two?"

"I wish I could tell you. But I can't."

"Why not?"

"Because you wouldn't believe me, love."

"God, please stop calling me 'love' right now! This is so irritating, I could scream!"

With no one behind us, Edward veered to the side of the road—a desolate stretch of swampland.

The truck angled toward the drop-off.

He killed the engine.

Still. Humid. Empty.

"What are you doing?"

"Go ahead. Get out of the truck and scream—at me. At the world. I'll wait."

I wanted to be mad at Edward, but he had an adorable grin—and I had to cover my face to conceal that he'd made me smile.

He caught me.

The diesel engine rumbled back to life as he rolled the windows up and cranked the A/C.

"Allie, you're fighting it, but we both know what this is."

"What, exactly?"

I turned slowly as he bit his lip—suggestively, infuriatingly.

"*Us.*"

"Edward, if Blake thinks we're sleeping together, he might kill you."

He chuckled under his breath, like it was a joke.

"Seriously. Don't dismiss it. I know Blake."

"I know him, too, love."

"Ughhh, you've *got* to stop calling me 'love!'"

"Fine." He shifted, eyes narrowing. "I know him well, *Allie*. Do yourself a favor—leave him."

"Why?" I asked. "Just so you and I can be together?"

"Well, that... and he's toxic. But you and I are going to be together whether you leave him now or later."

I laughed, but there was no humor in it. "What makes you think that?"

"The night we spent in each other's arms."

I felt the night all over again. Edward's lips. His hands. The *want*.

He reached across the seat, gently brushing his knuckles down my cheek.

I trembled.

"You can fight all you want," he said quietly, "but we're happening."

"You're so confident."

"It's not confidence. It's intuition."

He smirked as I nearly choked with laughter.

"Great—now you're a mind reader!"

"Does your heart not race when I do this?"

Edward's fingers traced my collarbone.

I swallowed.

My eyes darted away as I tried to hide the flutter in my chest.

"Maybe. But I think you're conflating sexual desire with..."

"With what? *Love*?"

The word hit like a lightning strike. I nearly gasped.

He leaned in, forcing me to meet his gaze—he saw my flicker of panic.

"Don't you want me?"

"Edward," I warned. "You're playing with fire right now."

But part of me *wanted* to get burned.

"Fair enough. It was a rhetorical question anyway. I already know the answer."

"So should we skip dinner and go straight to sex?" I blurted.

He smirked.

"Don't answer! It was a rhetorical question. You forget—I can play this game, too."

"Allie, I don't know why you don't see it. We're inevitable!"

I banged my head against the headrest, groaning.

"Please just drive. Or turn the music on. Anything."

Edward chuckled as the truck rolled forward.

* * *

Several minutes passed before he interrupted the music.

"Allie—why don't you head out to west Texas with the team for a driving course coming up? All high speed and off-road. Prep for a trip to Mexico."

"Maybe," I replied cautiously. "What's Mexico all about?"

"Cody's leading a small team down around TJ. One of Derrick's friends at the DEA got a tip—some D.C. elites are trying to fabricate an illegal arms shipment so they can do an intercept and pin it on 'right wing extremists.' We're just going down to spook them."

"You're going?"

"Yep. Very lowkey. I know Blake doesn't think you should—but I wouldn't ask if I didn't think you could handle it."

He grinned, then flexed his bicep. "Plus, I want you to see I can operate better than him."

I'd personally seen Blake operate—including when our teams got mixed up on an op.

Was that the time I caught him brazenly flirting with a 25-year-old agency contractor?

Blake. It was always something.

* * *

"You're sure our plans for tonight are nuked?" Edward asked.

I looked at my front door, a pang of disappointment hitting harder than expected—wishing our plans hadn't unraveled.

I'd been eager for our date all week.

But with Blake back, it was categorically out of the question.

"Any chance I can persuade you differently?" he asked.

I shook my head.

He nodded then hugged me in the threshold, leaning in—his lips brushing my cheek, lingering a breath too long—like he wanted me to take the bait.

I glanced up at the security camera overhead and felt a chill.

Blake might be watching. Somehow.

Edward sighed.

"I'll have James take care of that."

Then he squeezed my hands.

"Allie, everything will work out. Just... don't let him take more from you than he already has."

"Thanks. I'll let you know about Texas."

I slipped inside, tears in my eyes. And went straight to bed—where I laid awake for hours, wondering how I'd become the star of a drama I never auditioned for.

How the hell did I get here?

* * *

I drew a bath in my oversized tub.

The mirror fogged in steam, blurring my reflection—a fitting parallel to my life.

I sank in—warm water stinging my skin as I leaned back, letting the silence settle.

I sipped wine, the glass damp in my hand, bottle within easy reach.

And I tried not to think of Blake. Or Edward.

But thinking wasn't the problem. Analyzing was. It's what my mind did best.

Blake was muscle memory. Edward—adrenaline.

Blake spoke over me. Edward listened.

Both menacing in their own ways.

They had more in common than either would admit.

Like Edward, Blake grew up in privilege.

His father was an executive—suit, cowboy hat, and alligator boots— his mother—a beauty queen with giant hair.

Blake lived in a mansion in Houston until he was sent away to military boarding school.

His summers were spent hunting, fishing, and doing cowboy things on his family's ranch.

A Texan through and through.

As the oldest of three boys, serving in the military was Blake's job.

There was an expectation he would serve as a prerequisite for political office—after earning an Ivy League education at Yale like his father and grandfather.

I remembered Blake's uncle once talking about him being elected as senator, or governor, or even president early on in our marriage. It caused me to unintentionally roar with laughter—something I had to vehemently apologize for later.

His father's deep ties to Texas oil money—and alleged Skull & Bones membership—fueled his dreams for Blake.

But he knew little about him.

When Blake retired, he was hired at Ground Branch. How? I wasn't sure. He lacked popularity and allies within the special operations community.

When he quit, he claimed the persecution was my fault. In reality, he was about to be fired for questionable behavior. Still, Blake's father blamed me for his downfall.

I'd always had too many ambitions of my own, and his parents scoffed at me being a working woman—a Marine, then Program Analyst at USAID—my agency cover. Too modern for their taste.

When I reached thirty-eight without our marriage producing an heir, their attitude swiftly turned from lukewarm to ice cold.

* * *

Blake was a fun-loving cowboy with a bubbly personality.

He could be generous to a fault.

Cussed up a storm.

And though intelligent and well-educated, it didn't always convey when he spoke in Texas twang.

He didn't care—one of the reasons I'd fallen for him.

His pedigree bred boldness—and his big mouth often got him in trouble.

He'd once called a sitting senator "ol' boy" after he cut in front of me at a popular D.C. bar—knowing full well who the man was.

His next line: "Get your whiny ass to the back. I don't give a fuck how important you think you are."

And much to my displeasure—he treated women like his father.

As objects of a man's desire.

It took me years to come to terms with him calling other women *darlin'*.

I wished he could've called them anything else—sweetie, cutie, honey.

But he didn't, even though I'd asked.

Blake also firmly believed he was wiser than me—because he was nearly fifteen years older. And a man.

When I left the agency, he tried to convince me to be a housewife in perpetuity.

And after being unemployed for several years, his dream nearly came true.

Until Edward and Bright Sands.

I'd always wondered if the reason Blake pushed so hard for me to quit working was because he didn't want me around men.

That maybe he was frightened I'd meet someone and find that happiness was possible without him.

After meeting Edward, it all made sense.

Not because I was so easily swayed. But because Blake never really saw me.

He loved the idea of me—someone who made him look good. Fit the part. Played the role. Smiled on cue. A beautiful accessory.

But he didn't love the part of me that spoke up. That questioned him.

Blake offered structure, status, and safety—but at the cost of my freedom.

My voice.

Edward *understood* me. How? I still wasn't sure.

I pulled out my phone:

Count me in for TX and Mexico.

A minute passed, then Edward's reply:

Let's do this.

CHAPTER 29

By Sunday night, the Dark Skies fiasco had just barely stopped haunting me—Edward's fists, Blake's fury, my own fidelity.

But a question still hung: where did Blake and I stand?

Was the fight the final blow to our marriage? Or just another beating—something to leave us more bruised and battered?

I bit the inside of my cheek, body suddenly shaking. Angry. Not with Blake or Edward, but with myself. For being so foolish. So reckless. Actions like mine had consequences... potentially *deadly* ones.

The longer I sat with it, the more chilling the realization. I should've been afraid. Blake wasn't known for empty threats, and if he truly believed I was cheating on him... well, there wasn't just a target on Edward's back. There was one on mine, too.

The scrape of a key in the front door jolted me upright. My eyes went wide. Heart stuttering.

I stilled, straining for a clue—hoping it was Liv. Waiting for her cheerful voice to barrel down the hall with, "I'm here, don't shoot!"

Instead, I heard the door burst open, then the heavy clack of cowboy boots on tile.

Blake.

But, how'd he get a key to the house? I hadn't given him one...

I rose from the sofa, adjusting my sundress then I swallowed hard as he stepped into the kitchen with his go-to *I fucked up* accessories—a dozen white roses and a bottle of my favorite vintage Merlot—sporting a black and blue face and busted lip.

Brown eyes blazing, darting. Wild. Clearly sleep-deprived.

"Hey, darlin'," he said with feigned sincerity.

I forced a timid smile, a wave of anxiety washing over me.

Edward and the guys dropped by all the time because they lived nearby. But Blake had driven all the way out from Dark Skies, which was half an hour away.

This wasn't a visit.

It was either a cold and calculated ambush... or an apathetic apology. I prayed for the latter.

"Hey... good to see you," I said, moving toward my phone on the kitchen table. I slipped it in my back pocket unnoticed and flipped the kitchen lights.

He set the wine and flowers on the counter before giving me a lukewarm kiss, then waltzed around like he'd been there before—eyes sweeping the rooms, taking inventory in an unsettling way.

Almost like he was looking for something. Or *someone.*

I'd moved in while he was deployed.

He'd never seen the place in person—at least that's what Mike said. *Or had he?*

Blake was skilled in reading human behavior. I watched as he sized me up, observing my verbal and nonverbal cues, reading my emotion for vulnerabilities.

His stance was cold. Devoid. Not his usual bubbly and charismatic happy to see me.

I strategically positioned myself behind the island as he snapped, "Time's up. You gotta make a choice. You wanna keep me or work for him?"

I groaned as consequences caught up with me.

Here we go... he came for a fight.

"Blake, please. That's not fair," I pleaded. "You can't give me an ultimatum like that."

He grunted with a scowl. "I'm still your husband, ain't I? I can. And I will."

"No, Blake. You can't," I replied with a heavy breath, then lowered my voice, trying to avoid escalation. "You also can't drop in like this without any warning. I love you, but—"

"But?" he sneered. "You know what? Fuck this!"

He balled his fists, stewing, and turned to leave.

"Wait, hold on!" I shouted, stumbling around a barstool, grabbing his arm from behind.

He flailed as I leapt back—instincts flaring.

I softened my tone. Apologetic. "Will you please let me finish?"

He mumbled something I couldn't make out.

I quickly edged toward the opposite side of the island—giving him space. Giving myself a safe zone. Moving toward the drawer with my gun. Just in case.

Maybe I was in my own head, but Blake wouldn't really hurt me... would he? He had more sense than that. Right?

"Blake, I love you, *but* it's not fair for you to take this away from me."

I didn't love him—not the way I used to. But I said it anyway. I kept my tone cool and collected. To keep him calm. No sudden movements.

I continued. "You've been gone so much and I'm all alone. Please, I can work and *still* be your wife. I've been working most of our marriage."

Blake huffed. "Not for him, you haven't."

"Would you prefer I worked at the agency again? We both know how shitty that was."

"Darlin', make a choice. I'm telling you right now—you can't have both."

Though livid, I knew better than to poke the bear. I kept my tone gentle. "I can't be married and still work—or I can't be married and work for Edward?"

Then I dropped a line I'd soon regret: "It's not serious. It's just a security detail."

He exploded. "You think I'm stupid? That I don't know what's going on? That ass clown's been a thorn in my side for years. You're not working there!" he screamed. "End of fucking story."

Blake fidgeted again, his shoulder twitching involuntarily—like a Tourette tic. A classic sign of drug use.

Was he high on coke? Or amphetamines?

"Don't think about it again," he hissed. "I've already warned him once."

I laughed—stunned.

How dare he.

I was done with de-escalation.

"Blake, come back when you're not high. Then we can have an adult conversation."

"Oh fuck, Allie!" he shouted—then grabbed a paperweight off the counter and hurled it.

The mirror behind me shattered—

a starburst of silver glass. Raining down inches from my head.

He saw the terror on my face, then punched the wall and stumbled for the door.

Moments later, his truck roared down the street.

I remembered the time he threw a glass at the wall—

but that was after a friend died.

This wasn't the same.

* * *

As I swept shards of mirror off the floor, I tried to recall a memory with Blake—one not centered around sex. Or overshadowed by liquor or rage.

A trip we'd once taken to Australia's sunshine coast early in our marriage—lounging on the pristine golden beaches, exploring Brisbane, hiking—even holding koalas.

We spent evenings drinking wine on our apartment's balcony, taking in the panoramic views—and we connected.

Blake was happy—*we* were happy. I pined for those days—and for that man.

I sat on the kitchen floor, legs crossed among the shards.

Realizing—

Blake hadn't meant to hit me.

He'd been a star high school pitcher.

If he wanted to—he wouldn't have missed.

But maybe next time...

I shivered.

We were done.

Really done.

That was the final blow.

CHAPTER 30

Days passed.

I didn't hear from anyone except Tank.

He kept me updated on Blake's whereabouts as he decompressed at Dark Skies—hog hunting, drinking, and floating around the lazy river.

I expected him to come home at some point to talk or apologize, but after a week, he opted to visit a friend in Wyoming before hopping on another overseas contract.

* * *

On Wednesday, James texted, inviting me to join him and the guys in Tampa on Friday night. He had dinner and bottle service arranged for his birthday, and since I didn't have any plans, I jumped at the opportunity for merriment.

Our night started with drinks in Greg's hotel room before we dined at a steakhouse.

The ridiculously stereotypical Marine Corps stories the guys told were the pick-me-up I needed, reminding me how good it felt to belong.

Cody had us in stitches, retelling a story from MARSOC as an ASO tasked with recruiting local Afghans to provide intel on an al-Qaeda network making IEDs with fertilizer from Pakistan.

"So yeah... I'm working this dude like two months and he sends me a text to meet. 911." He grinned. "I roll up on a quad with my terp and bro starts going on and on about bomb-sniffing dogs."

"I'm like, what the fuck is this dude talking about? I ask my terp, thinking something's lost in translation. Nope. Sure as shit, this moron pulls out a block of C4, rubs a fucking tennis ball on it, and throws it like a sissy for this street dog. Bro! I kid you not—the dog comes back with it cuz it's a *fucking tennis ball.*"

Cody made a mind exploding gesture that made the table erupt in laughter.

"And this dude tells the terp the dog's trained... then he points at the rest of the dogs and says—eyes wide—'They all are.' I fucking lost it."

Cody wiped tears from his eyes. "Like what? Now I'm trying to explain that the last thing I need's a fleet of fucking street dogs retrieving IEDs for me. No thanks. But damn, bro thought he fucking reinvented the wheel."

James—who was usually the most reserved—thanks to his high IQ and superiority complex—even he told several hilarious Marine Corps stories.

Greg and Cody couldn't resist giving him shit—adding "and then you found a hundred bucks" to the end of each—but his comebacks were priceless.

* * *

By the time we reached the nightclub, it was a little past 11 p.m.

We were settled in—dancing, drinking, singing—when I caught a stare from across the club.

The room spun as our eyes locked.

My pulse quickened. Breath caught.

Of course *he* showed up.

He always did. On his terms.

Linen suit, hair slicked back, commanding the room with a single glance.

Strobe lights cut through the haze, each flash catching him mid-stride—frozen in frame.

He moved through the crowd like it parted for him—lights, music, motion swirling all around. But his eyes never moved. They stayed fixed on me.

Heads turned. Girls stared. People... noticed.

He greeted me assertively—a hug and kiss on the side of my lips.

The guys partied on, but they were quick to give me space—their flirty winks, gestures, and jokes stopping cold.

Edward had claimed me—whether tacitly or not—and the dynamic shifted in an instant.

While he spoke with Cody, I asked James if he'd expected Edward—he hadn't mentioned it.

"Nope," he replied. "But it doesn't surprise me he showed up."

"Oh, why?" I asked.

"Cody told him *you* were coming."

* * *

Edward stood behind me, music blaring—sparklers everywhere as VIP guests celebrated.

He wasn't shy with his hands—brushing them against my arm, waist, and lower back.

It seemed innocent. But our chemistry was scorching, and I knew better.

Edward was making *another* move—so when he asked if I wanted to grab fresh air, I agreed.

Every part of me was on fire.

"I didn't think you'd be here tonight," I said as we stepped onto the breeze-swept patio, stars glittering like diamonds in the clear tropical sky.

The bass still pulsed in my ears—my own heartbeat syncing to it, quick and rising.

Edward had a twinkle in his eyes, a subtle grin pulling at his lips.

He didn't answer right away.

"I wanted to make an appearance. I'd have joined you for dinner, but unfortunately, I already had an engagement with my political advisor."

Of course he had a political advisor...

Then: "But truthfully, I came to see you."

His hand wandered to my side, fingertips gently tracing the fabric of my dress.

"James told me."

Edward tilted his head, mock offended. "He threw me under the bus?"

"I'm afraid so."

"Betrayal," he murmured, eyes still on mine. "We'll be having words."

I laughed, brushing my hair back before the warm breeze caught it. It danced on my neck.

Edward drifted closer. "Allie, you look incredible tonight."

His voice was low, deliberate. Dangerous. Eyes dragging over me, unhurried.

"You want me to kiss you," he said. Not a question.

"Zack's watching," I managed, glancing to see him standing beside a pillar.

Edward didn't even look. "I'll make him disappear."

He started to lift a hand but paused, watching me squirm, then smirked.

"Unless... you're cool enough to go back in?"

For a moment, everything stilled—just the two of us under the stars, string lights floating above, music vibrating the floor.

I nodded—but I was far from cool. My entire body burned for him.

"Come on," he said, his palm pressed against the small of my back—guiding me toward the door. "Before I change my mind and take you home."

He winked—slow and intentional.

Every nerve in my body begged me to stop. To let him pull me back, kiss me senseless. Take me home. But I was trying—desperately—to be good.

Why?

We'd already kissed, touched—but for whatever reason, I was wavering.

I lacked confidence in my own decision-making. My own love life.

I was, sadly, the tease men complained about.

* * *

Edward grabbed my hand, guiding me to the crowded main dance floor—out of sight of the guys.

He moved against me, firm—his body like a silent command.

Every twirl, every touch, tantalizing.

Watching me like the room had vanished and I was the only one.

My hands slipped over his shoulders, body melting into his.

Everything about him, intoxicating—his heat, his scent, the weight of his gaze.

And I craved him.

God, I craved him.

* * *

We spilled out of the club into a perfect Tampa night.

The street was quiet, the air cool—but between us, the temperature kept rising.

He whispered, "Come home with me."

"Edward..."

A smirk. "Then what about a ride back to your hotel?"

He tickled my side, voice laced with mischief—the kind I was trying to avoid.

"It's fine. I can walk back with the guys."

"Allie, look at them. They're hammered. At least let us drive you."

He smiled—kind, persuasive—flagging down Zack.

And because I wasn't thrilled about walking six blocks in stilettos—I agreed.

* * *

Edward kept a tight grip on my hand as we reached my door.

I scanned the room quickly giving it an, "All clear," trying to hide my nerves.

But he didn't laugh. Didn't move. Just stood there—lingering in the threshold.

Still. Magnetic.

I knew that look.

He was about to kiss me... and if he kissed me, I wasn't sure I'd stop him.

"Edward, I—I'm not going to invite you in. I really—"

"Actually, I had a question," he interrupted softly, almost smiling. "Would you like to attend a black-tie with me and the guys tomorrow night in Sarasota—a fundraiser for disabled veterans? I have an extra ticket."

"*Oh*—sure. That sounds nice."

"Perfect! I'll pick you up at six."

He smiled, then stepped closer—pulling me tight.

I caught my breath just as he kissed me, his tongue tracing mine—tasting me, teasing me. Claiming me with quiet confidence.

One hand pressed me against the doorframe, the other held my hip. I moaned. Knees weak, spine arching.

When my heel slipped, he caught me as I crashed backward.

He steadied me, brushing a strand of hair from my face, then kissed me once more.

My cheek. Reverent.

"Good night, Allie. Now deadbolt this behind me."

I leaned against the door after it clicked shut.

Dazed—and grateful for the stumble that stopped me from leading him straight to bed.

Fingertips touching my lips. Not sure if I was drunk... or just drunk on him.

My skin tingled from his touch, but my heart ached with the weight of what it meant.

CHAPTER 31

Saturday morning hit hard.

A withdrawal of drinking, dancing, adrenaline—and *him*.

By late afternoon, I was back home in Siesta Key, standing in front of my closet. Recalling the glamour of my old life and hoping the right dress might make me feel like myself again.

I sifted through a sea of gowns until my fingers landed on blush lace—an elegant mermaid-cut. Sultry as the Florida heat.

It was unapologetically feminine, hugging curves I'd been hiding for weeks under tactical pants and polos.

Tonight I was going full glitz and glam.

Curled hair. Smoky eyes. Red lips. Diamonds. Stilettos.

All in.

* * *

I was halfway through a final once-over at the foyer mirror when I heard his knock.

As I opened the door, he nearly took my breath away.

Crisp tux. Hair perfectly styled. That confident smile.

Alarmingly handsome.

Almost too-good-to-be-true.

And suddenly, I felt like a teenage girl getting picked up for prom—butterflies and all.

He exhaled with a hand to his chest.

"Allie... wow," he said, his voice soft. "You're stunning."

He took my hand and twirled me slowly. "Absolutely incredible, love."

"Thank you. You look rather dashing yourself," I replied with a shy grin, praying he couldn't hear my heart pounding.

He kissed my hand, then led me to the Bentley, where Zack and Cody were waiting—also in tuxedos.

Cody gave a low whistle. "*Damnnn,* Allie. Rolling like a high-net-worth-individual."

Zack nodded, his grumble barely audible: "Or high-value target."

"I'll take that as a compliment." I smiled, adding, "Cody, for a guy who hates dressing up—"

"Yeah, yeah... doll, I'm not a monster. I own a tux."

I laughed. "Well, you both clean up nicely."

Zack offered a rare smile from the driver's seat.

Soon, I was probing Cody about his and Greg's evening with the girls from the club—two twenty-somethings in town for a bachelorette party.

After dancing around the subject, he finally admitted that the bride talked the girls out of leaving with such 'old guys,' so he and Greg went home alone.

"But damn, Greg was *so* close to sealing the deal with his tats." Cody shrugged. "Shame. I had my dick pills ready."

We all laughed before Cody launched into an obscene story about Greg's use of ED meds with a European supermodel weeks earlier.

With a wicked grin, he handed me his phone.

I took it hesitantly as Edward rolled his eyes, muttering under his breath:

"Thanks, bud."

On the screen—a zoomed-in video of a couple having sex in a luxury high rise.

The woman wore a spectacular rhinestone and feather corset with dazzling stilettos and a blinding necklace.

The man had on a Stetson, white long-sleeved western shirt, and cowboy boots with red, white, and blue stars up the sides.

He had amazing legs—which was obvious given he wasn't wearing any pants.

Soon, the woman filming from a nearby building gasped:

"Ladies, I wouldn't normally film this, but—Oh. My. God! These two have been going at it for two hours with no end in sight, and this urban cowboy keeps pulling twirly moves like I've never seen. Watch! He's about to do it again!"

Eyes glued to the screen, I watched as the man twirled the woman over on the kitchen island, sweeping her legs together in a slow windshield-wiper motion—still inside her—as she screamed in pleasure.

He twirled her back as she appeared to orgasm, her entire body spasming.

"Ladies, if anyone can help me identify this sex god, please, please, *please* send me a DM!"

"Wow, that cowboy's got some moves," I said faintly, handing Cody his phone back—my face surely red.

Wait—

"*That cowboy?*" Cody laughed. "Doll—that was our very own Rockstar. A sex god."

"Oh jeez," I blurted as I covered my mouth in embarrassment.

"Yeah, women on social media started a campaign to find him."

Edward shrugged apologetically as Cody and Zack chuckled, but he tended to forget I'd heard my fair share of locker room talk—in the Marine Corps, at the agency, and through my marriage.

There wasn't much I hadn't heard.

* * *

Zack and Cody escorted me and Edward into the yacht club upon our arrival—regrettably, not like guests themselves, but like part of our detail.

'Mr. Anderson' was greeted by the event coordinator, who led us to a private room with a dozen or so wounded warriors receiving gifts and awards.

Edward was then asked to speak.

He retold his story—

from his vehicle getting blown up, to waking engulfed in flames, to dragging a friend missing a leg to safety and applying a tourniquet, then going back for another buddy, to holding down the location and providing life-saving aid—all while gravely injured himself.

His voice was calm, but his words were heavy.

I could almost smell the diesel. The blood.

I blinked hard—fighting unexpected tears—as men in tuxedos and women in gowns nodded along beside me. They understood the situation Edward described. Many of them had lived some version of it themselves.

He paused before he began detailing his injuries and the dozens of surgeries he'd endured, and my mind wandered—picturing him with nothing on.

Not in a lustful way. Just... trying to comprehend the damage. The scars. The pain he still carried.

The thought made my chest ache.

Then he spoke candidly about his spiral into addiction—until a friend checked him into rehab.

He rebounded—establishing the foundation to fund rehabilitation for fellow wounded warriors. *His* foundation—a detail he'd strategically omitted.

Edward inspired. It was obvious as I scanned the faces around me—his words landed deep. Whispers cut through stunned silence. Eyes glistened.

His story wasn't unique—but it was devastating. And for the first time, I saw a tender, vulnerable side of him I didn't think existed.

Especially when he started talking about God. And destiny.

Suddenly, I realized his pain wasn't so different than mine.

I hadn't been burdened by physical injuries—but I'd battled my own demons. Depression. Prescription drug dependence. A brush with alcoholism.

And somehow, he'd helped pull me out of that darkness.

I couldn't explain it, but my gut told me Edward was somehow linked to my own destiny.

Yet as he stood there—vulnerable, exposed—a part of me bristled at the practiced charm and calculation.

Like the entire night was nothing but a performance for the cameras. Every word carefully crafted and rehearsed for consumption.

Unexpectedly, he motioned to me.

"I know our time is limited now, but Allie and I would love to connect with you throughout the evening. Please don't be shy."

He took a few minutes to shake hands—with me by his side—and his warmth lit up the room, even when the topic—the horrors of war—was heartbreaking.

After the small gathering, we were whisked off to cocktail hour, where Florida wealth was on full display. Everywhere I looked: bronzed skin, surgically sculpted bodies, gleaming smiles, designer gowns, and sparkling diamonds.

Sarasota's celebrities.

Edward introduced me to a series of people I'd never remember—men with strong handshakes and women who air-kissed with perfectly plump, glossy lips. All eager to impress the magmatic Mr. Edward Anderson.

He didn't call me his friend or an employee. Just *Allie*. Always delivered with an endearing grin that hinted at more, keeping a hand gently on the small of my back—protective.

I played along, but it wasn't until we were seated at the head table that it fully registered.

He'd indisputably brought me as his date.

* * *

I excused myself to use the restroom, stumbling across Cody, who was lingering in the hallway, talking into his earpiece.

"Where's the rest of the team tonight?" I asked. "I thought they'd be here."

"I mean, yeah, we're all here... but you won't be seeing anyone else unless shit gets ugly."

He pointed to a security camera overhead.

I took a deep breath.

"So, I'm Edward's date tonight?"

"Dunno what else you'd be. You're definitely not part of the detail—unless you're packing something I can't see under that dress."

He glanced me up and down, chuckling.

"Funny."

"Yeah, well—consider yourself lucky. There's nothing worse than wearing a stupid-ass penguin suit and not being allowed to get wasted and pick up these rich cougars."

I grumbled as I walked away.

Typical Edward.

* * *

It was another wonderfully balmy night, the ambiance at the yacht club enchanting as the party moved onto the terrace.

I stepped away to take it all in as Edward grabbed us more champagne.

When he returned, he placed his arm around my waist. Doting.

"Allie, thank you for joining me tonight."

"You're welcome, but... Edward, I believe I was invited under false pretenses."

He smiled—slow, knowing. Frustrating.

"You know I'm married, and it's obvious you brought me as your date. The team's going to give me so much shit for this—and people are already assuming we're together."

"What people are you concerned about?" he asked. "Blake isn't here. He won't find out. And if he does, well—"

I glared. "Edward, *please.* I know how you operate."

He met my gaze, unflinching.

"He won't be an obstacle much longer."

He smiled—like he hadn't just casually threatened my husband—then softened.

"Allie, you can blast me on this tomorrow—I probably deserve it. But not tonight. Let's dance and enjoy the rest of our evening."

He extended his hand.

And against my better judgment, I surrendered.

* * *

Under the glow of lights, something in Edward surrendered, too.

At the center of the dance floor, he pulled me close—our bodies fusing together.

His fingertips lingered on my skin through lace.

His scent—smoky leather and patchouli—wrapped around me.

The music faded. The room blurred.

I waited for what I knew was next.

He dipped me low—eyes locked, hands firm—like I was his.

And then his lips found mine—

tongue cool with whiskey.

Kiss long and slow—nothing but smoldering.

Maybe indecent.

My breath caught.

Heat surged through me, every nerve on fire.

He pulled away, grinning—lights twinkling around him like stars.

He didn't care who was watching.

He wanted a scene.

Applause broke out somewhere behind us.

I stiffened, suddenly aware of curious onlookers, my skin flushing as my chest rose and fell in shallow waves.

"I know I shouldn't have done that," he whispered. "But aren't you glad I did?"

He gazed at me, letting me bask in my desire.

Then—finally—I exhaled, biting my lip.

Cody stood a few feet away with a smug grin.

I could only imagine what the team was chattering about in his earpiece.

They were all watching.

And I'm sure they were all talking.

I didn't need to hear it to know—Cody's face said it all.

Not only had the entire team witnessed our kiss—worse, so had half the event. All eyes were already on Edward—people drawn to his charisma, his story, his fortune.

And now they were watching me, too. Trying to figure out who I was.

On the edge of panic, I excused myself from the dance floor.

I stood at the terrace railing, eyes drifting toward the house lights glittering on the water—still swooning, despite whispers clinging to me like static.

* * *

Edward held my hand in the backseat as we crossed the bridge to Siesta Key.

He leaned close, voice firm:

"Allie, I'd like you to stay with me tonight."

I turned toward the window, but there was no hiding what he was doing to me.

I was falling—fast.

The line between loyalty and desire had all but disappeared.

I wanted to say yes.

But I had no toothbrush. No sexy negligee. No plan for the morning after.

I wasn't prepared and worried maybe I'd subconsciously sabotaged myself.

My heart pounded.

"I shouldn't," I whispered.

"But do you want to?"

He stroked my arm, and I couldn't stop the sound that slipped out. "Ohhh..."

"Allie—I want you. All of you."

"Edward... not tonight. I just—can't."

He gently tickled my inner arm, promise in his voice, "Fair enough. Another night."

* * *

Alone in the dark, I let myself go—imagining Edward's lips on my skin, breath warm against my thigh, hands unzipping my dress, exploring every inch of me.

I moaned into my pillow—my skin still tingling from his touch—aching for the night I didn't take.

And wondering how much longer I could keep telling him no.

Chapter 32

My phone lit up at midnight—Edward.

Still awake?

I smiled, then typed back: *Yes.*

Seconds later, he called.

"Allie, I don't know if I can keep operating with this level of distraction. I got home, sat on the phone with Tanner for thirty minutes, and didn't hear a word he said. All I could think about was you."

I bit the inside of my cheek. "We've been drifting this way for a while. Maybe we need to reset—and figure out what it means to work together."

Wait—was that what I wanted?

No... far from it.

He exhaled. "How do I say this without spooking you?"

When he spoke again, his voice was careful. Sincere.

"I don't want to keep drifting. I want you to be mine. No borrowed hours. No split loyalty. I want you in every sense. In my life... and in my bed."

My heart raced.

He cleared his throat, then added:

"I'm trying to be patient. But I'm not used to being turned down. Tell me what I need to do to have you. Because I've never wanted anything—or anyone—like this."

I heard the vulnerability in his voice. The rawness.

"*Ohhh.*"

I recalibrated my response.

"It's just... the more this feels like a fairy tale, the more I worry it's somehow artificial. It's hard to explain."

"Don't you want a fairy tale?" he asked.

I didn't answer right away.

A part of me did—all of it.

His attention. The way he made my body—and my heart—feel.

But fairy tales weren't real.

Not for women like me.

Not after everything.

"I do, but..."

I looked out the window, moonlight casting fractured shadows, palms swaying watchfully overhead.

I thought of the crowd, the glamour of the evening.

Perfect. Almost *too* perfect.

And then it hit me.

I was already living pieces of the fairy tale.

The house. The job. Edward.

Or was it just fantasy?

A beautiful illusion?

"Edward, I'm scared I'm leading with my heart. That's not me."

"Love, if you need space, I'll give it to you. But..."

His voice lowered, edged with concern.

"I don't think the issue is you and me. I think this is still about Blake."

Edward wasn't wrong.

"I need to talk to him. He left again, and I don't know when he'll be back."

"I'll call Mike in the morning and have him back in the next twenty-four hours."

"No, please don't do that," I pleaded. "He'll have a full meltdown."

Edward chuckled. "Okay... I won't. But will you at least think about what I'm proposing? About a relationship—and intimacy?"

"Yes..."

"Thank you." He paused again. "I wish I weren't, but I'm flying to Puerto Rico tomorrow. Need to tie up some loose ends. I'll be gone until Thursday. But can I see you when I get back? Take you to dinner?"

"I'd like that, but—"

"But what, love?"

"It's—"

I wanted to explain that I didn't want my heart broken by a billionaire playboy, but I swallowed it.

"We can talk when you get back."

"Anything you want. I'll be in touch."

"Okay."

"Again, Allie, thank you for accompanying me tonight. You looked positively stunning. Good night, love."

* * *

Liv called around 7:30 as I was lacing my shoes for a morning run.

"Hey!" I answered, perky, refreshed.

"Want to explain why I'm seeing a picture of your boss's tongue down your throat in the gossip column this morning?"

"Tell me you're kidding..."

"They're saying there's a mystery woman dating Florida's Most Eligible Bachelor."

"Oh, shit," I gasped as panic surged.

I hadn't even seen the photo, but the fact that it existed made me nauseous.

"Girl, we talked about this."

I cut her off as I saw an incoming call from Edward.

"Liv, I know, I know... can you hold on a minute? I'm getting a call from Edward. Let me take it."

I answered. "I assume you're calling about the photo of us?"

"About that. It's grainy, so it's unlikely they'll identify you. James is independently working his magic in case anything pops up. Don't let it concern you. You don't know many people in Florida, and—"

"You're scaring me."

"Love, my lawyer's already talked to the paper, and they've agreed to pull the image within the hour."

My phone buzzed.

A screenshot from Liv—blurry but unmistakable.

I sucked in a breath. "My God..."

Liv wasn't kidding.

There was nothing casual about the way he kissed me or held me—like I was his.

And the worst part? I wasn't resisting.

"I'll handle it. Blake won't see it."

I hadn't even considered Blake.

My bigger fear was anonymity—and creeps like Joe Turner destroying the peace I'd found in Florida.

What was wrong with me?

"Allie, are you still there?" Edward asked gingerly.

"I'm thinking. What does the article say?"

"I'd recommend you don't read it."

He was probably right.

I didn't want to face what the image or article confirmed—

Edward wasn't just a flirtation anymore.

* * *

I called Liv back and told her the whole story.

She was stunned—and furious.

"Allie, you know Blake's going to flip if he sees that picture."

"I'm aware. *If* he sees it," I said quietly. "Edward promised it's being taken down."

"Aren't you the one that told me the Internet's forever? He's bound to see it."

"Well... let's hope he doesn't."

"Since when have you operated on hope? I'm starting to worry about you. You're acting reckless."

Her voice sharpened.

"With his temper? *Please.* I don't want him to hurt you."

"He wouldn't," I said on autopilot, though I wasn't sure I believed it. Not after our last encounter.

"You don't know that! You've never cheated on him before! What if he—"

"Liv, I'll be fine."

"Why are you being so dismissive right now?"

Her voice rose, almost breaking.

"Ugh, it's so frustrating... I'm hanging up."

"Liv, wait—"

But it was too late.

She was right.

I *had* changed.

She could sense it, too.

That I wasn't just falling—I was free-falling.

After years of playing it safe—by the book—recklessness felt intoxicating.

Liberating.

Instead of plotting every move, I was along for the ride—

almost undaunted by consequences.

It was ill-advised.

But the high was real.

* * *

The sun was brutal as I pulled into Bright Sands.

Sunglasses, hat, oversized sweatshirt—like someone hiding from the paparazzi.

James was waiting outside the ops center, arms crossed. He fell in step beside me.

"Looks like you and Edward had a nice evening," he said, voice low.

"Has everyone seen the photo?" I sighed.

"Yep. Cody left a copy on your desk. But I've heard the live version was better. Want me to pull the venue footage?" He nudged me playfully.

"Yeah, great."

I stepped inside.

The room whirred, then instantly collapsed to silence—all eyes on me.

My body tensed.

A giant poster covered my monitors—me and Edward, mid-kiss, blown up and encircled in a red Sharpie heart. Like something out of a high school yearbook.

Ugh.

I ripped it off in one slow motion, then dramatically crumpled it into a ball.

Cody cackled from across the room and smacked Greg's shoulder. But Greg didn't laugh.

I threw the poster into the trash with just the right force—making a point—as Edward strolled in.

Calm. Collected. *Courageous.*

"Hey, love," he said, smiling.

"What are you doing here?" I muttered as the guys looked on, curious.

"Oh, just wanted to see how everyone's doing. James says the Lance Corporal Underground has been on fire this morning."

"Not funny. I was hoping you'd be here to put this to bed."

"Superb choice of words, doll," Cody shouted, cracking up.

"It could've happened to anyone," Edward added with a wink.

"Dunno. Haven't seen too many pics of you kissing any of us," José yelled from across the room.

I didn't laugh. I didn't even smile. I just dropped my head and started rearranging my desk—the punchline of a joke I couldn't deflect. I'd walked into it.

But why was I the one under scrutiny? I hadn't initiated the kiss... Edward was the one that crossed the line. Very publicly.

He leaned in, lowering his voice.

"Hey, it's okay. When they give you shit, just dish it back, love. They'll forget about this by tomorrow."

"I'm *sure*," I huffed, eyes rolling. "You coming over to check on me doesn't help."

Rumors were already swirling—and he wasn't doing a thing to stop them.

Case in point.

"I'll get out of here," he said, hands up like he was innocent, grinning.

"I need to take some calls and pack, anyway. Everyone, get back to it."

Then he kissed the top of my head, causing the ops center to erupt in laughter. Commotion. *Gossip.*

His audacity was unreal. Frustrating. Incorrigible. Somehow still attractive.

I exhaled and managed a quiet, "Thanks a lot," as he walked away.

* * *

James approached while I worked, hovering for a moment before:

"Al, let's take a walk."

I grabbed my sunglasses and braced for a lecture.

A loaded silence stretched as we made our way outside. Only the birds filled it: nagging, noisy, and impossible to tune out.

When we reached the driveway, he started in:

"You know, Edward hasn't had a woman in his life in a long time..."

There was a warmth to his tone I didn't expect.

"I see how he looks at you. I don't have an opinion on the matter, but between dating and working, things could get messy."

"Yeah..." I conceded. I couldn't fault James for stating the obvious.

"Like I said, I don't care either way. He needs someone he can trust. You might be the first. He's never been able to talk about his work with anyone he's dated. But his life is unconventional—ours all are, you know? If this isn't a life you want, I'd tell him now. Save yourselves the heartache."

I nodded before he surprised me—pulling me into a hug.

Brief. Formal.

"Al, I'm saying all this as a friend."

"I know. I appreciate it."

Without another word, he turned and headed back toward the ops center.

In my mind, gratitude warred with doubt—wondering who else was secretly rooting for me to fall—or fail.

Chapter 33

I didn't hear from Edward while he was in Puerto Rico, and part of me was thankful for the space. Finally, Thursday evening, a text:

I just touched down. May I take you to dinner?

So formal. *So* him.

I stared at the screen, torn between boundaries and impulse.

The right answer would've been *no*, but I was past the point of smart decisions. And sad.

I thought the high that came with seeing Edward would make things better so I replied:

Any chance you want to come over and get drunk instead?

His response came instantly:

On my way!

* * *

The sun was setting on the Gulf, sky blazing with hues of red and orange, casting a glow around Edward as he stood at my door—ethereal.

"Hello, love!" he beamed.

His jawline caught the light, smile perfect.

My God, he was handsome.

He clutched a tall bottle of tequila in one arm while the other juggled an oversized floral arrangement—towering birds of paradise, spilling orchids, protea, fern fronds.

"Wow, this is spectacular! Thank you so much."

He set both on my foyer table before lifting me into a heartfelt hug, wet lips pressed to my cheek. "Oh, how I missed you! What's the occasion?"

He followed me to the kitchen, fingertips trailing over a sliver of skin at my waist, sending a shiver straight to parts of me I was still trying to behave.

I didn't want to ruin the mood. But something in me tightened—grief coiling to the tenderness of his touch. The sight of flowers. Tequila.

I shifted my weight, exhaling through my nose.

His smile faltered the moment he saw my face.

"Aw, love, what's wrong?"

"I was just notified my mom died." I swallowed. "Last week."

"Oh, fuck. I'm an ass!"

He pulled me back into his arms—his embrace longer, firmer.

"Allie... can you please forgive me?" he murmured, planting a kiss on the top of my head.

"It's not your fault... you didn't know."

I shook my head and broke away.

"We hadn't spoken in years, but it hit hard."

I turned to the China cabinet, pulling down two crystal shot glasses. They'd belonged to one of Blake's pretentious relatives—an unwelcome trinket in my kitchen.

I thought about switching them out but didn't have the energy, then pushed them across the counter before Edward filled them to the brim.

"Allie," he said gently, "will you tell me about your mom?"

Ugh. What was there to say?

"Well... she was beautiful," I started, grabbing a couple limes from a bowl, giving one a suspicious squeeze.

"A total hippie and free spirit with a bleeding heart. She met my dad while backpacking through the Balkans after leaving the Peace Corps. That kind of sums her up. We were total opposites."

Edward grinned.

"I know what you're thinking," I added. "No, she wasn't agency."

"You sure?"

"Positive." He wasn't the first to wonder.

"She was a good mom—well, until the affair..."

I stopped short, eyes darting to Edward. He didn't falter. Still, the words caught in my throat.

A quiet reckoning.

My mom gave in to something that felt good. A man that made her feel seen... and wanted. I'd judged her for it. Now... I understood.

Edward wasn't a fling or mistake I'd made one night.

Still, the word stung: *affair.*

"Well, then came the divorce, and my shithead half-brother... who knows if he's alive. The silver lining was Thomas, my stepdad. Retired Army. Amazing guy."

I paused to think. There wasn't much else to add.

"I wish he'd been around when the agency came after me... to help explain it. Instead, she assumed I was a criminal—like Tommy."

"Ouch," Edward grimaced.

"Yeah. I got really tired of it, so we just stopped talking."

I absently glanced toward the floor. For the first time, I wondered if I'd overreacted.

I'd become a different person since leaving the agency.

Softer. More emotional.

More like *her.*

"I'm guessing you knew about our estrangement from my background?"

He sighed. "I did. And for the record, Tommy's still kicking... and still a shithead."

"No kidding. I'm surprised he hasn't overdosed by now... or got himself killed in a drug deal gone wrong. What's that idiot up to these days?"

"Serving life at Folsom."

"Wow... well, good riddance. That would've destroyed my step-dad."

Edward nodded solemnly, then held up his shot glass with careful slowness, like he was trying to get the toast just right. He slid mine forward.

"Allie," he said, "here's to your mom."

My fingers curled around the crystal. I hesitated, hand trembling.

Was I toasting my mom... or apologizing to her?

"To Anita," I whispered.

His glass met mine with a gentle clink. "To Anita."

The tequila went down like fire.

I winced, biting a lime, then stared at the counter, shaking my head and blinking back the unwelcome sting in my eyes.

"Shit. Why'd you bring tequila?"

Edward smiled. "I thought we were getting drunk and partying. I totally misread the situation."

I outwardly laughed, but inside, I felt a pang of remorse. I'd never said goodbye to my mom. It was a regret I'd have to learn to live with.

"Whatever happened to your dad?"

My dad wasn't exactly a happy topic, either... unfortunately.

"He died in a Crystal City hotel room when he was visiting one Christmas. Jeez, that was almost ten years ago... awful way to go." I paused, remembering the call, the police report, the details that never added up. "I'm still convinced it was a hit."

"Really?" Edward asked, tilting his head in curiosity.

"Yeah, something about it never sat right. Growing up, I thought he was just a mechanic, but his behaviors were tradecraft. I swear he used to use me as cover on surveillance when I was little. We followed people around for *fun*."

"Who do you think he worked for?"

"Maybe Serbia's SID? The Russians? I don't know. I had a friend look into it, and I asked him about it. But he always had excuses. He never popped as foreign intel on any of my backgrounds, so... maybe he was agency, too?"

"Well, sounds like you joined the family business?"

"You, too," I replied softly, a nod to the mystery surrounding his parents' death.

He hesitated slightly.

"Wouldn't surprise me. A week after the crash, the bungalow got tossed in a 'random' burglary while I was at a friend's—I'm talking walls opened, floors torn up, lamps smashed. I wish I'd known better back then." He shrugged. "Were you close to your dad?"

"Not really. He moved back to Europe to take care of my grandma before she died, and I didn't see him much once I joined the Marine Corps. Then rarely at the agency. Plus, he hated Blake like he hated sleazy car salesmen."

Edward smirked but didn't comment.

The first wave of tequila hit—warm. Just enough to dull the edge.

Still, I bit my lip, heart heavy.

"Thanks for coming over. I didn't have anyone else."

On the verge of tears, I cracked a beer—the hiss loud in the quiet kitchen.

Edward rested his hand on mine. Gentle. Supportive.

"Allie, you could've called any one of the guys, and they would've dropped everything. No questions asked."

He laughed. "Greg and Cody would've zipped over in five minutes... that's how this team works. We're family."

I nodded before he brushed the corner of my eye, catching a tear before it fell.

"I mean it. What about your girlfriend Liv?"

"Uhhh," I exhaled. "We went out Tuesday... and the night didn't end well. She's mad at me."

"I'm sorry to hear that, love." Edward's fingers tousled the hair on my shoulder, a whisper of contact—but enough to break through the haze of tequila, sad memories, and Liv's voice in my head—chastising.

All of it slipped away as Edward inched closer.

The last thing I wanted was to cry ugly tears in front of him.

"How'd you two meet?"

"Oh... I worked with her husband, and we slowly became friends over the years. But she's never liked Blake much... especially after he got home from the Philippines and gave me—"

I stopped short in circumspect, tapping my fingernails anxiously on the counter.

I was referring to Blake's team returning from deployment with gonorrhea.

When I heard about it, I had myself tested—and sure enough, I was positive—something Blake couldn't explain away.

"Well, you probably already know about that little incident."

"I do," Edward nodded. "Heard about it through a friend."

He paused, pensive.

Then: "Allie, why on earth didn't you leave him after that?"

I stared at the tequila bottle—overwhelmed with an urge to drown myself. I'd made so many stupid decisions I wanted to forget.

"I don't know... because I'm a glutton for punishment?" I shrugged.

Unfortunately, the truth was darker.

"Blake promised it would *never* happen again, then I deployed and didn't have the time or energy to divorce him. When I got home, things seemed better, but if I questioned him, he gaslit me, so I let it go."

Despite being confident in my professional life, I'd struggled with my own self-worth.

I told myself Blake wasn't emotionally abusive—but all the signs were there.

Forced isolation, ultimatums, belittling, guilt-tripping, silent treatment, devaluation.

But the worst of it?

Gaslighting.

I took a deep breath, gathering my thoughts.

"I know that's a terrible answer. I shouldn't have stayed, but the alternative was starting over. And it's not like I could date normal people."

Edward chuckled gently—but his face showed concern.

"My options at the agency were either self-absorbed sociopaths or chauvinists. Not exactly great dating material. I took the path of least resistance. It sounds foolish saying it out loud."

His expression softened as he squeezed my side.

"No, love, it all makes sense."

He paused, his face morphing to a mischievous smile.

"But what about now?"

I sensed where the conversation was headed...

"Want to pour me another?" I asked, eyeballing my empty glass as it sparkled on the counter.

Edward laughed. "I *did* agree to get drunk with you, didn't I?"

He poured us both another shot and quickly took his, flinching.

Then: "I know a normal-ish non-sociopath that understands the work you're doing. He seems pretty into you... *Florida's Most Eligible Bachelor*, if I'm not mistaken. People tell me he's a catch."

He bit his lip and winked.

I should've teased him back. But the way he looked at me... it was raw. Honest.

I downed my shot—looking for anything to stop the next question forming in his eyes.

CHAPTER 34

I was trained to sit still—no tics, no nerves. But the excitement that Edward sparked in me was hard to contain.

The legs of the barstool whispered softly on the travertine floor as I fidgeted, leaning in, cool marble kissing my skin—a stark contrast to the heat rising in my body.

"So, Edward, why didn't you ever get married?"

"Because I've never met a woman I trusted." He grinned. "Sorry, I couldn't resist. I swear I'm not a chauvinist."

I giggled. He was delightfully clever.

"Candidly, women tend to chase my fortune. And once they learn I travel solo and can't father children, they move on like clockwork. My trust-fund girlfriend at Harvard dumped me the day I enlisted—her parents didn't approve."

He paused, thoughtful.

"I haven't had many meaningful relationships."

"That's crumby. I'm sorry."

"It's fine. It allows me to pour myself into our work. Sometimes I think... it's why God put me on earth."

"I respect what you're doing."

He smiled bright and sincere. "Thanks. You're one of only a handful of people in the world who knows."

"That's crazy," I murmured, nearly tripping over my words. "Gosh, I'm tipsy already."

"Well, I won't take advantage of you, love. Do you want me to leave?"

I shook my head.

"Then, let's slow down. Maybe have a few beers... you know, to rehydrate," he said with a wink.

He cracked open the fridge and pulled out two Coors Lights, the bottles clinking in his hands.

When he returned, he eased back beside me, like we were just friends catching up.

But my energy shifted—a shift that wasn't lost on him. His eyes lingered. Waiting.

He knew something heavier was coming.

Tequila loosened my tongue.

"Edward, is that story true? The one about your platoon sergeant dying under 'mysterious circumstances' after you got blown up?"

He nodded thoughtfully for several seconds before responding. "Depends who you ask."

"*Oh.*"

So, it *was* true...

"The Pentagon will deny it. But yeah—I did it. And he deserved it. Just... please don't repeat that, love."

I nodded nervously, surprised by his candor.

I didn't mind the act of justice.

But the way he said it—so matter-of-fact—made my heart race.

Because it wasn't a clean shot to the head.

It was something else.

Slower. Angrier.

Darker.

Merciless.

By other people's standards, he was a monster.

I reached for a topic that seemed safer.

Lighter.

Instead, I landed on: "Edward, how many women do you call 'love'?"

He shook his head. "I don't understand."

"You call me 'love.' How many other women do you call that?"

His eyes locked on mine—steady, unblinking. "Only you."

I half-smiled, surprised.

I'd expected something casual—like Blake calling all women darlin'.

He reached for my hand, his thumb grazing the inside of my wrist. Just once.

Then: "I'm not one to toss words around, love."

I gulped, scared of what he might say next.

And if he said it out loud...

He bumped my knee with his.

"What else would you like to know?" he asked—with a grin that made me want to lose all self-control.

Images slammed into me—

his mouth on my neck,

his breath in my ear,

a cool, controlling whisper telling me exactly how he wanted me...

The thought hit like a jolt of electricity.

My thighs clenched. I shivered.

And before I could stop myself—

"Out of curiosity, how many women have you slept with?"

"*Ohhh.*" He stilled as a look crossed his face. I knew it... not annoyance but something closer to calculation.

My heart thudded.

What was wrong with me? Why did I ask that?

I'd broken the spell. Shifted our conversation from seduction to stats.

Five seconds ticked by—maybe more—before he leaned back and exhaled.

"I'm not sure I have a respectable answer," he replied, the smallest hint of amusement in his voice. "Being the godson of a billionaire at such a young age, well... some years were a blur."

I winced.

"Since I got blown up, not many—if it's any consolation."

He shifted closer. "What else?"

"You're not going to ask me the same question?"

"No, love. It wouldn't matter if you said one or one hundred."

I narrowed my eyes.

"Okay," he started. "I'm guessing five."

I nodded as his smile widened, but he said nothing at first—just looked at me.

When the tension was almost too hot to handle, he added: "So lucky number sex? Uh, shit... I meant six."

He laughed and slowly tickled my knee with his fingers—lazy, teasing strokes like he was tracing shapes. *Hearts.*

"Allie, if the number of women I've been with is a deal breaker, I can't change it. Those rounds are down range."

I laughed at the pun.

"But if we get married—"

My head shook. "Married?"

He froze—his expression plastered in instant regret—then backpedaled. "Shit. Strike that. If we enter into a *relationship* like I'm hoping—" he blurted, dragging a hand through his hair, visibly rattled.

"I don't intend to cheat. If that's a concern—because you think I'm some rich playboy juggling girlfriends and mistresses—it shouldn't be. That's not me."

I tilted my head, watching him unravel.

"Wow. I think I need another shot." He exhaled as he poured. "And no, I don't know how many people I've killed, if that's your next question."

I laughed, shaking my head, as tequila sloshed in his glass.

"Anything else?" he asked with a chuckle, voice warm again—inviting.

Tipsy and flustered, the best I could muster was, "Gosh... um, how many houses do you have?"

Edward grinned and gently squeezed my hand.

"Excellent question. Jake could tell you—but I've lost track. I know how that sounds. Dreadfully out of touch... but my favorite's on a private island Ed developed in the Bahamas. It's peaceful. A good place for the team to decompress. The beaches are spectacular."

Then: "If you'd like to go this weekend, I'll fly us. I'm certain the guys won't mind."

Marriage... now the Bahamas?

He made it sound so easy. So normal.

I pivoted. "I didn't know you could."

"Fly? Yeah, Ed made certain of it. If he hadn't died, he'd have made me his personal pilot. He even tried to talk me out of Harvard for a while."

"I'm curious... why'd you go back after becoming a billionaire?"

"I barely attended classes between surgery and rehab. But my donations kept everyone happy."

I nodded, not fully trusting myself to speak.

"May I ask you something personal?" His tone shifted—serious.

"Sure," I said, though a flicker of hesitation bled into my voice.

"Why didn't you and Blake have any children? Did you not want them?"

"Ohhh... well, we tried a few times. His parents desperately wanted him to have the quintessen—ugh... I'm too tipsy to say it."

I paused, the memory catching harder than I expected.

"They wanted the perfect image—for a campaign, go figure. When I eventually got pregnant, I had a miscarriage and decided not to try again."

Not after that.

Not when I already felt so alone.

His fingers twitched slightly—like he wanted to say more but hesitated.

I smiled to lighten the moment. "I guess there's only so much those background investigations can tell you."

"You're not wrong."

He placed his hand over mine.

"So, what did you find out about me?"

"Only that you were boring." He winked.

"Hey!" I giggled, swatting him. "That's not fair."

He caught my hand mid-air and kissed it—smooth.

"No drugs. No tattoos. No high-risk sexual activities—*allegedly*. Not even a speeding ticket. I almost didn't want to bring you on."

We both laughed.

"I'm kidding," he added. "You're exactly what I need."

His gaze told me he didn't mean professionally.

My chest tightened in charged silence.

"I'll grab us another beer," I offered, already walking away. We didn't need it. I just needed the space. From his eyes. From *that* look.

Safely at the refrigerator, I asked, "What about you? No tattoos?"

"Just one. It's hidden. Something dumb I did when I was younger."

I shifted, uncomfortable, trying not to picture where it was...

"I hope it's not as dumb as Blake's blacklight tattoo."

Edward choked on a sip of beer. When he spoke again, his tone was sharper. More alert.

"He has a blacklight tattoo? Where?"

"His wrist... a college thing, supposedly. He got it a few years ago on a trip with his frat brothers. But please pretend I didn't tell you that. He told me never to mention it to anyone."

Edward nodded—slowly—processing something.

I tilted my head, curious. Wondering if Edward had one, too.

Maybe it was an Ivy League-thing. One of those secret societies no one admits to.

Another strange little thread between them.

"Well, to each his own," he said.

A beat.

"Next question. Why didn't you finish the last semester of your MBA?" he asked, casually—but I could feel his eyes absorbing my every move and mannerism.

I shrugged, fingers tracing the condensation on my beer bottle.

"I wish I had a better excuse. But I was bored. And over the liberal college scene."

"Have you considered going back to finish it? Wouldn't be that much work."

His tone was gentle, but the thought made me grimace.

"Nope. It'd require me moving back to D.C.—and that's out."

I shook my head firmly. "I know I should've stuck it out, but I realized it was just a stupid piece of paper. I didn't need it for anything... Blake still harps on me for it, but I really only went to collect the housing allowance. It paid for my—"

I hesitated. "Ah, I shouldn't say."

His eyes blazed with mischief as his fingers grazed my thigh. "Oh no, you've got to tell me now. I'm loving this."

"Only if you promise not to judge."

"One million percent."

"I saved up for a new nose." I giggled, embarrassed. "Stupid, I know."

Edward blinked, then leaned in, brow raised.

"You're kidding? What was wrong with it?"

"I got knocked out and it didn't heal right." I touched the bridge of my nose absently.

"Blake swore it looked the same, but I just couldn't stand it."

"It's perfect."

He studied me. Then, with a curious frown:

"But why'd you have to save for it? He's loaded."

I laughed dryly. "Oh yeah... he had no problem paying for my boob job but for some reason drew the line at my nose."

Edward nearly spit out his drink.

"Boob job? I wasn't expecting that."

"That I had one?" I squinted. "You can't tell?"

"Maybe I haven't looked at them enough," he muttered, grinning as his eyes wandered...

"*Shit.*" He caught himself—face flushed—then grabbed the tequila, poured a shot, and threw it back.

"I've also had a nose job, if it makes you feel better... shattered it in a bar fight in the streets of Morocco when Cody and I snuck out and got hammered. You'll have to ask him about it someday. I can't corroborate anything because I was blacked the fuck out. We tried stealing mopeds... or camels. The story often changes based on the audience."

I laughed, hard.

Edward paused, turning toward me—suddenly quieter.

"Allie, do you want to come over to the compound tonight? Tanner's turning thirty, and the guys are throwing a pool party. I didn't invite you earlier because—"

He chuckled to himself.

"Well?" I asked.

"Uh, well... because there will undoubtedly be female entertainment..."

He half-covered his face, a smile spreading across it.

"Nothing lewd. But come back with me and let's spend the night together."

My eyes widened.

"Shit—I didn't mean it like that. Just that we could spend *time* together—if you'd like."

"Pretty bold, asking me to a pool party just to see my boobs. You really can't stop thinking about them, can you?"

He smirked. "I can't. My background guy's fired!"

Eventually our laughter faded, but neither of us looked away.

The air shifted—thicker. Charged.

"Uh, okay. Bad idea." His fingers wandered my skin, tickling my arm. "What if I get your favorite Italian delivered and we have our own pool party here?"

"Edward, you have a hard enough time keeping your hands to yourself when I'm in normal clothes. You really think you'll behave once I'm in a bikini?"

"You have a good point, but I will... I promise."

He gave a playful salute with one hand, the other casually brushing my waist—a sparkle in his eyes begging me to believe him.

I took a shot.

"Okay—but under three conditions. First, you can look, but you can't touch. Second, no kissing. Third, you go home by eight."

"A.M. or P.M.?" he asked, then grinned scandalously. "And why no kissing? I can't stop thinking about our amazing kisses and—"

"There's no negotiation on the rules. And I'm setting an alarm."

He feigned a dramatic pout, then ran his hand down my arm—slow and suggestive.

"Edward, the first rule was no touching!"

"Fuck—I thought you meant your boobs!"

He laughed, flashing that dazzling smile, the silence pulsing with possibility.

A gorgeous moonlit night. Warm water. Way too much tequila.

The kind of night that ended with wet swimsuits on the floor, bodies tangled up in sheets.

Reckless written all over it.

And every part of me wanted to dive in.

"Quick, go throw on your swimsuit. I'll meet you outside."

My pulse raced.

Before I knew it, I was barefoot, halfway down the hall—

Head screaming *bad idea*. Heart saying *don't slow down*.

CHAPTER 35

I stood in front of a full-length mirror in a white triangle bikini, struggling to decide if it was appropriate.

Too much skin would send the wrong message—*but who was I kidding?*

We both knew my rules would be thrown out as soon as we were half-naked.

The energy between us sizzled—scandalous, scrumptious, irresistible—but beneath it, a connection deeper than anything I'd ever felt.

I settled on a more modest bikini top and cheeky bottom, then touched up my makeup, spritzed myself with a sweet scent, and made my way outside.

It was dark except for the twinkling lights overhead and the pool, glowing in a hypnotic turquoise.

Edward lounged, shirtless, his body gorgeously lit, exposing his scars and burns. He stared for a half minute with a boyish grin before I finally barked:

"Hey! Snap out of it, Marine!"

"You said I could look, didn't you?"

His grin was dazed.

"Holy shit! Your boobs are amazing. Your whole body. Fuck me... I'm in trouble tonight."

He was flustered and just tipsy enough, giving me a terribly naughty idea.

"Did you bring the salt out?" I asked, eyeing the two beers and shots he'd lined up on the table.

"It's still on the counter. Want me to grab it?"

"No," I said smiling. "Give me a minute."

I twirled around, giving Edward a full view of my backside.

Behind me, I heard a tortured, "Ohhh God..."

I returned with limes and a salt shaker, nudging Edward over so I could sit facing him. We flirted for twenty minutes, the tension buzzing between us like a live wire, until I whispered, "Edward, give me your arm."

He obliged hesitantly.

I squeezed lime over his inner wrist before dusting it with salt.

"Put this in your mouth," I ordered, handing him the wedge.

"Allie... oh God, you're not... oh my God, you are... oh... you're trying to kill me," he mumbled as I licked the salt in three long strokes, then downed the shot.

He sat, squirming—instantly hard—staring at me like I'd short-circuited his brain.

"Don't tell me you chickened out on the lime after all that talk?"

He set it on the table, then dropped his face into his hands.

"I can't believe you did that. What happened to no kissing or touching?"

I let him sit in silence.

When he looked up, I smiled, seductively running my tongue over my teeth.

"Love, you're not playing fair."

"Your point?"

He exhaled, subtly adjusting himself. "I'm barely keeping it together here."

I caught the flicker of strain in his eyes—then we both heard the doorbell. He exhaled, visibly relieved.

"That's the food. Do me a favor—close your eyes."

"Why?" I giggled.

"Do you really need to ask?"

"I've seen you before, haven't I?" I teased, biting my lip.

"Yeah... not like this."

He leaned closer, took my wrists gently, and pressed my palms over my eyes.

Seconds later, he muttered, "Okay, you can open now."

I peeked as he walked off, towel riding low on his hips, hands dragging down his face in torment.

He lingered in the kitchen, elbows braced against the counter, head bowed—like he needed a full tactical reset before facing me again.

When he returned, his eyes skimmed my towel, and he smirked. Like we both knew it wouldn't be on long.

* * *

After eating, he turned to me, a dare dancing behind his eyes.

For a moment, neither of us spoke.

Then, softly: "Would you like to go for a swim?"

My heart stuttered. I nodded before I could second-guess it.

Liv was right—I was reckless.

Edward set me on fire.

My inhibitions were dangerously low after drinking tequila, but I ached for Edward—to kiss me, to touch me, to take me—all of me.

I was ready. I wanted to be his.

As he sank into the water, I slipped off my bikini top—and eased in behind him.

In the darkness, it took a moment for it to register.

His eyes went wide.

"Oh my *God*... you look incredible," he said before adding, "But please, love, let's get something on you before you give me a heart attack. I'll grab my shirt."

He scrambled out of the pool and tossed his shirt toward me, eyes closed.

"Please put it on."

"Ugh, you're no fun!"

I pouted, half-teasing—but the look on his face made me pause.

It wasn't just restraint. It was respect.

Thirty seconds later: "Is it on?"

"Yes, sir," I replied as he opened.

"Oh, love," he sighed, reentering the pool—his pale shirt sheer in the glowing water.

"You look beautiful," he murmured, voice thick. "But maybe I should put you to bed before we do something we shouldn't tonight."

He glanced down. "You're igniting every inch of me right now..."

My eyes drifted lower, under the water.

Oh my...

"I can't help it... but I'm worried you won't remember this. Let's get you to bed."

He reached for my hand and led me out of the pool, sitting me on a lounger, still dripping. His shirt clung to me—soaked, translucent, completely useless at hiding anything.

He diverted his eyes fast, mumbling something unintelligible as he grabbed towels.

I peeled off his shirt just as he turned back.

"Oh, you're absolute chaos on tequila!" he sighed. "I love it!"

I winked, giving him a suggestive look that said *come get me.*

He drew a deep breath, a hungry grin spreading across his face.

A second later, he muttered, "I give," and lunged forward, scooping me up in one swift motion.

I squealed—pure exhilaration—as he shoved the slider open and rushed me inside.

In the kitchen, he set me on the cold marble counter.

"Edward—brrrr!" I shivered, nipples tightening.

"Yeah, terrible idea," he laughed. "Bedroom?"

"Yes, please!"

We didn't make it far before he pinned me to the wall.

His body pressed strong into mine, cool and slick.

I gasped, spiraling—out of control with desire.

Logic out the window.

He kissed me like he was starved, lips blazing a trail across my neck, then lower, brushing my shoulder.

My back arched. I ached for more.

His mouth found my breast.

I moaned, dizzy. Breathless. Insides tingling.

I wanted *all* of him. Now.

I pulled the string on my bikini bottoms, letting them fall away. Then his trunks.

My fingers inched lower, sliding around him. He was... flawless.

Well-endowed. Everything I hadn't let myself imagine until that moment.

"Edward," I whispered, body shivering against his chest, "what happened to you putting me to bed?"

He growled low in my ear, "Oh, I'm putting you to bed all right," before he stepped out of his trunks and picked me up, carrying me to the bedroom.

His eyes searched mine as he set me on the bed—asking.

Eyes locked, I nodded.

Then he lowered himself.

His weight on mine. Skin against skin. A tizzy of desire.

He pinned my wrists softly over my head, lips hovering—his face etched in a tenderness I hadn't seen.

I squirmed, anticipation pulsing through me.

"I want you so badly," I whimpered, wriggling one hand free.

I reached for him, stroking him gently...

But he didn't melt.

He froze. Muscles locked tight.

Then—his eyes shifted.

"Shit, what are we doing?"

He looked down at our naked bodies—glistening, tangled—and sat up, breath uneven.

One moment, fire.

The next, fog.

I blinked, disoriented. Cold air prickling where his body had just been.

"What do you mean, 'What are we doing?'"

Didn't he know?

Didn't he want this?

He exhaled, shaking his head.

"Love, you've had too much to drink. I can't—um—we can't do this tonight. Shit, I fucked this up. I want this to be perfect. Please... let me make this perfect."

My chest tightened.

"Edward, you *do* know I'm not a virgin, right?"

"That's disappointing," he teased, brushing hair from my face. "Allie, you matter too much to me to risk this on a night you might forget." He smiled brightly. "Let me take you to the Bahamas this weekend."

"I can't. I'm leaving for Texas."

"Ah, skip it!" he laughed, then flinched. "Fuck! Okay—what if we spend all day together tomorrow? Just us. No distractions. I'll make us breakfast, then we can take the chopper up, maybe spend a few hours at the beach, have dinner poolside... how's that sound?"

"That sounds lovely."

"Good, and then... um, maybe you'll spend the night?" He paused. "I mean, there's no pressure, but if you wanted, we could...?"

I smile slyly. "Edward—why not tonight?"

He shook his head again.

Was I that drunk? I must've seemed it. It was the only explanation. Right?

I tried convincing him to stay. He declined. I tried seducing him. He resisted.

He wanted perfect. So eventually, I gave up.

He tucked me in, kissed me fiercely, then turned to leave, looking torn—like it was physically painful to walk away. Still, he did.

After an hour, his text buzzed:

Party is raging here-surprised? Greg wanted to know how my shirt got soaked at the liquor store. are you good or should I cum check on you later ;-)

I replied:

I'm tucked in where you left me, but if you're worried...

Don't tempt me!

Then:

Breakfast 9am?

Sounds great. Have fun with the guys! Good night handsome! XO

* * *

I lay in bed restless. Heart pounding.

Edward was on my mind day and night—his energy addicting. Infectious.

His presence changed something inside me.

And somewhere in the silence, I knew.

It wasn't butterflies.

Or temptation.

Or adrenaline.

I wasn't falling anymore.

I'd completely fallen.

I was in love.

CHAPTER 36

Adull beat throbbed behind my eyes—not as bad as I'd feared, but worse than I'd hoped.

I didn't care.

I had one thing on my mind: Edward.

My hands trembled with excitement as I packed an overnight bag, adding a risqué lace bra and pair of panties I'd hidden away in my lingerie drawer for years—a set I'd never dared to wear.

It felt like the start of something new.

Something perfect.

* * *

On the quick drive to Bright Sands, I was lightheaded. Not from the tequila—but from sweet anticipation.

Edward and I would finally be together—bodies, hearts, everything.

After months of tension and restraint.

I tingled.

Zack waved as I approached the gate.

"Well, you dodged a bullet last night."

"Oh yeah? What'd I miss?"

"Hmm... drinking, drugs, strippers, fireworks, a flamethrower... flamingos. Thank God there weren't any midgets."

He laughed to himself... *clearly midgets had been involved in a previous party.*

"I bailed around one. Put Sammy in charge. But they partied well past six... oh, I'm getting too old to babysit this crew."

I smiled—then faltered, suddenly aware of appearances... me showing up when no one was working.

"I'm meeting Edward for breakfast."

Zack gave a knowing smile.

"He told me. Enjoy yourselves."

* * *

The mansion looked in order—except for a pair of abandoned swim trunks on the front step.

I rang twice before Greg answered, wearing nothing but an itty-bitty pair of red silkies, beer on his breath.

"Damn, babe! You look smokin' hot this morning! I like what's going on here."

He grinned and hugged me, leaning in to smell my perfume—lips lightly grazing my neck.

"Where were you? You shoulda come!"

"I stayed in," I replied with a half-smile, stepping into what looked like a frat house on spring break.

Cups, cans, and bottles littered the floor.

Three inflatable flamingos slumped lifeless on the couch. A painting tilted sideways. End tables flipped. All casualties of a wild night.

"Damn, the strippers were sooo hot," Greg mumbled before shot-gunning a beer.

I glanced out to the cabana—two scantily clad women passed out.

Tanner lay sprawled between them, completely naked—a large tattoo on his thigh answering my unspoken question about his call sign: Shamrock.

Not exactly my ideal view for breakfast...

As Greg turned away, I tiptoed down the hall.

Everything felt suspended. Golden light. Edward's scent in the air.

I passed the dining room, then the stairs—heart fluttering. Somewhere in the silence, I imagined him waiting. Shirtless. Smiling. Coffee in hand.

Then I heard it.

A muffled giggle.

A woman's voice—soft, intimate, close.

I froze where I was. Just in time to see her.

Naked.

Sauntering out of Edward's bedroom.

Dress in hand. Messy sex hair. Lips curled in a nauseating smirk.

My body locked. I couldn't move. Couldn't breathe.

No. Please, no...

I prayed he wouldn't see me. Willed myself invisible.

But it was too late.

His door swung wider.

Our eyes met.

Pain slammed through me.

"Fuck me... Allie, wait!"

He grabbed for my arm as I turned down the hallway.

"Allie, please—hold on!"

I wrenched free, staggering back like I'd taken a punch.

My whole body braced for the blow—humiliation, betrayal, rage.

I sucked in a sharp breath.

"You could've slept with me last night—but you fucked a stripper instead? What the hell is wrong with you?!"

"I didn't."

"Yeah, I'm *sure*."

I started walking away, but he caught my hips and pushed me into the dining room.

"Get your hands off me!" I shrieked.

He backed off immediately. "Shit. Allie—listen to me for a minute. I swear I didn't touch her."

"Then what happened? She was in your room. Naked!"

"She tried to give me head, but I was drunk and passed out. I asked her to leave when I noticed her on my couch."

I stared at him, pulse hammering—holding venom on my tongue—sharp and rising.

Edward scratched his head. "Wait—are you still upset?"

"Are you *fucking* kidding me?" I gasped. "Why wouldn't I be?"

"Nothing happened."

"So, nothing happened—except you were going to let her give you a *blow job*?"

My body trembled with hurt and fury.

"Seriously? That's your defense?" I blinked, stunned by his audacity. "Why didn't you just call me?"

He squinted. "Love, I'd never ask you for that."

"Edward. Explain. Now."

"Head's different—transactional. For hookers and escorts... and slutty girls. I'd never ask you for... *that*."

"You can't be serious!"

"I am."

My chest tightened. "Are you retarded?"

He scrunched his face, clearly still intoxicated. "Uhhh... I must not be explaining this right. You're actually upset?"

"Now you're just mocking me."

"No, Allie—"

I held up a hand, voice low and shaking. "Don't."

"I—"

"I thought I meant something to you. I'm leaving."

"Wait! What can I do?"

"Nothing! I stupidly thought we were in a relationship. I assumed that meant you wouldn't have strippers giving you blow jobs behind my back."

I moved toward the door, disgust curdling to disappointment... and something uglier. Shame, maybe. For letting myself believe he cared for me. Loved me.

"Clearly, I was wrong. That's my fault for being so naive."

He flinched. "I think we're talking past each other, love. We *are* in a relationship. I wouldn't even consider sleeping with another woman. Honest to God."

"Are you seriously this clueless? Have you never been in a relationship before?"

"You know I haven't!"

Realizing he'd nearly shouted, he lowered his voice.

"Allie, you know I'm used to doing whatever I want, whenever the fuck I want. This is... *new*."

"New?"

"Well, it categorically didn't happen. But even if it had, I didn't think it would be a big deal."

"So, we're exclusive... but blow jobs don't count as cheating?"

He started to nod yes—caught my look—and quickly changed his answer.

I glared. "Edward, we're too far apart on this. This isn't going to work."

He grabbed my arm—softer, more pleading. "Please. Let me shower and make you breakfast. Then you can name your terms."

"Terms? Relationships shouldn't need terms like this."

"Apparently ours does. Love... *please*. I'm willing to concede almost anything you want. But I need to know what we're talking about. Give me ten minutes."

* * *

I considered walking out right then. I should've.

But I sat. *Waiting*.

Because a small part of me still hoped he'd fight for me.

But the longer I waited, the more dangerous the silence, the clarity.

The more obvious it became:

A future with a man like Edward—a billionaire playboy with no rules—

no matter how thrilling, how addictive—

might always be just out of reach.

Even *if* he agreed to my terms...

* * *

He returned in slacks and a collared shirt.

The naked girls were gone. The kitchen cleaned. The chaos erased.

It had clearly been all-hands-on-deck. I wondered which of the guys helped—and whether they knew Edward had hidden me in the dining room.

I spotted the celebratory bottle of champagne I'd brought and cursed it under my breath before popping it anyway. I filled a flute, hands shaky. Trying not to spill. Or cry.

But my heart ached.

I considered myself a forgiving person, but was what Edward did forgivable?

I thought of Blake. The first time he cheated—during his bachelor party. The misfired text that gave it all away.

The same script with a different man.

Eventually, I found the nerve to speak.

"Edward, you ruined something I thought was so perfect. You know I've been cheated on... and maybe you thought it was okay because I never left him, but—"

I managed a deep breath.

"This devastates me."

I wanted to leave—I even tried—but Edward wrapped me in a hug from behind, holding my hand and kissing my fingers.

"Love, it was never my intent to hurt you. Please tell me what I can do to fix this."

"I don't know. Say you're sorry?"

He spun me around. "Allie, I won't apologize for something I didn't do."

"She was in your room!"

"Nothing happened. Why won't you believe me?"

"Can't you say you're sorry for letting it get that far?"

I stared at him, searching for guilt. Regret.

But all I saw was a blankness, like the wires weren't connecting.

Like he truly didn't get it.

I pushed him away gently, placing my hand over my forehead.

The day was supposed to have been a romantic start to 'us' but instead, all my hopes of our future had been almost instantly destroyed.

Then it dawned on me—if I *hadn't* seen him with the stripper...

Would he have mentioned it?

Maybe the day was a blessing in disguise.

* * *

He sat me next to the window overlooking the ocean.

The water glinted behind the glass. Waves crashed in a cathartic lull.

I didn't know if we were salvaging something—or saying goodbye.

He smiled shyly from across the table before tapping on a notepad.

"Allie, name your terms."

"This is ridiculous."

I couldn't believe I was still there.

"I know. But I want us to build a relationship. I need to know what that means to you. Tell me what's off-limits."

Chapter 37

I stared at the blank page in front of him. The space between us tense. Exposing.

Less than twelve hours ago, he'd kissed me like he'd chosen me. But now he couldn't even understand why I was upset. I wanted to scream. Instead, I crossed my arms.

Edward waited—pen poised, eyes sharp—like we were negotiating a postwar treaty.

In reality, it was a sex contract.

He expected me to name my relationship terms.

Like that was normal.

Like fidelity was somehow optional.

Like I was the problem.

Anger rose fast—but under it, a deeper ache—the kind I felt in my bones.

"I can't believe you're going to make me say some of these things," I muttered. "You should've known a stripper sleeping naked in your room would be a breach of trust. It's common sense."

"Humor me, okay? I haven't had a girlfriend since college—and that wasn't exactly healthy."

I sat in my own pained silence before: "Sure. No naked girls. On your lap. In your room. In your pool. On your boat. Anywhere."

Then slow: "Absolutely no blow jobs or hand jobs."

He stopped mid-scribble, eyes lifting from the paper. A flicker of confusion—or disbelief.

I repeated, slower. "No blow jobs or hand jobs—is that going to be a problem for you?"

He blinked. "No."

I stared him down, almost daring him to challenge me before he nodded. "Got it."

"Good. No sex of any kind. That means no threesomes or orgies."

"That's fine."

"And no suggestive contact or lap dances."

Edward raised a finger. "Wait—no lap dances? But what if—"

"If *what?*"

"Nothing," he mumbled, putting his pen back to paper. "Continue."

"Thank you. No late-night phone calls. No sexting. No 'emotional intimacy' loopholes."

I took a deep breath.

"That's it?" he asked.

I shrugged. "I'm probably missing some stupid billionaire-specific category of misconduct. But those are the big ones. Use your best judgment on the rest."

He glanced up. "So... what about parties? Like last night. If there's nudity or dancers, am I not permitted to attend?"

Was he serious?

"Edward, last night's why we—"

"Fine, no parties." He paused, formulating his next question. "But what if a buddy invites me on his yacht and there are... I don't know, let's say... orgies?"

I froze.

My God.

"Okay—amendment: if there are naked women or orgies, you leave. Or better yet—you don't go in the first place."

He looked slightly wounded. "Even if I don't participate?"

"Edward, if you're asking me to clarify what 'no orgies' means, we've got bigger problems than I thought."

"No nudity or orgies. Noted."

His flippant tone made my stomach knot.

I turned away, gazing at the ocean as my mind tried to escape, heart sinking.

He opened his mouth again, then closed it. "Never mind."

After reviewing the list one last time, he said, "The lap dance rule confuses me, and avoiding nude women will be tough—but if you insist, I won't argue. I'll just have to tell the guys."

He half-smiled before signing and dating the bottom of the page. "I agree to your terms—all of them—effective now."

Then he ridiculously folded the page and slid it into his back pocket.

"Why'd you do that?" I asked, flatly—with an overwhelming sense I was in some sort of warped reality.

"I'm keeping it as a reminder. Allie, I feel awful for upsetting you. I want you to know I'll stand by these promises."

Edward's hand crept onto my thigh. Not tender. Not affectionate.

Like he thought touching me could erase what he'd done.

I stiffened, then quickly pushed it away, throat tightening as I stood to leave.

"Love, I'm trying to fix this."

The way he said *love* suddenly killed me—it sounded more like a nickname than a word he understood. He truly didn't get it.

I shook my head. "Sex isn't going to fix anything. I'm heading home... please don't call when I'm in Texas. I need space to think."

"Allie, what else can I do? I'll do anything," he pleaded with a hint of panic. And for the first time—real desperation.

Instead of softening me, it irked me.

"You know what? I've had this spiny sense for weeks that something about this was just too good. And here we are. You confirmed it all this morning."

My tone was bitter. Ugly. Unlike me, but I was wounded to the core.

I looked around.

Half a bottle of champagne sweated on the counter.

Risqué lingerie waited in my bag by the door.

The sex contract creased and folded in his pocket.

I left all three behind—fairy tale dead—and walked out.

He followed, sulking, hugging me before I reached my car—causing something to crack—fast and uncontrollable—splintering every emotion I'd fought to hold together.

Tears blurred my vision.

The kind I couldn't stop.

The realization hit hard as I pulled away: I wasn't even his girlfriend.

Still—I sobbed like I'd been betrayed.

CHAPTER 38

I spent all night grieving the fairy tale I'd mistaken for reality.

By dawn, I accepted it for what it had always been:

A fantasy—too-good-to-be-true.

I threw on oversized sunglasses, yoga pants, and a light jacket—camouflaging my heartbreak—and headed to the airport. Texas bound.

The hangar was quiet when I arrived, the sky illuminating with a soft sunrise.

A single Gulfstream sat glinting on the tarmac.

Cody leaned against his truck, sipping coffee and smoking a cigarette.

"You look like shit," he said, grinning.

"Thanks, I feel it... how long's the flight?"

"Eh, about three hours. Wheels up in thirty." He tapped his Bluetooth. "Hold on, I gotta take this."

I drifted toward a picnic table, headphones in, watching planes vanish into a pink cotton-candy sky.

The hangar buzzed as the guys loaded crates and gear—but no one asked me to help.

Greg just blew me a kiss, flexed a bicep, and said, "I got you, babe."

I was in no mood to argue.

* * *

"Hey, pretty lady! Glad to see your smiling face this morning!"

I stood to greet Tank as he quickly wrapped me in a bear hug.

"Heard you had a bad day yesterday."

"Yeah, you could say that."

"Well, before I forget, Ed sent you a gift."

Good grief.

I rolled my eyes. "Whatever it is, I don't want it."

"Yep, he told me you'd say that." Tank offered me a box with a disarming smile.

I examined it for a split second before it registered.

"He's giving me a gun? Seriously? Ugh, what an idiot!"

He smirked as he opened the case. "It's a tricked-out custom Glock 19. Not a bad piece, if you ask me. What do you think?"

"I think you can tell him to shove it."

He chuckled. "Yeah, but he bought it for you a few weeks ago. Was just waiting for the right time. You know he's been crushing hard."

"Did he tell you what—?" My voice broke.

Tank nodded. "Yep... I'm afraid so."

Then: "Hey, let me finish loading. Let's talk on the flight."

"I'm not sure I want to talk."

I frowned dramatically before he squeezed my shoulder.

"I know. But who else are you gonna spill tea to, other than your bestest friend?"

* * *

Tank dropped into the seat next to me.

I lowered my glasses revealing sad, tear-stained eyes.

"Aw, Allie. You poor thing. For the record, I'm on your side. What he did? Way outside acceptable—for any normal person."

"Thanks."

"Yeah, but... Ed's not normal. He plays by a totally different set of rules than us peasants. I mean, he might seem normal sometimes, but he's not. It's an uber rich person thing. You can't avoid it. They're all a little... off, you know?"

He made a crazy hand gesture.

"That's what I'm starting to realize."

"Yeah, his godfather screwed him up pretty bad."

Tank glanced toward the window, weighing how much to say, then turned back to me.

"Hey, it doesn't mean you can't be with him. You just need to be prepared for stuff that's not normal. Hang with his friends. You'll see it... drug use, total disregard for human life, scary sexual stuff."

Tank looked around then lowered his voice.

"I'm gonna tell you something about Ed. He'll kill me if he finds out, so you can't repeat it. To anyone."

I nodded.

"So, um... things don't always work right for Ed. Down there."

He gestured vaguely.

"You should've seen him a year after getting blown up. He had a rocky recovery. Didn't expect to be with a woman again. And that's a hard thing for a guy, especially a guy like Ed, you know?"

"I had no idea."

"Yeah. He never talks about it. But I think that's why... uh... I think that's why the thing with the stripper seems so normal. I swear, he'll kill me if he finds out I told you. But he did a lot of that when he was trying to get things back to 'operational.' The guy hasn't been with anyone he's cared about in, oooh, more than ten years... uhhh, maybe longer. I know that for a fact."

Suddenly, I felt almost guilty. "Seriously?"

"Think about it. When you're the world's most sought-after billionaire, there's a lot of pride. He doesn't want to be spending an evening with pretty ladies in his social circle that might talk about his burns or tell their girlfriends he doesn't work."

I let the hum of the jet engines fill the silence—absorbing.

"That's just how things are. And I'm not telling you to cut him any slack. The opposite. If you're planning to... well, be a couple or whatever, you need to lay the law. Bolt the rules to the floor!"

"It's just insane to me. He didn't think blow jobs counted as cheating? On what planet?"

Tank chuckled. "His own."

"Is he going to be into threesomes or...?"

Tank snorted. "I mean, if you're asking whether he's participated..." He shrugged, his eyes telling me all I needed to know. "Doesn't mean he'll ask you to get into any of that. You're a different ball game."

"Am I overreacting? He said he didn't get a blow job, and I want to believe him—but the whole thing was such a breach of trust."

"Oooh, yeah, I don't know... if my ex-wife, *when* I loved her, did something like that, hell no! Damn, she was a nightmare. Took everything I owned while me and Ed were deployed. Even my brand-new Mustang."

With a smile, he added, "Look, if you can get past this, I'd try. Ed's got a big heart and he'll treat you like a queen. If you can't, well... he might throw himself off a bridge. But that won't be your fault."

I smiled bleakly.

"Let him sweat it out a while before you decide..."

"I wanted to think he was perfect."

"Yeah... he's not. Not even close. But, if it helps, he's *stupid* rich." Tank grinned.

"And I know your hubby's got money, but Ed's got *real* money. Like top hundred in the world kinda money... might help you get past some of his more serious quirks."

Tank was right. Edward had quirks—from his sexual past to his involvement in the deep and dark world of human trafficking.

If we ended up together, I was terrified I'd be conceding my normalcy for his.

"Thanks, Tank." I touched his knee. "One more question for you."

"We have the whole flight, little lady. Keep 'em coming."

"You saw the photo, right? The one of me and Edward... *kissing*. Do you think he set it up?"

"Oh yeah... Cody sent it to me." He paused. "Well, he mighta been the one that took it... but you didn't hear that from me."

"What?" I gasped—yanking at my seat belt, ready to stomp my way to the front of the plane and give Cody an earful.

Cody? Really?

He was scrappy, but I'd learned to trust him.

Tank abruptly put his hand on mine, tugging me back. "Uh... maybe not. I've been wrong once or twice." He grinned. "Total speculation on my part, so no firing squad just yet."

I exhaled hard, trying to contain the anger rising in my chest.

"But back to your question. Knowing Ed, yeah, he orchestrated it... and I'd bet he's already sent it *anonymously* to your hubby, so he's somewhere seeing red. Be prepared for that."

I gritted my teeth, dragging a hand down my face as I sank deeper into the seat, groaning.

"Great. Something to look forward to."

Outside, clouds drifted—bright white against blue. Inside, everything felt sad and gray.

"Why does he hate Blake so much?" I asked quietly. "Do you know?"

Tank leaned forward. "Unconfirmed, but I think he's got some decent dirt on him. Don't know the full extent, but Ed almost pulled him over to Bright Sands a few years back then changed his mind real fast."

"Interesting. I didn't know that." I tilted my head, watching him. "So... what do you think of Blake? And please be honest. It won't hurt my feelings."

He sucked in a breath. "Oooh, well... he's a decent operator. A good in a gunfight kinda guy. But he's not much of a team player, you know? I don't have a personal rub, but plenty of the guys do. There've been some scuffles."

"Yeah... that doesn't surprise me." I looked down at my lap. "It's weird. We've been apart more than we've been together. Part of me feels like I barely know him anymore. He's so angry and—"

"Violent?"

Tank didn't know the half of it... I just nodded.

Tank's voice softened as he looked me squarely in the eye.

"Hey... if you decide to leave him... Ed'll catch you. I guarantee it."

I stared out the window, sunlight glinting off the wing.

A memory came crashing back: Blake's phone buzzing at 2 a.m., face down on the nightstand. A woman's name I didn't recognize on the screen—with an X-rated photo and the words: *Wanting you.*

Blake caught me once, and I thought it was love.

But all he did was control my life.

I wasn't sure I needed Edward to *catch* me.

I wanted him to see me. To love me.

To let me be *me.*

I smiled, faintly. "Now you're trying to sway me."

Tank grinned, leaning back in his seat.

"He's an upgrade, no? We all heard about Blake getting booted from ground. The guy's a womanizer and you're never gonna change him."

He paused, letting the statement fully land.

And it did.

"You've learned to deal with his shenanigans, but should you have to?"

Tank was right. I couldn't change Blake.

I knew I shouldn't have to... but I was worried Edward wasn't much better.

I shook my head.

"I feel like an idiot for assuming we were something."

"I mean, from how he talks about you, it's obvious you're an item." Tank shrugged. "I'm not sure you need to label it."

I nodded, working up the courage to ask more about Edward's past—especially his experience with hookers. Tank gave it to me straight—no sugarcoating—and at one point, I physically covered my ears.

"Ah, I'm good now!"

He chuckled. "Well, if that freaks you out, don't ask Greg about sex—ever—cuz he's kinky. Way crazier than Ed."

"Oh God. Please don't tell me anymore!"

As I glanced at Tank, something clicked.

I wasn't just torn between two men.

I was torn between two worlds.

In Blake's world, appearances mattered more than reality. I was a trophy—his wife in photos. At galas. A prop for a potential political career.

I'd mastered that role.

And over the years, I'd outgrown it.

It wasn't for me anymore.

He wasn't for me anymore.

And Edward?

Edward's world was intriguing. Dangerous.

Perfect for an operator.

As far as I could tell, he'd built a life based on money, charm, and brilliance.

But was it for me?

Maybe it was just another illusion—another world shaped by seduction and control.

I'd convinced myself Edward was somehow different from Blake. That he saw me.

Wanted me for me—a woman with strong conviction, determined to make the world a better place.

But what if the only real difference between them was... more money?

Maybe I'd be just another woman on his arm at fundraisers. A name he muttered during toasts.

Shrinking to his personality...

Smiling on cue for cameras.

A slightly different filter on the same privileged life.

I didn't want to keep performing.

I wanted a life I could actually live.

One where I was finally free to be myself.

* * *

I folded my arms, suddenly anxious—like I'd been holding my breath for miles.

I needed a reset. To change the topic.

No more Edward. No more Greg. No more sex.

I forced a half-smile. "I'm done talking about Edward and Greg. Let's talk about you."

Tank grinned modestly.

"Why do you work at Dark Skies instead of Bright Sands?" I asked.

Tank gave a small laugh, but he didn't miss the tension in my voice.

He probably thought I was nervous about getting into Greg's kinky sex life.

I let him.

"I love Ed, but I have a tough time dealing with his crap—and it puts less stress on our friendship this way. I still get to hear about the cringe-worthy shit he and Cody and Greg do without having to live it."

He sighed, tone shifting. "Ed pulled me out of that Humvee. Saved my life. I owe him. One day he asked me to set up shop at Dark Skies—to back Mike up, be his eyes and ears, and that's what I'm doing. I'll be at Dark Skies as long as he needs."

Then he leaned back, thoughtful.

"You know, I checked him into rehab the day after he got the Silver Star. He was popping painkillers, doing hardcore drugs, drinking vodka like water. We all were, I guess—but everything hit him harder. He couldn't stand. Couldn't sleep. Needed help to do basic shit. He's lucky he got back on track."

Tank shrugged.

"Hasn't let me pay for a thing since."

"*Really?*"

"Not a phone bill or a plane ticket. Not even dinner. Pays every penny of my mom's Alzheimer's care. When my kid brother died... he was just there."

"Wow."

It didn't seem like generosity for show. It was deeper—rooted in love and loyalty.

And it didn't match the version of Edward I'd built in my head over the past twenty-four hours.

The player. The master manipulator. The billionaire who broke hearts.

"That's how good a friend he is. Yeah, it's easy to give shit away when you're stupid rich—but I knew him before he got his own fortune. He was generous and humble. Would've given you the shirt off his back, no questions asked. Hell, he almost gave his life for mine."

Tank's voice broke.

And just like that, we'd circled back to Edward.

I wanted out of that orbit.

I reached for Tank's arm, my fingers stopping on the tattoo of his brother's face.

"I've never heard the full story," I said. "Tank, what happened to him?"

He exhaled, gaze distant. "Poor kid was hit in the neck his first month in Afghanistan—ricochet round. Bled out before anyone even noticed."

My eyes filled. Death could be so cruel.

He stared at the floor, then grasped my hand—hard.

"Oh hun, I'm so sorry."

"It kills me. If I hadn't made it out of that Humvee... they'd have never let him enlist." He cleared his throat. "Sometimes I wish I could go back. Still haunts me. Kid should've had a full life."

"It's not your fault."

We sat in silence before:

"Yeah, dad stopped cancer treatment after that. Died about four months later. Then Mom finally got the surgery she'd been putting off to care for him... and it messed her up bad. She's never been the same."

He rubbed the back of his neck.

"Needed round-the-clock care after she almost burned the house down. Poor Mama Vincent." His voice softened. "Ed's been so good to her. Visits her every birthday and holiday."

Then he cracked the slightest grin. "Oh, but she loves herself some Cody, too."

I smiled, holding his gaze—and hand—realizing how small my troubles really were.

Edward. Blake.

None of it compared.

CHAPTER 39

There was an unmarked van waiting for us—keys on the dash—at the bare-bones airstrip. After loading up, we drove an hour to a sprawling 300,000-acre property—stark terrain under endless clouds and blue sky.

Once we passed the exterior gate, we kept driving... and driving.

The compound itself was mostly dirt roads and scattered cactus. Empty drums and rusted-out vehicles served as the only landmarks, like a post-apocalyptic Western.

I'd been to the compound before in a previous life—but this time was different. I was older, wiser... and more focused on survival. Not schmoozing.

Dust kicked up as we rolled into the checkpoint for the interior compound thirty minutes later—the first pavement we'd seen in miles.

Ahead, several acres were scattered with outbuildings and Porta-Johns, beat-up trucks and SUVs in every make and model, a dozen shipping containers retrofitted as bunkrooms, and giant "Rattlesnake Warning" signs every fifty feet.

While the guys bunked together, I was assigned my own room— one of the perks of being the only female.

In reality, it wasn't a huge perk considering the 'room' was a converted CONEX box with plywood floors and zero cell service—but I appreciated the privacy.

And I needed the space.

That night, teams from all over—some foreign—tore around the track. We watched them slide, drift, and burn rubber under floodlights.

It looked like a blast.

I hadn't been to a driving course in years and couldn't wait to get after it the next morning before the brutal west Texas sun made off-roading without A/C unbearable.

* * *

Before bed, Tank summoned me to Cody and Greg's container.

I assumed it was a quick team brief until I stepped in and the guys fell silent—the vibe quickly transitioning to somber as my cheerfulness faded to anxiety.

"What is this?" I asked, eyes locking on Tank—hoping for a clue.

He shrugged apologetically as Cody crossed his arms.

"Doll, you ever killed anybody?"

Greg coughed, covering his face before Tank elbowed him.

He let out a loud, "Ow," then the container returned to silence.

All of them standing there. Looking at me. Waiting for my answer.

I understood what was going on.

I'd even suspected something like this was coming.

"You're seriously making me kill someone to patch in?"

Greg giggled from the corner, this time failing to hide it.

Cody glared at him before: "Look, for this to work, we need trust. We've gotta have some dirt on you so we know you're never gonna talk about the shit we do."

I exhaled. "Okay, well, spit it out. Who do I have to kill?"

The question slipped off my tongue like I'd already accepted the challenge before I had a chance to second-guess it.

Was I capable of murder?

Yeah, but it was wholly dependent on the target.

Terrorists, pedophiles, and rapists—easy day. Anyone else... I wasn't sure.

Tank started, "Whoa, whoa—" before Greg interjected.

"Nah, babe, it's super chill."

He pulled a small pouch from his cargo pocket then grinned.

"Nobody's getting murked tonight. You just gotta take shrooms with us."

I squinted, skeptical. I had no intention of ever using my security clearance again. I could theoretically do drugs whenever I wanted. And the guys did them all the time when they partied—pot, Ecstasy, even coke. I didn't condone it, but I didn't judge them, either.

"That's the test? Drugs?"

"Yeah, but have you done drugs?" Cody asked, a knowing smirk spreading across his face.

"Not illegal ones," I muttered.

In hindsight, my moral high ground—that the drugs I'd done weren't technically illegal—was laughable.

I'd once popped Ambien like Tic Tacs. Borrowed Adderall from friends. Scored pills under fake names in foreign countries.

But never *real* drugs. Not the kind the agency tested for.

If it came in a bottle with a name that matched my alias, it didn't count...

I chuckled as Greg handed me a few shriveled pieces of mushroom.

"You're serious?" I asked, still half-convinced they were fucking with me—until he passed them around like communion wafers.

"Totally for real. Our team leader used to kidnap us and take us down to Mexico, then force us to trip on shrooms and record it so he had dirt on us. Made us pretty fucking loyal." Greg grinned. "We're just continuing the tradition... you're welcome."

He winked, then added: "Zack's standing by next door if we need him—but, we won't. We're taking just enough to chill out and have fun. Nothing psychedelic."

I sighed. "Uh... okay."

It sounded like a terrible idea, but what the hell?

I popped it in my mouth and crossed my fingers.

* * *

An hour in, something in me shifted. My stress melted. Happiness bubbled like champagne. I was lighter. Warm. My body almost humming with the music.

Colors glowing.

Laughter sparkling.

Even my thoughts felt more fluid.

"I feel so... floaty," I said, eyes exploring the container walls.

"Just a body high, babe," Greg smiled. "Super normal."

He tickled my side then grabbed my hand.

I nodded, eyes closed, letting music wash over me.

* * *

I woke in my dusty room, the smell of stale cigarettes still hanging in the air—a holdover from the previous occupant.

It was pitch black inside.

I flipped the light and sat up. Gear already laid out.

Ready to face the day.

Bits of the night flickered: Sammy's laugh. Cody's stupid playlist. Tank's watchful eyes. Greg's hands.

I hadn't felt much other than a buzz and suspected Greg gave me a purposefully small dose, which made me think:

Maybe the real test wasn't about the trip.

Maybe it was about the choice.

Trusting them and joining them against logic and my instincts.

Thank God no one handed me a gun.

* * *

We spent the day tearing up the off-road course—rock-crawling, bottoming-out, hauling ass, and even winching and digging one of our vehicles out of a soft sand wash not once—but three times—thanks to Cody.

And as we drove around laughing and joking, I realized I was *in*—an irrefutable member of the team, for better or worse. A membership fully independent of my relationship with Edward.

Doing shrooms with the guys consummated bonds of loyalty and trust, and a strengthened sense of camaraderie. Even family.

The feeling hit hard and deep.

For years, I'd told myself I was good on my own.

But being alone had been slowly killing me.

Being *in* meant more than I wanted to admit.

* * *

Greg and I ended up alone in a team room that evening as we waited for the rest of the guys to get cleaned up.

He'd spent the better part of the day as my co-pilot and hadn't stopped talking once.

If he wasn't talking about his favorite topic—sex—or his second favorite topic—working out—he was talking about guns and ammo and flashlights and gear and *haute horlogerie.*

Then boats and cars and real estate and Bitcoin and military history.

For a guy I'd initially assumed a dumb operator, he was a walking encyclopedia on a much longer list of topics than I'd given him credit.

Surprisingly intelligent. And annoyingly sweet.

"Allieeeeeee," he sang, barging in with a twelve pack—already half in the bag.

"Ready to get this party started?"

He handed me a beer and offered a quick toast: "To crazy nights and poor decisions."

Then: "I heard you might need a new guy. I know you think I'm simple, but I swear—I'll make your wildest dreams come true!"

I virtually spit out my beer.

Wildest seemed to be the key term.

Clearly he'd needed some liquid courage to approach the topic.

I smirked. "Wow, Greg, coming in a little hot, don't you think?"

"For an operator? *Nah.* I'll buy you a badass diamond and we can lock this down in Vegas at the end of the week."

He grinned as I laughed.

"Babe, I can't compete with Ed's money, but I've gotta few mil saved. I could buy us a beach house somewhere and we could just fucking relax for the next forty years with a boat and a buncha kids. Not a bad way to go."

He lifted his shoulders. "Plus, with all this chemistry, our sex is gonna be absolute fire!"

I giggled. "That's a tempting offer, Greg. *Very* tempting."

"I'm not kidding! Forget Ed! Damn, I'll even give you a test drive if you're up for it."

I felt a tingle in my cheeks as he playfully pumped his hips and blew a cute kiss.

"I know you wanna say yes. How could you not? I can tell you're super into me."

He was hard to read. *Was he messing with me or trying to conceal raw emotion and vulnerability with shock and awe?*

I should've stopped him right there... but a small sliver of me was curious about the Greg underneath the bravado.

"Um, well, Greg, you've got a decent pitch, and I'm tickled. It's not a definite no, but it's unlikely."

"Okay, scrap getting married. How 'bout just a fucking awesome rebound sesh? I'll be the best fuck of your life, *guaranteed.*"

"Oh." I fidgeted in my chair.

"Hold up, I'll give you a preview."

Greg's fingers grazed the hem of his T-shirt, teasing it upward, slow and theatrical. Then, in a practiced pull, he tugged it over his head.

I gulped.

Damn. Why had I not checked Greg out properly?

Every muscle was flawlessly sculpted, his body physical perfection.

Raw, athletic power.

My God.

I tried not to stare. Then I stared harder. Then I gave up completely.

My gaze dragged over his body.

Greg was nearly dripping with sex as he posed like a male centerfold.

Petrifyingly sexy.

An American flag tattooed on his chiseled pec.

A cluster of puckered scars—bullet wounds—on his rippling abs.

A Recon Jack on his perfectly contoured bicep.

Two pistols tattooed at his waistband... his obliques luring my eyes further down... I caught myself biting my lip.

"So, uh... those pistols—do they, um, go all the way downtown... or...?"

My voice cracked mid-sentence—like I'd never seen washboard abs before.

"Oh yeahhh..."

He began unbuckling his belt.

I waved my hands. "Oh no! You don't need to show me!"

"All good. Part of the 'know before you buy' preview."

He swiftly unbuttoned his jeans, letting them fall to the floor—eyes locked on me as he watched my reaction.

He wasn't wearing any underwear. And he was *massive.*

My jaw unhinged—equal parts stunned, horrified, and—unfortunately—impressed.

I'd never seen anything like it. Like him. The whole package was... new territory.

I clamped a hand over my mouth—not to scream, but to keep from laughing—as he licked his lips.

I was still unintentionally gawking when Cody walked in seconds later.

Greg yelled, "Sup, bro!"—standing completely naked.

Cody did a double take.

"What the fuck's going on here? Bro, put that away!"

"Uh, Greg was just showing me his tattoos."

I laughed, too loud, as Greg shook his hips.

He really didn't care what people thought. And I kind of admired that.

Why hadn't I looked away yet?

"If you wanna see this BWC at full attention, blow him a kiss."

With a wink, he added: "I'm a grower."

He was already giant. How much bigger could he possibly get?

I couldn't stop staring... oh my...

"What's BWC?" I asked as Cody tapped me on the shoulder, pulling me from my daze.

Greg grunted, a twinkle in his eye, moving toward me. A smile from ear-to-ear.

"Aww, you're so stinkin' cute. Come here!"

Cody extended his arm in an arm bar.

"Yeah, no! That's a sure way to get yourself fucking disappeared by Ed," he warned.

Edward. My stomach lurched. I could picture his face if he were to walk in.

Wounded. Disappointed. Even furious.

But that wasn't enough to stop me—or Greg.

Undeterred, he took another step.

Cody yelled, "Hey! I said *no* and I'm not fucking kidding. Keep your hands to yourself."

Then he turned to me. "But the guy's got an impressive *big white cock*, huh?"

I nodded timidly as Greg beamed. "Top ten percent of the top one percent *in the world*. Verified. Requires an ops brief."

He bit his lip, then lowered his voice. "Think you can handle me?"

"*Ohhh*," was all I could manage.

What was it about Greg that suddenly had me hot and bothered?

His body? My loneliness? Or revenge?

I was tempted, sure.

But not enough to hurt Edward back—not really.

Still, Greg would've made it easy.

Cody snapped, "Okay. Time to put it away before Zack shows up and fucking handcuffs you to your bed—*again*. And, please, leave Allie alone so Ed doesn't murk you the next time we go out. You know what he's capable of."

"Yeah, whatevs, bro."

Greg took his time getting dressed as Cody sat next to me sipping a beer.

"He's something else," I whispered.

"You shoulda seen him Friday. He was so hyped. The wheels in that dumb head started spinning and he started talking about proposing and shit."

"Oh, well, he actually already did..."

"Tell me he didn't give you a ring," Cody said flatly.

"Thankfully, no. But I feel bad for laughing at him."

"Don't! He's a fucking handful. You wouldn't believe the shit I gotta bail him out of. He's like my dumbass younger brother. Although that dumbass is *already* in prison."

A bonding moment with Cody.

"My loser brother's also in prison. Serving a life sentence. What'd yours do?"

"What?! You haven't heard? Well, shit..."

Cody howled enthusiastically, then readjusted in his chair.

"So, we're joyriding one of Ed's friend's dope sports cars one night in L.A. and I get pulled over for some bullshit like not coming to a complete stop or something, and the cop rolls up, takes my license, and before we know it, me, Greg, and Ed are being held at gunpoint with a helicopter fucking spotlighting us and I'm getting hauled off and arrested."

I gasped.

Cody laughed out loud. "Well, get this—cop tells me I'm wanted for multiple murders, gun running, a shit ton of other charges from all over. I'm telling this dude up and down I'm innocent and Ed's like, 'Whoa, bud. What the fuck?'"

"Not a fucking clue what the hell this cop's talking about, but sure as shit, my older brother's been using *my* fucking identity since I got outta the Marine Corps cuz he didn't think I'd ever notice or something. Had a dozen warrants out for his arrest—*my* arrest."

"Oh jeez..."

"Greg and Ed started calling me Con Man after that. It stuck."

"That's wild."

"Yeah. Not as hard core as Greg's L.A. story—that one's... rough." He paused. "His number one stupidest idea ever. Doll, note of advice, stay clear of L.A. It's the devil's playground."

Greg grabbed beer from the mini fridge and joined us—thankfully with all his clothes.

"Whatcha talking about now?" he asked.

"All your dumbass ideas."

Cody proceeded to provide color commentary on Greg's top five stupidest ideas—three out of five involving sex tapes—as Greg played along, butting in to make corrections—though they didn't help much.

His second stupidest idea? Making a sex tape with his CO's daughter.

He giggled. "Yeah, that'll get you kicked off a team pretty quick."

I had a sinking suspicion it was one of Major General Smith's daughters, if not the same daughter whose kids he'd rescued down in El Salvador...

The three of us laughed until the beers were gone.

But I couldn't ignore reality.

If I wanted to keep this wild, twisted family... Edward came with it.

There was no Bright Sands without him.

Chapter 40

We climbed into the van just after seven, worn out and starving, ready to blow off steam the only way we knew how: beer and bar food.

Zack took the wheel, music low, while Cody passed around road sodas like it was protocol. He handed me one with a wink as I wedged myself into the very back—accepting my fate.

Greg jumped in beside me, already shirtless and buzzed, cracked a beer and yelled, "Let's goooo!" as if we were headed to a bachelor party instead of a local dive bar—the only restaurant within an hour's drive.

A place built for the spooky types that passed through like the weather.

A friend of Zack's owned it—and the town—population fifty.

Just enough people to run the safe houses, off-grid training sites, and hush-hush projects.

And all the land as far as you could see.

Not that outsiders ever would.

The whole property was blurred on satellite imagery.

* * *

We rolled in loud, hungry—then ordered beer, food, and settled in like locals in a town that didn't officially exist.

I was halfway through a basket of greasy fries when Greg leaned across the table—eyes glassy, grin wide—and came in for a kiss.

I caught him by the chest and gently pushed him back.

Across from us, Zack stiffened. His gaze faltered, like he'd seen a ghost.

Sammy choked awkwardly mid-sip, coughing beer down his shirt.

From the bar, I spotted Cody mumble, shake his head, and nudge Tank.

He walked over to assist.

"Greg, I'm flattered—and in a different world, you might get lucky—but I'm married."

That was a stupid thing to say. Married but dating Edward. Real classy.

Fidelity wasn't exactly my strong suit these days...

"Well, damn!" Greg sat back in dramatic shock. "Consider all advances withdrawn, Mrs. Anderson."

"She's not married to Ed, dumbass." Cody hit Greg upside the head before Tank clapped a heavy hand on his shoulder.

"Hey, man, if you're gonna be dumb, you gotta be tough."

"No, I'm not married to Edward," I clarified, trying not to laugh.

"Then who?" Greg slapped the table like a total goof. "I needa know!"

Sammy squinted. "Bro, the dark-haired operator we took to Germany a few years back."

He said 'operator' in an accent—a dig, clearly.

"You know, the one Ed manhandled at the bar... Major *Bailey.*"

The name felt like a bruise.

They knew I was married. They'd *all* known. This whole time.

I'd been clinging to the illusion that I was in control of my mess—

Not trailing Blake like a storm cloud, stuck in the wake of his bad decisions.

"What?! Major Dickhead?" Greg's eyes bulged. "No way you're *still* married to that clown!"

"Bro, you knew that," Cody said, shaking his head.

Sammy snickered.

"That's my husband you're talking about," I replied, suddenly colder. "And he's one of you. I don't get all the hate."

Blake was an officer at MARSOC.

That was the line I always gave.

But even as I said it, I felt the thud of habit—hollow and automatic.

I never really believed it.

He served there, the same as the rest of them...

But Blake never fit in. Not with these guys. Not with real operators.

And still, I found myself defending him. *Why?*

Greg perked up like he'd just remembered something important.

"Hold up! He might be able to shoot, but no way he's one of us. Fucking Arty Officer that got dumped on us. Damn, after all the shit with the prostitutes, and you're still with him... *babe.*"

I froze.

Greg didn't just drag Blake through the dirt—he dragged me with him.

The woman stupid enough to stay.

"We're not going there. Knock it off," Tank warned.

Greg was too drunk to care. He grinned.

"Aw, babe. You deserve better! Like wayyy better. You should divorce him and marry me!"

Zack slid Greg's beer out of reach.

"Greg, I've seen your cowboy video and heard you're kinda kinky. I don't think we'd be a good fit."

"What? Who told you that?" Greg demanded before looking at Cody and punching him hard in the shoulder. "You needa stop talking shit about me to my future wife!"

Cody rolled his eyes.

"Bro, if you think Allie's gonna fuck around with your dumbass, you're a special kinda stupid. Let it go. It's *not* gonna fucking happen!"

"Take him out to the van," Zack grumbled, then: "Sammy, settle up, will you?"

Zack didn't need to bark orders. When he spoke, the team moved. He was the center of gravity—steady, seasoned. Respected.

In one swift move, Tank bear-hugged Greg before hauling him outside.

Greg staggered free, then swung once—wild and clumsy.

But Cody was already airborne. He landed on his back, locking him in a chokehold.

Seconds later, Greg slumped to the gravel, out cold.

Tank helped ease him down.

"You two look like you've done this before," I said as they hoisted him into the van.

"Too many times," Tank muttered.

"What's he on?" Zack asked, arms crossed.

Cody snickered. "I think he's just crazy into Allie. She's his *stardust.*"

"Stardust?" I asked.

"It's in a song he keeps playing on repeat. Hearts in his eyes. Cocaine-level obsessed."

Tank bumped me with his elbow. "Greg ain't the only one chasin' stardust. Seems Ed's got a pretty serious addiction, too."

* * *

"So why did Edward manhandle Blake?" I asked as we drove into the night—nothing but stars and a full moon illuminating the gravel road ahead.

Sammy and Cody exchanged a look behind me, both staying silent, so I asked Zack directly. "Do you know?"

Zack kept his focus on the road.

"Sorry, Allie, I shouldn't have brought it up," Sammy muttered.

Greg started to chime in, but Cody punched him. "Keep your fucking mouth shut!"

Zack took his time to reply:

"He wasn't where he was supposed to be. Put the team in danger. Nobody got hurt, but Boss lost it when he finally showed."

I nodded slowly.

Edward loathed Blake, but I knew it couldn't be over something as trivial as him not being in the right place at the right time. There had to be more to it.

* * *

A knock rattled my container door at 5:34 a.m.

"Hey, I came over to say I'm sorry."

Greg wiped his boots and stepped inside.

"Cody said I was super disrespectful. Sorry, babe. I swear I wasn't trying to be a total dick and insult you or anything. I think you're awesome. Will you accept my apology?"

I nodded. "Thanks, I will... look, I was trying to avoid mixing business with my personal life. It's obvious you hate Blake and think he's a loser... but could you guys keep it to yourselves? You know I'm still married to him."

Greg opened his mouth, but I held up a hand. "And I know you think you might stand a chance with me, but my life's a disaster and—"

Greg cut in. "Permission to speak freely, ma'am?"

I smirked. "Granted, as long as you never call me 'ma'am' again."

He winked. "Okay, so this is gonna sound super outta line, but babe... Major, uh... he doesn't deserve you. You're way too good for him."

I forced a smile.

"How long have you all known about Blake? That I'm still married?"

"Uhhh..." Greg shrugged. "A few years."

I studied him, puzzled.

He corrected. "I mean, yeah, I knew *he* was married... just not to *you.*"

Something about it hit... weird. Dishonest.

Greg continued before I could ask more. "So, I know Ed's gonna fuck up again... cuz that's what he does. And I'm not hoping for it, but you should give me a shot."

"Oh?"

"I'm not that kinky—just toys and bondage. Nothing gross or degrading. I'm always super respectful, and I'll treat you with such awesome care. Like it's my job."

I giggled. "Um... how about this? If things don't work out with Edward, I'll let you take me out on that date you've been dreaming of. And if all goes well, maybe you can tie me up afterward? Or whatever it is that you do...?"

I winked.

What the hell was I doing—flirting with a teammate about getting tied up while my marriage crumbled and I torched whatever was left with Edward?

Brilliant.

Greg's jaw dropped. "*For real?*"

"Sure, why not? I'll need some fun in my life. And you're fun, aren't you, Greg?"

"I'm *super* fun. The boss of fun! Damn, I didn't expect that," he said, practically blushing. "Thanks, babe!"

Then he gave me a kiss on the cheek and sprinted out the door—in a hurry to tell Cody, no doubt.

* * *

By 6:30 a.m., we were all standing at the off-road track as the instructors gave us a briefing—seventeen miles of brutal terrain in eighty minutes or less.

Cody stared at me, deadpan.

"Think I can beat the record, doll? Maybe I should I *tie* you in so you don't bounce around?"

Guess he didn't find my offer to Greg funny...?

"Handcuffs might be more effective." I drew strange looks from the rest of the team.

Soon, Cody grabbed my arm, practically dragging me to our beat-to-shit '96 Toyota Tacoma.

He tried shoving me in the passenger seat, but I punched him hard in the gut. "Get your hands off me!"

He wheezed as he doubled over, then laughed and jumped into the driver's seat.

"What the fuck? You told Greg he could tie you up and fuck you?"

"What? No. I mean—maybe. In a hypothetical world."

"You know how happy he was? He's in that Jeep naming your fucking children! Why didn't you shut his dumbass down?"

"I don't know. Greg might be what I need."

"You and Ed must've had one helluva fight. Are you outta your mind? You and Greg?" Cody shook his head.

"God, did Edward tell everyone?" I grumbled.

"Nah, Greg heard you scream and listened to your argument on the intercom. Cuz he's nosy as shit and fucking obsessed! Then he saw you leave all pissed off and told everyone else."

"Oh, jeez."

"Listen, he's in that truck plotting Ed's demise. He's infatuated! Stop. Giving. Him. Hope."

"Okay, okay!" I raised my hands in surrender. "I didn't realize he'd take everything so literally."

"Tell him you don't like him!"

"But I *do* like him!"

I laughed as Cody shot me a look.

"Oh, not like that."

"Doll, you're fucking with the team dynamic we got going. And Ed will seriously kill him. Zero fucks given."

He rasped, "You buckled in?"

I checked my seat belt.

"Focus. I'm about to break that agency son-of-a-bitch's record. You ready?"

"Yeah. Hit it."

Seconds later, we heard: "You're on the clock, gentleman."

Cody peeled out, leaving the rest of the vehicles in our dust. I clung to the grab handle for dear life as we jostled and skidded around for the next hour and twelve minutes.

We came in over the record—so he asked to go again. And again.

On the fourth run, he finally beat it.

For a bunch of former **MARSOC** guys, it wasn't just a win—it was bragging rights. And it demanded a rowdy celebration.

* * *

"You ready, little lady?"

I gazed out at the rugged landscape ahead—a course carved by thousands of years of wind and rain.

"Ready as I'll ever be."

I gripped the steering wheel tight, masking nerves—no room for mistakes—then pressed my foot to the gas.

The suspension creaked.

"Just take it slow," Tank said with a smile.

There was already a steady hum of adrenaline in my ears as we approached a boulder-lined ravine. Nowhere to go but up.

I'd watched Tank scale the near-vertical ledge an hour earlier through binos.

He'd made it look easy.

I wished it was.

As dust swirled around us—I realized there was a lot more than just skill involved.

Strategy. Laser focus.

The frame of the Jeep jolted forward, each tire clawing for traction as we inched along—bouncing, swaying, and crawling over rocks the size of cars.

The seat belt bit into my collarbone.

I winced. Breath short, heart thudding.

Rough, uneven movements—up-down, side-to-side.

I made contact with the ravine wall, the eerie scrape of metal on rough stone sending a chill up my spine.

"Shit!" I yelped. "Ahhh, I shouldn't ha—"

"Forget about it. Ease off the clutch a little. You got this," Tank said calmly, like we weren't about to roll sideways.

I hit the throttle, lurching us forward.

We tilted hard to the right—close enough to feel gravity shift—but Tank didn't flinch. I gripped the wheel tighter, pulse hammering.

His life was in my hands as he coached me through the most challenging five minutes of driving in my life.

Calm, steady, and reassuring.

"Almost there. You're killing it," he muttered as we reached the final boulder—our last obstacle.

Twenty seconds later, we crested, finally leveling out.

I looked at my white knuckles and gasped for air.

"Oh my God, we did it!"

"You did it!" He glanced at his watch. "In near record time. I was just along for the ride."

The guys jumped up and down on the adjacent ridge before Zack radioed, "That's our girl. Hell yeah, Allie!"

* * *

It was the last day of drills.

And I was doing more than keeping up—I was earning respect.

Over the radio: "Hey Rockstar, you got Stardust locked and loaded over there?"

Cody.

Greg sat like a sad puppy in the passenger seat. No comeback.

I smiled. "They're jerks. I've been called worse. At the agency, the guys called me Border Collie."

Greg perked up. "You know, Border Collies *are* the smartest dog out there. And they herd sheep. They probably meant it as a compliment."

"Doubt it, but thanks! Being likened to cocaine's much better." I raised a brow.

"Careful—Stardust might stick," Greg grinned. "Cody's not letting it go."

I floored it, blowing past Sammy and Zack.

"Nor should he."

I scanned the terrain ahead, then shot Greg a glance.

"Think I should pass Tank?" I asked.

"Hell no! You know he was a pro, right?"

"Of what?"

He shrugged. "He spent a year with NASCAR before 9/11. Baja 500. You name it. I dunno racing that well, but the dude can drift that truck like nobody's business. I've seen it."

"What happened?"

"Joined the Marine Corps. Ed tried to get him back into it when he got out. Even offered to sponsor him. Wrote him a check for a shit ton of money, he just wasn't into it."

"Why not"?

"The thought of crashing and catching fire. PTSD."

The fear of fire tracked—he and Edward had been in that explosion, the one that left half their platoon dead or scarred for life.

"Well, no wonder he's such a great coach."

"Yeah," Greg said, flashing a mischievous grin. "He's humble. Like me."

"Humble? Greg, you told me you'd be the 'best fuck of my life' the other night."

He tittered and brushed my arm. "Not to brag or anything, but..."

Greg was a menace.

And he lived to get under my skin.

* * *

We spent another three hours driving before flying home to Sarasota.

As we boarded the plane, Tank took a call from Edward and turned to me.

"Blake's back. A few days."

Perfect. Just what I needed—a pissed off husband to stir up more drama.

I wondered if he'd be at the house when I got home.

He wasn't.

No missed calls. No texts.

But he'd been there.

A handwritten note waited on the counter. He was headed to Germany for work.

At the bottom:

We need to talk. -Blake

Later, I realized he'd picked through my laundry, likely looking for signs of an affair like nighties or negligees.

In my lingerie drawer, he placed a single condom.

He even raided my medicine cabinet, stealing two bottles of my sleeping pills. No context.

The unnerving thing was, he didn't need *my* pills. His brother was a doctor. If he wanted a prescription, he had options.

So why take mine? Move things around—barely—like he was trying to make me second guess myself—to make me feel paranoid. Invade my space.

What if he'd ground them up?

Slipped them into my protein powder or food.

Would he try to kill me?

I wasn't sure anymore. It sounded crazy—not impossible.

I needed a camera in the house.

I needed to know when he came and went—what he touched.

What he planned.

Trust was long gone.

CHAPTER 41

By Wednesday, I was pacing. Anxious.

I was supposed to be getting ready for my first out-of-country work trip in over four years—but I hadn't even packed.

Instead, I'd been dodging angry, borderline threatening texts from Blake.

Where tf have you been all week?

I know you're home. Answer me.

WHERE THE FUCK WERE YOU

Allie, seriously??

WTF...

You're gonna ignore me?

My phone dinged again. Then again. And again.

I finally silenced it, tossing it across the bed. Screen down. I didn't want to feel the weight of the unread messages.

Grateful for the quiet, I exhaled sharply.

I knew I should've corrected the record—told Blake I'd been training, not off with Edward—but I didn't.

Why?

Defiance? Belligerence? Apathy?

I wasn't sure—but with Blake's temper, it was reckless.

Maybe I wanted him to spiral—to hurt—and make him regret how he'd treated me.

But mostly—I didn't want to be held accountable to him anymore.

I packed a gym bag and headed into Bright Sands after dinner. I needed endorphins. A distraction. I planned to close out a few tasks and speak with James after a quick workout.

* * *

I was doing squats when Greg and Cody walked in.

Cody waved while Greg winked—predictably flirtatious.

They were mid-conversation... something about Cody smashing a hot yoga instructor. Typical.

I kept lifting as Cody ducked out to take a call—but noticed Greg watching me.

"Hey Gunny," I called out. "Stop being creepy."

"Anything you say, ma'am." He giggled, looking away—briefly.

I racked my bar and wiped sweat from my neck, but when I looked back, he was staring—openly.

Our eyes met in the mirror. He didn't balk.

"Greg, seriously. Why are you watching me like that?"

"You've got solid form."

"That doesn't give you permission to gawk."

"What?" he said with a cute shrug. "I'm an ass guy. Dunno what else to do."

His voice oozed. Zero shame.

"This is literally why women hate the gym. There's always that guy checking us out."

"You forgot to say 'hot,'" he teased.

"Hot *what?*"

"That 'hot' guy checking you out."

"Oh God." *What a doofus.*

"Can I spot you?"

"No! I don't need a spotter. God, I'd seriously slap you if you weren't so hot..."

"Fuck yessssss! She thinks I'm hot!"

"Oh, please. You know you're hot. Don't be obnoxious!"

"Yeah, but all I care is that *you* think I'm hot."

"Greg, you're one of the most ridiculous men I've ever met—and that's saying something."

"But am I the hottest?"

I laughed. "What do you think?"

His whole body smiled. "So, I'm for sure the hottest? Yessssss!" He flung his arms up in a touchdown.

I playfully threw my water bottle at him. He caught it with one of his giant hands—effortless.

"Wow."

He grinned, teeth flashing. "What? I was a wide receiver."

Then he gave me a scandalous once-over.

"I'll leave you to it... gotta work on these biceps if I'm gonna keep my status."

Then lower: "Babe, lemme know if you ever got any pent-up cardio needs cuz... I can go all night."

I smirked. "Yeah, thanks. I'm aware of your *bona fides.*"

I made a beeline for the locker room, half-smiling, half-exhausted, then headed to the ops center.

Dread followed.

Edward would surely pop in, and I didn't feel ready for an emotional showdown.

* * *

Like clockwork, Edward arrived after I'd settled at my desk, immersed in work with James.

"Allie, if this was about payback, I wish you hadn't picked *him.*"

His voice was cold, cracking with something like rage.

I turned. "What do you mean, *him?*"

"Tanner told me."

"Told you what?"

"That you slept with Greg."

I managed a laugh, but my throat clenched shut.

My conversation with Greg made it back to him—garbled, weaponized, and wildly wrong.

But did he really think I was that vengeful?

Part of me wanted to let him believe it.

Let him feel what I'd felt—but then I caught his expression.

Wounded. His eyes... betrayed.

And it felt mean.

If he wanted the truth, I knew what to do.

I stood.

"Let's go."

* * *

"Hey guys," I said as we walked into the team room.

Greg filmed as Cody did bicep curls—both oblivious to the storm coming.

Cody gave a head nod but Greg responded, "Hey, you're back!" cheerfully—far too cheerfully considering.

"Greg," I said, slowly. "When exactly did we sleep together?"

The room stilled.

Greg lowered the phone, gaze flaring in surprise, as Edward's jaw clenched. He looked between us, panicked.

"No, um... Boss, I swear—bro code. Didn't touch her."

Edward's posture stiffened. He scowled like he was bracing for a fight.

Greg hadn't intentionally challenged Edward, but the damage was done. He quickly and unexpectedly backed down.

"So, why does Tanner think we did?" I asked, narrowing my eyes as Greg squirmed visibly.

"Ohhh, yeah... that coulda been my fault. I might've said you offered... like, dinner and handcuffs. I didn't mean to make it sound like we..."

"Yeah, I figured it must've been some sort of miscommunication."

Of course Greg had embellished—my offer was all too tempting.

"Would you mind correcting the record? Now."

"Um, uh, yeah. Sorry, ma'am," Greg stammered.

Ah, there it was, again—*ma'am.*

Nothing like a little guilt to bring out his inner Lance Corporal.

He scanned the room, looking for an exit that didn't require walking past Edward.

As Greg inched toward the back door, Cody grabbed his shoulder and muttered, "Bro, you are *so* dumb."

"Thanks, I appreciate it," I said before turning to Edward. "Are you satisfied or do you need me to take a polygraph, too?"

I pushed past him on my way out.

"Thanks for the vote of confidence."

"Allie!" Edward called, chasing after me. "What happened?"

"Nothing!" I snapped. "I told Greg if things didn't work out with us, I'd give him a chance."

"Then where'd the part about him fucking you come from?"

"I told him he could take me out for dinner and tie me up afterward if he wanted."

I shrugged without shame.

"What on earth? Wait—you'll leave Blake for *Greg*, but not me?"

"Those two things are unrelated." I stopped walking. "And can you please stop bringing up Blake? It doesn't look good on you."

I paused mid-thought to reconsider my words, frustration building.

"You know what? I was ready to leave Blake. And then you lost my trust by sharing an evening with a stripper!"

"Ouch!" James mumbled as I dropped back into my chair at the ops center.

I winced, regretting my sharp reply.

"Edward, I need to finish up here. Can you go?"

He didn't move.

Didn't speak.

Just stood there, like he wanted to say something but couldn't find the words.

Eventually, "God, Allie—"

His voice cracked.

He didn't say anything else.

Didn't slam the door.

Didn't look back.

Just walked out.

Gone.

* * *

I turned to James and forced a smile.

"Sorry about that. My attention's all yours."

But even as I tried to refocus, my thoughts weren't done with Edward.

My mind kept replaying his voice.

His face.

His exit.

Had we passed a point of no return?

Were we already too wounded—too jaded—to fight for what we wanted?

CHAPTER 42

Our wheels slammed into the tarmac—sun glaring, heat rising from the asphalt—fifty klicks south of Tijuana.

We were greeted by the usual suspects—all former CAG friends of Greg's. Now expats.

Salty, bearded, tattooed.

Mercenaries wearing kits more expensive than most people's cars.

Men who'd traded their uniforms for handshake deals.

Once driven by honor. Now driven by blood and money.

Beholden to no one.

The kind of men who made my instincts twitch—just a little.

* * *

We met with a cartel at a secret location—my first test.

And there was no room for weakness.

I had to prove I belonged.

We rolled out in armored vehicles, kitted up in case anything went sideways—faces and tattoos concealed. After tense negotiation, we reached an agreement and radioed Edward. He showed up in full disguise—black hair, bushy mustache—via an unregistered helicopter, duffle in hand: two hundred grand in cash.

I couldn't help but laugh on the ride back to the compound—three haciendas ringed by ten-foot fences, barbed wire, and top-tier security.

Edward was already larger than life—but the disguise tipped him straight into absurd. He looked like a narc from a '90s soap opera.

Whatever attraction I'd felt, it vanished in a puff.

That night, sitting around the fire pit with the guys, he sent me a text:

Nice job today!

I was crafting a snarky response as Cody blurted, "How you feeling, doll?"

"Good, why?"

"You need to talk through any trauma or anything?"

"No... *why?*" I asked.

Did he think I was that fragile?

He smirked. "Well, cuz Ed asked me to check on you."

"Ugh... what?"

"And he wants to make sure you feel..." Cody squinted at his phone. "Let's see... yep—'confident and emotionally supported.'"

"He didn't seriously write that."

"Direct quote."

The funny thing was, I could picture Edward typing it—erasing, rephrasing, overthinking.

Deploying a surveillance network to track my mood.

Not exactly sexy. And definitely not subtle.

I finished my drink in three gulps.

"Well, I'm going to bed. Please tell him I'm going to write in my journal then cry myself to sleep."

Greg rose dramatically, arms wide for a hug. "Aww, babe, don't do that!"

I walked right past him.

"Bro," Cody snorted. "You think Allie's got a journal? Come on. And I bet she's never cried a day in her life. Emotionally barren. Right, doll?"

"Thanks, Cody!" I shouted. "See you idiots in the morning!"

As I walked to bed, I groaned.

Edward thought he was protecting me—supporting me.

But his meddling made me look breakable.

It undercut everything I'd fought to prove.

I didn't need special treatment.

And I sure as hell didn't want it.

* * *

The next day, I went out with Greg and José while Cody and the expats met with local honchos—shady politicians and cartel-connected leaders.

We ran sources. Took pictures. Threatened blackmail. Flipped several of the DEA's informants—the ones coordinating the alleged arms shipment.

I even discovered the mastermind: the agency's own propaganda master, Joe Turner.

It didn't surprise me—the plan had all the right hallmarks: dishonest, audacious, and sinister. Pure Joe.

On the drive back to the compound, my mind drifted to my agency days—triumphs, failures, and the people I'd once worked with. Joe among them. The cartels were actively collecting biometrics on our team, and I worried he might ID me. If he did... it wouldn't just compromise me. It could put the entire mission—and everyone on it— at risk.

I wondered why Edward had brought me in—knowing I was recognizable in all the wrong circles.

Greg waved it off. "James has a handle on everything. I wouldn't worry. Slimeball's the least of our problems down here."

* * *

Before Mexico, I worried that working with Edward might soften me—make me forgive him.

Bizarrely, it had the opposite effect—he irritated the hell out of me.

Though he wasn't staying at the hacienda, he tracked my whereabouts through his proxies: Greg, José, and Cody.

Still, I managed to put my irritation on pause—I was too busy having fun with the guys to dwell on it.

High-stakes or not, I laughed more than I had in years.

José taught us just enough Mexican slang to get us slapped or arrested. Every night we cracked a new bottle of tequila. And, since José's family was from Rosarito, we even snuck past the compound guards on our third night to hit his family's beach bar.

I prayed we wouldn't need a non-standard reentry plan... though Greg *was* the expert.

* * *

Music blared, the bar and beach flickering with tiki torches and fire pits.

A Mariachi band gave way to a DJ spinning reggaeton remixes as bodies packed in tight.

After a drink and some harmless flirtation, I began dancing with an Aussie expat—special ops tattoos, muscles, a great smile.

Greg watched from the bar for a minute before cutting in.

He told the guy to "pound sand"—then helpfully translated it into Australian: "fuck off"—before he turned to me with a grin.

"You don't want an Aussie, babe. You'll barely understand his shit English. You need a real man."

He flexed, winked, and took my hand, leading me to the beach— a dance floor carved in the sand.

Where we proceeded to party. Hard.

* * *

The tequila burned warm through my chest.

Greg couldn't peel his eyes off me—every sway, every flash of skin.

He leaned back, watching me dance like he'd been waiting all night for it.

I twirled once, wind catching my hair.

He was already behind me, moving with the music, the fire, the ocean—letting the rhythm and glow do the seducing for him.

The bass thumped beneath our feet.

Firelight licked across our skin.

Waves crashed just beyond the flames.

Maybe it was the tequila.

Or the way Greg moved. But I didn't want to stop him.

Then—his hands and hot breath at my ear.

"God, you've got no idea what you do to me, do you?"

He gripped my hips, fingers gliding over warm skin—slipping them just inside my shorts.

Intimate. Brazen. Like we were alone in the dark.

Every second mouth-watering. Explosive.

* * *

We danced for hours—sweaty, teasing, bodies pressed close.

By the time we snuck back to the compound, the damage was already done—lines were blurred, and sex was all either of us could think about.

Between the tequila and our chemistry, I was shocked not to end up in Greg's bed that night, but it wasn't for his lack of effort.

We said goodnight with a hug. And a slow, delicious French kiss.

His hands lingered at my waist—until Cody muttered something about murder and peeled him off.

I stood there—breathless, body tingling.

There was no doubt a spark existed—and I worried it was only a matter of time before it ignited.

* * *

I nursed a beer the next morning on the patio as Cody settled into a chair beside me with an earful.

"Doll, you might not get how Ed operates, but Greg's dead if he finds out about last night. Not to mention the coronary he'll have when he finds out you were slow-dancing with a CAT..."

"Oh, are *you* planning to tell him? Because I seem to recall you having some sexy moves of your own."

Cody's hands had wandered to my butt at least twice before I swatted them away.

"Fuck no, I'm not telling him. And shit, look at the agency coming out of you. Should've known you'd use that as blackmail."

I looked him dead in the eye and grinned—I wasn't above weaponizing a little guilt.

"Well, it's not my first rodeo. And for the record, Edward has *no* claim on me."

"Yeah, well... you tell him that," Cody's voice dropped.

"I should! He's treated me like a child all week. All these check-ins. Spying through you and José!"

"It's your first time out with us. He's being cautious."

"You sound like you're defending him. You *do* realize I used to do this shit on my own, right? Places scarier than Mexico."

"You don't need to explain." He leaned back in his chair, eyes sharpening. "I'm just following orders."

"You don't need to!" I snapped—louder than I'd intended. "The handholding is humiliating."

"Doll, we're operators. It's our job to look out for the fairer sex."

He smirked as I rolled my eyes so hard it hurt.

Seeing my expression shift, Cody quickly added, "Oh, don't get bent outta shape! We're just being chivalrous."

"So, that's what we're calling it now? Chivalry? Was the dancing chivalry, too?"

Cody stood, stretching.

"You're a fucking force to be reckoned with, doll." He grinned. "Just stay away from Greg, you hear?"

"Yes, dad," I deadpanned.

He stopped at the doorway.

"He's got no idea what he's doing with you," Cody mumbled, eyes darting to me. "None of us do. And I don't think you realize what you're playing with."

A long pause, then:

"Be careful."

He walked off, his warning drifting in the air like smoke.

CHAPTER 43

As the tequila slowly faded, the consequences caught up. For me, at least.

But Greg looked unaffected. Way too chipper for someone who'd partied until 3 a.m.

"Mornin', babe! Get your ass-chewing? Cody said you called him *dad.*"

He slapped his knee, giggling.

"I did. I may still be slightly drunk..."

"Damn, you and me both." Greg winced and rubbed his temples. "Think you'll be ready to roll out in a few hours? We've gotta meet with that douchey mustache guy at noon—no, not Ed," he added with a grin. "Cody said we could go solo as long as I promised not to get you abducted or anything."

I raised a brow. "I'm still trying to figure out why you guys even brought me."

"In our defense, we're under strict orders not to let you do anything dangerous."

"*Ugh.*"

He nudged my foot under the table. "You've seen you though, right? I'd abduct you."

"Greg," I warned, laughing. "I worked in Eastern Europe. If I were going to get kidnapped, it would've been there."

"Not disagreeing," he said, shrugging. "Just don't want it happening on my watch."

Then he held his hands up like guns. "But you know I'd track 'em down and kill 'em."

I snorted. "Good to know."

Greg's grin faded as he looked at me again.

"Damn. Just wait 'til the Albanians see you on this yacht thing. Then Ed's really gotta worry."

His gaze lingered—too long. Too nervous.

Smile gone.

The shift in his energy—from cheerful to skittish—was instant. A tug in my gut told me something was off.

"Wait—what yacht thing?"

Greg paused. "*Uh*, the one Ed 'recruited' you for." Air quotes.

I shook my head. "He vaguely mentioned a trip, but we didn't get into details."

"Damn, I thought you knew. I shouldn'ta said anything." He rubbed his eyes. "Shit... maybe this is a convo you should be having with him."

"Why?"

"Cuz he probably doesn't want me to scare you off."

"Greg, seriously?" I sobered fast.

"Okay, yeah. I mean—you're gonna be guarded the whole time. But Ed's got this thing lined up with his bro, Vlad. It's for some child trafficking shit. Big shipment of girls."

"*What?!?*"

"I mean, he's not *actually* trafficking them. But damn, yeah—he buys a lotta women and kids."

"What the hell?" I gasped—goosebumps everywhere despite the warm sun.

It sounded noble—but the thought of Edward even pretending to trade in human lives made my spine crawl.

Greg put his hand up. "Hold up. Let me explain."

"Please."

"So, he buys 'em, then we put 'em into hiding. Rehab programs. Homes. Places to get their lives back on track. A lot of super sad situations, but at least they're not sex slaves anymore."

His tone was flat. Matter-of-fact. Devoid of emotion. Like he'd said it—and seen it—a hundred times.

Maybe he had.

But I hadn't.

I felt uneasy. I knew Edward's operations walked a tightrope—covert, gray, morally negotiable—but this? This wasn't just fighting with evil. It was becoming it—a deep cover.

Suddenly, I understood the stakes.

"Wait, so what does Edward *say* he does with them?"

"Sells 'em. Rich people, diplomats, other billionaires. Whoever's willing to pay."

My skin prickled again. Eastern Europe had taught me to trust my instincts—fleeting thoughts, whispers in my mind, the pit in my stomach. The same instincts flaring now.

"So, how does the yacht thing tie in... with me?" I asked, praying I wasn't needed as a decoy.

I'd played the decoy before. The escort. The girlfriend. The bait.

Let men think I was theirs. Smiled when I wanted to scream. Let hands linger where they shouldn't. Held my breath, counting exits. Been covered in brain matter when it was done.

Even if the mission succeeded, it came with a cost.

I wasn't sure I was willing to pay it again.

Greg hesitated, clearly wishing he could backpedal.

Whatever he wasn't saying was worse than what he was.

"Uhhh, he's meeting with some thugs to negotiate a deal. It's kinda shady... related to the A-team."

I shook my head, confused.

"Ummm, the Apparatus," he clarified. "Not exactly a mission for rookies. Or anyone with a conscience, but..."

"But *what?* Why does he need me?"

"Well," Greg looked away, tense. "I'm gonna leave that for him to explain."

Greg said he didn't want to scare me off, but I wasn't scared of danger.

I was more scared of what Edward hadn't told me—the truth.

I needed to know what, exactly, I'd been recruited into—before I was in too deep to get out.

Chapter 44

The sun beat down as we left the safety of the compound—armored vehicle, loaded weapons, high state of alert.

Even with backup, Greg insisted I wear body armor.

"You're not wearing it. Why do I have to?" I asked.

His response was blunt:

"Cuz I can operate in my sleep."

I grumbled. "So, it's because you have a penis?"

"I wasn't gonna put it like that, but yeah. I've got this badass body and a giant cock."

He laughed.

"You can take it off soon. Just wear it 'til I say it's clear—I don't want you getting shot."

* * *

We rolled toward the next meet—douchey mustache guy under an overpass—the cartel watching our every movement.

We'd negotiated safe passage, but Cody, José, and a few expat friends were staged nearby. Just in case.

Thankfully, the meet was clean.

But afterward, Greg veered off course—an unannounced stop on a secluded stretch of road.

He checked his weapon and hopped out of the vehicle—ordering me to slide into the driver's seat and take off if things got dicey.

About twenty yards ahead, he confronted a sketchy-looking white guy in jeans and a baseball hat.

Greg kept glancing back at me, tossing the occasional thumbs-up like everything was fine.

I wasn't so sure.

I scanned our perimeter.

The road was still. No cars. No people. Just heat shimmering off asphalt and eerie silence.

Then an exchange: cash for a medium-sized box.

"So what's in it?" I asked once we'd safely reached the main road.

"Couple of DEA hard drives. And shrooms."

"You're kidding! You bought shrooms. On the side of the road. In Mexico. When we're working something DEA-related. You see the irony, don't you?"

"Pharmaceutical grade shit. Wouldn't wanna run out."

Then he nodded toward me.

"You can take the vest off now. Wanted you to keep it on in case we got caught up."

"Wait—Edward didn't tell you I had to wear this?"

"Nah, but he didn't know I'd be buying shrooms outta a tweaker's trunk, either."

Fucking operators.

* * *

As the adrenaline faded and the road stretched ahead, our silence turned thick—until Greg broke it with a grin and, "God, you're so pretty."

I laughed out loud. "Greg, are we okay after last night?"

"Better than ever!" he beamed. "That was hot as fuck!"

He winked then reached for my hand on the center console. I moved it—nervous.

"Babe, give me your paw."

"What?"

"Your cute little paw." He gazed at my hand. "Gimme."

"We work together. We're not going to start holding hands."

"Well, I was gonna do this—" he started as he pulled my hand to his jeans.

"Oh my God! What the hell?"

I snatched it back like it burned—but not fast enough.

My blush gave me away. His body intrigued me. His bravado turned me on.

Still, I couldn't...

"What? *You touched it last night!*" He stuck out his tongue. "You make me rock hard."

"Gregory!"

"Aw, babe, you said my name so sweet, like my mom. Say it again!"

He shot me a half-smile that was pure flirt, no shame, then:

"Want me to drive around for condoms?"

"Oh my God—no!"

"What? I didn't pack any cuz we're working. Damn, I wasn't expecting us to fuck either, but judging by that look, I might get lucky and end up ten inches deep in you later..."

"Where did that come from?" I shook my head, dazed.

"I thought that's where this convo was headed..."

He played dumb—obnoxiously. *Adorably.*

"Greg, we're not. It's not a good idea."

"You're wrong. Just sayin'..."

"Why?"

I braced for a cocky one-liner like, 'Cuz it will be awesome!'

Instead, "Babe, we owe it to ourselves to fuck at least once. Our chemistry's on fire."

"You and Edward just love being provocative." I rolled my eyes. "Why is that?"

"Hah! I'm nothing like him in bed. *Guaran-fucking-teed.*"

"Yeah, well… I wouldn't know." My voice drifted.

He stared at me dumbfounded. Five seconds, ten seconds…

Then: "Whoaa, hold up! He never sealed the deal?"

"Never."

"At least tell me he blew your mind with awesome oral?"

I exhaled. Resignation. Disappointment.

"Nope. We never got there, either."

Greg let out a choked laugh. "Oh, damnnnnn! Whaaaat?!"

He covered his face, nearly shaking with glee.

It took a full minute for him to get it out of his system.

When he finally looked at me again, his grin softened to something else.

Was it care? Or just curiosity?

"But for real—why haven't you two fucked?"

"I don't know. I guess I didn't want to give myself to him too easily."

I looked away.

Why was I telling Greg this?

"You're so damn cute," he said, grabbing my hand again with a hard squeeze.

"Please don't make fun of me."

"I'd never—I like you way too much. Damn, I'm gonna rock your world so hard tonight!"

"Not happening."

I tried to keep my voice firm, but the air between us buzzed. Hot.

Pure gasoline. One spark, and we'd explode.

"Why not? Major Dickhead's outta the picture—as he should be—and Ed's Ed. Let's have hot sex like adults cuz we can."

"I can't."

"If you're worried about raising your body count to three—"

"It's not three," I snapped. But he wasn't far off.

"So, four?" he teased. "Babe, guys don't care about your number unless they're totally insecure. And you don't wanna guy that's insecure cuz he's gonna totally suck in bed."

He smiled. "Check it out—when a guy asks a girl how many dudes she's been with, he's tryna figure out how inexperienced she is. He's hoping she's not gonna know any better and think he's good. Nine times outta ten."

That sounded accurate.

No one had ever asked me—except for a few girlfriends. And Blake.

"So, when a girl asks, she's tryna figure out, is he just into one-night stands or boyfriend material?" He winked. "Go on. Ask."

"Greg, I *definitely* don't need to know."

"Two-hundred and twenty-seven," he blurted with an unapologetic smile.

My jaw dropped.

"There were a lotta threesomes. Some outta control orgies. Gets the numbers up quick."

"That's... so many."

I was still reeling as we pulled up to the hacienda. Greg shot me a look, putting the SUV in park.

"Nah, it's just a number. Babe, trust me, I'm gonna be super respectful—until you're begging me to rip your clothes off."

He paused with a grin. "Then I'm gonna fuck you like you deserve."

As I sat in a state of shock, he adjusted himself—openly.

Oh my God.

I unbuckled my seat belt with shaky fingers, heat rising up my neck, then hurried to the house, eager to escape my embarrassment.

"Hey, hold up!" he shouted.

I spun around to find him advancing on me.

He pecked my cheek before opening the front door.

Then in a breathy whisper—"Allie Elizabeth... for you, I'll be husband material."

Greg disappeared inside, but I stayed frozen—breath held, cheeks hot.

I was flirting with risk and forbidden desire.

But each step closer to the edge made me feel more alive.

A pulse-pounding thrill.

Free-falling.

CHAPTER 45

The marine layer rolled in, cooling the air and casting the compound lights in a soft, ghostly haze.

I hoped a relaxed mood would follow.

Wishful thinking.

The guys wanted to party again.

Back to José's family restaurant—same table, same tequila.

And the night played out like *déjà vu.*

Drinking. Dancing. Flirtation.

Temptation.

* * *

I opened my eyes to the sound of a door creaking—followed by the shocking sight of Greg nearly skipping into view with a grin. Naked. Practically glowing.

I glanced around with horror... I wasn't in my room.

I was in his.

Panic surged as I tried to piece together what happened.

Oh God...

"Hey there, babe," he said sweetly, jumping into bed and spooning me under the covers.

"Shit," I muttered.

"What?" He sounded concerned as he squeezed me.

"Did we—?" I rubbed my temples, bracing, then grabbed a bottle of tequila from the nightstand and took a swig.

He waited for me to return it, then pounced, his body pressing into mine. "I wish, but nah... morning sex is way hotter."

I froze—my mind and body resisting just for a second—before his mouth met my neck with wet lips and I found myself giving in.

Soon he was revving me up, fingertips teasing and tickling, before taunting, "Touch me," with a feather-light breath.

I exhaled and tried to own the situation—even as alarm bells blared in my mind.

I was already naked, moaning, and melting to his touch.

We were past the point of no return.

"Oh my *God*," I squealed, peeking under the covers.

Greg tossed them aside—and suddenly, we were naked and completely exposed—sunlight kissing our bare skin through stained glass windows.

I shivered, staring in admiration before reaching for him with nervous hands.

Thick, heavy, and—*my God*... my eyes bulged as he grew in my hand.

"Yeah, that was kinda your response last night, too..."

"How would we even—?"

He couldn't possibly...

I laughed.

Not true! He'd been with two-hundred and something other women—he was bound to fit inside me, too... though I was certain it wouldn't be without effort.

"Well, step one is I get you insanely wet," he growled, his hand trailing lower in a deliberate tease until—

"*Ohhh.*"

I trembled.

Eyes still locked, he slipped two fingers into me. Seconds later, he pulled them to his mouth with a sultry smile and a wink.

"Step one's achieved after the hottest makeout sesh ever, and…"

"And?" The specifics were still fuzzy.

"Well, I may have eaten your perfect pussy after you licked me a lil' bit."

My eyes flew wide, cheeks burning.

"Oh shit, I hope I—"

"Don't worry. You were super fun! You sat on my face and came three times. Made me explode."

Well, that was new…

He sighed. "Not too many women can cum back-to-back like that. It was sooooo hot!"

As I squirmed, he licked my neck with a flat tongue.

"Oh God… ohhh, wow… um…" I gasped, body spasming in delight—suddenly sexually supercharged. "It must've been your technique because… um… that's unusual for me…"

He pulled me close.

"So, what's step two?" I asked.

"Step two is I'm gonna slip my monster cock inside this tight, wet pussy… stretching you open 'til you're begging me to fuck you deeper than any man has before."

I inhaled the scent lingering on his chest—a dizzying blend—musky cologne, tequila, and sweat.

"Oh my *God*," I whimpered, intoxicated by everything—the warmth of his skin, the way his breath danced on my neck, his smell. Even Greg's dirty talk somehow turned me on.

The smart thing would've been to stop him. But I didn't.

Instead, I encouraged him, my fingers exploring him boldly.

Within seconds, we were kissing, my insides aching with want as I writhed under his body.

He reached for lube on the nightstand.

I paused nervously. "Greg, I don't know if we should without… um…"

The world had changed since the last time I'd had sex with someone new.

The guys always joked about going bareback.

But what if...?

I felt a pang of anxiety knot in my stomach.

I knew I should've cared more about risk, but as he kissed me again, I let it go—lust louder than logic.

"Don't worry, babe. I'm clean. And I'll pull out."

He tickled my inner thigh as our eyes met.

"I was gonna say, 'Just smile and look pretty,' but babe, you're *gonna* enjoy this. This is all about you and your pleasure," he murmured, slipping his fingers inside me again, slowly—his touch more intimate than anything I'd ever experienced.

"Deep breaths. That's it," he whispered, guiding my breathing with soft murmurs and kisses.

I found myself smiling wildly, then grasped for the covers, hoping to hide my face.

Greg grabbed them with his teeth and tugged them away. "Nope. I wanna see this gorgeous smile," he giggled before turning serious. "Babe, you ready?"

I nodded, trying to conceal my terror as he primed himself.

"I'm gonna use a tonna lube and go super slow, but give me a sec. It might hurt to start, so just scream... or bite me."

He nipped my shoulder like a dog, grinning scandalously.

I closed my eyes.

And then I started gasping.

Over.

And over.

And over.

I finally exhaled, then flung my head back as he continued pulsing into me, rolling his hips with a smooth, gentle rhythm—attentive to my every movement and sound.

It hurt, but it exhilarated me more.

As he nibbled on my neck, I felt myself tightening around him, my entire body starting to tremble.

He sensed it, sliding deeper with every breath until he filled me completely.

I opened my eyes, watching him move. Entranced.

He grabbed my wrists with a smile, pinning them over my head as I took a shocked breath.

"Had a feeling you'd like that." He paused, kissing my lips softly. "Now stop fighting it. Babe, take a deep breath and relax."

I inhaled sharply.

As the air left my lungs, he said, "Another"—a quiet command.

I obeyed—legs shaking as the feeling swelled.

His eyes locked on mine, completely focused.

"One more big breath and I want you to cum for me," he whispered. "You're so close, babe. I got you."

I moaned and took one more breath. Then I let go.

My back bowed off the bed, pleasure ripping through me. Hands clawing at the covers. Body bucking into him. Frenzied.

"Oh my God, Greg, *ohhh Greg...!*"

After a few seconds, he abruptly pulled free.

I lay dazed riding the rush of hormones and endorphins before he spoke:

"Damn... you're so fucking gorgeous!"

He ran his fingers down my chest and giggled—sweet and light. Perfectly Greg.

"Sorry, I didn't wanna pull out, but you were squeezing me so tight, and you started screaming my name, and fuck... I almost lost it. Uh... that doesn't usually happen to me."

He leaned down to kiss my lips—delicious and soft.

Hungry for more, I seized the moment, wrapping my legs around his hips, drawing him back—our kiss unbroken.

He surged into me without hesitation—this time thrusting harder, his pace steady—precise. Absolutely electric.

Pleasure swept through my veins like voltage. Surging. Sparking. Surging again.

With Blake, it was never more than once. But with Greg, the current built and broke in powerful waves, crashing through me on repeat.

Even as I was drowning in the overload, I caught the small things. The way his gaze devoured me. The way he treated me with care—attuned to my breath, my body, and my needs. The way we just... fit.

He flipped me with that signature cocky grin—a grin that melted all my inhibitions away.

I drifted dangerously toward feral—breath ragged. Screaming his name. Hips grinding. Hands scratching. Teeth nibbling.

All things I'd never done before in bed. It was like I was someone else entirely.

Almost... rewired.

The cross around his neck rocked with hypnotic rhythm, diamonds flashing with every roll of his hips.

I bit my lip, trying to stop my smile from spreading, my gaze betraying me as it raked down his glistening abs.

My God, he was gorgeous.

Greg caught it—his face lighting up, smug and playful. Heat rushed my cheeks.

"You like it, huh?"

I nodded, losing control of my smile. Letting him see exactly how much I liked it.

Eyes blazing, he added, "Good. Now cum for me again."

As the words left his lips, he drove into me. Hard.

I gasped, "Oh God!" before he surged into me again. Then once more—pleasure hotter, impossible to hold back—my breath hissing, "Ohhh, Greg..."

He froze, teetering on the edge. Pulse throbbing at his temples. Mouth stretching as he let out a deep, guttural, "Fuuuuck."

Unfiltered and primal.

My body shook beneath him as he rose to his knees, hands working in urgent strokes before I felt his release—warmth hitting my stomach in heavy, shocking spurts that felt filthy and obscene... and yet still unbearably sexy.

I slapped a hand over my mouth as I giggled, startled by my own reaction.

He shook his head in amusement—or maybe adoration—then kissed my cheek and collapsed beside me, the morning light hitting the stained glass just right, casting soft reds, golds, and blues across our bodies like sunlit tattoos.

Seconds ticked—bodies gleaming, breath heaving—before:

"Babe, that was fucking perfect."

CHAPTER 46

I smiled into the sheets—too stunned, too satisfied, too everything to speak.

And a little afraid I'd tasted something I couldn't live without.

Greg pulled me close, unbothered by the heat and mess.

"You good?" he asked, concern wrapping around me as tightly as his arms.

Surprised by his tender tone, I eased away from him just slightly. Enough to meet his eyes. It was the first time Greg had truly dropped his bravado. His voice, his hands, his face—all softened.

He tucked a strand of hair behind my ear.

I nodded, still searching for words. Not fully trusting my voice or emotions.

"It wasn't... too much, was it?" He glanced at where his hand rested on my hip—uncharacteristically unsure.

"No... it—"

Then a gentle grin: "Good. So, uh... full debrief—was anything too rough? Too fast?" He paused. "If there was anything you didn't like or—"

Suddenly, words rushed out before I could stop them. Or filter them.

"I've never felt anything like that," I gasped—exhilarated, exhausted, overwhelmed. "That was *phenomenal.* The best sex of my entire life!"

He hopped out of bed, cocky swagger returning.

"Yeah, well... hate to say *I told you so...*"

As he winked, he grabbed my feet, tugging me playfully toward the edge of the bed, making me squeal. A second later, he confidently scooped me up and carried me to the shower.

The experience was surreal.

Soapy. Steamy. Insanely satisfying as we flirted with our eyes and slippery hands.

I braced for guilt to hit like a sledgehammer.

But as water poured over me, all I felt was... free.

Whatever regret I'd expected rinsed down the drain.

* * *

I was melting into Greg's kiss, body pinned against the glass shower wall, when the bathroom door creaked open—and the moment snapped into a still frame. All in glorious detail.

A fog of desire. Water droplets tracing down Greg's skin. Steam swirling. Hands exploring. Horror on Cody's face.

One second, I was moaning into Greg's mouth.

The next, I was frozen against the glass, wide-eyed—caught.

"Oh shit!" I shrieked, diving into Greg's chest.

"Ah, fuck. I shoulda known!" Cody yelled before quickly disappearing back into the bedroom, leaving the door cracked behind him. "Sorry, doll!"

Greg laughed. "Uh, hey, bro. What's up?"

"Bro, what the fuck?"

"What the fuck *what?*"

Greg spanked me as I got out of the shower, grinning shamelessly through the glass.

"Bro, you *know* Allie's off-limits."

Off-limits? According to Edward, maybe. But I had news for him.

"Damn, I totally forgot," Greg giggled, winking and licking his lips.

I caught Cody's reflection pacing in the mirror.

"You two better fucking not! You know Ed's gonna murder you," Cody muttered, rubbing his face.

"Look, I fucked her, now I can concentrate on real shit again."

"You better promise, cuz I'm not covering for you if Ed asks."

"Fine! I won't fuck her again. She's outta my system," Greg replied—sounding resolute, even as he shook his head mischievously and hopped out of the shower behind me, clearly ready for another round. "But bro... it was fucking amazing. I think I'm addicted to this woman."

I started to wrap myself in a towel before Greg whisked it away with a low growl, "Oh, I'm not done with you."

He nudged me toward the bathroom counter with a grin.

"Well, you're on your own if you keep this up," Cody yelled. "You, too, doll."

"Damn, you're like a fucking morale suppression officer. Get outta here!"

"You're gonna fuck as soon as I leave, aren't you?"

Greg lifted me onto the counter, calling out, "What happens down in Mexico stays in Mexico!"

"Oh, for fuck's sake!"

I giggled before he shouted, "Now close the door and give us some damn privacy!"

The door slammed shut. Greg's hands were already back on me.

"I'm gonna make you cum again before we leave," he whispered, breath hot on my ear, fingers slipping between my legs. As he traced soft kisses down my neck, I clutched the edge of the counter, dizzy with anticipation.

My breath stuttered. *I needed more.*

"Greg... I want you."

"Fuck, yeah."

He gripped my hips tight—steadying me—then filled me, inch by inch. Slow and deep.

My body trembled, pleasure building again—not just from the stretch, the heat, or the way he moved—but the way he held me, like he knew exactly what I craved.

I drew him in, kissing him hungrily, his movements unhurried, each one drawing me closer to the point of no return.

"You're trying to kill me," I muttered.

Greg paused with a sultry smile. "Nah, babe. Just trying to ruin you for everyone else."

God. *He might.*

I dug my nails into his shoulders. And then it hit. My body quivered—tight, pulsing, every nerve alight.

"Oh *Greg...!*"

I shook against him, muscles locking, teeth finding his shoulder in a moment of pure nirvana.

"Ohhh, fuck yeah!" he cried out, voice booming as his body tensed, too.

Startled, I smacked him. "Greg!"

His eyes shot down, panicked. "Ah, shit, I forgot!"

I was paralyzed—a lump in my throat forming as he quickly pulled out, spilling onto the floor.

A flash of panic hit me, but he just grinned, giggling.

How was he so adorable?

"Uh, sorry... I swear I usually have like wayyy more control, but you bit me and grabbed me with your little lobster claws." He pinched my hands. "Totally your fault! I think we should be good, but damn— I haven't fucked up my pull-out game in, like, decades. Twice in one day."

He paused. Then, completely deadpan:

"Babe, let's get married and make a buncha babies."

"Oh, stop!" I shook my head, laughing as he kissed my cheek. *Typical goofy Greg.*

"What? I'm for real! Fuck what Cody and everybody else says! Let's fuck just like that twenty times a day for the rest of our lives."

"Oh my God! What?!"

"Too much? Ten times? *Pleeeeeeease.*" He flashed that large, incredibly sweet grin.

"You're not serious?"

"What if I am?"

I searched his face.

Was he?

Greg had been softer, gentler, and more affectionate than I would've imagined...

"I like you," I admitted, "but I don't think you're my type."

He guffawed.

"*Puh-lease.* You telling me chiseled, badass operators aren't your type? I'm not buyin' it. I'm *exactly* your type."

Shit. He had a point. His build, his job, his energy—it all matched my history.

Not that my history was a point of pride.

"Greg, I have a husband. That hasn't changed."

"Nah, don't worry. I'll murk him. Problem solved."

"Gregory!"

"Aw, babe..."

His smile made me want to give in.

To *him*—not his offer to kill Blake.

But as he kissed me, my mind wandered. To Edward.

And for a split second, guilt sliced through me. Sleeping with Greg wouldn't just hurt him. It would devastate him.

"Um... let's have fun and see where this goes."

Wait—that didn't sound like me at all.

I was trying to match the vibe I expected from Greg—casual, detached, no strings. But he'd gone off-script with babies and a future. Now I was stuck performing a version of myself I didn't recognize...

Still, it felt safer than being honest.

"Yeah, cool... let's have fun."

I grabbed his hand, sensing something had shifted. "What's wrong?"

"Nah, all good."

* * *

When I entered the bedroom minutes later, Greg was packing.

I pulled on my dress—body still tingling—then crossed the room to kiss him.

"That was amazing!" I gave his side a playful pinch.

He drew me in, arms tight around my waist, then nuzzled his face in my hair and kissed the top of my head, letting out a heavy breath.

"Babe, I know you think I'm all talk," he whispered. "But I need you to know—I'm fucking crazy about you."

He leaned back, forcing me to meet his gaze. Bravado gone again.

I moseyed back to my room after one final, lingering kiss—wishing I'd been brave enough to say what I felt.

That he wasn't just incredible in bed.

That he was dangerously lovable—and I might've been crazy about him, too.

Not yet.

CHAPTER 47

As sun streaked through my windows, I smiled. The brightness matched my mood—blinding, euphoric. Unbelievably alive.

I jumped on my bed, giddy, thrashing. Every nerve in my body still buzzing.

This is what I'd been missing?

Why had no one told me?

I closed my eyes, trying to etch every part of the morning into permanent memory—Greg's body, his breath, his moves. How he took control—flipping me like I weighed nothing.

I let out a giggle. *God, that move alone...*

The rawness of his touch.

His power. His stamina.

Phenomenal. All of it.

I wasn't sure I could go back to normal sex ever again.

Maybe Greg was the piece of the puzzle I'd been missing in my life—the man I needed to make my life—and my body—feel complete.

In the span of three hours, Blake's shot at ever weaseling his way back to me was gone. Done. Goodbye. *Never again.*

And Edward's?

He didn't stand a chance if Greg kept up like this. Tender. Doting. Almost loving.

Wholly unexpected.

I hopped out of bed, bound for the shower, then stopped dead, catching a glimpse of my afterglow in the mirror.

My spirit lighter—brighter. I even looked younger.

All from a morning of sex.

I giggled again as I dialed the water to hot.

As steam rose around me, giddiness made way for a satisfying serenity.

I was a woman reborn.

* * *

I padded barefoot toward the kitchen—still on a cloud—until I heard familiar voices wisping around the corner—Greg and Cody.

My feet glued to the ground mid-stride.

"Bro, no *way* she hasn't fucked him! He's been talking about getting with her for months. She just didn't want you thinking she's sleeping around."

Greg laughed. "Nah. If she was sluttin' it up, she woulda let me hit it already. Damn, her body was thirsty. I thought for sure she was gonna be a pillow princess, but she's so fucking sexual... blew my mind!"

I stood still, but the coffee mug shook in my hand. I gripped it tighter, breath shallow.

I knew I should've left.

But some awful part of me needed to hear everything.

"So how was her—?"

I cringed, waiting for Greg's reply.

"Started out tight."

Cody snickered as I caught it—the distinct sound of a high-five.

"That woman's a thoroughbred, bro. Fucking flawless!"

"Calm down. You're obsessed. She's not that special."

"Nah, she is! We smashed raw and it was so hot, I legit almost dumped a load in her."

"Whoa, bro... you gotta be careful!"

"She's amazing! God, I kinda hope I knocked her up. Our kids would be star fucking athletes."

"Chill out! She's never gonna fall for your dumbass. Seriously, you fucked her—now let her go back to Ed." Cody sounded annoyed.

Greg giggled. "Damn, he's gonna be crying himself to sleep when he finds out I fucked her first."

Fucked her first?

That's what I was now? A point scored?

My stomach turned.

"Yeah, well he can't find out. He probably already got her a ring. I'm not playin'—he finds out, he'll fucking kill you." Cody laughed, but nervousness carried in his voice. "You hit it, now quit it. For real."

I backed away on unsteady legs, breath trapped in my throat.

I didn't cry until the door shut behind me.

Then I collapsed—face-first into the pillow—muffling the sob that ripped through me.

I'd heard worse, but Greg's comments...

Less than an hour earlier, he'd touched my face, kissed my cheek, and whispered—

"I'm fucking crazy about you."

He'd looked me in the eye and said it like it mattered.

So how the hell was he out there laughing—bragging—like I was a conquest?

Was any of what he'd said genuine? Or was it just a setup?

It hit me as I cried:

All I wanted was a fairy tale—the one Edward destroyed.

I lay there until it was time to leave for the airstrip.

Then I buried my emotion—all of it.

I straightened my shoulders and wiped my eyes.

Smile on my face. Bruise to my heart.

Back to business as usual.

Chapter 48

We found our Cessna waiting on a sun-bleached stretch of pavement. Cracks spiderwebbed across it—filled with sprouting weeds. It didn't look remotely fit for a tarmac, but it would have to do.

Greg jumped out, loading our gear with practiced speed, the engine idling in a low growl.

Cody provided overwatch as José spoke with the pilot in Spanish—a friend of Zack's from Delta Force.

We all kept a close eye on our surroundings—M4s ready.

Edward called. Irritated, I ignored it—glancing around, wondering if he was surveilling me from a tree line or maybe a drone overhead.

His protectiveness was starting to flirt with condescension.

* * *

We deplaned in Sarasota late that afternoon.

The whole flight, not a word from the guys—even José. I was puzzled, even wounded, and wondered what else had been said behind my back.

I expected Greg to say *something* about our morning together. A joke. A backhanded compliment. Anything.

Instead, he reverted into fun-and-flirty mode like nothing happened.

I should've expected it.

His call sign was Rockstar, after all. And he had a reputation to match.

Still, I felt a twinge of disappointment and tried not to sulk.

But as I stood by the team van minutes later, he approached.

With no one watching, he lifted me off the ground—feet dangling—grabbed my butt, and kissed me hard—tongue and all.

Off the charts sexy.

"Babe, can I *puh-lease* take you out tonight?" he muttered. "Drinks, a fancy dinner, dancing... maybe some super hot playtime if you're not too sore from this morning."

The mischievous twinkle in his eye made me blush.

I'd misread the situation.

Or had I?

Greg's voice was warm. His touch was gentle. But I couldn't shake the memory of his laughter. The way he'd said *fucked her first.*

I forced a smile, hoping it reached my eyes.

"So that's a yes?" he asked, setting me down.

I nodded, a clandestine grin.

"Fuck yessssss!" he exclaimed, giving my butt a naughty pinch before boosting me into the van.

My heart skipped as he closed the door.

Not just from the excitement he sparked with his fingertips. There was something else—a flicker of unease, even distrust. Concern that maybe he was playing into my emotions. My vulnerability. Just for sex. But why?

He hopped in the front passenger seat, winking at me in the rear-view mirror.

Cody sat beside him, already scowling.

"Shit, you two are acting like you just lost your virginity," he grumbled. "Can you tone it down? It's nauseating."

Our eyes met in the mirror as he added, "Doll, that was a side of you I didn't need to see... or hear. I'm gonna need some major Ayahuasca therapy for that shit. And I'm sending you the bill."

"Oh jeez! Don't be so dramatic!" I said, shaking my head, dishing it back. "You watch porn on your phone all day."

Greg snickered. "Bro, I'm telling you, it was hot as fuck!" He turned to me. "Babe, on a scale of one to ten, how awesome was it?"

"What?!"

"It's just Cody. I already debriefed him."

Yeah... sadly, I'd heard.

"Tell me!"

"How was it for *you*?" I teased, trying to flip the question without answering. My score was a solid ten out of ten. But I didn't want to say ten if he was going to say seven.

Greg looked high off the memory, sighing. "Nineteen. Maybe more."

Cody groaned and rolled his eyes. "Bro, please."

"I swear! Hands down best sex ever."

Greg turned back to me. "I was *not* expecting you to be such a wild animal! Oww!" He touched one of his nipples dramatically.

I nearly choked—mortified. Cody looked like he wanted to jump out of the van.

"So I was thinking, after dinner, maybe we try some super light bondage?"

"Oh God," I mumbled.

"See what you did, doll?" Cody shot me a look. "The last thing I need is his dumbass making *stupider* decisions cuz all he can think about is chasing tail. This is fucking superb."

"Bro, you're just jealous," Greg scoffed, laughing.

"Literally a billion women you could fuck, and your dumbass decides to fuck the only one Ed says is off-limits." Cody shook his head. "I don't get it."

Then flatly: "Now shut up."

The van door opened and José climbed in.

* * *

As we drove, I caught Greg eyeing me in the rearview mirror every few minutes—until Cody punched him in the shoulder.

"Bro, chill out."

José's interest piqued. "What'd I miss?"

"I'm stoked," Greg beamed. "I'm going out with a sexy little thing tonight."

Cody muttered, "What the fuck?" just under his breath.

José smirked. "Got any pics?"

This seemed to be routine banter, but I prayed Greg wasn't about to reveal my identity.

"Nah, bro. She's married. Gotta be kinda discreet."

"Jesus," Cody groaned.

José's eyes snapped wide. "Uhhh... dude. Married's a bad choice."

"Wasn't asking for judgment—just explaining why I'm not gonna be sending you jerkoffs any pics or vids of us banging later," Greg replied.

The moment was thankfully interrupted as Cody's phone rang. He answered on speaker.

"Hey," James said. "Sorry to ruin your vacay, but Ed needs you to head back out tonight."

"Fuck, why?"

"Oh no," James teased. "Did you have plans with your imaginary girlfriends?"

Cody half-laughed. "Bro, you *know* I had hot dates lined up all week."

"Yeah, I'm sure."

Eyes already rolling, Greg asked, "Where we going?"

James didn't hesitate. "You know where."

"Yuckkk. Not again. We've been there ten fucking times in six months," Cody added as Greg slammed his head against the headrest. "And it sucks every time. Bro..."

"Sorry, same deal. Take it up with Ed." James paused. "On the bright side, he chartered you knuckleheads a spiffy jet. Leaves at seven. Said he'll catch you tomorrow. The usual spot."

Cody grumbled before hanging up.

Beside me, José pulled up the weather on his phone—Stuttgart.

And the rant about Germany began.

* * *

A faint sheen of sweat clung to my skin as I walked into Bright Sands—whether from the thick Florida heat or the lingering afterglow, I wasn't sure.

Inside, fluorescent lights hummed overhead. Air cold.

Cody tapped my shoulder.

I slipped out an earbud and glanced up.

"Yes?"

"We're gonna be out of pocket a while," he said low. "So don't expect any calls or texts from your *sweet Gregory.*"

"Thanks, dad. I know the drill," I muttered, turning back to my screen as he griped:

"Call me 'dad' one more time and I'll bend you over my knee and spank you. Fuck around and find out."

I snickered as he walked away.

* * *

After thirty minutes, I felt it—movement behind me.

My shoulders tensed.

Please don't be Edward.

I kept my eyes on the screen ahead, pretending not to notice.

Then, a left hand down my back, the other snaking around my waist.

Greg.

He pressed his chest into me, shooting a tingle up my spine as he whispered—breath warm against my ear:

"I've got an hour 'til I gotta get on the road. Can I drive you home and have you as my early dessert?"

His hand grazed my stomach, tiny electric sparks dancing on my skin.

"God, all I can think about is my cock inside you," he growled. "I want you so fucking bad."

My breath seized. The words should've been offensive—but I'd never been more turned on. I nearly purred. All I could think was the same.

A grunt sounded from Cody a few feet away. "Well, stop thinking about it, cuz it's not happening."

"Nah, you're outta your lane, bro." Greg turned back to me. "Babe, we can do whatever we want. I need you again before I leave."

I bit my lip.

Cody's voice dropped an octave. "I'm not playin'. Get your hands off her. Walk the fuck away before James sees you and tells Ed."

Greg laughed him off but Cody looked ready to snap.

"Hey, dumbass," he cracked. "Either Major Dickhead's gonna kill you—or Ed is. Can you apply a little brainpower to this situation?"

"*Puh-lease!*" Greg scoffed. "Major Dickhead doesn't scare me."

Then, with a cocky grin: "And Ed might be cool as long as I share."

My eyes flew wide. "I'm sorry—what did you just say?"

"I mean... I know you're not into girls, but we could get into some super spicy MFM."

I didn't know what MFM meant, but any type of sharing was categorically out of the question.

Greg giggled.

"Greg," I said calmly, "there won't be any that. That's non-negotiable."

I was into Greg—too much, maybe—as long as he didn't try to impose his Rockstar antics on me.

Was he testing my boundaries... or was that what he really expected?

"Then let's get married in Vegas," he said with a shrug. "Would give me such an awesome reason to tell Ed to fuck off."

Cody broke. "Jesus, like how many times do I gotta tell you? Leave her the fuck alone and go pack your shit or I will fucking fight you!"

Greg finally relented, smirking as he turned to me one last time.

"Babe, you're the best. See you in a few weeks."

Then he was gone.

And I was left with Cody—who was fuming.

After five minutes, he turned to me. "You've gotta knock this shit off."

His tone wasn't playful.

"You think it's all fun and games now, but you're fucking around with a guy who doesn't understand boundaries. If Ed finds out, he's not gonna be pissed—he's gonna fucking lose it. You think I'm joking, but he'll put a bullet in Greg. For real."

I stayed quiet, worried that maybe he wasn't wrong.

"I like you, doll," he added, softer. "I really do. But for all our sakes—drop it. Before this gets ugly."

I gave him a tight nod and cautiously agreed.

CHAPTER 49

I walked through the front door just past seven—sunset casting a dusky gold across the floor like fire.

I kicked off my shoes, opened a bottle of wine, and threw on a risqué nightgown to match my wildly sexy mood. Then I ordered a pizza and caught up on laundry while unwinding to music.

I'd never felt so alive.

For a second, I considered calling Liv to dish on my scandalous life—but she was probably recovering from bedtime mayhem.

I sauntered barefoot across the cool tile, still humming from the memory of Greg's hands on me. My cheeks flushed just thinking about it.

At seven-thirty, he sent me a dick pic—a spectacular erection in tight jeans.

Thinking of you, babe! Miss you already!!

We swapped a handful of flirty texts before he left me with a heart emoji.

Aw, Gregory.

* * *

Around eight, Edward called three times in close succession. I ignored all of them, each one chipping away at my mood.

I debated heading to bed but curled up on the couch with a movie instead, waiting for sleep to find me.

At 9:10 p.m., a familiar knock.

Two sharp taps—precise, proprietary. My heart jumped.

Edward.

Of course it was him. I didn't move.

We'd barely spoken in weeks—only when absolutely necessary.

He had to know I was still upset.

If I didn't answer, I wondered if he'd use his key... so I threw my hair into a messy bun and tiptoed to the door. All I heard was silence.

My fingers hovered near the deadbolt. I considered waiting him out, pretending I wasn't home.

I jumped as he rapped on the door again, then took a deep breath and cracked it.

"Hey, what are you doing here?"

"Can we talk?" he asked, voice uncharacteristically soft.

"Can it wait until tomorrow? It's late and I'm tired. And I'm in my pajamas."

I glanced down at my nightgown—not the best choice.

"Allie, please."

Ugh. He sounded... wrecked.

"Fine," I replied stiffly as I walked toward the kitchen. "What's so urgent? Are you here to apologize for treating me like a child all week?"

For a moment, I panicked, wondering if he knew about Greg.

No... he couldn't.

If he knew, his mood wouldn't just be grief. It'd be vengeance.

"I didn't treat you like a child."

"What are you talking about? You questioned my judgment—repeatedly! What was the point of even hiring me?"

We spiraled into a bickering session, circling the same tired debate.

I finally spun away from him, ready to walk away from the argument—

But he stepped closer and grabbed my wrists.

I flinched, ready to knee him out of instinct.

"Stop—I treated you like..."

He hesitated.

"Allie, I lo—"

He didn't finish.

I reeled.

Did he just—?

And why did he stop?

For a second, neither of us moved—our gaze locked in a tense, fragile silence.

Then he rushed forward, closing the distance.

Eyes lit with something wild—hands cupping my face, thumbs sweeping my cheekbones.

His mouth crashed into mine with the sweet taste of whiskey.

I stumbled backward with him—breath fast, heart thumping.

He lowered me onto the couch, his body heavy, pinning me into the cushions.

His kiss deepened—greedy.

I heard his belt clink. The tug of his zipper.

I gasped as he pushed down his briefs—warm and hard against me, pulsing with urgency.

I whimpered as his fingers slid my panties aside.

He pressed into me harder—hot and hungry with desire.

We were seconds from oblivion.

Everything disappeared—the room, the week, even Greg.

Then his breath changed—ragged, not with lust... but restraint.

With his face in my neck, a guttural whisper:

"Fuck me."

He stopped. Pulled back.

Eyes glazed, he stared at me. Face pleading.

I didn't recognize him.

Who was this man? It wasn't Edward.

My eyes twitched—quick, disbelieving—disoriented as heat drained from my face.

My body still burned, but the mood was broken.

I wrapped my arms around myself. Vulnerable.

"I shouldn't have come here like this," he started. "I just... needed to see you."

My skin crawled with shame and fury.

"For what? A booty call? Closure? Control? What the hell was that?"

So much for Edward's promise of *perfect.*

He flinched like I'd slapped him. I nearly had.

"None of the above."

"Then what was it?" I shoved myself upright, fumbling with my panties as I glared at him. "Because you came here uninvited, threw me on the couch, almost fucked me—and now you're just walking out?"

He leaned in for a hug, but I stopped him cold—a firm hand to his pounding chest.

No. Not like this.

"Edward, go."

He looked gutted. "Allie, please. I didn't mean to..."

"Just go."

He nodded before fastening his belt and making his way to the foyer.

Not another word. No explanation for why he'd hit the brakes.

He paused at the front door, looking back—his expression hollow. Almost like he already knew he'd lost me.

When he opened the door, he nearly jumped out of his skin.

A tall shadow stood in the doorway, backlit.

My heart seized.

Blake?

I moved fast—backpedaling toward the kitchen, hand reaching for my gun as Edward yelped, "Fuck me! What are you doing here?"

A familiar voice answered coolly.

"Man, I was about to ask you the same thing."

James.

Thank God.

I inhaled sharply, pulse slowing as I leaned against a wall. Mind and muscles calming. Catching my breath.

James pushed Edward back into the house, stepping through the threshold.

He paused mid-stride, his gaze hitting Edward first, then me—taking in my nightgown and hair.

Brow raised, he said, "I've been trying to reach you for an hour. You know you're supposed to be on the jet to Germany right now."

"Fuck, I lost track of time."

"Yeah, well, change of plans." James narrowed his eyes on Edward again, glancing down as he added dryly, "Be respectful. At least zip your pants."

Edward promptly sorted himself out.

Then: "Al, why don't you grab something to cover up?"

"Shit." I turned, examining myself in the hallway mirror. I didn't look much better. My barely-there nightgown was nearly sheer under the light—my nipples showing straight through.

Maybe that was the reason Edward jumped me—he thought it was an invitation.

Why did I even open the door?

And why did I let him go that far?

I darted into the kitchen for my robe as James followed, making himself at home on a barstool, arms crossed—scanning from me to Edward.

"Well, the reason I'm here at this hour is because you need to get your asses to Greece. The Monaco thing's getting pushed up, and Vlad wants to meet. The jet's ready. And Andrew's still waiting..."

James rolled his eyes as I mentally left the room.

My thoughts spiraled back to the couch.

I'd let Edward in at an unreasonable hour.

Had him all but admit he loved me.

Let him kiss me. Touch me. Nearly take me.

And then... he stopped.

Why?

I wasn't sure what shook me more—his hesitation or the fact that I'd wanted him.

When had I turned into such a slut?

I hated that word, but my behavior astonished even me.

* * *

James tapped my shoulder. "Al, you with us?"

I teetered against the kitchen counter, dazed.

"No... sorry, what'd I miss?"

He chuckled. "Alright. Let's take a time out. What's going on here? What's with all this tension?"

The question hung thick—like an invisible weight pressing down on the room.

I eyed Edward blurting, "I'd love to know that myself."

Edward appeared shell-shocked. Pale.

"Bud, we haven't exactly figured that out yet."

"Well, I'd suggest you figure it out quickly... before you hop on that plane tonight," James replied with a smirk. "You're about to play lovers in front of the world—paparazzi, royalty, the agency... oh, and let's not forget, the Apparatus."

My heart skipped. Not with joy. With confusion.

Then came the rage.

I let out a wry laugh, suddenly comprehending why Greg had been so cagey about the trip. "What the *hell*, Edward?!"

I opened my mouth to speak again—to scream—before gnarling my teeth instead.

His nerve.

Edward just shrugged. "Allie, I wanted to tell you, but—"

"Seriously? This is what you needed me for? You're unbelievable!"

I threw my hands in the air. "You know what, why don't you take someone else? I'm sure there's a long line of women just dying to play your lover."

"I'm paying you instead."

James leaned back, chuckling. Glancing at him sideways—for a split second—like they'd made a bet and Edward had lost.

"You don't have to *pretend* if you want to make it official," Edward added with a faint smile.

My eyes pierced through him.

"Shit, Allie, it's not like that. I'm not paying you for... *that.*"

"It better not be about that!" I shouted, scowling. "Edward, you need to leave."

James stood. "Hey, okay, let's all calm down."

Edward weighed his options, clearing his throat. Levelheaded, he said, "Allie, this is the trip we talked about—with the Black Roses."

The yacht trip with the Albanians. The one so harrowing Greg didn't want to explain. Where I would *also* be role-playing his lover.

What a trip.

For a second, Edward's eyes flicked to James—clearly unfazed by the smoke billowing from my ears. "You're *sure* she's good?"

James nodded. "Yep. Backstory's ironclad. Backstopped. You met at a foundation gala and have been dating ever since. They've got plenty of photos of you together... your truck at the house—it's solid."

James snickered as our eyes met. "Al, the agency won't know what hit them."

That's why Edward set up the photo of us kissing? And the late nights at my house? Part of a backstory for an op?

I shook with anger.

"I can't believe you," I growled, hands flying as I paced in the kitchen. "Both of you!"

Edward examined me carefully, then asked, "Love, do you feel ready for this?"

"Stop calling me *love*!" I snapped.

"Okay, we can get into the details later." He half-smiled. "I'll send for you in a few weeks."

"Wait—you're not taking her with you tonight? I thought that was the whole point?" James asked, skeptical. He shot Edward another look, suggesting they'd already made plans behind my back.

Typical.

"Bud, to Greece? With Svet—?" Edward stopped short.

"Yeah, okay... your call. Forget I said it." James peeked at his watch. "Doesn't change the fact that you still need to get to the airport."

Edward nodded. "Got it. I'll give you a call from the road."

"Man, you're drunk! No way I'm letting you drive anywhere else tonight."

"Fine, then just give me a minute with Allie, please."

"Roger. I'll wait outside." James smiled. "Al, let's grab lunch tomorrow. I'll catch you up."

He gripped my shoulder then left. But Edward lingered in the hallway, tired, pale. TV light flickering across his face.

He was off. Not just drunk—but jittery, erratic. Too many tells at once: his eyes, his stance, the way he stared. Almost pained.

"Edward, spit it out. Whatever it is you need to say."

He softened his body and tone.

"We might not be able to talk before I get back. Don't worry about packing anything other than toiletries. I'll have a friend in Paris prepare your wardrobe."

"Great, thanks." My reply was flippant. I thought Edward would get the hint to leave, but still he lingered. "And?"

"Allie—" he hesitated, glancing at the floor. "Please remember, you can't break character."

I frowned. "Yeah, I'm tracking. Something about us being lovers?"

"You're my girlfriend."

The word landed like a slap.

Everything else failed—now he was forcing me to be his *girlfriend* under the auspices of work?

I laughed under my breath—just once, not out of humor—then pointed to the door.

"Edward, go."

He nodded.

Twenty seconds later, I watched as he and James sped off down the road.

* * *

I collapsed into bed, adrenaline still ripping through me.

I couldn't believe what happened.

Every time I closed my eyes, I saw it—Edward's belt, his hands, his mouth on my skin.

What man starts something like that and doesn't finish?

I stared at the ceiling, thoughts tearing in every direction.

Was it lust? Power? Or a smokescreen?

Maybe I was never the woman Edward wanted.

Maybe I was just someone he needed for a role.

Rehearsal for something bigger.

None of it real.

Chapter 50

The water was too hot. I didn't care. I sank into the tub anyway, letting it sting.

Mind and body burning.

And I deserved it.

I used to be a good person. Loyal. Disciplined. Controlled.

I knew my lines—and I didn't cross them.

But now? I was flirting with danger and enjoying it.

Sleeping with Greg.

Almost letting Edward seal the deal—

I stopped the thought cold.

I was used to operating in dangerous situations—hostile enemies, war zones. But that danger had rules. This one didn't. For the first time, I was in a moral freefall—leading with my heart... and maybe my libido—my mind locked in tug-of-war between desire and discipline.

Still, somehow, I felt alive.

I didn't know if it was the taste of true freedom or my slow unraveling—marked by questionable men and worse decisions.

* * *

I had plenty of time to reflect—and to regret.

Edward had reawakened something dormant in me—danger and temptation reviving parts that had withered after years of emotional starvation.

Like a hunger I couldn't shake. I was ravenous. Reckless.

I sensed a darkness beneath his polished surface that only made him more interesting. Magnetic. Perilously attractive.

His intensity electrified me.

And yet, I'd cheated on Blake with *Greg*.

Crude, cocky, chaotic—and absurdly charming.

A walking contradiction who made me laugh, then took my breath away.

I hadn't planned to sleep with him, but he made me feel something I never had.

Wild. Out of control.

Being with him was hot and steamy.

Somehow still loving.

It defied everything I thought I knew about sex.

But in his absence, guilt crept in. Heavy and loud.

I worried Greg wanted me for a sense of supremacy over Edward—the billionaire used to getting whatever he wanted.

What if I wanted Greg for the same reason? Revenge.

Two men circled me in an unspoken, animalistic power struggle—like possession would prove something.

But I wasn't sure I belonged with either of them.

While I longed for Greg's body, he wasn't right for me.

He was unpredictable when I needed substance—and stability.

Edward might be—but he'd require work. And the thought of coaching a man of Edward's age and pedigree to be the man of my dreams?

Daunting.

* * *

I was still sorting through the wreckage of my life when, ten days later, I heard a knock.

I opened my door to find Zack standing at attention, illuminated by the entry light.

"Good evening, ma'am."

His body language was tense. Stiff. And there was a tightness in his face I didn't like.

"Hey Zack. What's up?"

"Got something for you."

He forced a sympathetic smile, but his voice gave nothing away.

He extended me an envelope.

No markings.

No return address.

My hand trembled as I took it.

"It's from your boy."

My mind spun.

Was he referring to Edward? Or Blake? Jeez... or even Greg?

God, when had my life gotten so complicated?

"Want to come in?" I offered.

"Why don't you read it first?"

It was one of those letters. Great.

I opened it slowly, gazing at the ominous words.

Zack nudged me. "Allie, what does it say?"

I glanced down again, then turned it toward him.

A single line.

Handwritten.

HE KNOWS

I staggered slightly.

"Zack, who's this from?"

It wasn't Edward's handwriting. Or Blake's. Or Greg's.

He shrugged. "Shit, I thought it was from the Boss. It was dropped off by our regular courier this afternoon. Tanner said it was for you."

I swallowed hard.

It's what I'd feared.

I'd laid low for years—then stopped hiding.

Edward. Bright Sands. Mexico.
Just long enough to be found.
I didn't know which threat I'd triggered—
or if it was already too late.

Glossary

AFSOC — Air Force Special Operations Command

AO — Area of Operations

ASO — Advanced Special Operator

Arty — Slang for artillery

Black Roses — A fictitious Albanian-led criminal organization involved in large-scale human-trafficking across Europe

BRC — Basic Reconnaissance Course

C4 — A military-grade plastic explosive

CAG — Combat Applications Group (also known as Delta Force)

CAT — A derogatory nickname for Australia's Special Air Service Regiment (SASR), as in "scaredy-cat"

Clear — The process of moving room to room to ensure a building is free of threats—and surprises

CQB — Close Quarters Battle

DEA — Drug Enforcement Administration

EUCOM — United States European Command

Ground Branch — A paramilitary branch of the CIA; often referred to as 'ground' or 'GB'

HALO — High Altitude, Low Opening parachuting technique

High and tight — A dead-giveaway military haircut

HUMINT — Human Intelligence

IED — Improvised explosive device

JSOC — Joint Special Operations Command

JWICS – Joint Worldwide Intelligence Communications System; used to store top secret (TS) and sensitive compartmented information (SCI)

Lance Corporal Underground – A suspiciously accurate intel network, and the predominant source of rumors in the Marine Corps

LNO – Liaison Officer

MARSOC – Marine Corps Special Operations Command; now known as the Raiders

MFM – A threesome between one woman and two men (Male-Female-Male), where the woman is the center of sexual attention and the two men aren't sexually involved

Morale Suppression Officer – An officer who can ruin fun and destroy team spirit on contact

Murk – Slang for kill or murder

NVGs – Night-vision goggles

PJs – Also known as Pararescuemen

Recon – Short for reconnaissance

RSO – Regional Security Officer; a position within Diplomatic Security at the State Department

Salt dog – A nickname for a Marine who is very experienced—and likely very cranky

SCIF – Sensitive Compartmented Information Facility; used for viewing classified material

Silkies – A term for tight-fitting nylon military shorts; beloved by Marines, feared by civilians

Special Activities – A division of the CIA responsible for covert and paramilitary operations

SPIE – Special Patrol Insertion/Extraction; a method to extract personnel from terrain that doesn't permit a helicopter landing

Terp – Slang for interpreter

USAID – U.S. Agency for International Development; a cover frequently used by the CIA

ACKNOWLEDGMENTS

DH, NJ, CW, GW—thank you.

About the Author

Chrissy Johnson is the author of *Bright Sands, Dark Skies*—the first in a multi-book series that blends psychological suspense, emotional intensity, and cinematic heat. Influenced by the grit of military life and the shadows of covert operations, she crafts heroines who rise through darkness and the dominant, battle-hardened men who challenge them. Her stories unfold in a world of ruinous truth, exploring what happens when desire becomes its own kind of danger.

A Note from the Author

Some stories begin quietly—like a slow, steady whisper.

This one did not.

Before Allie ever walked onto the page, there was Edward—a decorated Marine with a relentless sense of mission and purpose.

For a long time, this was his story—Bright Sands navigating covert operations in a shadowy underworld.

But then Allie appeared, and the story changed.

Or maybe it revealed itself.

Because it was impossible for her not to be drawn to him.

Not to be seduced by his power.

Not to love him.

Bright Sands, Dark Skies grew from that tension—the collision of men walking the thin line between good and evil and a woman trying to rediscover herself in a world that once destroyed her.

What followed was a love story I didn't expect to write, and one I couldn't stop once it began.

Thank you for stepping into the darkness with them.

There are more truths still buried.

More dangers still waiting.

More of Edward—and Allie—and Greg—to come.

—Chrissy

COMING NEXT...

BOOK TWO:
BRIGHT SANDS, DARK SKIES—A RECKONING

Every secret starts in the dark.

And on a billionaire's yacht in the Mediterranean, surrounded by glittering water and blinding sun, Allie is about to learn that the brightest places cast the darkest shadows.

Pretending to be Edward's lover was supposed to be simple.

A role. A lie. A brush of skin she could resist.

But chemistry has consequences—especially with a man like Edward.

It coils. It burns.

What begins as torturous heat becomes something deeper... right as the world around her starts to collapse.

Loss shatters the team.

Truths threaten to ruin her.

And when the darkness finally comes for her, it hits harder than anything she's survived before.

In the aftermath, desire ignites in the most forbidden place.

A touch she remembers too well.

A man she shouldn't want—but can't stay away from.

Temptation sparks. Loyalties shift. Lines blur.

And one truth becomes impossible to outrun—

light comes as a cost.

Not all love will survive.